RELEASE

THE TANDRO SERIES - BOOK ONE

NAOMI E LLOYD

To lovely Gayle,

Lots of love,

[signature]

xxx

Charmed
Chameleon

To all the diamond philosophers out there.
Each and every one of you helped to make this book
journey a truly enlightening experience.

JOIN NAOMI'S TANDRO DIAMOND TEAM

Members of Naomi's Tandro Team gain access to the exclusive Tandro Diamond Energy Cave for free books, treasure hunt competitions, behind the scene photographs and unique items to accompany the books.

Members are always the first to hear about Naomi's new books and publications.

See the back of the book to find details on how to sign up.

INTRODUCTION

Most of us dream from the outside. Even in a nightmare we know we are observers. For as real as the bear chase, the passionate kiss, or the falling from a great height may feel, we know our mind is playing with the desires and fears we hold within. The reliving of what has already happened to us whilst we sleep.

Tiegal did not dream in this way. She lived her dreams as though she were awake. Her dreams shared little connection to her personal memories, hopes, or longings.

But they had everything to do with her future.

These were auspicious dreams.

The kind of dreams that filled her with desire and hope.

But then came the portentous dreams.

The kind of dreams you did not always want to believe in.

DREAMSCAPES

Tiegal inhaled the air inside the pink bubble which contained her, ever aware of her tendency to feel claustrophobic whenever her dreams placed her in this scene. It was imperative that she keep herself here – for as long as possible this time – hovering over this river in her energy capsule, where she could observe the fair-haired male she was so drawn to.

A combination of pleasant tastes filled her mouth. They were delicious, but also, deeply unsatisfying. For she knew they were only her reaction to him, the sense of him - and not a real perception of substance in her mouth.

"Honey," she whispered. "And citrus, combined with damp wood."

He couldn't see her. She knew that much about this dream. That she would be given a few minutes to watch him, from afar, as he played with some stones on the bank of the river, twisting his wrists back and forth to flick and catch them in one swift maneuver. It always fascinated her; such a carefree act, with no purpose other than pleasure.

"Why do I keep coming here? You must mean something to me,

to my future?" she announced. Her words echoed around her. The pink globe of energy that encapsulated her swirled its thin sphere of liquid, as though responding to her words. Tiegal sighed as the colours of her surrounding bubble grew denser. She hated it when her view of him was obscured in anyway. For once, she wanted to stay in the dream long enough to glean some clues. To finally understand more about her connection to this beautiful looking male from another world.

Where is this? And what kind of being are you? You look like me and my kind. At least in body and form. Perhaps a bit shorter than the males in Tandro? But your frame is strong and muscular as theirs are. And you move and breathe just as we do. Still, I can sense we are not the same species.

Your skin is different. So much lighter. Like pale sand, crushed shells, and cream. And yet you smell of wood and bees and the lemons that grow on the trees. A sublime perfume. It's like none I have ever encountered. Even from this distance, you are filling my senses with your scent and the taste of your essence. You are familiar, but somehow not of my world - or even from my time.

How do I know this? I don't know. It's a feeling. Perhaps it's in the sights and the sounds that surround you? The rushing river, the strange upside-down trees, the sound of wooden wheels being pulled, and of animals working, rather than being nurtured.

It whispers of an older world, one still full of variety, and of difference. One not yet aware of the power of energies and diamonds, or, how it is possible to rebuild again when all has been lost.

Tiegal reached up to pull her dark hair away from where it stuck to her forehead as she waited for the scene to unfold. Although her naked skin was exposed inside this hovering colour surround, she was always warm when she experienced this world in her dreams. There was no question that this male, who she was so drawn to, lived in a hot climate. His skin gleamed sweat as he batted away flies from his face. He pulled at his cream cotton shirt to detach it from the sticky wetness of his under-arms.

Her heart raced as she watched him. She knew there was not much time left here. The dream would soon end. Unless, that is, she was able to move her bubble a little closer to him. If she could just get near enough to see his eyes, then she would know, could finally understand, this magnetic force that existed between them.

"Hello!" she called out to him.

The colours intensified around her once more. Now a rich amethyst in place of the soft coral hue of before.

"I want to see him! I need to see his face!" she demanded. Her right foot lifted and stamped down on the liquid substance beneath her before quickly disappearing from her view. She had to extend her arms to the side to steady her balance.

"Please?" she tried again, not knowing who or what she was pleading with to change the course of her sleep journey.

Sighing, she closed her eyes, accepting that her request would go unheard. She let her head fall back, preparing to transport to her world of awakening - to the world in which she never felt she truly belonged.

Look into his eyes Tiegal!

She gasped at the sound of her own voice instructing her from inside her head.

"I can't!" She pointed at the opaque colours in front of her.

You can't? Or you won't?

"I'm not in control of this though," she spoke back to herself, annoyed that another part of her – one perhaps more in control – had a clearer perspective than she could see in this moment.

The smell filled her nose again. Breathing him in, she smiled at the realization that she had somehow moved herself closer to him. With her eyes still closed, she squeezed her arms around her chest and willed the coloured fog to clear, even for a moment, so she could take a look at his face.

1,2,3,4,5…

Tiegal counted out loud. When the sense of him close to her threatened to overwhelm, she opened her eyes and gasped. It was just one look, a glance, but she saw it in the shape and colour of his eyes- a large circle of green centered by a smaller circle of black. They did not flash out light from the pupils. These were gentler, slower, pools of colour. More like the eyes of an animal.

Confirmation that he was a different creature than her. And yet, somehow, a new awareness, a promise that she would one day become just like him.

PART ONE

TANDRO
2065

1. THE ESCAPE

"I am an Island.
I am fire.
I am light.
No one can douse my fire.
No one can dim my light.
No one can enter my island."

Tiegal watched them all carefully, assessing each of the kimberlings as they chanted the morning mantra. They were all so trusting. There was not a hint of questioning from any of them. But then, this was all they knew; this was their way of life. They relied on this ritual to start their day. All the Tandroans did. It was their instruction, their purpose: to maintain their own fire!

Tiegal recognised herself in each of them; at least, her younger self.

These words were as familiar to her as her own breathing; their rhythm as recognizable as her heartbeat. They were imprinted into her brain like the strongest glue. Never to be removed. She had chanted them when she was a kimberling, and now, almost eighteen and a teacher to these young ones, she was hearing them chanted back to her.

You learn what you live

This thought came into her head, as she stood before them. They were all living like robots. It was the same, every day: arise, eat, chant, work, eat, chant, sleep and repeat.

Every morning, her assigned group met on this large decked classroom, the eating and meeting place for this floating camp. They ate their morning meal in silence and then turned to face the rising sun, ready to declare their dedication: to preserve their own fire, their energy, their gift from the ultimate star in front of them.

A doctrine that used to make sense to her when she was younger. It brought her comfort, security and purpose. But that was before. She was older now, stronger, and becoming more aware of her own power. After last nights' dream, Tiegal was more determined than ever to find a way to reach beyond this ordered sameness. She had to *find* her destiny; one that she was convinced lay beyond this group of islands they were all confined to.

The chanting stopped and the young kimberlings turned their attention from the sun to her face, staring at her with dogged intensity as they had been trained to. After all, it was their *duty* to assure her of their loyalty to the Tandro life.

They waited for her to speak. She opened her mouth to start her talk but then had to steady herself on a nearby pillar in order to prevent herself from falling.

One of the male kimberlings, seated at the front and closest to her, cried out to her:

"Teacher Tiegal you are too close to the edge. You will fall in!"

She looked over her shoulder to check her surroundings. The young male was right: she must have swayed a little during their chant, moved too near to the water.

"It's such a beautiful lake though. I am sure I would enjoy the dip!" she answered him with a smile.

The young kimberling frowned at her.

"But you would lose your sun energy if you got wet so soon after we..."

"That's okay, don't you worry. I don't plan to lose any energy at all. You have all shared plenty this morning with your dedication. Now it is my turn to extend some of my energy back towards all of you," she assured him, moving herself forward, to a safer distance away from the edge.

"Okay, you have five minutes to ask me some general questions and then we will move on to the procreation process. I know you are all so keen to learn more about this."

She was anything but keen on discussing this.

A female kimberling put her arm in the air.

"Yes?" Tiegal asked.

"Can you tell me when we can be part of the Jarm matches?" the kimberling called out.

Tiegal did her best to disguise her sigh –and her yawn –by flicking away the mosquitos that had gathered around her ankles. It was already stifling hot now the sun had made her appearance and everything else on the Kimberrago Island had burst into life in response. The cicadas were particularly excitable this morning; their noise seemed to have kick-started a gibbon monkey chorus in the jungle behind them. The urge to run up the hill to join them all was almost overwhelming. She had always believed that the jungle was where the real energy could be found.

Abandoning the class was not an option though. She was here to answer their questions.

"We will get to the Jarm Matches in good time. I just need you to understand the process of carbon donation first," she explained.

The kimberlings all looked at her, wide-eyed, each of them wearing identical expressions.

We've made robots.

"Okay then, first of all, who can name the two most abundant elements in our Tandroan bodies?"

All twenty-five of them answered in unison:

"Oxygen and carbon"

Tiegal nodded. "That's correct. Now, who can name a *pure* carbon substance?"

"Diamond!"

The young male nearest to her was the first to answer. She threw him a piece of dried mango in reward.

"Very good! Now, who can tell me where this carbon came from, originally? And the first to answer gets not one, but two, dried banana pieces."

This was one of her favourite parts of teaching – throwing out rewards- because it was *her* invention. It inspired competition between them; something she was not supposed to encourage, which was exactly why she did it anyway.

One by one the kimberlings responded with their theories about supernova explosions and the elements that are released from them.

"We are like the ashes of dying stars! We must be, if we are all so abundant in carbon."

One male kimberling declared with confidence.

"We are *more* than just ashes of dying stars. We are part of something even deeper. We are *children* of diamonds!"

Silence.

They all knew this – it had been drummed into them since their creation day - but just saying those five words always created a surge of vibrational energy underneath them. The decking on their floating island shook a little in response to their excitement. Tiegal glanced behind her to check the activity in the lake. As expected, a shoal of puffer fish had already made their surface appearance in response to the ripples in the lake.

She yawned again, keen now to move to the next stage, so she could finally satisfy the kimberlings' curiosity, and then get back to her bed. Her dream journeys to the other world and the mysterious fair-haired male were finally starting to catch up with her.

Reaching behind her, where her favourite bamboo chair was tucked in the corner, she picked up a palm-sized device, octahedron in shape, and placed it on the table nearest to the edge of the decking. Careful to balance it so that its small lens faced the lake, she twisted her finger and thumb on either side of it as she had been trained.

"Okay everyone. I want you to watch carefully. This here is a Holomac. It is an innovation in visual imagery that we have just received from the Rungar Island. The mechanical designers over there have distributed these across the camps so we can start using them for our educational needs. I am going to press this one more time now to prompt it into action. Please don't be alarmed by what you see. The machine will project an image across the water and then you can watch a show! I think you will all enjoy it! It's the story of our creation process. It's called the *Journey of Our Energies.*"

As expected, they all gasped in amazed anticipation. She pressed the Holomac firmly and stood back to allow them a clear view of the image that quickly formed into a suspended screen over the lake.

Let them be amazed by this. It's the best version of their life they will ever see!

She was grateful that these young ones were not yet capable of accessing the thoughts she still found so difficult to hide.

A voice boomed out from the device; a narrative to accompany the moving depictions of bloody wars; chemical experiments; dark skies; icy, deserted lands – the days of destruction, when all who had survived made their way to the centre – to what became the bundle of habitable islands of Tandro.

The narrator, was their ruler, Atla, of course"

"For centuries a wider world existed, a species who spread themselves across the lands, divided in their desires, fighting to exercise their choices, often to the detriment of others. There was only ever going to be one ending to this way of life: destruction. Only the fittest could survive, and only the strongest did; the ones most adaptable to change.

And so, they gathered together, the best of them, from each of the lands, to find the stable zone, where the sun could still provide the energy for us to survive and thrive."

Tiegal fought to prevent herself from rolling her eyes as the dark, grey images changed to reveal the bright blue skies and sprawling green jungle terrains of the Tandro islands.

Here come the beats! She mocked the creators of the show inwardly.

On cue, the repetitive Tandro beats boomed out to announce the glory of the new world these young ones were – apparently - so fortunate to have been created in.

Atla's voice spoke over the beats again:

"This was a new dawn; a chance to take control of the energy around us and to make more of it, to thrive as we moved forward, together united, into the new procreation era."

Tiegal pressed the Holomac lightly, causing the current image - of an exploding star – to still. It created a magnificent scene across the lake: a contrast of shimmering water and sunshine, stars and space.

"Kimberlings. For the grand prize of a whole pineapple, who can tell me what Atla means by the 'new procreation process'?" Tiegal challenged them.

This part was always interesting. It was rare to find a kimberling with a higher level of instinct, a dreamer, who could connect with their beginnings, or even their future. She waited for a few seconds. Eventually, a small, hesitant hand, reached upwards at the back of the decking. Tiegal smiled. She had sensed there was something more vibrant about this one.

"The process by which pieces of hair and teeth are donated?" The voice was a tremble.

"Go on...your pineapple awaits. Can you tell us more? *Why* hair and teeth?" Tiegal challenged again.

She could see the others looking shocked. This was natural. If you had not dreamed it, how could you believe it?

"Erm, I *think* it is because of the carbon contained in them; they are used to make the pods they plant in the creation lagoon." The shy female kimberling answered.

"Good! And who do you think donates these parts of themselves?"

"Erm, I'm not sure? I think, maybe, that *many* Tandroans can contribute? Perhaps the ones who win the Jarm Matches?" she suggested.

Tiegal shot her a flash of encouraging light with her eyes. It was bright out here, even in the early morning sun, but this kimberling was highly attuned. Tiegal's look was all the encouragement the kimberling needed. The young female continued:

"And, also, I *think,* that maybe, the combination of these donations, from the different Jarm winners, mixes together to create the final energy colour in each of us?"

"The *colour* of your energy determining what..." Tiegal urged again.

This kimberling was the most interesting one she had taught. She reminded her of her younger self; which did not augur well for the kimberling. In fact, she probably shouldn't encourage this young one to reveal her dream memories so publicly. It could raise too many warning flags. But it was too late now; the valve had been opened.

"Your diamond colour energy!" the kimberling exclaimed. "The colour of the diamond you will one day wear in your Derado!" she added.

Tiegal nodded, allowing the news to wash over and sink into these young minds.

"One pineapple coming your way! You answered perfectly. And that's why you hear the older ones referring to how *everyone* is made of *everyone*! It is the constitution of our peace." she recited.

With this deliverance, Tiegal then reactivated the Holomac once more. It was time for them to watch the speeded-up stages of the procreation journey: the implantation of the carbon donations deep under the cave lagoon; the pouring of diamonds into the lagoon water; the gradual growth of the creation lily pods; and the final stage nine months later, when the pods reach the surface of the water, bobbing in the glow of the cave lighting, before finally opening to reveal a baby Tandroan.

She hated watching this. There was something so disconnecting about it all. It made her feel nauseous; to think of the myriad of teeth and hair, from strangers she had never met, and probably never would meet, that had made her. It sometimes made her dream of drowning. These nightmares haunted her, made her yearn for the boy on the river even more, to save her.

It was more comfortable to look across the screen to the other side of Kimberrago Island. That was her favourite spot, where she could re-energise, just by being near the wildlife that preferred to congregate over there.

There's a kayak tied to the decking. It wouldn't take me long to row over there!

She thought, biting her lip as she mentally weighed the risks of carrying out her urge.

But tempting as escape was, she realized she couldn't afford to create any more discontent in the camp. The leaders were already raising eyebrows at her tendencies to form close bonds in the groups around her. She just needed to round this all up.

When the show finished she pressed the Holomac one more time to switch off the light source so that the screen would disappear. With the exception of the more attuned female at the back, all the kimberlings looked utterly stunned.

"So...what did you all think of that?" she dared. This question was not on her sheet. Such opinions were not considered relevant for this programme, but she always asked for them anyway.

The young male at the front, the eager one, threw up his hand in the air. She nodded.

"Is it a good thing to be a donator?" he asked.

Silly question, she thought, but useful, as it seamlessly led her to the next section of this lesson: the Jarm Matches.

"What do you think?" She asked.

"I think ...yes?"

The piece of fig she had in her hand, ready to throw to him, was now soggy and his answer didn't really warrant the reward, but she threw it to him anyway.

"It is indeed a good thing. *And* it is what you are going to train for during your development years. Those who win the Jarm Matches are given the privilege to donate to our future generations. It is the greatest honour afforded to a Tandroan: to contribute your energy to new life!"

Now I sound like a robot!

Even though she was doing what she was supposed to do – following the teaching programme on the sheet – she bristled with frustration. It seemed ironic that she was meant to teach them to think of themselves as individual islands; to preserve their fires and energies; to only exchange their energy with others from a distance and to not let anyone drain it away! As so often happened during these teachings, she felt her own fire burning inside of her; a sudden, uncontrollable rage. There had to be a way to enjoy the search for connection with another, to be more than just single units who cannot love each other or form bonds.

Like the fair-haired male who plays with the stones by the river in my dreams. We are already connected in some way. I just know we are!

Just thinking of him again – how she yearned to reach him beyond her dreams – fuelled her frustration further. All this talk of preservation of energy was just a smokescreen for maintaining control!

"This is how you suck out energy from someone. You force them to say words they don't believe in!" she blurted out.

The moment the words left her mouth – when she realised she had spoken her thoughts out loud - she knew she was in deep trouble. The lesson was almost over. The camp leaders would be nearby and there was a strong chance that her outburst had reached their audible range.

On impulse she ran over to the edge of the decking and untied the ropes so she could free the kayak and jump in. Without pausing to check which camp leader was approaching - she could hear loud footsteps running on the decking between the floating sleep tents and the classroom – she grabbed the oars and began to row.

As she glanced back to wave at the kimberlings, who had all run to the edge of the decking to bear witness to this unbelievable act of rebellion, she cried out:

"And this is how you get your energy back!"

2. THE CAVE

Tiegal clenched her hands into tight fists and then rubbed her eyes with such vigour that it made them hurt. She was already wishing she had brought her sun-protection glasses. The way her pupils were flashing their light with such an alarming intensity, they might draw too much attention to her.

Curse those stupid prophecy dreams again! Now I'm tired, over-emotional, and my eyes are flashing more than they should be! All things that will count against me today. And just when I need to put on my best performance! To show I'm not too different to all the others! To prove that I have truly redeemed myself after my act of rebellion during class last week.

She shuddered at the sight of the light from her eyes flickering in her shadow as she approached her two best friends. Even though Zeno and Rinzals' eyes were also radiating more brilliance than usual– a clear indication of how excited they were - she knew her light was more vibrant than anyone else around them. That her anticipation for the day ahead veered on the brink of fear rather than pleasure.

"And here she is. The great teacher escapist extraordinaire!"

Rinzal teased as she reached him. She rolled her eyes at him, an action which created a kaleidoscope of light flickers in both their shadows.

Rinzal chuckled and gave her a gentle nudge as he rolled his eyes in unison with her, joining in with her shadowy light dance.

"I'm only teasing you Tiegal," he whispered, "I'm just grateful you weren't punished. And I'm still amazed the camp leader believed that story you gave him about over-heating on the decking."

Tiegal shrugged and nodded at him. She was more than aware of just how lucky she had been to escape punishment.

"So then, this is it! The day has finally come. How do you both feel?" Zeno bubbled. Her excitement was contagious.

"There are no words to describe how I feel right now. It's the moment we have all been waiting for!" Tiegal lied, managing a forced smile.

She saw no benefit in revealing the foreboding feeling that rumbled inside her. How she feared her true self would be revealed inside the energy cave, that she may no longer hide how alien she felt amongst her kind.

Or, that she still dreamed of a male from another time and space. A male she had never spoken to and yet somehow felt more connected to than anyone who existed with her here, in Tandro.

Tiegal lowered her eyes from the concerned looks around her, realizing too late that once again she had failed to hide her deeper thoughts. She cursed herself inwardly. Rinzal and Zeno didn't need to hear her fears. It was not fair to dampen everyone's spirits with her negativity. This was their special day.

"Is that Jovil? The energy lagoon master?" Zeno asked as they approached the entrance to the cave. A line had already formed in front of an exceptionally tall male, who wore his coal-black hair longer than most males, and who was counting each of the young Tandroans as they joined the queue.

"It must be," answered Rinzal, "I was hoping he'd be here today. I've always wanted to meet him. I mean he *was* the one who monitored our pods! Surely that kind of makes him our creator." Rinzal enthused.

Tiegal frowned at her male friend. The enthusiasm he was exhibiting today, for this milestone moment and all its big reveals, confused her. She had always thought that Rinzal was the one Tandroan she could count on to share her disdain for the secrecy that contained them all; about who they really were, where they came from, and what they could do.

"I thought it annoyed you that we have to wait until we are eighteen to enter the cave and finally understand our energy colours?" Tiegal challenged, careful to keep her voice low. She could have focused her thoughts to him in an inaudible way but there were too many others near them who would pick up her internal dialogue. It was far safer to whisper and encourage him to lip-read when they were in such a busy environment like this.

Rinzal didn't pick up on her question. Or, if he did, he was choosing to practice selective hearing again.

"I don't recognize everyone here. Do you think some of them transferred from the other islands?" Zeno wondered, scratching at her neck as she surveyed the young Tandroans ahead of them, standing in an orderly queue. Tiegal wriggled her nose. She could smell Zeno's anxiety. It was a spicy odour. And another contagious emotion. One she was determined not to absorb. Not today.

"Stop scratching your neck Zeno! It could interfere with your colours," she advised her friend in her gentlest tone. Rinzal nodded in agreement.

"Tiegal makes a good point Zeno. They do say the water in the cave lagoon is very sensitive to your emotions. Best to keep calm if you can. We want to make sure we get the best reaction from Atla's diamonds as possible," he added.

Zeno and Tiegal exchanged knowing looks. They both knew he was putting on an act. That Rinzal, just as much as any of them, harboured genuine fears of what the milestone ritual they were all about to face could entail.

"And in answer to your question Zeno, yes! This is the *only* energy cave. This is where *all* pre-releasers have to come when they reach of age. Why? Did you think there was one for each island?" Rinzal queried.

"I've never given much thought to it. I'm not as obsessed by it all as you are Rinzal." Zeno mumbled, shrugging her shoulders at them both and turning in the direction of the excitable chattering that sounded out from the queue ahead. She craned her neck as though she were looking for someone in particular.

Tiegal and Rinzal laughed in perfect unison. They both knew Zeno had given a *lot* of thought about what would happen in the cave. Everyone on Tandro did! How could you not obsess about this rite of passage: the day you finally discovered where you came from *and* how the diamond would react to your energy?

"Oh, come on Zeno. We all know that's not true. You're the one who's spent the last two years training to be a mine engineer, just so you could get as close to as many diamonds as possible and absorb their energy. At least you have a clue...a *feeling*...about how the cave diamond will react when you touch it? Not like me and Tiegal! We're just teachers! We don't get near any precious stones doing what we do all day!" Rinzal remarked, giving Tiegal a gentle nudge with his elbow.

"We have no idea what colour they will assign us!" he added.

Tiegal took a few steps back from them. The challenging exchange between her friends had released an unpleasant odour that made it uncomfortable for her to breathe. She shook her foot out in front of her to get rid of something inside her shoe. Both Zeno and Rinzal frowned at her. It was clear her stealth efforts to create some distance between them had failed.

"Sorry! You know my senses are heightened when I'm nervous." Tiegal explained, realizing too late that she had also failed to conceal her thoughts from them, once again. "And, I *know*...I'm also really bad at hiding my thinking too!" she admitted.

Zeno shook her head as she moved herself closer to Tiegal,

putting her arm around her shoulders. A strand had fallen loose from her copper brown ponytail. Tiegal reached out to tuck it behind her friend's ear.

"Hey, we're *all* nervous. You know Rinzal and I are only debating with each other. It's not this bad energy that you always assume it to be. It's good to challenge each other like this. It gets the fire inside of us sparking! But I do worry for you sometimes Tiegal. The way you pick up on things so...so..."

"Emotionally?" Tiegal offered.

Rinzal and Zeno nodded in perfect symmetry to each other.

"I *know*! I am a strange one. Maybe there was something in the cave water when I was being made, something other than diamonds... something that made me this way?" She tried to joke, but the tremble in her voice gave her fears away.

Rinzal suddenly clapped his hands, nodding his head towards the man they suspected was Jovil, the energy lagoon master, and who was now beckoning the people at the front of the queue to follow him.

"Well, we'll find out soon enough. The line is moving. Looks like we're going in!"

Rinzal said.

———

"Stop overthinking it Tiegal! Just relax and enjoy the experience," Rinzal instructed. His voice trembled across the space between them. The radiant light from his pupils pulsated out into the darkness of the tunnel entrance to the cave. Tiegal turned her face to his, eager to return light from her own eyes, and highlight the features of his face. To find comfort in the familiarity of him and his light, which she always found much warmer than the others in her camp. They had already lost Zeno to a group of engineers she worked with as they entered the tunnel. Keeping Rinzal close by was now more important than ever.

"I *am* enjoying it Rinzal! I'm just scared that's all! I've just got a bad feeling about what's going to happen when it's my turn!" she whispered back to him, berating herself for being so dramatic. The last thing she wanted was to ruin this day for him, but he was the only one who knew about her dreams - and her fears.

Rinzal touched her arm, ever so lightly, careful enough that no one could have spotted their contact in the darkness.

"Tiegal. Come on now. It's just because you let your dreams control your emotions. We've talked about this. You have to stop believing they're predictions of your future. It's not like you've ever dreamed something, or someone, *into* your life before," he reasoned.

"I know Rinzal but it's just so real to me when I go there that I can't help feeling it's trying to tell me something. That something is going to happen," she responded as she pinched her nose.

A strong aroma had wafted across the tunnel. A distinct combination of airborne molecules that made the hairs on her arms stand on end. It was the scent of doubt, uncertainty, and excitement oozing from the pores of her fellow Tandroans. There was no doubt they could all feel the powerful energy they were heading towards; that this truly was an auspicious day in their lives.

"Shh...Jovil is coming over." Rinzal had moved closer so he could whisper to her.

Tiegal froze as the line in front of her parted to allow the alarmingly tall lagoon master to make his way over.

"Tiegal Eureka! Come!" he both announced and instructed as he reached her.

She managed a tiny wobble of her head, hoping it resembled an assent. Without daring to glance back at Rinzal, for fear she would say something inappropriate, she followed Jovil through the narrow parting of the crowd until they reached the end of the line of participants.

"You will be called out individually when it is your turn to enter the lagoon. Stay in line for now. The wait should not take too long."

Jovil directed his instructions across the top of the heads of her fellows who waited patiently along the tunnel. Their eye-lights all flickered bright lights back at him from the darkness.

We all look like bats in here! Why can't we have the animal eyes? The ones with circular pupils that don't flash! Like my dream male across the river!

The thought came into her head in a flash, leaving no time to hide it. The sound of sniggering from the line behind her made her flinch. The ones near the front must have heard her deeper thoughts.

Jovil didn't turn around but carried walking into the darkness ahead. She could only just make out his hand beckoning for her to follow him.

"Careful as you go Tiegal. There can be some tricky gaps to navigate in this cave. It is fortunate that our eye-lights *help* us to see in darkness," he commented, without turning around to face her.

Tiegal bit her lip in frustration. Now she had managed to insult the lagoon master with this inability of hers to hide her deeper thoughts.

She stopped in her tracks, closed her eyes, and counted down from ten to zero, inhaling and exhaling with care, as Rinzal and Zeno had both taught her.

"Have you always struggled with compartmentalising your thoughts?"

The sound of Jovils' deep voice close to her, so near that she could smell his essence - coconut, orange, and bonfire - startled her. She swung around to check how far they had moved away from the tunnel and shivered when she realized that it was just her and the lagoon master in the deeper parts of this ancient cave. She had never been inside such darkness before.

Flashing her eyes to the side of her, she made use of their torch effect and grabbed hold of a protruding stalactite to steady her balance. Its wet, frigid texture made her flinch.

"Erm, I guess I have, yes. I'm working on it though," she eventually answered him. It was a shaky whisper.

"I see. And what else have you found a struggle so far?" he probed further.

"I'm not sure what you mean?" she replied, aware that each of her words sounded like clipped responses from automated voices.

"I think you *do*. You're easy to read. For example, I know that you think about your dreams all the time. You believe them to be real. *And* you think about how different you are than the others. Do you have any thoughts as to why this could be?"

The light from Jovil's diamond-shaped pupils had become stronger, pulsating in and out more rapidly and with more intensity, as his determined questioning probed further.

"I don't know. I'm just not normal. It's like I'm some kind of anomaly. Maybe the diamonds will reveal why?" she dared, not wanting to discuss the details of her dreams. Who knew what happened to those who delved too deeply into their emotional thoughts? Her way of thinking was *not* in line with the Tandro ways; that was the only certainty in this life that she did have.

I'm really cold. Can we go to the lagoon now please?

She crossed her fingers behind her back, hoping Jovil would respond positively to her attempt at silent conversing. Rinzal had forewarned her that the seniors preferred to communicate between minds when their energy reserves were low. And she doubted there were many activities more energy sucking than standing inside a freezing cold cave in the dark.

Jovil stood statue still. He seemed to be waiting for her to reveal more.

"I'm *really* cold," she tried, audibly this time.

When he made no further signs of moving, she chattered her teeth in an exaggerated manner, desperate now to display her discomfort to him.

"Okay then Tiegal, I hear you. It's hard not to. Let's go and see what reaction you create in the lagoon. Something tells me it's going to be interesting!"

The way he spoke his words, with more lightness now, seemed to cause a shift in the energy between them. It made Tiegal smile as she followed him into the abyss of darkness. She could swear he had laughed just then. That he was more than just interested in what reaction she would create. He seemed positively excited by the prospect.

This gave her hope. She could feel it flickering inside her; the possibility that, perhaps, she was not as misunderstood as she had always thought?

3. THE LAGOON

As she lowered herself down the slippery metal ladder a flurry of frustrated thoughts ran through her mind:

No one mentioned all these steps! Why isn't this something we are warned about? That you have to climb down even further into the cave to get to the lagoon!

Tiegal took a deep breath and twisted her neck so she could shine her eyes down to the darkness, willing her eyes to flash as brightly as was possible, desperate to see what lay in store for her down below.

She had already descended fifty steps and now her legs were shaking violently.

"How many more to go?" she called down to Jovil.

Two flashing eye-lights beamed up to her in response.

"You are half-way there now. Count down twenty more and you should start seeing the colours," he shouted back to her.

Only half way! Great.

"You are stronger than you think Tiegal Eureka. Keep going."

Everything burned. Her hands felt as though they could catch on fire.

Wincing, she loosened her grip on a ladder rung so she could move down to the one below, supporting her weight with the other hand in-between.

Come on Tiegal! You can do this!

Two inner voices echoed together in her mind. She wasn't sure which one belonged to her and which to the lagoon master below, who was now waiting patiently in the darkness. But as she continued to descend the steep cave walls, she could feel the skin on her forehead pinching together. None of this made sense. Why was she alone on this long and increasingly treacherous journey to the lagoon? They had left at least sixty participants waiting back in the tunnel. Surely Jovil wasn't going to endure this ordeal with each of them in turn? The ones at the end of the line would be waiting for days at this rate! Rinzal and Zeno must be going crazy waiting in anticipation for their turn.

"And why was *I* chosen first?" she hissed through gritted teeth.

"They are not going to the same lagoon as you are Tiegal. They will already be at their destination by now," Jovil yelled up to her.

His voice resounded across the deep cave.

Tiegal sought him through the darkness. She could both hear and smell that she was getting closer to him. But his words frightened her – the revelation that she had been sent to an isolated area, separated from the others.

Jovil called out to her again:

"That's it. Ten more steps down and you're there. Can you see the colour glow yet?" he urged. There was a dance to his lilting tone. A part of her wanted to seek out the source for his enthusiasm – this colour glow he referred to - but she resisted turning her gaze away from the metal strips and the damp cave walls directly in front of her. It would be just her luck to fall off, right on the last few rungs.

Five more steps Tiegal! Come on now. You've got this!

The touch of Jovil's warm hands reaching around her waist made her gasp with relief.

"Thank you," she breathed as he pulled her down. Her ankles

wobbled and knocked together as she reached the safety of the cave floor.

"There you go! Give your hands a really good rub together to circulate the blood flow again," he urged before adding, "In answer to all those questions I could hear you torturing yourself with up there... you went first because you're the *only* one who was made in this *particular* lagoon."

Tiegal froze. There was something in his choice of words that didn't feel right. She could sense he was holding back.

"By particular? Do you mean secret?" she whispered, meaning to ask the question to herself and not out loud.

Jovil spun round in a startling flash. It was clear her question had surprised him.

"Did you hear me think that just then?" he demanded.

"Erm..."

"Tiegal. I am not here to hurt you in any way. I want to help you. But I do need you to be honest with me."

"Grrr!" She stamped her feet in frustration. "I did hear you think that, sorry. I don't mean to dig too deep into someone's mind. The words just pop into my head!"

Feeling reluctant to register even a hint of disappointment from him, she kept her eyes lowered. He was the lagoon master. As Rinzal had said, he was like their creator. And now she had invaded his thoughts.

"I'm sorry," she managed.

"You have no need to be," Jovil assured in a gentle tone, "nor do you need to be so fearful of me. And all these assumptions you and your friends have made about me. That I am this looming figure, or *creator*. Is that what you call me?"

His deep laugh filled the cave with lively echoes. The sound bounced back warm, happy vibes, that Tiegal gladly absorbed. The temperature had dropped significantly since she had reached the end of her descent and this renewed warmth was already helping her clarify their confusing methods of communicating.

"Of course!" she exclaimed. "Our minds are playing opposites. I always forget this.

You heard my thoughts - the ones I *should* have hidden- and I heard the ones you *did* hide, even though I'm not supposed to be able to! I guess I really am a mix-up!" Tiegal let out a nervous giggle.

"No, Tiegal!" Jovil exclaimed. "You're not mixed up. You're powerful. More than you realise. But...it wasn't meant to happen the way it did. It was -" His voice broke off and he turned away from her, his mood taking a drastic turn.

Tiegal shivered and hugged her arms around her chest, intense fear engulfing her once more. She was not sure she was ready to hear the rest of it, about what could have happened in the lagoon to make her this way, so different, and perhaps more powerful?

Turning back to the ladder, she considered whether she had the strength to pull herself all the way back up again. To escape from the difficult truth Jovil was leading her towards, one that she knew would forever change the way she felt about herself...who she was... and where she came from.

It was a mistake! It was supposed to be a safe experiment. And it was all my fault.

Jovil's guilty thoughts echoed in her mind. She shook her head in desperation, anxious to turn down, or turn off, this power to hear the things she was not supposed to.

His words hurt, like a blow to the stomach that sent shock waves across her arms and legs and strangled in a knot in her throat. It made breathing almost impossible. She cupped her hands around her mouth, inhaling and exhaling as slowly as she could; a trick she had learned as a younger one to help redress the balance of carbon dioxide and oxygen in her blood whenever a panic attack threatened.

"I was a mistake!" she nearly gagged the words as she bent her head between her knees.

Jovil came closer to her again.

"It's not that *you* were a mistake Tiegal. It was *me*! I made a mistake. But don't worry, *please*, all is not lost. Far from it! I have a feeling you are going to change everything. That you were an accident that was *meant* to happen," he enthused.

"What? I d...don't understand?" she trembled.

Tiegal can you hear me?

She flinched in surprise. It was Jovil's voice – his inside voice – talking to her, inviting her to converse through their deeper thoughts.

Yes, I can. But why are you talking to me like this? I thought we were alone here?

She channelled her anxious questions back to him.

I think we are Tiegal, but you can never be sure of these things. And, what I have to tell you is not something I find easy to verbalise out loud. I'd rather explain it to you in this way.

Jovil made a strange, sorrowful sound then. The strangeness of it unnerved her. She quickly raised her body to search for his face, once again reaching her hand out to the side to grab hold of a useful rock formation to steady her balance. What she saw made her feel dizzy.

His expression looked sad - more than that - tortured by an emotion that Tiegal could sense, and smell from him, but if pressed could not find a word to describe.

Yet it was more than just his emotional distress that had caught her off-guard, it was the sight of the coloured glow that now haloed behind him; an inviting light that danced around in swirls, dimming in and out in vibrant pulsations.

"Where is all that glowing colour coming from?" she breathed.

Jovil just shook his head at her and then raised his index finger to his forehead to indicate he wanted to talk in silence.

It's from the diamonds in the lagoon water. I'll take you there in just a moment. It's why I brought you here after all. But, please Tiegal, just listen to what I have to tell you before we go there. It's something I have needed to say for a very long time.

As Jovil's body swayed from side to side whilst he prepared to transmit his deepest secrets to her, Tiegal noticed how the red diamond of his Derado neckpiece glowed underneath the thin white shirt he wore. She had not paid any notice to it before but now it appeared the neckpiece had come alive in the cave. That it was revealing its power in reaction to his feelings.

Just looking at how the gemstone radiated its red glow excited her, the knowledge that soon she would receive her own, personal, Derado – her *own* diamond energy control centre. At least, she *hoped* she would receive it. If she could get past the unexpected turn of events.

I didn't think the Derados connected to our emotions?

She started to transmit to Jovil.

Tiegal, please, can we focus on one thing at a time. We will get back to the Derados, but before that, I need to check that you have been taught the basics of how the creation process works.

She nodded at him.

I teach it to the younger ones. They always find it quite a surprise. I do too, every time I activate the Holomac projection. But, I was hoping that seeing the lagoon would make more sense. Perhaps bring me some comfort.

As the red diamond burned around Jovil's neck she found herself transfixed by the allure of its glow, as his words filled her head:

I'm not sure if what I tell you will bring you comfort but I have always believed that knowledge is power. And you, Tiegal, deserve to know the truth. That there was something in the lagoon water during your creation process, something that I believe made you more power-ful, and different than all the others.

Tiegal still couldn't breathe properly. Her throat had closed in tighter with each second as she battled to register the words she was hearing.

Jovil...please can we just go to the lagoon now. I want to know everything, I do, but I can't stand being in this freezing spot any longer whilst all that colour glows behind you. It's beckoning me to go to it... and it's making it hard for me to breathe!

She stumbled onto the floor gasping for breath as she let her thoughts move towards him. His hands were around her arms in an instant, pulling her up.

"You're right! I should have realised you would feel a connection with it when you came this close. Sorry. It was unfair of me to make you stand in the darkness like that. It's my darkness, this guilt, not yours. We can go there now. Just hold on to my arm for support. You're shaking!"

As she grasped her hands around his bare arms the heat from his skin transferred through her veins. She buried her face into his biceps, desperate to fill every part of her body with his warmth. The smell of him engulfed her once more and she inhaled its comfort, suddenly aware of how holding onto him in this way made her wish she was younger and smaller again; that this tall male who smelled so familiar and warm, would look after her and protect her.

"Just like a creator," she mumbled into his skin.

"Well, here it is. The lagoon," Jovil announced. He pushed her forward with a gentle but firm maneuver.

As she pulled her face away from him, tears instantly filled her eyes, blurring her vision of the spectacular sight before her.

"It's so beautiful!" she managed to splutter, whilst wiping her tears away and scanning the circumference of the cave surrounds. The light from her eyes danced over the colours that illuminated the cave walls, creating a stunning shimmer effect as she swung her head from left to right, to enhance the iridescence before her.

"Look at this!" She laughed, in-between her tears.

Jovil came to stand beside her.

"It's been like this ever since you emerged," he whispered. "Look at the water Tiegal."

Despite knowing it was there - the glistening teal-coloured pool of water in front of her - she remained reluctant to let her eyes rest on its surface. It was as though a part of her was afraid to confront her origins, whilst another part was enjoying savouring the moment.

Jovil made a grunting noise, clearly listening to her internal debate.

"Okay, you look at the lagoon when you are ready. Enjoy playing with your light and the colours and I will explain as much as I can."

He coughed, scratching his shoes on the dusty cave flooring. The obvious unease he was experiencing was distracting, but she continued to flash her eyes side-ways as she waited for his explanation. The story of her beginning:

"When our great ruler, Atla, first designed the lagoons, he made it clear that no one should tamper with the water. Once the carbon contributions are planted and the water is filled with diamonds no one is allowed to go near it for the nine-month period it takes for the pods to develop."

"Why can't you go near it?" Tiegal whispered, still not ready to look at Jovil, or the lagoon.

"Because water is receptive to thoughts, particularly positive ones. We can accelerate the vibrational energy in water just by being near it. Atla didn't want that to happen at the start. He believed the diamonds in the water would provide enough energy to develop new Tandroans successfully. He reasoned that too much energy could cause problems, and..." he hesitated, "as it turns out, he was right."

His confession hung in the space between them, daring for one of them to push the story to its conclusion. Eventually, Tiegal spoke up:

"And so, let me guess, this is where you come in?"

Jovil sighed. She could hear him crouching down next to her.

"Production was going so well. Every time we increased the amount of diamonds in the lagoon, for each creation period, the better the survival rate. Not to mention how much healthier and stronger these new Tandroans were too. It was quite exciting. Each time I entered the cave after the nine-month gestation period I was amazed by how bright-eyed these newborns were. I wanted to see how much light and energy we could create for the future generations. So, I tried a little experiment, to help push things along.

"The year you were created we planted a hundred pods, all of them full of the carbon donations of others, of which I personally vetted. This was a new lagoon I was working on to increase production... sorry, procreation." He coughed.

"Go on!" She urged.

"Atla agreed I could try adding even more diamonds this time to see if we could speed up the gestation period ...or perhaps even create Tandroans with a greater energy potential. I was excited by this idea. I kept having this dream..."

He paused to take a breath. She sensed he was hoping she would react to the last part of his confession, but she could already feel a bubble of rage rising up to her throat.

Keep talking. What happened!

"I kept dreaming about talking to the water. I saw visions of myself sitting for hours by the lagoon, channelling positive thoughts. It was so *real* that I decided it was a message and I ..."

"What did your dream tell you would happen if you did this?" Tiegal interrupted.

"I knew you would understand this."

Jovil stood up and walked in front of her so she was forced to face him.

"You really believe in dreams Tiegal? That they are more than just jumbled up memories playing back to us?" he urged, running his hands through his thick black hair, which shone from the coloured lights surrounding them.

"I experience the dreams as though I am there. I can feel, hear and smell everything. It's not a case of believing in them. I *live* them," she answered.

"The male across the river you always think about?"

"Yes! But, that's not important right now. What did your dream of this lagoon tell you?"

"That I was meant to do this...to interfere with the vibrations of the water with my thoughts. I didn't experience it like you described. It was more like a viewing dream, but it kept coming to me, and I just kept hearing the same words."

"What words?"

"That there will be a powerful one, a female. And she will emerge from this lagoon

and one day she will transform everything."

As soon as he finished his sentence the water in the lagoon burst into life, bubbling like a hot spa, enticing them to turn their attention to its excitement. Tiegal, without realizing she was doing it, raised her hand up in the direction of the water and motioned up and down. The water stilled in an instant.

"What happened when you sneaked in here to talk to the water?" she demanded.

"Nothing at first. I noticed the diamonds seemed to glow more than usual when I talked to them but everything else seemed normal. It was only on the last day, before the pods were due to emerge, and I could see them rising just under the surface, that I noticed the change in the water, how it fizzed and spat. I knew then that it was over-charged. I backed away and came back with Atla and the others to witness the opening but when the pods arose and opened... they were ruined," he stammered.

"The babies had died?" Tiegal flashed her eyes at him.

"All but one," he answered her carefully.

Tiegal nodded at him. She had heard his thoughts a few seconds before he uttered the words from his mouth. There were no more surprises coming her way. The truth had been delivered. Now she finally knew what she had been searching for: who she was and where she came from.

With her right hand she reached out to press her palm to Jovil's arm.

"You don't need to feel shame about this. I can smell your pain and it's not justified. Atla created this new world and this new procreation process. You thought you could help create an even greater future, full of Tandroans that were so abundant with diamond energy that they would live forever," she reasoned with him.

"But it went very wrong. It was too much. I had tampered with the vibrations...over-cooked them!" He cast his eyes downwards, his lights danced on the cave floor.

"And I was the only one to survive?" she checked.

"Yes." He seemed to hesitate at first, but then he looked her straight in the eye and stated:

"You were the only one."

Tiegal sighed. Her body felt weighed down with all these revelations. A sadness swept over her as she walked over to the water. The very place from where she now knew she had survived what no other Tandroan had; a power too great for them to sustain.

Or did I take all the energy? Was that why they all died around me? Because of what I can do?

Without pausing to think about the consequences she took off her grey cloak, kicked off her boots, and then, only wearing her thin cream jumpsuit, she stepped in to the lagoon. The water bubbled furiously in response to her entry. Jovil screamed for her to, *"Get out"*, but she ignored him. Her heart raced and her whole body shook. Still, she could not stop herself from moving forward. The water seemed to be calling for her.

Taking a deep breath, she turned away from Jovil's anguished calls and then swan-dived under the water. Her eyes instantly lit up the dark bed of the lagoon, making it easier to scan her surroundings. It was deeper than she had expected, but it only took three strokes before she reached the bottom. And there she sat herself down, watching in amazement, as hundreds of different coloured diamonds arose all around her, glowing their fluorescent magic in response to her return.

4. LIGHT

Tiegal sensed fury and fear. The hairs on the back of her neck bristled. Since yanking her out of the lagoon and ordering her to climb back up the ladder Jovil had not said a word. The unnerving noise he had made during the steep climb back was a strange animal-like sound from inside his mouth; a combination of teeth grinding mixed with a growling noise that grated on her. It was only when they had made their way back down the tunnel and found a resting spot on some rocks at the entrance of the cave that he quieted.

Taking a deep breath, she finally resolved to push him for more answers:

"How did you explain the deaths of all those pods to Atla?"

Jovil nodded and gave a little shrug, wiping the sweat off his brow.

"If you must know, that part was easy. Atla knew it was an experiment. He just assumed we had included too many diamonds into the water. And, that we had planted a smaller batch of pods than we usually did. I don't think he felt any great loss. Getting carbon donations is not difficult." He yawned, shaking his hair out in front of him to rid it of excess lagoon water. Tiegal flinched as she heard his frustrated thoughts pounding through his mind; his fury at how she had made him come in and rescue her.

I didn't need rescuing. I can breathe for a long time underwater. I've always been able to.

She wasn't sure if Jovil was listening to her inner voice, or if he was, he was choosing to ignore her protests.

"The lagoon at the other side of the cave is much larger. That's where your friends, Rinzal and Zeno, went earlier. They were made in the other lagoon, like everyone is these days. No one goes near your lagoon anymore. And clearly no one should. I thought the lagoon was going to explode the way it reacted to you Tiegal. You must never do anything like that again!" he scolded, still catching his breath after their frantic scramble up the ladder.

Folding her arms in defiance she watched him gasping for air, surprised at how such a strong and able man would need to source more oxygen after what now seemed like an easy feat. Climbing back up the steep ladder had been a joy for her this time, like a release in pent-up energy. In fact, the way her muscles had responded to the physical challenge – contracting and relaxing with such rhythmic ease – had fascinated her. And when they reached the top, she had wanted to push her body even more, to test this new strength she suspected the lagoon water had given her. Even now, as she stood before him, her breathing easy in comparison to his, her body buzzed with power.

"So, are you going to tell me why you brought me here today?" she pushed. Jovil nodded again.

"To tell the truth! To see how you are. To check if you are struggling with this extra energy that *I* was complicit in giving you," he answered, managing an apologetic smile. "Are you? Apart, that is, from your mixed-up mind-reading abilities and limitations," he teased, giving her a wink. His shock and anger appeared to have already simmered.

The sound of her own laughter made her jump in surprise. It was a happy sound like none she had ever made before; one full of joy, like a carefree birdsong. A sound that evoked the feeling of freedom and balance.

Like the way I feel when I am in the dream bubble, near the male across the river.

Just thinking of him now had a sudden, physical effect on her. A strange heat burned between her hips, an urge, a burning desire to be close to him in a way she could not understand. Self-consciously she raised her hand to her lips and sighed.

"Sometimes, yes, I do feel torn by something. It's not easy being so unusual. All my senses are so much stronger than everyone else. I smell things with more intensity than the others do. Sometimes, I even *taste* words. And then, there are the dreams, and the feelings, the *yearnings* that I know I'm not supposed to have. I've never understood why I have all these wants and desires that none of you seem to have..."

"Like what?" Jovil quizzed. He had got his breath back now and seemed relaxed chatting with her as he leaned on the sign that had welcomed her and the other young Tandroans to their pre-release day.

Perhaps it was this – the way he stood before he with such ease - that lulled Tiegal into a false security, that encouraged her to reveal more of her desires to him. The thoughts that, despite her limitations, she had been able to hide until now.

"I want to feel affection, to know what it is like to be touched. To make a real connection with someone. I want to feel love," she confessed. Her fingernails pinched into the skin of her palms as she waited to see his reaction.

Jovil grabbed both her arms, almost shaking her. He looked frantic with worry again.

"No Tiegal! It's not our way. Atla forbids it." He sounded alarmed, frightened even.

"But why? Why do we all have to live as single units and only protect our own energy, our own fire? Wouldn't we burn brighter if we could light each other's fires? Our desires?" she pleaded with him.

Just saying the words out loud was a huge release, as though she had been holding back all of her life and was only now finally breathing as she was supposed to.

Jovil shook his head at her and then threw his arms in the air in such a furious manner that she felt compelled to step back from him, unsure of where his anger was directed.

"Because if you even try to do something like that...any kind of intimacy... with someone, then I can guarantee that *both* your fires will be stamped out. Atla will see to it."

A vein on his forehead throbbed and he wrung his hands together.

Seeing him so distraught was too much and she threw her arms around him, ignoring the way his shoulders twitched at the shocking sensation of her gesture.

"Why though Jovil? Have you never questioned why Atla is so against us making connections and bonds with each other? We grow up learning of the beauty and strength of the diamonds that gave us our energy and our eye-light. And yet the very reason why a diamond is so strong and can reflect such incredible light is *because* of its tightly-bonded carbon atoms! We should be embracing these parallels we share with diamonds. Perhaps we would become even stronger, and brighter, if we did! I mean, think about it Jovil, I know you are a senior, the lagoon master, but you are *also* a child of diamonds. You too were born in diamond water!"

"But Atla isn't even one of us! He doesn't have the diamond-shaped pupils that pulsate light and he can't read minds like we can. And yet we all follow him like robots, under his control, never listening to our needs and desires – what our energy wants us to share with others!" She shouted her rant out over his shoulders, her warm breath releasing mist into the cooler early evening air. Jovil pulled away from her, buried his face into his hands, and then let out a frustrated growl.

"Oh my, this is worse than I feared. What have I done? Tiegal you can't let anyone else hear such thoughts. You could get yourself killed with this kind of thinking. Atla is the one who created this new world for us, so we could live across these beautiful islands, and thrive, and grow for longer, and be healthier than any generation in our world has ever lived before."

"If it is a creator you seek then you should look to Atla, not *me*. You need to respect him Tiegal because if you don't then I can promise you this - you *will* be destroyed."

He stepped forward then, his hands clasped together in front of her as though willing her to agree with him, to promise him that she would be a faithful Tandroan and bury such treacherous thoughts.

"Jovil, I'm sorry but I just don't think I can keep respecting this life. Not after today. Not after what I have seen, heard, and experienced in that water. My heart wants, it *needs*, something more than this. I sometimes feel like I'm breathing in the wrong atmosphere and it suffocates me. I know you are scared for me Jovil but I'm not sure I want to live this way. Not if it means enduring this loneliness. This lack of oxygen..." she trailed off at the sound of repetitive drum beats ahead.

Jovil nodded at her. They both knew the beats signalled they would have to leave each other now, to meet the members of their respective camps. Supper would soon commence.

"I feel like I have known you forever. You were familiar to me from the moment I saw you," she whispered sadly, aware that she would have to separate from him now, this figure who represented a security – the scent of a warm, fresh, blanket.

"I thought I smelled of coconut, orange and bonfire?" Jovil mused as he listened to her thoughts.

"You do. But you also make me feel safe, hence why I was thinking of the smell of a soft blanket," she giggled.

"I can live with that," he smiled, "but can you promise me something before you go?"

"I will try," she promised.

"Well, two things please. First, that you will work hard to conceal your deeper thoughts from others. You, more than anyone on Tandro needs to learn to do this. I cannot stress this enough. And, secondly, that you *please* be careful on your Release Day. After seeing how the diamonds in the water reacted to you in the cave, I fear for what will occur when you receive your Derado."

He gave her a long, flickering stare.

"I will do my best, I promise. But won't you be there? On my Release Day?" she queried, already feeling a tightness in her chest. The way he was talking indicated he would be leaving for a long time, and even though they had only known each other for a few hours, she felt as bonded to him as she did to Zeno and Rinzal, perhaps even more.

Jovil breathed a heavy sigh. "I'm sorry Tiegal, but I have to leave now to get back to the Jarm Island for the forthcoming match. We need to find more contributors for the next creation period. But I *will* come and find you and check up on you - and soon," he promised.

Tiegal bit down on her lip, determined not to let her tears betray her again. He turned to walk away, but then swung himself round to face her once more.

"Ugh! I'm probably going to regret this, but I can't bear to leave you feeling you are alone in this world like this. Because you're *not* Tiegal. Look, I don't know how much you know about the old-world ways, and I don't want to encourage your yearnings, but I will tell you this. The ones who lived before us were very different in the way they interacted with each other, almost opposite to the Tandroan ways. You see, they encouraged the forming of bonded groups. They actively sought family units, and they procreated in the *bodily* ways." He stammered and covered a nervous cough with his clenched fist. "Humph... between each other. So that the females, the mother, bore the children and the male was named a father and..."

"Yes! That's what you are. The *father* of me!" Tiegal interrupted, clapping her hands together in little beats.

The way Jovil's face contorted, so that he had to cover his mouth to hide the huge smile that had broken out on it, confirmed that *they* had already formed a strong bond.

"And I thought you would hate me when you knew what I had done with the water."

He kicked at a pebble near his shoe.

Tiegal threw her arms around him once again:

"I could never hate someone who smells of happy and safe."

With great reluctance she let go of her grasp on him, turned away without a glance backwards, and then broke into a run, heading in the direction of the drum beats and back to her camp.

It was only as she approached the decked entrance to her camp's kitchen area, where the smell of pineapple mixed with rice and beans engulfed her, that a terrifying thought entered her mind:

I missed something back there! There was another scent in the cave. And it wasn't mine or Jovil's. Someone else must have been there!

Biting her lip, she rocked on her ankles, torn between moving forward to take her place with Rinzal at the supper table, and rushing back to find Jovil – to warn him that they had not been alone in the cave of her origins after all.

But just as she was about to turn back to the cave, two hands pressed down on her shoulders. The voice of her camp leader boomed its annoyance into her ear, "In you go Tiegal Eureka. Supper has already commenced."

5. MINT

Tiegal hurried along the sandy pathway which connected her sleeping camp with the elephant compound. Rinzal was only a few feet ahead of her but she didn't dare to shout out to him. They had already exchanged awkward looks during supper.

"You're late. That will cost you another breakfast voucher," he had hissed at her across the table.

"I couldn't help it. I slipped on a ladder in the cave," she had lied to him.

That's when she had relayed the rest of the day's remarkable events through her open thoughts to him, secure in the knowledge that none of the other Tandroans near her were interested in accessing her mind ramblings.

She had hoped Rinzal would wait for her after supper, so they could take the fruit and figs over to their elephants together, but he had made a quick exit from the table without waiting for her.

Well your loss Rinzal! It's not my fault I was taken to a different lagoon.

She thought now, already wondering whether it had been a

mistake to relay all the findings of her day with Jovil - and the secret lagoon.

"You never learn!" she reprimanded herself, kicking some pebbles in her path as she walked, not caring that doing so caused bursts of dusty mist to obscure her vision.

But the second she saw Namnum, in the far corner of the field, she hurried over to the food buckets. They were full to the brim with bananas and figs. Selecting the nearest one, she then ran at full speed towards her elephant.

"I'm so glad to see you!" she called out to Namnum. The elephant shuddered as Tiegal neared her.

"Oh, I'm sorry! I didn't mean to scare you. It's been quite a day. I have so much to tell you." She buried her face into Namnum's grey, rubbery skin, keen to inhale her comforting scent.

"You know something. I think I should have been born an elephant... like you," she whispered into Namnum's giant ear, glancing over her shoulders to check that none of the other members of her group had heard her. They hadn't. They were all were busy tending their own elephants.

Namnum waved her trunk from side to side, a clear tell that she was getting impatient.

"You must be ready for food hey!" Tiegal reached down to her bucket and rolled a fig in a pile of salt at the bottom before holding it out to her snout. Namnum didn't hesitate, flicking it around in a circular motion so that she could cradle the fig securely on its journey towards her mouth. The morsel disappeared within seconds.

Intuitively, Tiegal collected a couple of bananas and some bamboo from the bucket and quickly fed the hungry elephant some more nourishment.

"So...I finally know why I'm so different. I'm full of too much energy!" She breathed out slowly. "And you know what Namnum? It feels good! Knowledge is power. At least now I can find some acceptance with who I am. And It's reassuring that it's not my fault too!"

As if to justify her comment, she pinched both her thumb and index fingers together and blew out a gush of her pent-up breath in Namnum's direction:

"Now I can just breathe and accept!"

The elephant reacted by pointing her ears forward.

"Oh, I'm sorry Namnum! I'm supposed to be feeding you, not breathing over you like that!"

Her smile quickly turned into a frown at the sight of Namnum's tail, now standing out, erect: a clear sign of distress.

"Hey, what are you afraid of?"

As if on cue, the air became heavier and dank. Out of stillness came an unexpected breeze. It billowed her cotton trousers and lifted her dark hair above her ears, followed by a sudden rush of wind that surrounded her in a vortex of dust and carried with it a strong scent of eucalyptus and mint. The dust instantly filled her nostrils causing her to sneeze in five rapid convulsions.

Before she had time to check for the source of this sudden elemental change, a rich, deep, female voice commanded her attention from behind her:

"You are an *abundance* of energy Tiegal Eureka!"

Tiegal froze at the sound of this unfamiliar voice, unsure whether to turn around to face it. There was something disarming about hearing her full name spoken from an uninvited source. It was also highly irritating. Feeding Namnum was her favourite moment of the day; her quiet, peaceful time, that had now been disrupted.

"You do not need to fear me. Please, turn around. I think you will be pleasantly surprised," the voice urged.

Unable to prolong the inevitable, she gave Namnum a reassuring stroke on her cheek and then swivelled around on her heel in one determined move.

"How do you know my name?" she demanded.

Out of habit, she raised her right knee, ready to stamp it into the ground, but then quickly changed her mind, registering the features of the figure in front of her: a young female whose face suggested she was of a similar age, and one, who despite wearing the standard

Tandroan uniform – thin, cotton jumpsuit off-set with a long flowing cape – had an entirely non-uniform face.

"Your eyes? H...h...h...how are you flickering them like that?"

The female responded with a broad, confident smile.

"What do you find so surprising? I have the same eyes as you do, as all we all do."

Namnum let out a low-frequency rumble behind her, another indicator of distress. Tiegal reached her hand behind her and stroked the elephant's back. Normally, she would have been furious with anyone who upset her favourite animal, but for some unfathomable reason, she could not stop staring at the eyes in front of her.

"Yes, but *your* eye-light is magnificent! It's like looking into a hall of mirrors! How are you doing that?"

Namnum let out another rumble. The unusual, nervous sound sent shivers down Tiegal's back, but still, she ignored the animals' warning. Instead, she tiptoed towards the female, determined to get closer so she could see how she was achieving such a scintillating reflection from her pupils; her initial curiosity of how she knew her name already forgotten.

"Wow!" Tiegal gasped, as her own eyes adapted to the brilliant light before her.

"I have never seen this before. It's almost like it's leading you to a portal of infinity! That's quite magical!" she enthused, wiping the sweaty palms of her hands down the side of her trousers. The light was beckoning her closer, drawing her in. The female leaned her upper body towards her, so that their faces were only a few inches apart.

"That's right Tiegal. But, what can you see when you look *deep* into my light?"

A myriad of possible ideas passed through her mind as her own eyes adapted to the light.

Who is she? Why does she feel so powerful? And what is this magical secret appearing from inside her light?

As her eyes gained a clearer focus, an enchanting display of feathery threads of golden light dispersed from the mysterious female's eyes.

Fireworks!

Tiegal thought, at first. But, then, as she watched more closely, she noticed how the golden fibres radiated from the centre of the light, and then curved in a sway, as though they hung from an animal of great strength, and power.

"Oh, there it is!" She jumped backwards, unable to hide her excitement. "Wow! Your diamond light has a *horse-tail* inclusion inside it! I can see it clearly now."

The female moved her head up and down slowly, as though playing with time.

"That's right Tiegal. I knew you would see what others cannot. That, like you, I absorbed more magic during my creation. That I have hidden secrets inside me - as you do. Magic, and ...*dreams!*" She hissed the last words out at her and then laughed.

Tiegal shivered at the sound, unsure how to place this strange female's laughter.

"Who are you? What do you know about my dreams? I know I'm not good at hiding my deeper thoughts, but it's rude to try and extract them from someone," she protested, all at once aware of how vulnerable she was under the seduction of this powerful female.

And yet, even as she launched her defence, a flurry of thoughts rushed to the forefront of her mind before she could hide them. They flashed through her in bursts:

I dream about him all the time!

But I'm always in this energy bubble that hovers over a river and I can never quite reach him...

When I was submerged in the lagoon, I saw him again...

It was like a vision from the diamond light that glowed around me...

And he was there in front of me... like magic!

The female made a satisfied purring noise as her golden threads of eye-light dispersed, hypnotising Tiegal with their repetitive sway. A chanting, lulling voice, filled her head:

Release it Tiegal! Release it! Release it!

Really focus on what you feel. On what you want. How you long for his touch. Let your desires out. Release them Tiegal. That is what you are meant to do! It is your power, your magic.

An eerie silence followed the mysterious female's silent words, shortly accompanied by a gust of wind that surrounded Tiegal in another exclusive vortex. The whirlwind lasted no more than five seconds, but it was enough time to obscure her view and for the female to leave the elephant field before Tiegal could call her back.

"*Who* are you?" she shouted out.

Namnum released another rumble at the side of her.

"I know, I know!" she acknowledged, returning to her elephant's side once more.

"You tried to warn me there was something powerful heading my way. The problem is though Namnum...I have no idea who she is. *Or, why I feel we are connected in some way!*"

———

As Parador strode away from the swirl of dust, she popped a handful of fresh mint in her mouth, relieved that she had remembered to fill her pockets with this essential herb: the only one that could restore her senses to their optimum levels. Her nostrils felt as though they were on fire after being in such close proximity to that elephant. For, not only was the animal's scent particularly abhorrent to her senses, just hearing the name "Namnum" had filled her mouth with a disgusting taste; one so abhorrent she couldn't even identify it.

Still, there were more pressing concerns she needed to deal with after that exchange.

Tiegal is more of a threat than I feared. All this emotion inside of her! It carries great power! I could feel it manifesting. Damn that stupid lagoon master. He reunited her with the water where she was made ...where WE were made... and now she is even more dangerous. The lagoon water has made her even stronger.

As this dark thought entered her mind, it twisted its rage deep inside, conjuring bizarre images in her mind of a venomous snake that had crawled inside her and was now in battle with her internal organs.

But she doesn't have MY ability. Nothing could be more powerful than the control of a mind.

A smile formed on her thick red lips at this more reassuring thought and the snake of rage calmed its attack on her insides. Her balance was already restored. She silently praised herself:

You made an excellent choice exercising your power over Tiegal just then. She will not be able to hide her thoughts on her Release Day now. Once Atla hears what she really thinks about, how she longs for real connection with another, he will destroy her!

Invigorated by these thoughts, she picked up her pace, navigating the small rocks on the dusty road that led to Atla's estate, aware that she could not afford to be late for her meeting with their ruler. He had instructed her to meet with him by his favourite fountain; a good sign that she was considered a worthy member of his advisory team.

The shell beads on her rope belt banged against her hips and her hair bounced on her cheeks, now flush with excitement. The more she thought about her plan, and the characters who she would manipulate to play their parts - Atla, Tiegal *and* the other two – the more certain she was that her true destiny would soon be realised.

Pushing open the wooden gate to the rose gardens of Atla's estate, she hesitated before she carried on, feeling the need to have a quiet word with herself.

Go careful! Don't get carried away with your ambition. It's hungry, but it needs to be controlled. You need to think this through carefully. What do you want Atla to do? What needs to happen now?

The sight of Atla's long purple jacket, gleaming against the light of the glass fountain in the gardens ahead, made her smile. There was no doubt in her mind now. She knew what she needed to get him to do, where she needed him to be – and, at exactly the right time too.

All she had to do now was use her power, to play with his mind.

"Atla!" she called out to her ruler, careful to make a graceful approach as she negotiated the maze of rose beds that led to the fountain where he was waiting.

"I have some news!"

6. THE PYRAMID

"I am not scared anymore. I can do this!" Tiegal mumbled her words into the material of her black cape, which she had wrapped around her mouth to guard from the tropical winds blowing across the island. The sand had risen from the banks to join the harsh breeze, which now threatened to land on her tongue and settle in her teeth.

"Did you say something Tiegal?" Zeno asked.

"I'm just talking to myself again; trying to get prepared," she answered

Tiegal nodded at her friend. They still had five minutes to wait outside the Erasmati Pyramid before the doors would open. Her body shivered next to Zeno, so calm and poised in comparison.

"So! This is it then Zeno. Our Release Day. How many nights have we spent together talking about this? Little kimberling Tiegal and little kimberling Zeno, sneaking out of the sleep tents to stare at the stars. Do you remember how we used to ask the sky if she could tell us the colour of our energy?" she mused.

Zeno nodded, amusement registering on her face. She pulled down the hood of her cape, allowing her hair to sway freely and then rest on her shoulders in that perfectly angled bob they all wore.

Tiegal mirrored Zeno's actions. Her own bob settled too, just not quite so squarely.

"I don't want to mess up, that's all Zeno. You always know the right thing to say and do and I'm really nervous about this. I still can't believe I was given a place at this ceremony. I assumed I would be at the Estate Hall with Rinzal and the others from my camp, not *this* pyramid with all these superiors. I'm way out of my depth here," she argued.

"Yes, you are! But you are still better off being here. I have no idea how your energy will behave when you release it. You just need to demonstrate that all the extra power you have is positive. And Atla is going to be here too, which should help." Zeno put her hand on Tiegal's shoulder, willing her to stop shaking.

"Is it a good thing though? Atla might think I'm dangerous! And then what will happen?"

Tiegal thought she was going to cry – or be sick. Zeno sat down on the marble steps that led up to the imposing doors to the pyramid.

"I think you should sit with me and just breathe slowly for a bit. Get yourself in a settled state. It's my first time too so I don't know what is going to happen either, but I do know that it gets highly charged in there." Zeno raised her eyebrows at Tiegal. This made them both laugh. Their time together as kimberlings had provided plenty of opportunities for Tiegal to show how reactive her hidden energy was.

"Do you remember that time when we were supposed to be learning how to polish diamonds and you made one of them glow blue just by touching it?"

Zeno reached her hands out to encourage Tiegal to join her on the cold steps. Tiegal groaned at the memory as she sunk down beside her.

"I *still* don't understand why that diamond did that. It made the teacher so angry with me. I just *touched* it."

"I know why it happened Tiegal. It's just *you*...your energy. It's obviously very powerful. That diamond must have had some other, hidden, element trapped inside it which reacted to your touch. I think you have a unique energy source inside you." Zeno suggested.

Tiegal dropped her head in between her knees. Her chocolate brown bob swung forward, blending in with her cape as one dark coloured swirl. She *did* know why the diamond reacted that way. She had seen how they fluoresced in the secret lagoon when she swam near them, as though they had been waiting for her to return; the one who possessed the power to unlock their hidden light.

Still, she didn't feel like discussing that today – her unusual beginnings - even if she suspected Zeno could hear what she was thinking.

"How do you think this male, my match today, will react to my energy then?" Tiegal whispered.

Zeno nudged her, a gentle reassurance.

"I have no idea, but I guess we will soon find out!"

He was so clear in my dream last night. It was like I had dreamed him into life. And those eyes! They were just like animal eyes. The colour in them, a circle of emerald green with a black dot in the middle. He must exist in another world...and I want to meet him...

Tiegal jumped at the sound of Zeno's hissing in her ear:

"Tiegal! Why are you thinking about your dreams of aliens right now? You need to concentrate. Get yourself in the zone!"

"Well don't access my thoughts then." Tiegal snapped.

"Well learn to hide them then!"

Tiegal shook her head from side to side, determined to banish the fair-haired male in her dreams from her mind, despite how a lingering voice inside her head kept urging her to think of him even more! She reached out to touch Zeno's arm.

"I'm so glad you're here Zeno. I feel so out of place. These people...they are so important, so elite. I just wish Rinzal were here too." Tiegal whispered, mindful of the need to keep a low profile. No one around her seemed to be conversing.

Zeno smiled at her and then beckoned her to follow to the centre of the pyramid, where a crowd of Tandroans were gathered around a large circular pool. Tiegal stood up high on her tip-toes to get a better view of the two figures in the pool who stood facing each other: a young male and a young female, both knee-deep in water, their black capes floating around them on the surface of the water.

Tiegal frowned and turned back to whisper to Zeno.

"Why are they standing in water?" she asked.

"Shh...you must keep your voice down. We are not supposed to talk."

Zeno paused and then turned her back to the crowd to lean in close to Tiegal so she could talk into her ear.

"The water is the source of supreme power because it is brought in directly from The Big Hole. I think it is supposed to help intensify the releases! Listen, the music has started. The ceremony is about to begin." Zeno nudged her and then pushed Tiegal through the gap between the two males in front, so they could get closer to the main event. Loud beats boomed out and the crowd responded in an instant, forming an orderly circle around the pool of water.

The nervous tension amongst the crowd was palpable. The young males in particular were responding to the sounds, their feet banging on the floor in time to the rhythm of the beats.

The young male and female in the pool both seemed to be ready for action. They arched their heads back and looked up to the roof of the pyramid.

"What are they looking up there for?" Tiegal asked Zeno, nodding her head at the male and female who were standing in the pool, staring up at the roof of the pyramid, their eyes both fixed on the point at the top where the four sides of the glass pyramid joined.

"Wait and see Tiegal. You must be patient. It will all make sense very soon. Watch this couple first and then you will know what to expect when it is your turn," she answered in a soft tone.

Tiegal nodded. "Okay, I'll be quiet."

The pyramid walls slowly started to open outwards, filling the room with a cool breeze from above.

"Look up there Tiegal. The Derados have arrived," Zeno squeaked, pointing up above their heads. "Our Derados are in that Argyle up there. And there's Atla's symbol on the side. Can you see it? Atla must be in there!"

Tiegal was already looking up. She recognized the whirring sound the Argyles made when they hovered for lengths of time and the one suspended above them was the most prestigious Tandro aircraft she had ever seen. The underside of the barrel-shaped machine was adorned with gem stones that reflected purple and red lights on the glass above and around them.

"I can't believe the pyramid can spread outwards like that. Does it open completely?" Tiegal asked.

Zeno shook her head. "No, not completely, or the energy exchanges could be lost if we became too exposed. I think it has stopped now," she answered in a quiet voice.

The sides of the pyramid did appear to have stopped moving further outwards. The three triangles now jutted around the crowd at a four-pointed star above them, swaying back and forth in precarious action as the Argyle's propellers pushed at the air around them.

Tiegal shuddered.

The unmistakable sonorous voice of Atla filled the pyramid:

"On this day, our millennial Derado Ceremony, I join you. We have an opportunity to generate an unprecedented level of power amongst us in this pyramid today."

There was a short pause. The music stopped, replaced with an eerie silence as the significance of Atla's words were allowed to sink into the crowd around the pool. Everyone stood statue-still, necks arched, as they looked up to the imposing machine above them. Atla's commanding voice filled the pyramid:

"Let it commence...First, we deliver Derados for Indramia Langton and Mocodiza Chaponi. Raise your hands to receive them."

Without further instruction, they raised their hands above them, reaching out to receive the two oval-shaped boxes as they were lowered down from the base of the Argyle towards their heads, attached to thick, red, ropes.

Tiegal leaned over to Zeno. "What's in the boxes?"

"Their Derados of course! Indramia is in my engineering team. She should have a very nice diamond. Just watch and learn okay!" Zeno sounded frustrated. Tiegal nodded at her friend, turning back to watch Indramia and Mocodiza as they received their boxes.

Her toes wriggled in her sandals. She felt an overwhelming urge to shake them off and jump into the pool; to let her skin soak in the power of the diamond water.

Atla's voice boomed out from above them again.

"Indramia and Mocodiza, as part of the team who developed the most advanced diamond sensor to date, you have both been granted Derados which contain real coloured diamonds. Open your box. Attach your Derado around your neck. This will be yours for life. You must promise to obey the laws of Tandro and in exchange all desires will be fulfilled."

Indramia and Mocodezia did not hesitate. With regimented obedience, they both opened their boxes, took out their collared neck pieces and then pressed the diamond pendants to their chests.

On cue, the crowd burst into an excitable chant:

"All laws obeyed, all desires fulfilled. All laws obeyed, all desires fulfilled."

"Okay, they are about to release their colours Tiegal. This is where it will get interesting." Zeno whispered.

Mocodiza and Indramia, both with serious, but nervous looking expressions, pressed their diamonds in perfect timing with each other. Their mutual actions created an instant release of colourful mists from their Derados; orange from hers and a vibrant blue from his.

Tiegal watched them in amazement. It looked as though Indramia and Mocodiza had both just liberated their inner desires from their physical beings; as though they had released another person from within them, which was now dancing around them, creating a stunning spectacle of colours, the intensity of their energies submerging their bodies and obscuring the shapes of their figures.

The chanting continued around the room as murmurs of approval emanated from the pool.

"Ooh it sounds like Indramia is enjoying herself. You can definitely hear her voice more," Zeno giggled and winked at Tiegal.

Hearing Indramia's obvious pleasure and the release of her colour made Tiegal feel hungry for something she could not place. Once again, she tried to push the image from her dreams away, but to no avail. His face and his smell overwhelmed her.

"Oh no!"

The alarming sound of Zenos' shriek broke her trance, forcing Tiegal to look back to the pool to see what all the commotion was about.

"Where did all the colour mist go? And why is Indramia sitting down in the pool?"

Zeno shrugged and pulled on her arm, encouraging her to walk with her over to the pool.

"I don't know. I think she just fell backwards! That didn't take very long and Mocodiza doesn't look happy. Can you help me lift her up?" Zeno called out.

Tiegal scurried around to the other side of the distressed looking Indramia and reached out to grab hold of her arm. As soon their skins connected Tiegal jumped back, thrusting her fingers into her mouth to relieve them from the burning sensation she had received on making contact with the girl.

"Ouch! What did you just do then?" Indramia cried out.

"Do I know you?" Tiegal asked. The girl smelled familiar, of orange blossom and peonies.

I know this smell! I have been near this before.

She recognised the feeling it conjured inside her too – of happy and safe, like Jovil.

"What did you say your name was?" she asked Indramia, who had now pulled herself off the floor and was pulling the Derado neck-piece away from her skin.

"I don't know you at all, but when you touched me just then the diamond in my Derado burnt my skin!" Indramia complained.

Zeno rolled her eyes at Tiegal. "Oh great! So sorry Indramia. I'm sure it was just the after effect of the release," Zeno apologised on Tiegal's behalf.

Before Tiegal had a chance to offer her apology a group of exasperated looking females, all wearing silver-coloured cloaks, came over to whisk Indramia away. Unable to restrain herself, Tiegal grabbed hold of her wrist to pull her back, accidentally catching her skin on Indramia's bracelet as she did.

Indramia winced and turned her head back to face Tiegal. Her eyes flashed with an extraordinary brilliance, reflecting a prism of stars around her beautiful face and caramel tinted hair.

"I have to go!" Indramia said, nodding at Zeno over Tiegal's shoulders.

Zeno waved goodbye and then turned back to Tiegal, huffing an exasperated sigh aimed in her direction.

"Tiegal! Why did you ask what her name was in the middle of all that? I told you her name was Indramia and Atla announced it to the whole pyramid!" Zeno grumbled.

"Because I think I am connected to her somehow." Tiegal interrupted in a hush.

A thousand thoughts rushed through her mind:

How could her smell remind me so much of Jovil?

Why did her diamond react to my touch in that way?

And why did her eyes reflect images of stars when she looked at me?

"Whatever connection you share with that girl, you really need to clear your mind right now Tiegal. I thought you promised to stay focused today! And, oh great, another distraction for you now. Look who's just arrived."

The sound of the familiar male voice behind her made Tiegal squeal with delight.

"Rinzal!" she cried out.

Ignoring all rules of etiquette for such a solemn occasion she threw her arms around him, almost knocking him into the ceremony pool just as a group of older males, each wearing tight-fitting black uniforms, instructed them to move away from the sacred diamond water.

Rinzal steered her over to where Zeno was staring at them, her eyes flashing with fury at them both.

"Honestly! This is embarrassing," Zeno said.

"I know, sorry Zeno, I didn't mean to make such a grand entrance. And Tiegal! When are you going to learn not to display such physical affection in public? Atla is observing from up there for goodness sake!" Rinzal shook his head at her. "And also, you really need to turn off those thoughts of yours. I could hear you loud and clear when I entered the pyramid just now."

"Never mind that. What are you doing here Rinzal? I thought you were at the Town Hall for your Release Day?" Tiegal demanded.

She glanced at him first, and then at Zeno, before glaring at them both:

"Were you both in on this?"

Zeno shrugged. "I knew nothing about it."

"All I know is that I have been matched with someone with an unusual energy. Now, let me guess who that is?" Rinzal chuckled raising his eyebrows in Tiegal's direction.

Tiegal gasped in surprise. Of all the Tandroans, across all the islands, and her match for her Release Day was Rinzal!

This has to be Jovil's work. What a superstar.

She silently thanked her adopted "father", vaguely aware of how Zeno and Rinzal frowned at her at the same time she did.

"Stop listening to me you two! It makes sense in my head. It's not meant to be understood by anyone else! That's why I didn't verbalise it," she complained, with a sigh of irritation.

Zeno put her hands on her hips, clearly frustrated by this unexpected turn of events.

"You think Jovil did this?" she asked.

"I think it's highly likely that he..." Tiegal started but the whirring sound from the Argyle as the machine hovered above them interrupted her mid-sentence. They all looked up to the top of the pyramid as Atla's voice filled the room again:

"The second Derado initiation today is to be between Tiegal Eureka and Rinzal Udansty. Take your positions in the ceremony pool."

Tiegal started to shake. She didn't feel ready for this just yet but there was nothing she could do to pull it back, no way to press the pause button she so wanted to.

"Go on Tiegal, you'll be fine," encouraged Zeno, giving her a gentle push on her lower back to urge her in the direction of the pool. "You can't keep Atla waiting."

Tiegal shook her head, let out the breath she had been holding in, lifted up her cape and stepped into the pool. The temperature of the water made her flinch. It was almost glacial.

She looked over to see Rinzal step into the pool from the other side. He didn't even flinch as his skin met with the frigid water. Fixing her eyes on his, she matched his stare. The room quickly became silent, the crowd watching on; at least a hundred pairs of flashing curious eyes.

A brief moment of tranquility followed, quickly interrupted by the return of Atla's voice, now impatient and instructive:

"Tiegal Eureka, you have proven to be an interesting addition to both the teaching and elephant camps. Your energy has continued to be utilized in the work amongst the farmers in this area."

Tiegal looked down at her feet.

An interesting addition to the elephant camp!

It sounded so pathetic in comparison to developing innovative diamond sensors and robotics like the previous couple.

"For this, you have been awarded a natural pink diamond to match your unusual colour energy," Atla continued.

She couldn't believe it! This had to be the best day ever. No one in the teaching or the elephant camps had come close to being granted a Derado with a *real* diamond in it. Her whole body buzzed with excitement. She glanced back to Rinzal who appeared to be in a trance as he fixed his gaze on her.

Hardly able to breathe she watched as he moved closer to her, only about an inch, but enough that she could see the pulsations of his brilliant pupils.

I can't believe it's you and me here, like this!

She channelled her thoughts to him, willing him to respond with a friendly smile. To her surprise, Rinzal looked at her in a strange way – with a deep intensity and determination.

Play this properly Tiegal.

His voice, in her head, sounded frustrated, or perhaps fearful. It was difficult to determine and did little to settle her nerves.

Responding to his gaze, she willed her pupils to match the action of his, knowing this was the correct precursor to their exchange; an acknowledgement that they were ready to immerse themselves within each other's deepest parts.

"Rinzal Udansty, you too have shown a dedication to teaching. A record number of kimberlings have requested a seat on your learning deck. You have shown you have a gift for conveying the wonders of our origins and the great promise for our futures; an ability that carries great power. I thus grant you a yellow diamond."

This news did not seem to have an effect on Rinzal, who had kept his eyes locked on Tiegal's throughout Atla's commendation of him.

Since when did you become such a supporter of Atla's robot regime?

Rinzal shook his head at her in a way she knew was meant to silence her. Frustrated, she gave a little stamp with her right food, sending ripples across the water in the space between them. Rinzal sighed at her, cocking his head upwards to urge her to pay attention to the box making its way down to her.

As soon as it was close enough, she reached up to release the box from its hook and watched as the red rope it had been attached to retreated back up to the Argyle above. Excited now, she removed her Derado from the box, wasting no time to ponder the beauty of her diamond, and pressed it to her chest as she had seen Indramia do before.

The effect was instant. As soon as she placed the Derado around her neck and pressed her precious stone in time with Rinzal she felt a release from within her that made her whole body convulse, followed by a rush of warmth that flooded up and down her legs and arms.

Swirls of pink mist danced around her face and an identical cloud of vibrant yellow mist surrounded Rinzal. The entire experience had already exceeded her expectations.

The music may have been beating, the crowds may have been watching, but she couldn't tell. All she could allow herself to focus on was trying to gain some control over the heat building up inside of her, as it became stronger with every breath she took. It was a liberating sensation, coming from somewhere deep inside; a place she had not been aware existed. It made her knees feel wobbly and unsteady. Her mind was no longer fully in control of her body. She realised it was a feeling that was equally pleasing and unnerving.

Rinzal's eye-light flickered at her amidst his yellow cloud. They nodded at each other. Tiegal squeezed her fingers into the palms of her hands, bracing herself as Rinzal's yellow mist moved towards her pink energy cloud and their connection was made.

Oh...what is this? This sensation...

The impact of their energies mixing was so forceful it knocked her body backwards. At least that was what she assumed had happened. An electric shock reaction, perhaps? At first, she wondered if she had fallen out of the diamond water pool, as Indramia had done before her. It was hard to tell, everything was so blurry, making it impossible for her to make sense of her surroundings since she could no longer see her own body.

A rushing, vibrating sound resonated up and down and around her. A part of her wanted to scream. Yet another part of her wanted to lie back and enjoy this strange feeling; to embrace this floating sensation. It wasn't painful, it was the opposite. It felt as if she were being transformed in some way, like she was in her chrysalis, soon to emerge into her new, more elevated state.

Where these thoughts came from, she had no idea. None of this was happening the way it had been described to her – her first Derado exchange – but it was better than she had expected.

A fleeting vision of Rinzal flashed in front of her and she wondered if he was also transforming into something higher than before. This thought made her smile - at least in her head, she was not sure could feel the nerves and muscles around her face anymore.

Yet something told her that Rinzal would be pleased with how their energies were exchanging together. That was assuming they *were* still exchanging with each other; if she was even still with him in the pyramid?

It didn't feel as though she were still there, since the atmosphere had changed from the heaviness of before; a lighter air now, one that was instantly easier to breathe.

Blinking, she scanned her surroundings, allowing the immediate sense of joy to engulf her.

"Zeno? Are you here?" she heard herself cry out whilst swallowing down a surge of excitement – at the possibility of what could have just occurred.

Her hands jolted out in front of her, as though someone else was in charge of her bodily reactions; a remote control that she did not have hold of. She tried to move forward but she quickly realised she was trapped in a statue-like paralysis. The only part she had control of her were her fingers, which she wriggled around frantically in the space in front of her, trying to break through this strange, pink, glowing, substance that surrounded her.

"Who is there?" she shouted out to the moving shapes ahead of her. But as she looked down to her feet, she gasped.

"The river!"

Without hesitating she lurched herself forward, managing to break herself out of her trance and regain control over her body. She knew who the moving shape must be on the other side of this bubble thing she was trapped in. It was him. The one she had dreamed about. The fair-haired male from the other world!

I knew I would make it to him!

"Hello!" she called out, twisting her body to urge the bubble to move her across the water somehow. To find a way to reach him.

Her heart was racing with excitement. Every part of her - body *and* mind - had all connected together again, and she could think of nothing else but getting over to him. It didn't even matter what this could mean, or where Zeno, Rinzal, or the others were. The male was on the other side of the river. She *had* to get over to him.

"Zeno did say they had no idea what could happen when I released my colour energy!" she giggled into her bubble space.

The bubble moved slowly but she could feel she was getting closer to him. His shape was becoming clearer. He had his back to her. And it appeared he was leaning forward, as though his arms were wrapped around something.

"Hello!" she called out again.

The male turned around. Unable to contain her excitement she waved her arms above her head, desperate to gain his attention. But then she saw why he had been leaning forward. That he had not been wrapped around some*thing* at all. It was some*one* – a female!

"Oh!" She heard herself cry.

Who is she? This was not how I dreamed this scene? Why would you draw me to you like this if you already have a love?

She wanted to cry, but another, more physical pain, distracted her.

"Ouch!" she cried out again. Her Derado burned hot around her neck. Yanking at it she pulled it away from her scorching skin.

"Damn!" she screamed as she struggled with her neckpiece, quickly realising the reason for its stubborn refusal to budge: she was releasing her energy again!

A thick, dark, pink-coloured energy burst out of the diamond in the pendant and made its way towards her frame. Feeling both helpless and drained, she watched as the colour mist wrapped around her once again.

So that's it! You drew me over to you like this and now I have to go back!

"Good-bye," she managed to whisper as she closed her eyes, aware that she had no choice but to let herself go to wherever her energy would take her next.

And I was so sure I was meant to be with you!

Heavy, confused thoughts drifted across her mind and then... nothing.

7. GAMES

How did she disappear like that? Her first diamond energy release and she just vanished from the pyramid! I misjudged her power. And now... Atla is downright furious!

Parador took her seat at the round mosaic table and then placed her hands on her knee. It was imperative that she projected confidence whilst she waited for him to make his appearance. It was a well-known fact that this was Atla's favourite time of day: his morning coffee break, always taken in the rose gardens of his vast Estate. And Atla was notoriously punctual, which is why her heart raced as she registered that he was already late. Even taking a deep inhale of the floral scents surrounding her did little to settle nerves. There was no question in her mind, being kept waiting for him like this was intended as punishment.

My plan should have worked. It WAS working. Atla was made aware of Tiegal's vile thoughts during the release ceremony. All her ridiculous yearnings for this male she dreamed of. Every Tandroan heard it! It was almost comical how loud her deepest desires were - her weakness.

Parador dug her fingernails into the skin on her thighs with such force that her blood seeped through her teal-coloured trousers.

I was sure Atla would take her away then. Lock her up before she could pass such destructive ideas on to the others. Perhaps even destroy her altogether? But, no. She got away!

The sound of a chair being dragged across the tiled floor made her flinch. Atla sat down directly opposite her and clicked his fingers to the side, signalling to a male waiter nearby to fetch him coffee. His short, heavily waxed black hair glistened in the morning sunshine and his severe side part exposed a sore redness to his skin where it had been unprotected from the scorching sun.

Not for the first time did Parador question his decision to sport such a different and distasteful hair style. Surely there were more profound ways to indicate his superiority over them all.

When I am in charge, I will have more hair than anyone else. I will let it tumble down my back. There will be no doubt who is in charge of the pack then!

The toe-curling sound of Atla's barking cough interrupted her thoughts. Careful not to show her distaste, she flashed him one of her most charming smiles as he leaned towards her.

"So, then Parador! We seem to have a problem on our hands: a case of a vanishing young female."

"Yes, most unexpected..."

"It was quite a spectacle, wouldn't you agree?"

His interruption silenced her. She bowed her head to offer her submission.

"There she was one moment, a vision of pink energy, and then... nothing! Just a pile of clothes floating in our sacred diamond water!" Atla raised his arms, palms face upwards and to the side, waiting for her to offer an explanation.

Parador lifted her chin, giving him a flash of her eye light. She had prepared herself for this.

"Yes, it was most unexpected Atla. However, I have given it great thought and I feel certain that her disappearance was inevitable and necessary. Her presence in our world was simply not healthy. Tiegal Eureka's thoughts were full of rebel ideas. She held great desire for the older ways of connection and..."

Her pause was dramatic and deliberate. It was crucial that Atla understand that Tiegal posed a genuine threat to his ideology. "And *intimacy*." She uttered this last word with a heavy exhale and a raise of her right eyebrow.

Atla shuffled back into his chair, folded his arms and then shuddered.

There you go. You really hate that word, don't you?

Parador felt her shoulders relax as she waited for her reasoning to settle Atla; to restore his confidence in her.

"Ah yes, Parador, but it was *your* idea to get her upgraded to the Erasmati Pyramid. And didn't I question this idea? That a mere teacher, a lowly elephant keeper, be granted a *real* diamond in her Derado! A place at my finest Release Day venue! And for what? So that she could humiliate our ways and all that we stand for? Do you not think I *know* what she was thinking? My aides tell me everything they hear from your Tandroan minds. And in Tiegal's case, it seems she is...was... unable of concealing any of her corrosive thoughts."

That was the idea! I WANTED you to hear how damaged she is!

Her fingers dug even further into her thighs. Keeping this frustration in check was unbearable. Still, she knew how to play him. Patience was the key.

Let him vent and then make your move. Remember...he is easier to manipulate when he feels out of control.

"And now the others are starting to wonder... to question our Tandro ways."

He growled at her as he leaned across the table. His face now much closer than she felt comfortable with. So close that Parador could detect the acrid scent of coffee on his early morning breath. Repulsed she managed to nod her agreement.

"I can see this may not appear ideal Atla..."

"Not ideal? They heard her thoughts! About her dreams of

touching and kissing and other disgusting things!" Atla squirmed in his seat. "And this is exactly why we give you the Derados! So that you don't need to lower yourselves to such weaknesses. All laws obeyed. All desires fulfilled. *That* is what I promise you all: controllable desires, longer lives and ... to keep your own damn fires burning! To not let anyone else dampen your flames."

Atla grabbed the silver mug full of steaming coffee and lowered his nose to the rim. For some reason, the scent of coffee beans always seemed to calm him. Parador suspected that it reminded him of another time, of memories that he still struggled to let go.

There you go! You got yourself all worked up then! Thinking about the old-world times. When making bonds with others left you open to being hurt. Like, I suspect you were way back then...when someone you connected with damaged that side of you! You are exactly where I want you now!

"Atla, my esteemed ruler, what you have created - this remarkable new world - and what you have given us all is a gift. Please, let me assure you that my reasons for suggesting Tiegal Eureka be present at the Erasmati Pyramid for her Release Day was in the best interest of Tandro - *and* our way of life."

Pausing to let these words register, she focused her eye-light towards him, knowing she would need to practice a little bit of her mind magic to convince him.

"I told you I had found someone who possessed an unusual energy that would be powerful when released. And I also knew that it was a dark energy that could threaten our world. I felt then, and still do, that it was important that the others saw how destructive such energy is. So much so, that it destroys you! Obliterates you into thin air. Like vapour, never to return."

"You knew she would disappear?"

"Yes. I did," she lied. "Trust me Atla, she *strengthened* the Tandro rule. Tiegal Eureka demonstrated the consequence of giving in to such dirty thoughts. If you release too much of your energy, you lose control of your fire, your island. And *then*... you simply disappear! It is a validation of your philosophy! Of everything you have created."

As her words ran through his mind, she finally relaxed her fingers from their painful grip on her flesh. Atla clicked his fingers to the side again. The male waiter appeared at their table in a flash. More coffee was poured into Atla's mug and a matching one was placed before her. A clear sign that she had presented her argument well!

"You do make some interesting points Parador. They please me, greatly. I only wish you had shared your ideas before with me. I do not like surprises. You know that!"

That was a close one, but he seems to have bought it!

"Yes, and for that I apologise. I will make sure to let you know when..."

The sound of pounding feet approaching the courtyard made them both jump and turn. A flush faced female ran up to their table. She wore an alarming expression that suggested she was caught somewhere between panic, fear, and euphoric excitement. Her forehead glistened with sweat which had attracted wisps of her black hair to stick in spider-like webs across her unusually pale skin.

This will be entertaining! Anyone who dares to approach Atla in such an inappropriate manner, and during his morning coffee, is going to be met with a nasty surprise – even if she is wearing a purple cloak.

But the female's announcement stalled her thoughts and sent a rush of fear coursing through her:

"She's back! The pink energy one who disappeared!" The female panted out her words.

"And...she ...she's naked!"

———

Parador jumped out of the open side-door of the trolley cart that had driven her to the Erasmati Pyramid and ran up the steps to the door as fast as she could.

Stupid, stupid, stupid Tiegal! Now Atla will think I am the dangerous one! That I lied and betrayed him. How the hell did she get back?

As she flung open the heavy doors to the Erasmati Pyramid she screamed her anguish into its vast inside space.

"Tiegal Eureka! Where are you?"

Nothing! Not a single sound reverberated back. "Ouch!"

Her Derado burned around her neck

"Stop it!" she demanded, slapping her hands over her turquoise diamond in a bid to prevent her colour mist from emerging. Releasing her energy in such circumstances would not help anything. This was her fear, her adrenaline, seeping out of her. It needed to be contained.

"Hello! Anyone there?"

Again, nothing.

Turning back to the open doorway she shouted down to her female driver.

"Hey, you, get in here, now!"

The female looked terrified as she ran up the steps. Her black bob kinked at the edges in a jarring fashion. Parador had already noticed that she had a habit of smoothing it down with her sweaty hand at regular intervals. It made her want to slap her, and hard.

"What is your name?" she demanded as soon as the female reached the step below her.

"Jingishi."

"Ugh! Tastes like monkey dung." Parador shuddered as the taste of the female's name filled her mouth. She popped a sprig of mint between her lips and took a deep breath, waiting for the vile taste sensation of the female's name to leave her.

"Tell me again what you heard this Indramia and Ochrani saying to each other. And I need the words verbatim."

The female took a deep breath and then launched into her detailed account.

"Well, I was just finishing off delivering some catering goods to the engineering camp before my shift at Atla's Estate was due to commence, because I have lots of different jobs to attend to and in a very short time..."

"Get to the point!"

"Oh, sorry, yes." The female took another step down, removing herself further from Parador's personal space.

"I, erm, well, I don't really know them very well, but I've seen them a few times together and I always notice them as they just seem a bit too close!"

Parador made a low growl.

"And...sorry yes, one of them, the smaller one, Indramia I think, said she knew when the pink energy one would come back here because she had *seen* her return?"

"You have already told me that. *Where* exactly did she say she had seen her return?"

"As I already told you. The diamond lagoon pool."

"Hold on there, she didn't just say diamond pool...she said *lagoon* pool! I said verbatim! Do you not understand what that word means?"

Jingishi nodded her head and then took yet another step down.

"Give me the keys to the trolley cart. And go back to your camp."

"But...I am supposed to go back to Atla for my shift..."

Parador dug a clump of mint out from between the back of her teeth with her tongue and stared at the female, long and hard.

"Go to your camp and forget this ever happened. You will have no recollection of hearing of the return of the vanishing one. Leave, now!"

Without uttering another word, Jingishi handed the keys to the cart, ran down the steps and then sprinted off in the direction of the sleeping camps.

As Parador watched the female leave she scanned the entrance to the Pyramid to check that she was safe from prying eyes. Once satisfied she was alone, she stamped down the pyramid steps, threw herself into the driver's seat, turned the key to the right to kick-start the cart and then swung the steering wheel to a severe left. The energy cave was only ten minutes away from the pyramid. She *had* to get there before anyone else did!

There were too many tectonic plates shifting all at once. Her mind was struggling to piece all the ruptures together. But, there was still time. There *had* to be. If she pushed this vehicle to the max she could stop Tiegal and the rest of her sisters from getting too close - before, they manifested their powers together - and made this whole situation even worse!

8. THE RETURN

The voices echoed above the surface of the water, each of them calling out her name.

I can hear you! Help me, please! I can't breathe under here.

The voices kept on calling. Wherever she was, under which waters, and in which time or world, it was clear her silent pleas could not channel through to them.

I am under here! Under the water? Can't you see me?

Determined to reach them, Tiegal kicked, wriggled and punched the space around her. But with each desperate move she made everything around her blurred. Swirls of pink coloured energy mist danced around her matching the exact movements of her intended actions. Horrified, she tried to scream as the realisation hit her: she had not yet reassembled her body into a physical form.

Damn! I'm still just matter.

The sheer terror that this awareness brought to her sent her into instant panic mode. But the more she fought, the stronger the current seemed to pull her further down into the water.

"Are you absolutely sure she would return here? And at this exact time?"

She knew this voice! Hearing this familiar, deep, comforting male tone stilled her frantic struggle.

Jovil! You are here? Help me, please! I feel like I'm drowning.

Once again, her silent pleas had no impact on the figures above the surface of the water. Despite this, she already felt calmer. Because a female voice had answered Jovil, one that she didn't recognise, but was filled with promise:

"As we told you Jovil. Our powers can only do so much. When I make a location perfume, I need a substantial part of a body to work with. To be honest, it was highly fortuitous that Tiegal cut herself on Indramia's bracelet when she did. That little piece of her skin provided me with just enough of her essence to form the necessary ingredients we needed to locate her."

"It's more than fortuitous Ochrani. It is quite remarkable!"

Jovil's answer was only just audible against the unmistakable sound of his feet pacing up and down a dusty, scratchy, stone floor; a sound that clearly identified where they were.

I must be in the cave lagoon again. Jovil! Look at the water! I need you to see me. Pleeeease!

Jovil's anguished voice reverberated above her again:

"Tell me again how these powers of yours work? Not that I don't believe you. If you two are anywhere near as powerful as Tiegal is, then, anything is possible. I just need to get this clear in my head."

Jovil's voice sounded gruff, anxious even.

A different female voice responded to him this time, one that sounded more like bird-song; a high-pitched melodic lilt. It was also strangely familiar.

"Our powers are very different, but they are complimentary to each other. Ochrani has the unique ability to create a location perfume. That's what we call it anyway. We have not heard of any other Tandroan with such an ability.

"She can create a distinct perfume that allows her to locate someone, no matter where they are. As long as she knows the ingredients of their scent, and can work with a sample of their DNA, she can make a perfume oil to pinpoint exactly where they are. It's quite magnificent!"

Hearing this revelation - that this female had made a perfume to locate her - was all Tiegal needed to find her strength to rebuild herself again.

That's Indramia's voice! The one who fell over in the pyramid pool. I knew there was something special about her!

Scanning her surroundings, she realised that the current had dragged her to the bottom of the lagoon, and yet, she somehow also knew that she was safe. She only had to twist herself a little to confirm that her physical being had almost fully reformed. And that her brilliant eyes were now fully functioning again. Their reflection finally revealing that she was still contained and protected within her energy bubble.

I'm not drowning! I'm safe!

A new feeling burned inside her now; an animal-like instinct that screamed at her to fight – and to survive. Her every instinct assured her that these fellow Tandroans above the water were part of her somehow, possibly even intertwined with her destiny. She *had* to find a way to get their attention.

Looking up to the surface of the water she could just make out Jovil's tall frame. He appeared to be shaking his head as he paced back and forth in front of the two female figures, waving his hands around in an exasperated fashion.

His voice echoed above her:

"And you, Indramia? How does your magic work with Ochrani's once she has made this location perfume?"

"Ah, let me answer that one if you don't mind."

The one she assumed was Ochrani, spoke again. Her deep voice was filled with excitement.

"Indramia is always so quick to applaud my gift, and yet hers is just as compelling. You see, Indramia has the gift of sight! If she can connect with the energy of someone, she can see things that have happened in their past... and in their future!"

As if on cue, Indramia stepped forward and placed her hand on Jovil's shoulder.

"That's how I know she will return here, on this day. It's not an exact prediction, to the minute, but she *will* be here, and soon."

Indramia's voice travelled down through the water to where Tiegal sat in her bubble on the bed of the lagoon, mesmerised by the words she was hearing.

"But how will she appear? Where should we look?" Jovil said.

"In the water, of course!" the two females chimed.

"I saw her reappear in this diamond lagoon! You will know when she is here." Indramia clarified.

I'm already here! Why can't you see me?

Unable to restrain herself any longer, Tiegal let out a roaring scream. Then, using both her fists she pounded on the bubble wall that surrounded her.

"I'm in the damn lagoon!"

A gush of water filled her mouth as she tried to shout out, realising too late that her screams had burst her bubble and she was now rapidly ascending to the surface of the water.

"Ooh we might not have to wait too long either. Look at the lagoon Jovil! It's glowing and... there's something moving... that looks like..."

The rest of Ochrani's delighted announcement was drowned out by the sound of breaking water, as Tiegal exploded out of the lagoon and landed straight into Jovil's arms.

The four of them sat shoulder to shoulder, in a circle of the cave floor. The cold, stagnant air had drawn them all together to share their body heat. Still, despite being wrapped in Ochrani's silver cloak, Tiegal's body refused to warm up.

"You have started to get some colour back in your cheeks again, but you're still trembling. You need some more clothing. I'm so sorry

Tiegal, if I'd known you were going to appear...erm...well..." Jovil stammered.

"Naked?" Tiegal finished for him. "It's okay Jovil, you can say the word out loud. We can't pretend that didn't just happen. That I just flew at you like that when I was... well, in a state of nature."

Ochrani and Indramia both let out a peal of giggles, which echoed around the cave in perfect harmony.

"Tiegal! You are just fantastic. I don't think I have ever heard anyone speak so, well, so... honestly! When Indramia told me that she had found another one of our sisters, I knew you would be special, but I wasn't expecting someone *this* exciting."

Ochrani's eye-light reflected brilliant prismatic light around their circle.

"I agree with Ochrani. You really are splendid Tiegal," Indramia whispered, her eye-light also shimmering with excitement. "I'm so glad you touched me at the Pyramid."

Hearing the word 'sister' made the hair on Tiegal's arms stand on end. That, and the fact that she recognised these females; their scents, and their energies.

Turning her face to Jovil she flashed her eyes at him, ensuring he received a deliberately blinding radiance.

"I think you need to do some explaining here Jovil. Why do I feel that you didn't tell me everything the last time we were here?" she demanded.

Jovil shifted to the side, removing his much-needed body heat from her as he did. The smell of regret permeated through him.

"Well, she is not entirely naked, is she? I mean, amazingly she is still wearing her Derado! It seems our energy controls have the power to both transport and transform us."

Jovil gripped the collar of his own Derado with both his hands, as if he were willing them to follow his distracting lead.

"I asked you a question Jovil?"

Tiegal reached over to give him a nudge on his shoulder, knocking him off-balance so that he rocked from side to side. No one said anything as they all watched him regain his balance and then bang his palms down on the cold cave.

"I'm not sure I understand it all myself," he finally muttered.

Ochrani made a tutting noise:

"Tiegal deserves some answers Jovil. She's been through a lot don't you think?"

Jovil looked at them all in turn.

"You're right, she does. You all do! And that's why... I think you should all get into the lagoon. Together! It will help you all understand. Please, just trust me."

Before waiting for a response, Jovil stood up, smacked away the cave dust that had caked around the legs of his black trousers, and then raised his arm in the direction of the pool.

Ochrani stood up first, then Indramia, closely followed by a reluctant Tiegal. All three of them took two steps back away from the edge of the water, and then folded their arms across their chests.

"Is this some kind of sick joke?"

Tiegal could hear a jumble of words coming from her two companions, their own minds scrambling with ideas of how all these connections could fit together, but all she could focus on was a furious rage with the male in front of her, the one she had assumed was her protector.

"First, you separate me from the others on my pre-release day. Scare the life out of me by telling me that I was made in a secret lagoon of death. That I was the only one to survive being born into a pool of diamond water that YOU over-energised with all your thoughts. Then, you declare that this is the reason I am now so different from everyone else on Tandro. And, that I needed to contain my wandering mind during my Release Day, in case my energy went into overdrive."

Jovil squeezed his eyes shut as she pounded him with her accusations.

"Well, no exaggerating there, hey, Mr Lagoon Master? I just transported to some other world, saw the beautiful male I have been dreaming about all this time, finally looked like I was going to reach him and get out of this hideous robot show that is Tandro, only to find that he was kissing some other female!"

Indramia and Ochrani placed their hands on her shoulders. She could feel both their intense body heat and their energies gently urging her to calm her fury, but she shrugged them off, unprepared to submit her emotions to anyone else until she knew exactly what was going on.

"And then... THEN... I find myself vanishing away again, only to end up back in that lagoon. And NOW! Now, you want me and my SISTERS to get back in there, under your command?"

With each sentence of rage uttered, Tiegal stamped her foot down and punched her fist out in his direction. Slowly, Jovil turned to face her, his expression unreadable.

"What do you see when you look into each other's eyes? Your sisters, as you have already referred to each other," Jovil finally asked, looking at each of them in turn.

Indramia responded first, by releasing her hold on Tiegal and then taking two strides towards Jovil.

"I can see it. There is definitely something different about our eye-lights." She turned back to face Tiegal. "Look at Ochrani. There's an image of an angel in her reflection. And you, Tiegal. There is clear heart shape radiating out from your eye-lights."

With one swift move, Ochrani took a giant leap forward, landing with both her feet next to Indramia.

"Yes! I can see it too. And Indramia's eye-light reflects the image of a star! It's obvious when you look for it!"

Jovil nodded. From the way he slumped his shoulders forward it appeared he was both exhausted and relieved.

"That's right. I think that these are your markers. It's like your hidden magic. It's what makes you all so unique, and so gifted."

Ochrani beamed both a huge grin and a blinding flash of eye-light. It was almost too much to absorb, and yet, as Tiegal allowed her own eyes to focus on Ochrani's reflections she realised that she was right: there really was the clear shape of an angel pulsating out from her optics.

Just like the strange female who approached me when I was feeding Namnum! The one with the eyes that radiated a golden horse-tail!

Tiegal opened her mouth to share this until-now-forgotten information, but Ochrani got in there before her.

"I get it now! Wow! After all these years of wondering why we had what we thought were mistakes, that we had defections, or even birthmarks in our eye-light, it turns out they are our symbols of power! So that's why Indramia reflects a star, because she has the gift of sight! And my angel must represent my ability to locate and guide," she declared, clapping her hands out in front of her.

Indramia put her hands on her hips and puffed out a satisfied sounding sigh:

"And, also, why Tiegal's reflection contains a heart! It explains why she has such a powerful energy. Because she is an abundance of love! That must be how she has connected to this male from another place and time! It is all starting to make sense now."

Tiegal watched them all in stunned silence. Jovil nodded at Ochrani, relaxing his shoulders in the manner of a long-suffering teacher, relieved to finally get through to his reluctant students. Indramia's skin glistened an apricot hue as she swung her silver cloak from side to side, revealing the smooth curves of her cleavage visible just above the tightly-fitted dark, green, bodice she wore. Ochrani, swayed back and forth, as though tuned into some meditative music only she could hear. Her rich smooth, chestnut-toned skin contrasting beautifully with her white-bodiced suit.

Tiegal had never felt more confused and alone.

"Argh! What is going on? Why are you all saying these things? I just told you that I saw my dream male from that other world kissing someone else! I'd hardly call that a beautiful destiny journey that my *powerful* love energy sent me on! And Jovil still hasn't explained how we could be sisters if I was the only one to survive this lagoon! Oh, and let's not forget that we are all using this old-world term "sisters" as though this is normal for us all. None of this makes any sense! What are you trying to do to me?" Tiegal dropped to the floor like a dead-weight, not caring that she banged her hip and scraped her toes in the process. Exhaustion finally winning, she buried her face into her bunched-up knees, not sure if she could hold off her need for sleep for much longer, never mind get back into the water again.

"I don't belong anywhere. I'm lost."

As these desperate words escaped her mouth, a confusing mix of emotions flooded through her; a deep shame over demonstrating her weakness to them all; and, worse, so much worse, an engulfing sense of loss for something that she couldn't quite place.

"Tiegal, that couldn't be further from the truth. If anything, you have only just been found."

The sound of Jovil's soothing voice near her ear made her shiver. His warm hands gathered around her arms and under her knees. Before she could protest, she felt her body lifted from the cold ground.

"Please, just trust me Tiegal. That's all you need to do. Trust me. I won't let you all down again," he assured her.

Before she could think of an appropriate response, the sound of splashing water and her sisters' laughter filled the cave.

"Come and join us in the water Tiegal. We have so much to share with you. So much to tell you. Jovil's right. You can trust him." Ochrani and Indramia spoke together in that remarkable harmony they shared.

Their excitement was so contagious that Tiegal's fingers tingled with a yearning to touch them. And as she reached her hands out in their direction, it was as though her body needed to seal a connection with them, that she instinctively sensed they used to share.

Seeing their identical, encouraging smiles beaming back at her from where they were floating in the lagoon, she jerked her body out of Jovil's arms and let herself fall into the water, crashing into it with an ungraceful splash.

Fuelled by a desperate urge to find this elusive truth they promised to share with her, she swam over to them, entwining her fingers with theirs as soon as she reached them, so that they formed a circle in the centre of the lagoon pool.

The water reacted to their connection immediately, treating them all to a glorious display of fluorescent colours. Tiegal's eyes widened, her light enhancing the colourful glow from under the water.

"The diamonds! They are glowing again...as though they are reacting to something? They did this the last time I was here, with Jovil."

As she said this, Ochrani broke their circle and gave a playful leap in the air before crashing down under the water, and then quickly resurfacing with both her hands full of luminescent diamonds.

"I feel so...so powerful; so strong! It's like magic! Here, try touching them," Ochrani enthused, holding out her hands to both Indramia and Tiegal. But then, Jovil called out to them from the water's edge. His voice was a trembling echo in the vast cavernous space:

"You *will* feel powerful! The diamonds are remembering how you grew out of their energy in this lagoon Tiegal. And...as Ochrani and Indramia did too!"

Tiegal shook her head at him and then smacked her hands down onto the surface of the water.

"But...you said I was the only one who survived?"

She watched as Jovil shook his head, bunched his hands into his pockets and then let his shoulders slump. His whole posture displayed his shame.

"I'm sorry I didn't tell you the whole truth Tiegal. I was just trying to protect you. All of you," he finally answered.

Tiegal shivered at the sound of his confession.

9. THE REVEAL

From where she crouched, behind one of the larger boulders at the other side of the cave lagoon, she was perfectly placed to hear and see everything, whilst still remaining hidden from their view. Everything about the scene before her offended her senses: the blinding glow of the diamonds; the acrid smell of Jovil's shame as he delivered his confession; the taste of their names, her "sisters" - Ochrani, Indramia, and Tiegal - that had blended together into one disgusting ball of solid vomit at the back of her throat.

Careful not to make any noise, she reached into her cloak pocket in search of a sprig of mint. If ever there was a time to ensure she maintain control of her senses, it was now.

Who do they think they are? They look ridiculous holding each other's hands and praising their unique powers! They have no concept of what power is! So what if one of them can make location perfumes, or, if the other one can supposedly see into the future. None of that is a match against what I can do.

This was more dangerous than she had feared. The females in the lagoon appeared to be getting more powerful. She could tell by the way their skin shimmered and their eye-lights beamed an extraordinary intensity that their energies were manifesting the more they stayed in such close proximity to each other.

But it was the heart-eyed one that worried her the most. Although her deeper thoughts were more difficult to detect this time, it was obvious that she was the one who posed the greatest threat to her ambitions. She could transport herself to another world! She couldn't deny that this made her a worthy opponent as the most powerful Tandroan that existed.

But then, she knew only too well, that there was a thin line between power and weakness. She only had to think about Atla to realise that simple truth.

The sound of a hand smacking the surface of the lagoon made the hairs on her arms stand at attention in anticipation. Tiegal was getting impatient.

"Why, Jovil? I just don't understand why you told me only half-a-truth? How is denying me the right to meet my sisters, who were also created in this lagoon, protecting me, or them? You knew how lonely I felt. I trusted you!"

Parador clasped her hand over her lips, suppressing the urge to laugh out loud. What foolish words! Could Tiegal not see the obvious answer to this ridiculous question: the lagoon master kept us all hidden from each other, because he knew he had seriously messed up his experiment! That he had created four supremely powerful Tandroans whose powers would get even stronger if they were ever to meet.

Oh Jovil, you can't even see your own powers. Why do you think you were able to have such influence over the water in the first place? You started this powerful fire that burns inside us all, with YOUR power! This elemental power you must possess! How can you not see this?

She watched, gripped by the scene before her, as Jovil sank down on the water's edge and let his feet dangle over the surface of the lagoon.

"I didn't tell you all because, well, if you realised that you each existed then you would want to know more and that would just..."

"Attract unwanted attention from Atla?" The one she now identified as Indramia interrupted him.

"Yes! Exactly!" Jovil sighed. "I have watched all of you from afar, all these years. I needed to be certain that you were all thriving and that you were not vulnerable in any way. It did concern me, at first, when Indramia and Ochrani ended up in the same engineering camp but, well, you were just drawn to each other. And it didn't seem to be causing any problems. So, I left you alone. It was only really Tiegal I was truly worried about, because of her dreams...her desires for more connection, her loneliness."

Tiegal made a whimpering sound that resonated throughout the cavernous space between them.

"Is that why you brought me here, before my Release Day?"

The lagoon bubbled around the circumference of Tiegal's body as she spat out her question, through gritted teeth.

"Yes! Trust me, I debated it many times, but in the end I decided that you were heading towards danger now that you had reached the age to receive your Derado. But I also knew that I had to be fair to you. That knowledge is power. That's why I begged you not to think of this male from your dreams during your first release. Or at least, to learn how to hide your thoughts from the others; especially from Atla's aides! I had this terrible feeling that something disastrous would happen if you released your energy once you connected with the pink diamond in your Derado. And, well, it did!"

Parador could feel her own rage surfacing as she watched Tiegal's expression visibly change from one of anger to calm understanding in the space of a split second; at how her hands immediately reached for her glowing Derado, and then out towards the lagoon master.

"It's okay Jovil. You were trying to protect me. I can see that."

Tiegal's soft, reassuring words reached Parador's ears like painful blows.

It's that easy, is it? He played a deceitful game on you and all it takes is a few pitiful words for you to simmer down! Do you really think he is telling you the whole truth? Isn't there something missing here Tiegal? I think this happy bonding party needs a little more shaking up. There is one sister here that you haven't yet bargained for!

But just as she was about to emerge from her hiding place, Indramia delivered another blow:

"You must hold on to your dreams Tiegal! It's not over. You will see him again somehow! The male you dream of! I have seen a vision of you together."

On hearing this, Parador skulked back into the shadow. Indramia's revelation had just turned the tables once more.

Damn! These seeing powers are actually quite useful! But then... If Indramia is telling the truth, that Tiegal will see this dream male again, then she must surely be capable of transporting to this other world again. And if that is the case...then I am back in the winning seat. My reasoning with Atla will still stand: that Tiegal must be an example to the others, what happens to those who dare to defy Atla's philosophy. The question is, how and, when will she vanish again?

Crouching down on her knees she leaned forward to catch the rest of the conversation, something that was becoming more difficult as the water bubbled loudly and more ferociously with every minute that Tiegal and her sisters remained in the lagoon.

It was Ochrani who urged Indrami to reveal more, her voice booming out in excitable bursts as she clapped her hands loudly with each syllable she spoke:

"Do tell us what you see Indramia! Where, when, and how, will Tiegal see him again? And is he still kissing that other female?"

Stop that damn clapping you stupid caramel-haired idiot! I can't concentrate when you smack your hands together like that every time you get excited about something. No wonder you have a power that means you have to use a diffuser to get any results. I could quite happily diffuse you right now!

Parador's head was pounding now. The mint had stopped being effective and the scents and sounds in the cave had begun to overwhelm her again. It made her feel nauseous, and weak. But there were no more mint sprigs left in her pocket and the information being exchanged in this cave held too much importance for her future. She had no choice other than to bite her lip and persevere.

Tiegal had pulled herself out of the water now and was being wrapped up in Jovil's black cloak. Her shoulders were slumped and the glow from her Derado had already dimmed. She looked both exhausted and defeated.

"I don't think I want to go back there again though Indramia. Not now that I have found a real connection with the two of you, my sisters! And, not after seeing him with someone else! It broke the connection that I thought we shared somehow! I felt like such a fool. And, if I'm being honest, being transported and transformed like that was not exactly pain free either!"

Parador could hardly breathe as she waited to hear Indramia's response.

"Tiegal, I don't think you saw everything clearly when you were in that bubble. But, I did.

Just now, when we touched the diamonds together. It gave me a glimpse into your past, as well as your future."

"What do you mean I didn't see things clearly? I saw him kiss a female. It was nothing like I had envisioned in my dreams. It made me feel...hollow, as though everything had been sucked out of me!"

"Yes, Tiegal."

Indramia swam over to Tiegal, managing to reach her in just two gentle strokes.

"He kissed someone else just as you appeared. And then..."

"What?"

"He saw *you*, and then he let her go!"

Parador held her head in a vice-like grip with both her hands as the pain behind her eyes pounded in persistent beats. Her head felt as if it could explode at any moment. There were too many smells, colours, and emotional energies swirling round this draughty cave for her senses to deal with all at once. It was oppressive, and also danger-ously close to sending her into a panic mode.

Dammit! Why didn't I bring more mint?

It was now clear that her original plan - to make a grand entrance and then expose Jovil and all his pathetic lies - would no longer work. Her current physical and mental state would not give her the neces-sary upper hand.

Does he really think he can ignore me, and my existence? I was made in this lagoon too! By him! Who does this lagoon master think he is?

A dark green mist seeped from under her cloak: the tell-tale sign that her anger was releasing its colour from her Derado. She quickly covered the neckpiece with her hand before her angry colour energy alerted her presence to the others.

This enclosed space was too much. *They* were all too much. Jovil, with his fiery coconut scent, long hair and constant pacing. Ochrani, with her enthusiasm for this birth-scene reunion: "Look at the light and magic we are making in the water together!" Her loud voice, bouncy mannerisms, and overpowering scent - a strange mix of lilies and basil.

Indramia, with her pathetic whisper of a voice, and slow, swan-like movements. And her grating over-confidence in the power of her visions.

"Between us, we will keep you safe from Atla before you are ready to return to him again," Indramia declared.

And then, Tiegal the 'sister', whose name tasted of red grapes and who released a scent that

could change from velvet rose to wild bluebell, with even a slight change in the direction of

the wind. She was just... sickly sweet!

How could I have been made amongst you? I am nothing like any of you!

She watched each of them as they either exited the lagoon or moved away from the edge, and then reconvened in their strange communal circle on the cave floor. And then, how they all gathered their cloaks around their shoulders and turned their focus to Tiegal, waiting for her to speak up:

"Can you tell me more Indramia? About what you saw, in your vision?"

Parador flinched at how Tiegal shook whilst waiting for Indramia's response. This desperation of hers - to find an old-world version of a love connection - was nothing short of offensive.

"I only see things in flashes, but I saw how he let go of the female he was with. It looked like he reached his hand out to you and then called out for you to come over to him. But your energy bubble took you away. I guess your release at the Pyramid was not enough to keep you there long enough that time?"

"No! It was Tiegal's jealousy releasing. I think that's what sent her back here again," Jovil interjected. He placed his hand on Indramia's knee, as though offering an apology for interrupting her.

"Can't you see? This is the conflict of releasing emotions. On one hand, having feelings towards another can build us up, make us burn brighter! But... it can also dampen our fires and take away the control we need to have over our lives, our individual islands."

He sounded exasperated.

"And it's exactly why Atla's philosophy teaches us that we should never be prisoners to our emotions. It's why we wear our Derados; so that we can control our energies, and exchange our desires with each other without the need for all these connections with each other! They make you weak, and out of control."

Parador trembled as a forgotten feeling of excitement flurried through her. Her eyes no longer pounding, she let her left hand release its hold on her forehead and her right hand fall away from its grip on her Derado. Jovil's words had given her an idea.

Without making a sound, she stealthily slipped off her cloak and unclasped her rope belt so that she could unzip herself out of her jumpsuit. Then, careful not to make a splash, she lowered herself down into the darker end of the lagoon, where she knew the others could not see her.

The moment the icy water met with her skin, she grinned. Being naked and exposed like this felt deliciously enticing. Her turquoise diamond on her Derado lit up in response to her excitement and her entire body flooded with endorphins in anticipation.

Let's see what happens when I remind them how controlling your desire brings more power.

Now that she was submerged under the water the voices of the others were muffled but she was no longer interested in hearing the rest of their pathetic attempts to search their deeper selves. Whatever vision Indramia thought she had seen for Tiegal's future, it had not yet been written. Not as far as she was concerned. *She* would be the one who determined how the rest of Tiegal's story developed. For now that she understood their individual powers, and their weaknesses, she held all the winning cards.

She swung her head from side to side, enjoying how her jet-black hair floated around her face as she moved. Then, on impulse, she wriggled her hips in a similar fashion, relishing how light her breasts felt as they danced in the water; and how dangerous the desire that burned inside her felt as she succumbed to the temptation to touch herself between her hips.

We all have forbidden desires Tiegal Eureka. You just need to learn how to keep, and enjoy them - all for yourself!

Within seconds of receiving her expert touch her body reacted, instantly rewarding her with a flurrying sensation that rippled through her, whilst simultaneously releasing a burst of turquoise energy colour from her Derado.

A buzz of noises from the other side of the lagoon reverberated across the surface of the water, signalling that the others must have finally realised that they were not alone.Delighted, she pushed herself upwards, gulped as much air as she could, and then broke into a fast breast-stroke towards them, all the time keeping her head just under the surface.

As she emerged from the water, just in front of the edge where they had gathered, she heard Jovil cry out: "Parador? Is... that you?"

Parador couldn't hold back her laughter. The lagoon master looked utterly terrified! And she? Well, she knew that she looked positively resplendent in her naked form; both radiant from her release, and from the glowing diamonds that surrounded her in the lagoon.

"You? I know you! You're the one with the horse-tail image in your eye-light!" Tiegal slapped her own forehead. "How could I forget this? You came to me, just before my Release Day! You knew my name! And you said that you had magic secrets inside of you... from your creation. Just like me! And...I suppose both Ochrania and Indramia do too!"

Parador smiled as she rested her arms on the side of the lagoon and then pulled herself up and out of the water so that she stood, dripping wet, in front of them.

"That's right Tiegal. Anything else?"

Quite predictably, Jovil rushed over to her and wrapped her up in a cloak, before Tiegal had a chance to respond.

"For goodness sake, Parador. Cover yourself up!" He demanded.

The scent of his fear seeped out of his pores as he brushed past her. The smell made Parador retch in response. She pushed him away from her and then turned her gaze back to Tiegal again, aware that Indramia and Ochrani were both staring at her with stunned, flashing eyes and wide, open mouths.

This was all proving too easy. She could feel an incredible rush of energy inside of her. Could even picture new synapses connecting together inside her brain. It was like she had just been re-born all over again!

Thank you, sisters! Your cosy little lagoon reunion has just made me even more powerful than the three of you put together!

Determined to capitalise on how her surprise appearance had rendered them all powerless with shock, she flashed her eyes at them each in turn. Jovil made a move towards her. Without hesitating, she shot him an extra brilliant flash of eye-light before he could advance any further. He stilled instantly. Satisfied she had him under her control, she then turned to her sisters. Not one of them made a move. Her eye-light had successfully stunned them, but they were all flashing their own eye-light back to her.

"This will be fun. I can't wait to see which of our magic markers can out-shine the others. Let's see, Ochrani. An angel? Hmmm...it is a useful guide but it bears no relevance now. Angels are relic ideas from the old-world."

Parador gave a dismissive wave of her hand.

"But what about Indramia's star? Definitely more of a competitor. I can't deny that there is a more useful magic in this kind of energy. After all, it does symbolise a reading of one's destiny!"

She rubbed her chin as she surveyed the three females, marvelling at her own power to render them paralyzed in front of her.

"In fact, I would say that this is where I need to intervene!" She stepped in front of Tiegal, pulling on a wet strand of her chocolate-brown hair that had stuck to the side of her nose so she could tuck it behind her ear for her.

"There you go! I'm sure that must have been irritating you!" She raised her eyebrows at her in a deliberately sardonic manner, relishing the satisfying feeling of control, and the fury she could sense coming from Tiegal when she touched her.

"Because Tiegal here has too much heart. And that, my sisters, is problematic! You see, I for one, do not want her messing things up around here. It just won't fit with the big plans that I have for shaking things up. My own dreams, that exist in THIS world, that I fully intend to turn into reality. So, angels, stars and hearts will need to forget about each other...vanish! You work too well together."

As she spoke her knees quivered with excitement. Consistent turquoise energy vapour released from her Derado in exquisite bursts around her as her body became intoxicated by the exercising of such intense power. Golden threads of her magic reflected on the faces of her puppets as she scanned her eye-light between them, all the time channelling words inside her head to ensure she could master them into behaving as she wished:

You have never heard of or have seen this lagoon.

You have no memory of meeting your sisters.

You have no knowledge of your powers.

You will exit this cave silently and retreat to your camps.

Despite her confidence, she held her breath as she watched her three sisters walk away from her in silence, one by one. Each of them ascending the steep ladder that led to the corridor of the upper section of the cave, quietly and robotically obeying her orders.Once they were out of sight, she exhaled slowly and then turned her attention to Jovil, who was staring at her. His eyes were firmly locked on hers. Dim flickers of light sparked from his pupils.

Careful not to break his trance too quickly, she sauntered over to him on her tiptoes. Using her index finger she pressed the red diamond that sat in the eye-shaped pendant of his Derado and waited for him to return to a state of consciousness.

"Hello Jovil! Remember me?"

His eyes flickered and his pupils dilated, a look of horror filling his face as he registered who she was.

"Parador? Wh...wh...what are you doing here?"

"I came here with you, don't you remember? On Atla's orders. To wait for the pink energy

female to return."

"Tiegal? She came back?"

She grabbed him by the arm, aware that he could too easily faint.

"Yes, she did. And she played some nasty little mind tricks on us when she did. You collapsed before we could stop her from escaping. If we go now, we can probably catch her. Atla was clear in his instructions that we should bring her back to him. She is very dangerous."

Jovil trembled under her touch as he absorbed her words. She could hear his mind scrambling to make sense of why he was here, with her.

"Why are we here though?" He gasped.

Ah, you think no one knows about your secret lagoon then? That I hadn't worked out your dirty little secret?

"Call it an intuition. I figured if she were to return then it would be to one of the diamond lagoons. You were the one who told me there was this other one, hidden down here. Don't you remember?"

She gave him one of her most innocent - and practiced - smiles, followed by another bright flash of her eye-light.

Don't ask questions you don't want the answer to!

"We should go! Tiegal left a few minutes ago. I think she was heading back to her camp. We need to get to her, before any of the others see her. She needs to be contained!"

Jovil raked his hands through his long wavy hair and nodded at her.

"Yes, sorry, I don't know what happened to me just then. It's like my memory was wiped."

"That's because Tiegal played some nasty little tricks on you when she emerged from the lagoon. Don't worry I won't tell Atla her magic worked on you and not on me. But we do need to get her before anyone else does. And...NOW!"

Without hesitating, Jovil turned and ran towards the ladder.

"Come on then Parador. Let's go and get her!"

PART TWO

**Earth
2065**

10.JOURNEYS

Johannes let his head sink into the pillow and closed his eyes, already feeling awkward - and slightly foolish.

"Kagiso, you know I would do anything for you and I've always believed in your methods, but don't you think this is taking it a bit too far?" he whispered, wriggling his bottom around to find a comfortable position on the old sofa Kagiso had insisted he lie down on.

"And I've got to go and help Frederick with the chores. One of the cows is sure to go into labour soon and I promised to keep watch over her..." he continued, hoping Kagiso would come to her senses and let him go find his brother-in-law, who was no doubt struggling to manage the animals in this stifling heat. It was hard enough for them all to keep up with the demands of the farm as it was, the last thing they needed was distractions such as their beloved housekeeper, Kagiso, holding one of them back.

"Johannes Smit! Stop this nonsense complaining and let me do my magic. You're no good to anyone when your head is full of dreams you still haven't bothered to understand! I keep telling you, you've got to listen to the messages or they'll just keep plaguing you. And then what? You'll go crazy!"

Despite his frustration Johannes couldn't help smiling. He rubbed at his eyes, still tightly shut, and waved his hand in the air to signal his compliance.

He could hear Kagiso shuffling her feet on the stone floor of their kitchen.

"How long will this take Kagiso? I don't think Annarita or Frederick are going to be impressed if they see me lying here in the middle of the day when there's so much work to be done on the farm," he pleaded.

"Shh... your sister is having a nap with the baby. Henri was awake all night, bless him. And I've told her she *must* rest when the baby does. And as for your brother-in-law, he is a good, strong man. Frederick can manage fine without you for a little while longer. We need to do this *now* Johannes, whilst the house is quiet and peaceful. It's the only way I'll be able to connect with whatever it is this spirit guide of yours is trying to tell you."

Johannes sighed. There was no use arguing with Kagiso when she laid down her law. Kagiso laid her clammy palm on his forehead and mumbled something about the turbulent journey her bittersweet boy had travelled.

"I'm eighteen now Kagiso. I'm not a boy anymore, remember." He dared to open his eyes, just a fraction, but she quickly drew her hands over his eyelids to smooth them back down.

"Not in your dreams you're not. When you go on your sleep journeys you visit another time, an earlier time, when your Ma was still here. I hear you in the night my boy. And that's why we need to know what she is trying to tell you." Kagiso's voice trembled with each reference to his late mother. It made him feel sick, a revulsion that called for him to run away. And he would have done, if it were anyone else speaking of his mother like this. If he didn't love Kagiso so much, then he would have pulled her hands away from his face, and run away, back to the cows, carts, and oxes that needed his attention.

Instead, he inhaled and exhaled slowly, as she instructed, letting her voice carry across him, relaxing and soothing.

"Go back there Johannes, to where you were last night, when you were talking to her. And tell me what you remember, what you can see around you," she urged.

He let his arm fall down to the floor from where it had been resting on his stomach, Kagiso's gentle, deep voice already lulling him into a hypnosis. He felt his body shrinking, regressing, as though he were falling back through time.

"What can you see?" Kagiso asked.

"People, lots of them, by the river. Some standing, and others eating, sitting on blankets. A gathering of some kind? A party?" he whispered, vaguely aware that his voice sounded higher, squeakier.

"Okay, good, now walk to where you feel drawn," Kagiso instructed.

Johannes squirmed from where he lay on the sofa, whilst simultaneously walking towards the people he saw in his mind; his body engaging in different actions in parallel conscience.

"I can see where I want to go." He smiled as he spoke, fully immersing himself in this scene by the river, strangely aware, and in awe, that his feet were a good five sizes smaller and that he was running towards his mother, in the body of his seven-year old self.

It was the karros he noticed first; the woollen shawl she often wore around her shoulders. The one his father had traded with some Xhosa people who had been exploring the area from the Eastern Cape. He remembered how it was his mother's favourite.

His mother's face lit up as he approached her, and she reached her arms out to him, pulling him easily onto her lap. He fell into her embrace, barely able to contain his tears.

"Come here my son, you look like you need some love," she whispered into his head, snuffling into him.

"Look at you, with all this golden hair," she marvelled, running her dainty fingers through his thick blonde curls, "still as fair as it was when I first laid eyes on you. And just like your father. A beautiful

Dutch boy sparkling in these hot African lands, showing us all how we can live and journey together."

"I missed you!" he choked. "You left me."

His mother jerked back from him, her hands grasping around his cheeks.

"Johannes Smit. I will never leave you. I'm always here. You know that really. You've always known it."

"But you're not Ma! You're not in the house with us anymore. You've missed so much. Annarita is married now and they have a baby..." he broke off at the sound of his sister – the eleven-year old version – giggling with her friends just behind them.

"Yes, your sister is indeed lucky. She will find it is easy to love; and to be loved. But what about you, my boy? What do you seek where you are now?" she questioned, her voice soft and reassuring as she wiped his tears with her hand and then kissed the soft, wet skin of his cheeks.

"I'm supposed to marry Elna. Just like Pa always said I would," he answered her in a child-like voice he had forgotten he had once spoken. His mother frowned at him.

"You must not be constrained by what is easily reached. Sometimes you have to travel further to find what your heart truly seeks." Her voice trembled, and this time it was his hand that reached out to her cheek. With his right thumb and index finger he pressed his mother's skin, using the soft pads of his fingertips to soak up her salty tears.

"Does that mean, perhaps...my destiny is *not* with Elna?" he dared. The strange sound of his pre-pubescent voice referring to such an adult concept made him both squirm and squeak.

He waited for her response, but none came. Instead she looked at him, her eyes wide and sad.

"What is worth having is never easy to obtain," she finally said.

"Ma!" He reached out to touch her again, but she had already started to fade. Her features now lost as his vision blurred and the sound of Kagiso's frantic voice called him back to his eighteen-year old body filled his ears.

"Where did you go? You looked like you were shrinking right before my very eyes there boy." Kagiso exclaimed, her hand already pulling on his arms to shake him back to reality.

"I saw her Kagiso. I spoke to her," he managed, gently pushing Kagiso away so that he could stretch his legs out and regain a sense of his size and form once more.

"Your Ma? Or the girl? You kept saying something about that girl you've been courting, the one from the neighbouring farm."

Kagiso shook her head at him with such force it looked quite painful. Johannes smacked his lips together, as he always did when Kagiso was exaggerating her irritation about something - or someone.

"The girl being... *Elna*, who you have known since she was little."

"Yes, yes, okay but why were you talking about her just then. You were supposed to be connecting with spirits, not girls who you can speak to every day!" she grumbled.

In spite of himself, he laughed at the woman who had taken over the role of mothering him, and stood up to place his arms around her, drawing her close to his chest. Her head only reached the base of his sternum. He leaned his mouth down to kiss the top of her head, his nose wrinkling as her hair tickled his nostrils.

"I did find a connection Kagiso. I found my Ma again," he whispered.

He felt Kagiso's shoulders relax in his arms as she registered his words.

"What did she say?" she breathed into his chest. He could feel the movement of her shaking body; the tell-tale sign that she was holding back her tears. He gave her a gentle squeeze.

"She said..." he hesitated, unsure how much he should, or indeed wanted, to share.

"That she hadn't really left. And that she was always here," he finally answered.

Johannes desperately needed to scratch his back. He twisted his left arm at an awkward angle, struggling to balance holding onto Henri, whilst using his other arm to wipe away the nervous sweat that was now trickling down between his shoulders.

Annarita had asked him to bathe his baby nephew and he hadn't felt he could refuse her. To be fair, his sister was usually soft with him when he tried to bow out of household chores; it rarely took more than a wink before she would give into him, but tonight her instinct – more motherly than sisterly - seemed to keep him from venturing away from the house.

Johannes clenched his jaw as he splashed water over the rolled-up baby fat of his baby nephew's legs. Henri was an easy baby, always happy kicking his feet up and down in the tin bath. Johannes normally enjoyed spending time with him, just not tonight.

The sun was still stifling and despite moving the large bath into the shade of the garden, his clothes were drenched in sweat. Damn! He would have to go back inside and change his shirt before meeting Elna.

He couldn't afford to be late. Elna would expect him to be at the river at six. They always met at this time and she hated it when he was late.

"Why are you acting so jittery today Johannes? Are you up to something, yes?" Annarita probed.

"I'm just going to be late again that's all!" he responded, careful to avoid looking in her in the eye. The last thing he wanted was to engage his sister in a debate about the merits of his choice in girl-friend. Annarita had made her objections about Elna's possessiveness clear, on more than one occasion.

"I keep telling you Annarita, she is not who you think she is. If you just spent time with her you would see what I see," he grunted, whilst his hands slipped under Henri's wet body, forcing him to grab the baby's arms and swing him upwards before his sister caught sight of his negligent uncle duties.

"I saw that!" Annarita muttered, in a tone that indicated she was neither worried, nor concerned about his mistake. He knew his sister loved her baby dearly, but he also knew how much she valued her rest and that she was grateful for any help she could get – careless brother or not.

Johannes frowned as he watched his sister struggling to rise from her garden chair, her hands clutching her hips before she steadied herself on the nearby fence. This was not the sight of a healthy, twenty-two-year old girl and he cursed – not for the first time - the doctor who had taken too long to arrive when Annarita went into labour three months ago. Their mother would turn in her grave to think her daughter had endured such pain with no medical help.

"Sorry Annarita! He's getting quite strong."

Johannes pulled Henri out of the bath, wrapped him up in the thin cotton towel Annarita had thrown his way, and then squeezed him, as tightly to his chest as he dared, breathing in his addictive smell.

"Why do babies smell so different?" he whispered into the edge of the towel where it rested on the wet hairs of Henri's soft head.

"It's God's way of ensuring we don't drop them so easily! That we like them enough to keep them safe. Even if they do poo and cry all the time."

Annarita groaned and then stretched her legs out in front of her, her mouth widening into an exhausted yawn. She looked almost ten years older than her age, splayed out in her chair in the shade of the evening sun, her cotton dress and dirty apron buttoned unevenly.

Just seeing her like this made Johannes furious, almost to the point of tears.

"Ah Henri's a good'un. You just had a harder time than most bringing him into the world. But you do look so tired sister. I wish that you had more help. That between us we could make it all better."

He held Henri close to him, rocking him from side to side, all thoughts of an impatient girlfriend waiting by the river for him now gone.

"I have more than most do. Between you, Frederick, and Kagiso we are doing just fine."

The way his sister smiled at him, with such a determined effort to hide her pain and fatigue, conjured the dreaded, but faithful, feeling of grief that lived within him. She looked exactly like their mother when she pulled such an expression.

"I know you have a great husband and Frederick is a really good dad but we both have so much work to do if we are going to keep the farm going and Kagiso is ... well, just Kagiso!" he managed to chuckle.

"Oi! Who you calling *just* Kagiso?"

Johannes and Annarita laughed in unison at the sound of their beloved housekeeper; the woman who had not only raised them after their parents had died, but had also given them more love and laughter than any other parent they knew in their neighbourhood.

"She has a point Johannes. Kagiso is more than a *just,* she's well, everything!" Annarita leaned forward, this time with more ease, as she reached her arms out to take her baby from Johannes' arms.

"Ah, now, don't you even be thinking about doing that. This baby is already fatter than most six-month olds and you have got little more strength than a baby bird. Sit yourself down Annarita," Kagiso instructed, batting flies away from around her face as she stomped over to Johannes and promptly yanked baby Henri from his arms.

"And you, young man, need to get cleaned up before you think of meeting that girl of yours," she scolded, shooing him away with her over-sized apron. It was remarkably clean and pristine in comparison to Annarita's.

Johannes gave Kagiso his broadest smile, planting a kiss on her cheek, another on baby Henri's wet head, and then finally one more on his sister's cheek.

"That's right! I really do have to go! The sun will be setting soon, and my girl is waiting!"

11. STONES

After taking care to change his shirt and leave the house in an inconspicuous manner, waving casually as he closed the kitchen door, he started to run as soon as he was out of view. The point on the river, where Elna would be waiting, was close to her house but far enough away from both their residences to put them safely in the no-man's land between the two. At least, he hoped it was safe. If her father caught sight of him, he would surely order him over to join him for a 'gentlemanly drink' – the kind that was impossible to get away from in any hurry.

He saw Elna pacing by the muddy banks under the shade of a large tree. She was banging a long stick against her grey cotton skirt and humming to herself. It made him smile as he listened, keeping a little distance from her before making his presence known.

"Hey there, I'm sorry I'm late," he called out to her. She looked startled.

"I was beginning to think you would not be coming to see me Johannes and I cannot stay too long. My family will be wondering where I am. I said I would be back for a cake later!" She rushed her words out, averting her eyes from him as she spoke, in a tone that sounded close to tears.

Damn! How could I forget it was her birthday today?

He scolded himself silently, frantically thinking of a gift he could promise her that would soon arrive. When nothing came to mind, he resorted to a tried and tested tactic he had seen Frederick use on Annarita, on more than one occasion:

"Elna, Elna, Elna. I think I could keep saying that word a thousand times. It makes me think of a beautiful girl one may be driven to write about in a poem."

He paused and waited for her reaction. When none came, he decided to try option two: distraction.

"Hey, were you named after anyone Elna? I can't believe I have never asked you that before."

He had no idea where such a bizarre question had come from, or why he thought talking to her in such a florid manner would distract her from his forgetfulness. Fortunately, Elna did not seem perturbed. She nodded at him slowly, her huge oval blue eyes staring at him, and then looked down to her feet, scuffing her brown shoes into the dusty earth, clear evidence that her father had been serving out field chores for her once again. He looked at his own feet, covered by the boots he wore, but just as worn and calloused underneath. He had this sudden urge to rub her feet in warm water, the way his mother had done for him when he was younger, to ease the pain of long days tending the fields. In a strange way, she reminded him of his mother. Not her face - they could not have been more different in appearance - but the way she held herself, her calm, deep-thinking gaze. He didn't understand why he found it so difficult to connect with her; or at least, in the way he knew she was longing him to.

At last, she finally answered him:

"Yes, it means 'reborn, or born again.' I have been told that when my father first saw me, he shouted the name out at the top of his voice, 'Little Elna. She is born again!', because he thought I looked so much like his grandmother who had passed only the week before. Strange hey? And you? Johannes? What does your name mean?"

She had such a melodic voice, a much lower tone than Annarita's, or even Kagiso. It made her seem older than her years, but also wiser. Again, she was a perfect match for him, and yet something always held him back.

Stop being such a fool! She's a lovely girl. She needs looking after and caring for! Stop over-thinking it.

He sighed as he moved closer to her, keen to catch her scent on the breeze that rushed through her long blonde hair. She didn't back away and so he leaned towards her, feeling brave enough to press his lips on her neck. It was brief, and careful, and he felt her body shudder at his touch, but there was something in her scent that made him step back.

"Oh..." he exclaimed out loud without thinking.

Elna frowned and her bottom lip trembled.

Stupid Johannes!

He scolded himself silently. Why did he retract from her like that?

Because your heart is telling you different.

It was his mother's voice in his head; she always seemed to visit – or plague - his thoughts when it came to matters of the heart. And yet, marrying Elna was what his father had always wanted for him. She was the *right* choice: a respectable girl from a similar Boer family; a white farming family of Dutch descent who had also settled here in Hopetown, on the banks of the Orange River in the Northern Cape.

He forced a smile in her direction:

"What does my name mean? Oh, now you have got me. Hmm... this is not something I have ever been told. Our family names all follow a pattern. As you know, I am the second son so it was decided I would be Johannes, before my parents even saw me!"

He laughed a nervous chuckle then, shoving his hands in his pockets.

"The second son? Oh yes, of course."

She raised her hand in a salute to shade from the low-lying sun.

"Erm, yeah, you know how my mother lost a baby boy before I was born," he admitted, not able to meet her eyes. He never let his thoughts wander too near the idea of an elder brother he would never meet.

"I'm sorry Johannes. Truly I am." She hesitated. "But, thinking of names...perhaps you need to find your meaning then?"

She smiled at him. It was a stunning smile; one that brought a youthful vigour to her face, more suited to her age. And yet another reminder that he was faulty in some way. He had to be. If he could not fall head over heels with a girl like Elna then he was quite clearly damaged in some way!

Johannes frowned. "I didn't know I was looking for a meaning but... I am beginning to wonder."

He paused, waiting to see if she would respond. When she didn't, he moved towards her, just close enough so that he could use his body to provide shade for her squinting eyes from the low-lying evening sun.

"Happy Birthday Elna. I have a gift for you, of course. It's just not finished yet," he lied, before quickly adding, "But, whilst you are here, shall we gather some sticks for a birthday fire for your family. I still find it gets cold in our house once the sun goes down so maybe you could enjoy some warmth as you eat your cake?" he babbled nervously, reaching down to pull out a stubborn stick entrenched in the hard, dry mud by the edge of the tree. Elna nodded amiably, accepting his hand so that he could lead her down towards the banks of the river.

"Aren't you going to show me your game?" Elna asked shyly.

Johannes reached into the pocket near his free hand and pulled out five small stones, each about the size of a penny. He knew he was probably a little too old to be playing such games, but then, he had always excelled at it amongst his peers and he hoped it would impress Elna, make her laugh on her birthday – perhaps, even, help them to make stronger bonds with each other!

He let go of her hand, gave her a wink and stepped back a little, ready to show her his special trick that he had become renowned for during his younger days.

"Are you ready for this Elna? I think you are going to be mighty impressed. In fact, I don't think you will be able to resist me after you've seen this."

Elna folded her arms and raised her eyebrows at him. She looked amused and not in any rush to leave. Johannes took a deep breath, threw the stones in the air, as high as he dared, twisted his wrist in a quick motion and then bent his knees just in time to catch the falling stones on the back of his hand.

"Ha, ha! Look at that, eh. First time! Not a single one dropped...and it's not as easy as it looks."

Johannes grinned and did a little victory dance in front of Elna. He quickly stopped when he realised she was no longer looking at him, but was instead, staring at something near the edge of the bank.

"Hey there, did you see what I just did Elna? What are you looking at?" he asked, trying to hide his disappointment that she had not seen his trick.

"Johannes, I think I see something special over there," she answered, pointing to a muddy section of the grass. Johannes could see she was right. There was something glistening in between the dull grey stones and dark, wet, mud. He grabbed Elna's hand and walked her over to investigate further.

"Woah, you are right. I think this *could* be something special." He bent down and reached out his hand to pull out the glassy looking stone, encrusted into the mud. He held it up to the space between his mouth and Elna's nose as he pulled her hips close to his. The stone really was beautiful; a translucent gem which seemed to reflect different coloured lights from its rough edges as the sun began to set behind Elna, creating a soft yellow glow around her hair.

"I think we have found something important, maybe...yes?" Elna asked in a whisper.

"I think we have Elna," Johannes muttered, his breathing raspy, excited.

It's a sign! It has to be! Mother said I should not be constrained by what was too easy to reach. And now, we've found this ... together! Perhaps it is a sign that I should stop holding back from her?

"And life is too short," he muttered, more to himself than Elna. He *wasn't* going to hold back anymore. It wasn't fair on her, or on him.

The timing was perfect now; better than he could have imagined for this evening. He reached his hand behind Elna's neck as gently as he could and pulled her face towards his, allowing his lips to melt into the fullness of hers, as he clasped the gemstone discovery in his hand. The feeling of his tongue moving inside her warm mouth, the heat of the sun behind them, the moment was flawless. He felt elated, elevated, and effervescent even, as he separated his lips from hers so they could catch their breath. He wanted to see her face, to try and read her expression, her reaction to their kiss. It was a shy, happy smile.

But then it wasn't. Elna's bottom lip suddenly pulled back and stretched across her jaws to reveal teeth and fear.

"What's wrong Elna? Did you not like me doing that?"

Elna looked terrified, her eyes wild. It startled him. *Was it that bad?*

"A g...g...ghost, Johannes, look!" Elna grabbed hold of Johanne's arm. Her body was trembling.

Johannes turned around to look behind him, to see what could be so terrifying to her, before jumping back himself in shock. It couldn't be right? It must be a mirage caused by the sun or something he had not yet learned about? How could he be seeing this?

Just over the river, they could see a huge luminous bubble of pink hovering above the surface of the water. It appeared to be fading in and out. Sometimes dimming into a faint misty circle and then pulsating out into a clearly defined balloon type shape. It was translucent enough for them to see there was a girl inside: a young, dark-haired girl. Her entire body was shaking, or vibrating, it was hard to determine. And...she was naked!

Her hands were clutched to her neck, holding onto a gold collared necklace encrusted with a sparkling pink gemstone in the middle. One that looked very similar to the gemstone they had just found in the mud.

And just as alarming, this girl - or this ghost, whatever she was, trapped in this pink misty bubble - was looking straight at them, shock and confusion registered all over her face!

"I think we should get out of here Elna. I don't know what that is, but we need to get out of here, and fast," Johannes urged, unable to hide the tremor of fear in his voice.

Johannes felt a surge of panic flood through him. Grasping hold of Elna's shoulders he twisted her around to face the thorn bushes that separated the river from their farmhouses.

"Let's get out of here!" he urged. Elna started to run. He could hear the fear in her heavy breathing. Every natural instinct told him he should follow her, to protect her. He lifted his right leg to move towards her, but then, something pulled him back and pivoted him back to face the river. It was like an invisible force had gathered around him, had taken control over his actions.

"Johannes! What are you waiting for?"

He heard Elna's anguished cry as a distant, muffled sound, like he was hearing her voice from under water. It was as though he too was now encased inside something that separated his body from the rest of his surroundings.

"Like being in a bubble," he whispered.

"Who are you?" he called out.

As the bubble moved closer to him, he noticed the girl had her eyes closed and that her face looked crumpled and distressed. He flinched in sympathy, as though he could feel her pain, despite having no idea who, or *what* she was.

"Johannes, will you please get away from the water!"

He heard Elna's screams, but he didn't retreat from his position.

He couldn't have, even if he had wanted to. Instead, he waded into the river, unable to resist this strange gravitational pull that lured him towards the girl inside the bubble.

The closer he came to touching it, his heart quickened. It was almost in his reach. He was still holding the stone that Elna had spotted earlier. It burned the thin skin of his palm, as though it was reacting to something. Yet even though it stung, he gripped it even more tightly. And then he reached his clenched fist out towards the girl in the bubble, not knowing why he felt the urge to offer her this burning gift.

Just as he was about to release his fingers from its grasp, the sound of splashing water made him jump. The stone dropped from his hand and he fell back into the water, landing hard on the stoney riverbed.

"Johannes Smit. I am not going to ask you again. COME BACK!"

Elna's hands grabbed his shoulders.

"Get off me!" he tried to shout, but his voice was lost in a rush of wind, followed by the eerie sound of cracking lightning that flashed across the sun-filled, midday sky.

Blinking away the river water and mud that had splashed his eyes during his unexpected fall, he scrambled himself upwards in search of the girl in the bubble.

"NO!" he screamed. The river was clear and still. The bubble had vanished, leaving only a spittle of pink froth around his soaking trousers.

"Wh...wh...what came over you? Why did you do that?" Elna cried.

He looked over his shoulder, to where Elan sat sobbing on the edge of the riverbank, her skirt now drenched, and her blonde hair caked in sand and mud.

He didn't answer her. How could he? There were no words to explain what he had just discovered. Or, for the engulfing sense of loss that now washed over him.

12. BEATS

The beats were back. Boom...boom...boom. This was her favourite part of the day: when she was still alone, and no one could see her dance! Tiegal opened the window as far as it would go, enabling the sounds of the nearby chanting to fill her tiny living space.

Life was abundant on Kimberrago this morning; she could hear, smell and feel the excitable energy outside her little cabin as the cool air filled the room. She tapped her feet in time to the beats, moving a chair out of the way so she could maximize the limited floor space she had to move around on.

"I am an island, I am fire..."

She clapped her hands along to the words, smiling to herself at how free she felt. It was a paradoxical freedom, but she had made it hers. She was locked up and yet she still had choice! Atla had separated her from the others, but *she* had separated herself from his rule! At least, she could for these few moments, when she was alone, and no one could see her acting out the scenes she saw in her dreams.

"No one can douse my fire, no one can dim my light," she sang quietly, swaying her hips from side to side. She twirled her fingers into her hair, pushing it up high above her head and then letting it fall again on to her shoulders.

This was joy! It filled her entire body as she flicked her fingers in different directions in front of her face in time to the beats. Jolts of pink-coloured energy darted out of them, responding to her rhythm. This was a new development. She had only discovered she could release her energy in this way during one of her morning dances, a few weeks ago. Another secret gift! It had filled her with purpose and hope. She was getting stronger. Her dreams were getting clearer. And this could mean only one thing. Soon there would be enough power inside her to get back to the river again. She had to believe this; it was the only thing that she could hold onto; her only means of surviving this life of experimentation and isolation.

There was one more round of the chanting left before the sun would rise and she wanted to absorb the opportunity to be a part of it. She grabbed the material of her long skirt and hitched it up higher, still fascinated by how her feet moved as they darted across the floor. She was determined to mimic what she had seen in her dreams last night, how the male and the female had danced together, around a fire – a *real* fire. Her sleep visions had become more vivid over the last week. And last night's dream journey had been the most spectacular yet. It had felt so real, as though she had transported herself back there again - to the river that belonged in another world.

And although she knew it was a dream, she believed in it; it was her prophecy.

The setting in the dream last night was different than the others:

Night-time: a vast back sky, lit up by a billion stars. The male and the female looked just as connected to each other as always, only this time they were dancing. They spotted her, suspended in her bubble, floating across the water. And they didn't run away. This time, they smiled at her.

The girl looked happy, at first, but then her expression changed. Her face clouded over as though she could feel great sadness. She pulled away from the male, shook her head at him and then...she disap-

peared! Her body evaporated into a colourless mist, joining the smoke of the fire.

At first, the male looked shocked, waving his arms around helplessly in the space where the female had been. But soon he stopped searching for her, watching calmly as the fire went out. The sky became lighter and the sun rose, enhancing the glowing circle around Tiegal's frame. The male turned his attention to her again, laughing freely as he waved in her direction, calling out for her to come over to him! She could feel herself moving towards him...

Tiegal had woken up smiling. Her jaw still ached from it! The dream was a promise, she was certain of it, something good was going to happen to her - and soon!

The beats and chanting stopped in time together, interrupting Tiegal's rhythm. She unclasped her grip on her skirt and sank down onto the bed in the corner of the tiny room. Her mouth was dry with thirst.

"Drink Tiegal!" she willed herself out loud. The tiny sink attached to the wall was almost in reaching distance – everything in this insignificant room was – but she was back in prison-mode again now. Her dance had stopped; she no longer felt like being kind to her body.

She was about to lie down on her bed again, hoping that if she closed her eyes, then she could transport herself back to the river again, even if it was only in the dream-sense, but a loud rapping on the door startled her. She jumped up from the bed in shock, bumping her head on the slanted ceiling.

Who could be here so early? she grumbled. The Team Atla had assigned to "work with her" did not usually appear at her door until after breakfast.

"Tiegal! Are you in there? It's me...Rinzal!"

Tiegal didn't hesitate. She yanked the door open.

"Rinzal!" she cried when she saw him standing there. He looked just as she remembered him. The same wide-set eyes, small straight nose, thick, burgundy-red lips, and that lovely warm, smell that always emanated from him. The scent of comfort!

"Buttered popcorn!" she blurted out as she threw her arms around him.

Rinzal pulled back from her.

"Did you really just call me that?" he chuckled.

Tiegal could feel her cheeks burning.

"I've been on my own a lot recently. I guess I've forgotten social norms!" she explained, as they stood facing each other in the doorway. She glanced over his shoulder, anxious that he may have others with him, or even – dare she contemplate it – be with the *Team!*

Rinzal shook his head at her:

"So, your smell senses are even more enhanced, but you *still* haven't learned how to place a barrier to your thoughts."

His eyes looked beyond her, to the darkness of her room behind where she stood.

"Don't worry, I'm not with anyone from the Team. I'm here alone. Can I come in? It's best if we talk inside," he requested.

Tiegal grabbed his hands and pulled him inside. She couldn't quite believe he was here with her. They hadn't spoken since her Release Day.

Rinzal positioned himself in the centre of the room, reaching both of his arms out like a scarecrow. He was able to touch both sides of the walls with the tips of his middle fingers.

"Something tells me you didn't choose this place?" he joked.

Tiegal shrugged at him, treating him to one of her wry smiles:

"I was hoping for something a little bigger, yes, but I did ask if I could be near to the camps and the water. I like to hear the morning noises. It has really helped me over these last few months," she explained.

They stood looking at each other for a while. She could hear his sadness – how it hurt him to see her trapped in here.

"It's been more than a few months Tiegal. It's a year, to this day, since your...well...when you..." he attempted.

"When I transported myself?" she filled in for him. "Wow! A whole year! I hadn't connected that. So, it's Release Day time again then?"

Rinzal nodded at her. He looked concerned, almost anxious.

"Your Derado really suits you. I always suspected yellow was your energy colour. So much less complicated than a pink, like me," she teased him, avoiding the obvious direction he was trying to steer their conversation in. She wasn't ready to face the implications of what the one-year anniversary of her disappearance could mean.

Rinzal frowned at her:

"I can't imagine there will ever be any energy colours as complicated, or as powerful as yours Tiegal."

She squinted her eyes as she looked into his, trying to read what his words really meant.

Why did you let yourself release so much energy like that?

She heard him say, from somewhere deeper inside his mind – a place he thought he had hidden from her. She didn't want to lie to him. Someone had to hear the truth about her.

"I can hear your thoughts you know; not just the communication ones. I mean, the deeper ones," she whispered.

He nodded.

"I had a feeling you could. It's a bit of a mix-up! Well, *you're* a bit of a mix-up!" He grinned at her then. "Why don't you sit down with me on this miniature bed of yours and tell me more. I want to know what you have discovered about yourself."

Tiegal felt her whole body relax with relief. She was desperate to talk about this, with someone she trusted. She crawled onto the pillow and pushed her body back against the wall, crossing her legs under her skirt to allow enough room for Rinzal to squeeze on to the bed and face her.

"Okay, where do I begin? Let's see...me being a mix-up is actually a perfect way to describe what I am... *and* what I am not! I guess explaining my mind is the best place to start?"

Rinzal nodded in encouragement. He didn't seem to be in any rush.

"I know that I can hear deeper thoughts; the ones others think they have hidden, which is useful, but sometimes very disturbing. But I *still* haven't mastered any control over my *own* thoughts, and this drives me crazy."

"I bet it does. I could hear you replaying your dreams when I was outside your door, before I even knocked. That can't be helping you get yourself out of here." His voice sounded a little sad. Not angry, more concerned.

"It's impossible Rinzal! Atla and his Team have complete control over me. I can't use my extra mind powers to my advantage because they're always one-step ahead of me! They hear all the plans I devise from *their* secrets and then they get angry and make me sit in solitude like this for even longer. What's the point of having extra abilities when they just cause you even more trouble?" she argued, slapping her hands onto her knees. Rinzal covered her fingers with his palms. He was warm and soft and just what she needed.

"Stop it Tiegal!" he ordered her, in a gentle voice. "I mean, stop feeling guilty about how you are enjoying me touching you and offering you comfort. I'm not going to judge you for wanting physical affection the way you do."

Tiegal drew back from him. She took a big gulp and held her breath, desperately hoping it would help her close off the deeper thoughts she didn't want him to hear in this moment – about how she knew how he felt about her.

To her surprise, Rinzal burst out laughing.

"Okay, first of all, holding your breath will *not* help you to shut off your thoughts. It requires a lot more concentration than that! And secondly, since I *did* just hear what you were trying so hard to hide from me, I can assure you that I am not in love with you...well, not anymore anyway."

Tiegal gasped. She coughed her embarrassment into her cupped hands, hoping they would conceal her face from his amused gaze on her.

"I didn't think you were in *love* with me Rinzal!" she protested. Her voice was a raspy squeak.

Rinzal rolled his eyes.

"Look Tiegal, I *did* have feelings for you that I knew I wasn't supposed to have. And it truly scared me - for many reasons. Mainly, because it was such hard work hiding those kinds of thoughts from everyone else, but more so, because I knew *you* could hear it no matter what I did."

"But you don't feel it now?" Tiegal dared to ask. Much to her shame, she felt quite deflated at the idea that she had lost his affection.

"I still adore you and feel connected to you, in a way no one of our kind is supposed to. But...it is different, and safer now."

"Because I'm a freak? Because they treat me like an experiment now?" she spluttered, unable to look at him.

Rinzal made a growling noise. She could hear the fury inside him; not towards her, but to the *Team* that Atla had assigned to experiment on her.

"Tell me they don't hurt you," he pleaded in a soft whisper.

Tiegal let out a snort. "What's the point. You can hear the truth inside me Rinzal. I can't hide it from you, as much as I want to."

She turned away from him to look out of the window, pointing her face towards the sunlight that was now streaming through her window. How could she explain how violated she felt every time they made her watch the scenes from the old days? The way they tormented her with visuals of girls, some as young as ten years old, being padlocked into coffin-like boxes that were suspended onto the walls of dark and dirty rooms. How they played with her emotions, testing her reactions to what she saw? Or, how she felt when the screens showed sweat-drenched men forcing their way into the coffins and onto the girls.

She knew Rinzal was listening to her re-playing these scenes in her mind. His short, raspy breathing made it obvious how distressed he felt by what he heard.

"So, they don't actually touch you in any strange way then?" he whispered. "They just make you watch horror scenes of what can happen when you let desires become physical? To see what it does to your energy release?"

Tiegal shook her head, wiping away her tears.

"A few of the males have tried, when they think they are not being watched, but there is this female who always stops them from doing anything. Well, before they take it too far anyway. They call her Parador."

"Parador? Yes, I know of her. She is one of Atla's favourite aids. Apparently, she is quite gifted, in a way he finds useful. To be honest with you, no one really knows what she can do, or what her agenda is. But whatever it is, she certainly has Atla entranced. He seems to do everything she tells him to! Although, I shouldn't complain since she was the one who gave me the all-clear to come and see you! Atla would be furious if he knew, particularly considering our history together."

With his index finger and thumb he pinched the skin between his eyebrows, in the way he had always done when he was feeling stressed about Atla and his rule over them all.

"Anyway, you might want to watch out for her Tiegal. I have a feeling that she can manipulate what you see and what you think. That's probably how she is creating these scenes they make you watch," he warned her.

Tiegal jerked her head back in his direction.

"It *feels* real Rinzal. And it hurts too. It's like they're trying to break me. Make me feel dirty and ashamed. That I'm a monster, because I have desires and dreams. That I want to make a real connection with someone. I don't believe that if we were allowed the choice to love and explore physical connection, the majority of us would choose to behave in such horrific ways. But, the more they make me endure these visuals, the more they drain me of everything that I believe in," she admitted.

Rinzal reached out to pull on a strand of her hair that had fallen loose from her ponytail.

"This sure is a tiny space they have given you in this bamboo hut. But you've still managed to make it seem cosy."

She managed a smile in response. Rinzal always had been good at creating distractions from awkward discussions.

"Rinzal! What are you talking about? I have a miniscule bed that is so small my feet stick out when I lay down. You and I can barely fit on it sitting as we are. There is one tiny sink and a bowl that they give me for...well, I'm sure you can imagine. Cosy is not the word I would use. It's a prison!" she complained.

With one quick movement, she swung her legs over his head to allow them to them to hang down from the elevated miniature bed. Her toes scraped across the dusty floor, narrowly missing a beetle that scurried out from under the bed.

Rinzal let out a heavy sigh.

"Tiegal, y'know I used to feel the way you do, about desire and choice. That's why I was so ecstatic when I heard I was your match on Release Day. I thought that maybe we could experience the desire between us via our Derados, in a way that Tandro would accept. But then...you disappeared. Your true desires were stronger, and you were drawn to someone else. And I can tell you the truth now. I was angry, and hurt, and jealous. Basically, all the emotions we're supposed to be protecting ourselves from by living as single units here. It wasn't a good feeling either. And it made me realise that there is a lot to be said for the way Atla has designed our life."

He paused then, as though waiting for Tiegal to protest. When she didn't, he shuffled himself even closer to her and continued:

"I'm in a better place now. I think I've come to accept the difference between what I thought I desired and what I can have. I'm enjoying life with my Derado. I can see the benefits now I have it. And do you know something else? I actually love the feeling that comes from releasing my colours *and* exchanging. I mean, it *feels* amazing. I can't imagine the old ways - the physical connection ways you and I talked about - could be more satisfying than what we have now. The experience of releasing is unbelievable Tiegal. You finish off feeling re-energised and then you can walk away from whomever you exchanged with, without having to deal with any emotional debris afterwards. You can keep your own fire burning all day long! It's all in your control!" Rinzal explained matter-of-factly.

There was something about his words that made her feel twisted inside and even lonelier.

"Oh!" was all she could think of to say in response.

"But that's not you, Tiegal. You are different, and that's okay. As I said, I'm here to help you now. To find a way to stop all this bullying experimentation they are conducting on you. But you are going to have to get yourself armed."

"Look, tell me more about what you can do. I want to know!" he urged as he placed his hands over hers.

This was music to her ears. She squeezed his hands in gratitude.

"Okay, let's see, what else. Hmm... for some reason I can sometimes *taste* words."

She paused to see how he would react to this. He didn't flinch.

"It's mainly names, which is mostly okay and sometimes nice, like yours for example."

"Butter popcorn?" he asked.

She managed a chuckle. "That's right Rinzal. One of my favourites. You always smelled like that to me anyway, but now I can taste it too. It's so strange!"

He winked at her, a little flash of eye-light. It was so good to see him, even if he did seem more typically Tandroan than before.

"But not everyone tastes good. Sometimes it can taste revolting. There is one member of the team they send over who is called... *Quintel*...urgh!" she gagged.

"That name tastes like dirt and worms, although I have no idea how I know that's what dirt and worms would taste like, it just does," she said.

Rinzal raised his hand indicating for her to slow down, but she couldn't stop. It was all pouring out of her now.

"And there is one new thing I have discovered. You will like this Rinzal... I can conjure little jolts of colour releases from my hands! When I dance or feel joyful," she added, in one big burst, almost running out of breath.

Rinzal shrugged his shoulders. He didn't look impressed.

"That's nothing new. I knew you had that ability. I saw you do that a few times during the morning chant, when you were still on the camp. I just didn't want to alarm you before you were ready to see it yourself. And that was before you were given your Derado. Where is yours by the way?" he asked, glancing at her neck.

"They won't leave me alone with it. They bring it to me every day to see what I can do with my energy and then take it away again. I guess they want to make sure I don't do anything crazy with it again. You know, like transport out of here!" she answered, hoping he wouldn't ask her too much about this part of her daily routine with whoever came to see her from the Team. She didn't like to think about it too much. It made her feel something strange inside.

Rinzal stared straight past her, as though fixated on something on the wall. His posture indicated his reluctance to hear any of the uncomfortable details. Finally, he looked at her again.

"Show me!" he requested. "The little releases from your fingers."

Tiegal smiled. This was more like the Rinzal she remembered, the curious male kimberling she had grown up with.

"Well, I've only ever done it when the morning beats sound, but maybe there is another way?"

She looked around the room, desperate to see if there were any objects that she could use to re-create a beat. There was only the bowl, the one they had given her for necessity. That was the last thing she wanted near to him. She hated having to use it herself!

Rinzal took control, pulling her fingers to his chest so they rested underneath his Derado.

"Don't worry," he reassured her "I'm not trying to engineer that kind of exchange," he added. "But I do think I can help you fix something that you really need to function effectively."

Tiegal gasped. "You mean the mind barrier? You know how to fix this part of me?"

She tensed her body, afraid to hear a negative answer.

Rinzal shrugged. "Don't get your hopes up, but it may be possible. I wasn't sure if you would have enough power inside you anymore, but from what you've just said about your fingers..."

"You said this ability was nothing new?"

"I think I was too quick to dismiss it. I can feel the electricity running through your veins when I touch your wrists. The Team haven't managed to drain you of all your energy. Not at all! Whatever they think they are extracting from you and storing into your Derado every day, is only a portion of it. You are abundant with energy. And... it seems you can hide it! So *now* you just need to learn how to also hide what is in your head too."

"How?" she whispered. Her entire body was trembling in anticipation. Something big was about to happen; she could feel it again. Her dreams had prophesised truthfully after all.

"Look into my eyes Tiegal. Keep silent. I only want to hear your thoughts. Don't try to screen them from me just yet. Let them flow at first," he instructed.

Her fingers burned on his skin. She could feel a charge of electricity running inside of him.

Can you feel my heart beating Tiegal?

She nodded at him. Tears of love and gratitude filled her eyes. He was showing her how to dance to a beat she could finally control.

I want you to feel how my beats sound. Listen to the sounds of my body. See if you can conduct it with your fingers and absorb the rhythm so that it stays inside you.

She watched her fingers as they moved across his chest, as though no longer connected to her mind. Pink sparks released from them in jolts on his skin. She pulled back from him, afraid she could hurt him.

Don't worry Tiegal. You won't stop my heart. I'm strong. Keep absorbing until you know it is ingrained in you.

They sat together in harmony for a few more minutes. It was Rinzal who finally broke them apart, gently removing her fingers from his skin. His head slumped forward on to his chest.

"I think you have got it now," he managed to grunt before falling forward on to her lap.

"Oh no, Rinzal. What have I done? Wake up! Please! I'm so sorry." She leapt off the bed so that she could let his head fall onto the pillow.

"I'm okay Tiegal. I'm just a bit drained. I'll be fine in a minute. Just sit with me and talk to me so we can see if it worked. Think of things you don't want me to hear but make sure the rhythm we just practised is in your head when you do. That's how you will know how to hide them," he managed to reassure her.

She sank down onto the cold floor and let her tears run down her cheeks.

"You do like a good cry Tieg!" he teased her. The colour had returned to his face again as he sat up and faced her, long legs stretched outwards at right angles.

"Go on! Think your craziest thoughts," he urged her.

I love you for doing that. Is that okay? To love someone but not in that big, unexplainable way?

Rinzal raised his eyebrows at her.

"I heard *some* of that Tiegal." He gave her a reassuring smile. He wasn't offended. "Try again. Keep the rhythm in the background all the time. Remember, you are different than others, you are too loving and open, but it causes you pain, so you need to armour yourself. That's why we are doing this. Try to use what I have given to you so that you have more control; so that they *can't* hear everything inside you."

Tiegal closed her eyes and tried again, conjuring Rinzal's beats as a backing track to her emotions.

I want to find the fair-haired male. I don't want to be here anymore. I don't belong here.

"Did you hear that?" she asked.

Rinzal shook his head.

"Not a word!"

They both jumped up at the same time and embraced each other in one big, non-Tandroan style hug.

"Thank you Rinzal, for everything. I can't believe you came here and did this. No one ever comes to see me...other than the Team."

She whispered the last part.

Rinzal pulled away from her then.

"I *am* part of the Team Tiegal."

Tiegal gasped. She wanted to scream.

"What? You set me up?" she shouted.

"Shhh, please. No, I didn't set you up. I meant what I said. I came here to help you. Look, today is the anniversary of when you disappeared and came back. Atla is obsessed with it. You must realise that by now. That's why he keeps you in here like this. I don't know the details, but I think he is planning to use this day to see what he can generate from you. He plans to manipulate your emotions, to show others what these kind of old world longings can do to someone."

He paused then, as though not sure whether to say any more. But she heard him anyway.

"He is planning to use *Zeno*, to get to me?" she asked.

"Yes! And me too. He thinks that it was your connection with me that created the big release."

Tiegal felt a wave of panic knock her off her feet. Rinzal grabbed her to prevent her fall.

"Tiegal! Stay strong now. This is your chance. To get out of here! Now you are fully armoured. You can hide your thoughts now *and* still access the thoughts others think they have hidden. You have all the mind power now and that hidden energy too. They can't win. *You can!*"

Rinzal turned away to head to the door. He stopped to look at her straight in the eye, flashing his pupils at her to let her know he wanted her to read him:

I will tell Zeno what you are now capable of. We are on your side Tiegal. It won't seem like it when you see us at first, but I can assure you that we are. You must use the mind barrier ability now that you have it. Play Atla at his games, but do it better, and then find your escape. You have done it before. You can do it again. Follow your dreams and go find him Tiegal. Find the male from the other world. Find your destiny!

13.POWER

Rinzal had tried to prepare her. The Team arrived only an hour after he left, but no amount of warning could have prepared her for the way they stormed into her cabin, all grimace-faced, ready to cause humiliation and pain. They were not usually so brutal in their handling of her, but they had almost yanked her arms out of their sockets in their efforts to move her from the cabin to this stark, industrial-looking room.

Rinzal had said she had all the power and yet she had never felt so weak. Her screaming sobs of rage and panic must have frightened the kimberlings on the nearby camps. They had been forced to drag her, kicking and fighting, across the rose gardens as they led her towards a corridor at the back of Atlas' Estate.

And now she was here - strapped on this cold, hard slab of metal - she was struggling to find any reserves of strength at all. All she wanted in this moment was to sleep. To disappear into the euphoric bliss of her dreams.

But there was a lingering odour taunting her nostrils. It made her want to vomit everything inside; to release her from anything they were planning to extract from her.

Zeno had just arrived. And she had brought a scent of danger with her. Even though Rinzal had promised that she was a secret ally, Tiegal couldn't hide the obvious body tremble, because she just couldn't shake the feeling that her oldest friend was not really on her side.

Zeno's diamond pupils were flickering extreme bright light, responding like automatic torches to sudden darkness. This was the first thing that alarmed Tiegal. This experimentation room was the opposite of darkness. Zeno's eye-light was far more intense than needed for a room with such a strong electric light source.

"I have come to show you something. Are you able to sit up a little?" Zeno's question was delivered with an unfamiliar curtness.

She spoke with superiority, showing none of the gentleness in their friendship before.

Zeno loosened the belts that contained her and stood back. Tiegal nodded at her and pushed her hands down on the cold metal underneath her so that she could rest her back on the wall behind. The pressure forced her left arm to unbalance. Her elbow gave way causing her body to bang hard against the side wall. She slammed her head into the concrete with one quick blow.

"It's no good pretending to be weak Tiegal. We know you have more to give." Zeno paused, flashing her eye light more furiously towards Tiegal. Her sockets were all brightness, not a hint of the darkness normally seen around the pupil.

"You know, I did want to help you Tiegal. We shared some useful connections before. I always appreciated your atypical ways. I even considered that it helped me connect to a higher intelligence, just by being near you."

Tiegal stared at Zeno, willing her to stop playing this charade; hoping it was all an act, and that she was still the ally she remembered her to be. They had shared so many memories. They had been friends.

Surely Zeno could not really be so changed?

"You can change a lot Tiegal. And *you* did!"

Tiegal gasped. Zeno could still hear her deeper thoughts, which meant Tiegal was no longer armoured. Zeno laughed; an uncomfortable snigger. It didn't fit the scene; it wasn't a match to her obvious anger.

"Of course, I can hear what you are thinking. You are still an open book for all to see. I can't understand why they are all so afraid of you!"

Tiegal didn't respond. She needed to think about this, yet she didn't *dare* to think about it – or anything else. This was power; one that Zeno had over her right now.

Empty my thoughts. Put them somewhere else.

"Oh no, you don't want to do that Tiegal. There is nothing you can do to prevent me from accessing your thoughts. There is no off button for this with you. You always pledged to develop a barrier that would enable control over who could read your mind. That was always your plan. You told me *many* times, even in your sleep. But it's just not in your power!"

Tiegal managed a weak smile.

"Yes, I guess I am the odd one out! I never did manage to work out how to do that. I always hoped you would help me find the barriers Zeno. You were always the smart one."

"YOU put the barriers around yourself. You created a storm when you disappeared the way you did," Zeno spat back.

So, *this* was the problem. Her suspicions were confirmed. Her energy release had disrupted the peace. She had raised the bar, made them want more, to connect the way she had with Rinzal. At least, that's what they all seemed to have assumed; that it was Rinzal who created her big release.

"Yes Tiegal. *Now* you are thinking again. Too many others saw how your colours blended with Rinzal in the water. It was intense, powerful, and dangerous; all of those things. And, not only that, they all heard your vulgar thoughts about connecting physically with a male too. Your dirty desires!

"It's caused chaos here. Almost a quarter of the engineering compound have displayed changes in their colours in the last year and have started spending more time exchanging with only one other – like a form of monogamy, as it used to be – and some...some have even tried a bit of the physical intimacy...kissing...and other disgusting things!"

Tiegal watched her old friend - she still wanted to think of her that way, despite how unkindly she was behaving towards her now – and she saw her, the real essence of her.

The trace of colour around Zeno's frame was no longer pure blue. The mist of particles that seeped out of her Derado had changed colour. Even the diamond in the pendant had transformed too. It looked more like the one she wore. It was pink! Zeno was feeling more, she was deepening.

"And you asked for it Tiegal! You brought it upon yourself! I told you not to yearn for more. We all told you this love connection they used to practice only brings you darkness, that it will just drain you, that it would douse your fire. But you never listened!"

Zeno grumbled these last words. It wasn't an angry noise, more helpless frustration.

"You *willed* a perfect love match and you got him! Pronto!" Zeno shouted at her.

It was this last word that got Tiegal's attention: *Pronto* – that was their secret word, when they were younger, as little kimberlings sneaking out on their camp decking together, to marvel at the stars and share secrets. It was Zeno who came up with it. A trigger word she could use to kick-start Tiegal into using her powers when she forgot she had them, on the days when she was too tired to remember the special things contained inside her.

Listen to me Tiegal. Come on, you are stronger than this. You need to hear me. Dig deeper!

Tiegal heard this loud and clear. And, at the same time, she felt her fingers spark with jolts at the fingertips. She could feel and hear the beat of Rinzal's heart inside of them. She was ready to be powerful again. It was time.

She flashed her eye light at Zeno, to let her know she was armoured again. Zeno nodded, her shoulders relaxed in relief.

You took your time Tiegal. Listen, Atla is on his way. You need to keep the rhythm going that Rinzal gave to you. It's your only way to make sure you are always one step ahead of everyone else. Zeno communicated.

What is he planning? Tiegal channelled her response between the light of their pupils.

I'm not one hundred percent sure Tiegal. All I know is that I was ordered to come in here and make you feel drained by showing you my anger and resentment at how you have affected everyone. Of course, you know I don't feel that way. I just have to pretend I do. But there is not much time and I don't know who is watching us. I think you should pretend you're tired again and close your eyes for a few seconds, so that it looks like I am actually draining your energy. They won't give you your Derado if they think you have anything left inside you.

Tiegal flashed a 'yes' response with her eyes. She then closed her lids. As she counted to ten in her head, she concentrated on the rhythm of the throbbing beats in her finger tips, relieved to know her reserves of energy were building up inside them. She reached ten and turned her focus back to Zeno, who was facing her. She had more to communicate:

Okay, good, see the long mirror behind me?

Tiegal flashed a yes with her pupils.

There are nearly fifty Tandroans watching you from behind there. Atla has placed them there as both a punishment and a warning. They are all being kept in isolation because of how they responded to your transportation; because they engaged in physical intimacy. Today is Release Day, as you know, but they have all had their Derados taken away or have been denied their day to receive one. Atla wants to use this day to show them the darkness you have brought them with your emotional release last year.

The sound of footsteps nearby quickened the beat of Tiegals' heart, distracting her from Zeno's communication. She willed herself to hear the last words before they were interrupted by a new presence in the room.

It's time Tiegal. Whatever happens next, please know that you will always be my friend. I am only playing the game he wants me to play. But remember, you have the upper hand. You just have to use it!

The foul odour of durian fruit filled the room in one heady burst: Atla.

Tiegal fingers sparked in response. She rolled onto her side, burying them into the sheet the Team had wrapped around her naked frame when they strapped her in earlier.

"Release Tiegal Eureka!" Atla ordered two male Team members, who stood the required two feet behind him at all times. Zeno had moved herself out of Tiegal's eye line, but she could still smell her. She was no longer the scent of fear. Now, Zeno released her familiar scent: morning dew; the smell of promise, and hope – of more innocent times when they were younger.

Atla approached the metal table, his arms folded as he waited for two male Tandroans to unclasp the buckles that constrained Tiegal. As soon as she felt her arms were free, she swivelled herself around, so that she could hide her hands under her bottom. The sparks were burning at her fingertips. She could not afford to let Atla see what was building inside her. Not as he was just about to place her Derado around her neck. She dared herself a lingering glance into his strange eyes – dark brown irises with black pupils, the identifying marker that connected him to the older world - as he clasped the rose gold collar around her neck.

She could hear his excitement inside him. He was planning to build her up into an emotional frenzy, for the spectators behind the mirror to watch and learn from. He wanted them to see how she was an abomination to their evolution. And there was more – an indecision. He had also not yet decided whether he would let her live through it!

This knowledge should have frightened her - that she could be facing imminent death – but she felt a strange sense of acceptance settle her breathing.

"What superior being do you think you are Tiegal Eureka? Do you think you can corrupt over a hundred years of order? My Team have reported their findings to me. How you have tried to manipulate them into believing that we will get more energy from the old ways. Two of them have suffered the consequences of this already."

Atla squeezed his hands around her throat. She could feel his breath panting with venomous anger on her hair. He spattered his words out with such rage they pricked at the skin on her shoulders, like the tips of daggers that threatened to lunge deeper with each contact.

"We did value your power Tiegal. That is why we have kept you in isolation this past year. To allow you to recover from your energy transportation and to see what else you could offer. But you have only tried to manipulate some of our greatest minds like Zeno here. What-ever you were conversing about just now, it was not good for her. I could see how her Derado colours changed to that emotional colour of yours. I cannot accept this kind of control you seem intent on acquiring," Atla declared.

It was a judgment; a resolution. *I cannot accept.* Atla had come to a decision. Tiegal, and her energy, must be eradicated. It was clarity of the purest kind. Her life would soon be ended. She would vibrate no more. Her fire would no longer burn.

As if on cue, Atla yanked her arm so that she had no choice but to cower in a crouch on the floor. He then grabbed a bucket from one of the male members of his Team and chucked the entire contents of it over her.

"There! See how you like it when your fire is extinguished. Because that's what your energy does Tiegal. You douse everyone's fire with your vile thoughts!"

Tiegal jerked as the icy cold water hit her but she did not say a word in response. Instead, she closed her eyes and waited. For him to resort to such a strange, almost immature act, suggested to her that he had gone off script. Which could only mean one thing: she really was in danger of reaching her demise.

And no one knew how Atla ordered the end of disruptive beings. The modern ways had never been revealed. The older ways were quite simple and quick; beheading, strangulation, hanging. She had a feeling, from the way he was holding her down, her knees on the floor, that he would opt for something clean and quick too.

But then a new body entered the room. It carried a familiar smell with it. A mix of wood, lime and ginger, followed by the undeniable taste of buttery popcorn in her mouth.

"Rinzal!" She opened her eyes as she shouted his name, spinning around to confirm he had indeed entered her oxygen space once more.

It *was* Rinzal. He shot out desperate warning flickers from his eyes. Orange and red flashes that signalled he was surrounded by danger. Tiegal managed to stand up, only just aware that Atla was no longer holding her down and was now leaning against the wall.

Why has he let me go?

It only took a few seconds for her to realise the answer: it was a trick! Atla was very much back on script. He wanted – *expected* - her to fall apart with emotion at the sight of her energy match.

He really has underestimated me then. And...grossly misunder-stood me too!

Stealing a glance over her shoulder, she clocked Atla's body language: arms clasped across his puffed-out chest. It was clear he was waiting to see how her reunion with the male from the Pyramid unfolded.

I have more power now! Your aides can't hear all my thoughts! Not now that Rinzal has shown me what to do!

Her fingers sparked underneath her body where she still hid them. And it was Rinzals' words who came to her mind - one of his theories he had shared with her during their earlier days on the teaching camp:

If you try to fight power with power, you give it power. The only way to reduce the strength of another's power is to withdraw from where it wills you to go!

Tiegal processed this carefully, quickly calculating how this theory applied to her conflict with Atla. The ruler always wore purple and black. His energy assumed he was right, that his power was the only way for good, even if that meant oppressing the energy of others. It granted him a narcissistic allowance to take energy from whoever he wanted, without replacing it with his own. He didn't exchange. He simply took. Aggression, oppression, intimidation were his weapons; like the blood sucking vampires of stories told in the older days, before the new rule. He was an *energy vampire* - the secret nickname that Rinzal had given him.

If only she could speak directly with Rinzal now - without anyone else hearing - and ask him for answers to survive the danger she now faced. How do you fight a vampire? That would be her first question. She knew they had written about this, in lifetimes before, when imagination – that wonderful concept, *fantasy* – had been encouraged.

Tiegal could feel her control slipping away. She was losing the strength she needed to connect with Rinzal's beats for much longer. The members of the Team who stood close by were trying to access her thoughts. Atla was getting impatient.

"What is she concocting in that devious head of hers now then?" she heard him say.

Time was running out. If she was going to survive, she needed to give him something.

What if I choose not to fight it? This energy game Atla wants to play with me? What if I let him take some of it, my fear? I can't hide that. It is too easy to extract what smoulders on the surface.

This was another one of the insights Rinzal had shared, one she remembered now:

Fear is like a gullible food source for energy vampires.

It had sounded so ridiculous before. Now – it was a lifeline.

She *was* scared. It had manifested into a thick, black smoke that seeped out of her. She willed it to leave her; to go to Atla.

Let him have it, this much he can have.

Atla inhaled her smoke of fear. She could tell she was magnifying him. He appeared larger in form, more vibrant. And he was watching her, keen to see how Tiegal reacted to the next part of his plan: to illicit jealousy from her.

Tiegal watched as Rinzal and Zeno faced each other from the other side of the room, and how they pressed the diamonds in their Derado at exactly the same time. Their connection was powerful. Their energy colours instantly blended into bursting blue and yellow supernovas. And their bodies radiated an alluring glow as they released and exchanged their inner desires to each other.

It does hurt! I didn't think it would but seeing them doing this together does feel strange.

Although she had not thought of Rinzal in the same way she dreamed of the fair-haired male, she had granted a place for him in her heart as the one she shared her first release with. But she understood this emotion now. She was not so special. She was not *so* chosen that Rinzal could only make powerful releases with her. There was a space across Rinzal's colour spectrum that belonged to others – like Zeno.

It's almost as if I feel...jealous!

As soon as this thought entered her mind, she realized this was the reaction Atla had intended to elicit from her. The execution would come later. There was more of her to be absorbed before then. Atla was thriving on her emotional reactions.

She allowed the feeling to flow. Let it free. He could have this too. This *was* her jealousy - and her pride. And it was a strange colour. One she had never seen from a release before. It looked like the feeling of being uncomfortable: dirty, cold and stuck. Like a day when outdoor working dragged you down. It smelled like wet manure. It was a murky green, at first, then darker, like the puddles in potholes, amongst fields of brown grass. It didn't flow easily. It was more like water travelling upstream.

And it delighted Atla. He glowed under the surge of her pain.

But then, a wave of calm reached her, like a cloth of cumulus settling above a mountain; white clouds of clarity, concealed underneath the black smoke around her. That's when she knew she was safe, that the fog would soon lift. And that when it did, she could reveal her serenity to this oppressor who had arranged her distress.

But she needed to act fast. And there was another part of her she could use, the real power source; her ability to see and experience a connection, to feel love. It was her playing card. One that Atla did not have!

Rinzal...Rinzal...come to me...connect with me again...why are you standing with Zeno? Rinzal...

These were the thoughts she needed Atla to hear. It was what he wanted from her. One of the male Team members started to chuckle at the side of her.

"She is calling for Rinzal to connect with her Atla! It's happening."

Atla couldn't hide his delight, or the satisfied smile that emerged on his sweaty, eager face.

Is this so enjoyable for you that you can't see how I am playing too? Against you!"

Tiegal knew what she needed to do now. She needed to release *everything*.

Something deep inside her burned. It was the antithesis of pain. It was euphoric. It was the stirring of creation. Something had awakened inside; a realization of her purpose, of knowing she was capable of generating what she desired.

A vision of Namnum, her beautiful elephant friend, giving birth filled her mind.

That is what it feels like to create something that has never existed before. It must be how it feels to give birth.

She could not create a baby, not in that way, not in this world. But she could create her own journey, her own release, a way to free herself – a method to transport her very being from darkness into light – perhaps even, back to the place where she had been before. Where she had felt that *she* was light.

I am not trapped. I am discovered.

She touched her pink diamond, hot now around her neck, and let herself absorb the colour scene around Rinzal and Zeno. The glow that demonstrated how her friends were enjoying themselves together. It would be wrong of her to deny them this. She was not the only one to share a connection with them. This fact dulled rather than sparked. It was bearable. It was shaping. Her fingers traced the facets of the diamond, cut so expertly to enable the stone to reveal its inner glow.

And it occurred to her then that this was how she was too, like a pink diamond. A stone made under pressure, a forming structure of parallel lines, absorbing the other coloured lights on her journey, enabling her to glow with her own unique colour. In the same way, she had absorbed traces of the elements of others she had encountered in her life: Rinzal, Zeno, Namnum... and even the short moment near the male and the female by the river.

It was time for her to get back to them again now, to the other world. Somehow, she knew they would be there again, that she would be invited into their world. The fog was starting to lift now. Her clarity had increased her strength.

Atla must have noticed, because he was striding towards her, a look of fury on his face.

"What are you doing Tiegal? How are you making yourself change like this?" he demanded.

It was happening again. She could feel the buzz of excited vibrations inside her. The skin that covered her arms was no longer solid. Once again, she was transforming, matter and colour, hot and rising.

A faint sound of a door opening and closing reached her ears and a long-forgotten, but somehow familiar scent filtered into what remained of her sensory connection with this world.

Mint? I know that smell somehow. A female with an unusual eye-light...I think?

Just as quickly as it reached her, she brushed the thought away, only vaguely aware of noises in the room: shouting, barking, orders being thrown. But they were getting further away with every second. Just like before, her oxygen supply had changed, the air-tight around her breathing organs, as though she was submerged under water, unable to see or reach for light and air. Once again, she was in a fog, drowning. She wasn't sure how long she could withstand it. She wasn't even sure she could survive this if forced to sustain this environment for much longer. She tried to scream. It was worse than last time. Everything seemed slower and more painful.

This time she was completely on her own. It wasn't the easy ride, like the time with Rinzal, when she had first connected with him in the diamond water. This was a ride fuelled by pain, desperation and escape. And it hurt. It was destination dangerous. She was losing control, could feel herself slipping away.

But then, just as she thought she would lose her battle to stay in this world she heard a voice. A happy, joyful voice! One that sounded out from somewhere ahead of her, in the direction of a bright light that beckoned ahead. Opening her eyes, she glanced around. What she saw made her smile despite the tears that were now streaming down her face. She was back again, in the strange, lighter world. This world where she could float above water in a haze of pink.

And it looked *just* the same. There was the river surrounding her. And the trees that lined the banks with their thorny looking branches and sturdy old trunks.

Desperate to locate the fair-haired male from her dreams – with, or without, the female - she turned around in her bubble and scanned her surroundings. It did not take long for her to realise that he was not waiting for her. That her dreams had failed her, yet again.

In frustration she tried to clasp her hands together, but they swept through each other like two breezes crossing each other from different directions.

"No!" she cried out. The glow of the bubble that contained her above the river was already starting to dim in response to her disappointment. Her energy was depleting, rapidly, and she had no idea how long she could sustain herself in this world. She needed to find the male!

"Dream male! *Where* are you?" she called out in desperation, falling on to the floor of the hazy cloud-like bubble below her. Distraught, she watched helplessly as her knees melted in and out of the particles of pink, and then, how the river rippled in response to each vibration that her body made. Already, she could feel herself losing solidity. The tides of fate had turned against her once again.

Now resigned to her doomed fate, she decided to cry out for the male, one more time. Taking a deep breath, she started her call, only to be stunned into silence by the unmistakable sound of an excited shriek nearby. It was coming from the banks of the river ahead. Pulling herself up, she managed to spread her hands in front of the pink haze.

"Hey!" she called out to a group of young males on the grassy banks in front of her. They did not seem to have noticed her, or her cries for help. It appeared they were preoccupied with an object one of the males was now holding high up in the air. At first, she couldn't be sure what it was, but then a reflection danced across the water.

"Oh! He's found a diamond!" she whispered into her bubble.

The young male was dancing now. He shouted something out, a word that she instantly recognised:

"Eureka! Eureka!"

She gasped.

"Yes! That's me! I am Tiegal...Tiegal Eureka!"

Not one of the males turned in her direction. Unperturbed she willed herself towards them. If she had any chance of surviving this journey she *had* to get herself over to the river banks before she got propelled back to Tandro again.

Right now, she didn't care that the fair-haired male from her dreams was not waiting for her. Because there were *some* young males here, and one of them had called out her name!

14. ROOTS

Johannes took another swig of whisky and then slammed the glass back down on the table. The alcohol had already started working its magic. And it felt good. He couldn't remember the last time he had lazed away an afternoon like this; a few hours with nothing todo but enjoy the simple pleasure of drinking, putting the world to rights with his brother-in-law, and perhaps even, revelling in a game of billiards. That is, if the billiard table ever came free!

Even Mrs Francis, the legendary hotel owner, seemed in a good mood today. Johannes grinned a bleary smile as he watched the older lady holding court at the door, welcoming the men of Hopetown to her establishment, 'The Royal Arch', the town's one and only non-religious meeting place.

He looked forward to coming here. Although not much of a hotel - more of a straggling chain of rooms without windows - it did offer this small billiard room, where men like he and his brother-in-law could gather for some much-needed respite on a Sunday afternoon. A place to escape from all the things that taunted your mind. And it was just what he needed right now, just a few hours where he could forget all the shameful things he had done, with only the sound of balls being smacked by cues and the splashing of dark brown liquid into glasses. Right now, this was as close to heaven as he could have wished for.

"Agh Johannes! Really? You're not going to be able to walk home if you keep knocking it back like that. And we told Annarita and Kagiso that we'd only be gone a couple of hours too."

Frederick scowled at him. Johannes clenched his fists, thinking, not for the first time, that fatherhood seemed to have a nasty habit of turning good men into holier-than-thou characters who thought they held a bigger moral compass than anyone else.

Perhaps I should count my blessings that I am a single man after all!

It was all he could do to hold back from sticking his tongue out at him.

"Come one Fred! We never get to relax. A few drinks never harmed anyone! Why don't you actually drink *your* drink too?"

"Really? Is that what you used to think when your father knocked them back then? As well as knock back anyone who got in his way?"

Johannes' entire body stiffened.

"Don't compare me to him," he growled, clasping his hands tight around his glass so that his knuckles turned pure white.

If only you knew Fred, if only you knew!

The sound of Frederick's exasperated sigh made his skin prickle with irritation, a reaction that forced him to take a deep breath so that he could restrain himself from lurching his fist at him across the table. The alcohol may have dulled his pain, and his regret, but it had also ignited his brimming rage.

"I am nothing like him!" He gave Fredrick a hard stare and then waved his hand at a concerned looking Mrs Francis to indicate he was in urgent need of a refill.

When she shook her head at him and waggled her index finger in front of her nose, in the manner of a disappointed schoolteacher, he slammed his fist down on the table. The sheer force of his rage made the table rock so that what remained of Fredericks's whiskey fell crashing to the floor alongside a sticky mess of broken glass.

"Johannes Smit!" Mrs Francis called out to him as she scurried over with a cloth and brush.

Her long dark brown dress swished across the dusty floor as she stomped over to him. "I think you need to simmer down young man. People are starting to talk about you around here.

I don't know what has gotten into you!" She ruffled his hair and then shook her head at him once more, causing her oversized felt hat to shift further down the back of her head.

"You look very glamorous today Mrs Francis," Johannes tried. She tutted and rolled her eyes at him, a genuine look of concern etched across her face.

"Your poor Ma would have been so worried for you."

Mrs Francis smacked her lips together and then rested her hand on Frederick's shoulder, as though to offer him her full support in the campaign against Johannes' path to destruction. Just as he feared she would launch into a full-blown lecture, a chorus of loud voices in the corner made her stamp her feet.

"Eh! You boys over there! I've told you what the rules of billiards are a hundred times now!"

Johannes let out an exaggerated sigh of relief as Mrs Francis rushed across to the billiard table to attend to the boisterous group of boys who had all adopted the postures of wild animals, squaring up to each other, posed and ready to fight.

"That was close, hey!" Johannes winked at Frederick in the vain hope he could divert his attention to more a more jovial conversation. To his dismay, Frederick did not appear to be happy to take the bait.

"She's right y'know. You have changed. And it's been driving Annarita and Kagiso crazy. It's all they talk about; Johannes this and Johannes that. They are both stumped by your recent behaviour. But I think I know what has gotten into you." Frederick rubbed his eyes and sighed.

"The question is though, do you?" he challenged.

Johannes could feel tears of angry frustration brimming his eyes. Embarrassed, he shook them away with a flick of his head.

"I'm just tired. I don't need you to get all parental on me Fred!"

"And there you go again. Venting all this anger again. It's so not like you Johannes. It's been like this for over a year now and it's only getting worse! It's like something took over your body and replaced it with this confused, angry boy who wants to drink all the time."

Frederick glanced around the room before leaning across the table, his voice lowered into a deep whisper:

"Look, ever since Elna left you've been a mess, a totally different person. More like...your father was! I know I shouldn't say that, but someone needs too. I mean, surely you can see the parallels! After your mother died your old man was so broken that he drunk himself to his death!" Fredrick's voice trailed off. Johannes could hear his foot tapping nervously under the table as he waited for a reaction.

"Watch yourself!" Johannes warned. "It is nothing like the same. I didn't ask for Elna to leave. She just decided to go live with her cousins. I don't know why she did, but it's her life, her choice, and it's got nothing to do with me! I've told you before, she just said she needed some space!"

Frederick slammed his hand down on the table, clearly exasperated.

"Which doesn't make sense! Everyone knows that girl was crazy in love with you. Annarita said she cried her heart out to her. She was utterly heartbroken. Apparently she just kept talking about how you abandoned her. That you went all crazy when you were down by the river. And on her birthday too!"

In spite of himself, Johannes laughed.

"Crazy is one way to put it." He trailed his finger over the table, soaking up the remnants of whiskey that still lingered there.

How could he explain the events of that day to anyone? What possible explanation could he give for how he had hurt Elna, ignored her. Basically, completely failed her. What sane man would have ventured into the river when something so extraordinary loomed towards them? He should have picked Elna up, carried her over his shoulders and run away. He should have given her another kiss. Assured her that he would always protect her and keep her safe.

"She was beautiful," he muttered.

Frederick clapped his hands in front of his face.

"Yes! She was Johannes. Elna was perfect for you. But you let her go. I just don't know why. And, to be honest, I'm not even sure I want to know." Frederick took a deep breath and then stood up from his seat, letting his chair fall back so that it made a loud slamming noise on the stone floor.

"Look, what's done is done. She may come back again. You never know. But, in the meantime, maybe try not losing sight of what is right in front of you, hey!"

Johannes gave a shrug. There was no point arguing with Frederick about this. It was easier to let him believe Elna's absence was the cause of his broodiness. It was better this way. He didn't even want to imagine what his brother-in-law would think if he knew his brooding was really about a fantasy. Even though, the more he thought about it, the more it made sense to him. A fantasy girl was safer than a real person. Unlike Elna who knew too much; who knew the secrets he needed to keep hidden.

Careful not to lose his balance, he stood up slowly, allowing Frederick to take his arms and lead him away from the temptation of the hotel bar.

"She will come back Fred. I know she will. That's what I'm counting on."

As he said these words, he whispered under his breath, "The girl in the bubble *has* to come back."

Johannes stumbled along the grey, stony plains that led from the edge of the town towards the riverbanks, counting the umbrella-shaped thorn trees as he passed them by. He had assured Frederick that he was just taking a walk to clear his head, but he now wished he had taken the offer to ride home with him in the wagon.

Everything hurt. His head was pounding, the beat as consistent and repetitive as Kagiso's pan call for supper. His mouth felt as dry and parched as the heat-hazed horizon ahead of him. His stomach lurched in nauseating waves. Frederick was right. He really did need to stop drinking.

It had been a year. A whole year since the day that he had finally kissed Elna, finally let his fear of making a genuine connection subside; the very same day that everything had changed.

"Why can't I stop thinking about it? I mean, who the hell was she? *What* was she?"

It was not the first time he had asked himself this question. He was even starting to bore himself.

He started to pick up his pace but then the unmistakable sound of an ox-wagon creaking across the trackless plain not far behind him made him stop. Turning around to check whose company he now shared on his path he waved when he saw a group of boys.

"Hey Johannes, you talking to yerself again?"

He managed a smile when he saw that it was Erasmus Jacobs who called out to him from the group that huddled together on the cart. He was a young, gregarious boy, who lived close by. The kind Johannes would have gladly socialised with not so long ago. But that was when he was still the old Johannes - the fun, sociable version of before.

"Something like that. Where y'all heading to then?" he answered, careful to hide the evidence of his afternoon excess in his voice.

"Just going down to the river to catch a breeze. It's like an oven out here today. Do you want to join us? Heard you're a pretty fine player of five stones. Fancy teaching us?"

Johannes couldn't help but laugh, much to Erasmus' obvious confusion.

How ironic! He thought. They were playing five stones together, just as he had with Elna, a year ago.

"Ag, no thanks Erasmus. I should probably get back to the farm. Another time, hey?"

He watched them tie up the wagon to a nearby fence and then run down towards the river ahead. Erasmus moved the ox into the shade and gave Johannes one last wave before running after his friends.

I bet his mother is proud of him! A kind, considerate boy who looks after animals and invites his drunken neighbour to play five stones with him and his friends. Mrs Francis was wrong. My mother would have been more than worried if she had seen me like this. If she knew what I was capable of, she would have been heartbroken!

Johannes shook his head to clear his thoughts. The sun must have gotten to his head as much as the alcohol had.

He reached the clearing in the trees which led towards his house and then stopped in his tracks. He needed to have a word with himself. Kagiso had promised to make bobotie for supper, his favourite meal, and his stomach was rumbling with hunger, but he wasn't sure the delicious mince dish was worth the fury he would face if he turned up in his current state.

He pivoted around on his heel and headed back in the direction of the river, close to where he could hear Erasmus and his friends playing with the stones.

As soon as he reached his favourite thorn tree, closest to the edge of the river, he slumped down the side of the bark, pulled on his brown felt hat so that it covered his eyes from the low-lying sun, and closed his eyes. Now he was here, he realised he was much too tired to join Erasmus and his friends with all their boundless energy.

He needed to sleep, even if doing so meant enduring the memory of the last time he had seen Elna and the words that always tormented him before sleep would finally come.

He drifted off into the first stages of slumber as their last conversation replayed itself in his tortured mind.

"Why can't you see what is in front of you Johannes? It's like you're always looking for something else, something sparklier than you already have. You even dropped that stone we found together. It could have been a diamond. I think it *was* a diamond and you just let it go. Like you let me go too!"

"Elna! Do you not remember why I dropped the diamond...I mean the stone, or whatever it was? Do you not remember what we saw?"

"We saw an illusion that's all! It was just the sun and the heat playing tricks on us. But you have become obsessed by it. You kissed me, and then you just ignored me. You abandoned me because of some naked girl that you thought you had seen."

"No Elna! That's not true. You saw her too. I know you did."

"I think you have actually gone mad Johannes. Your mother would be ashamed of the way you have treated me. Not to mention your dirty little secret!"

Those were her last words to him. He heard her spit them at him as he fell asleep. The hatred in her words that always encouraged his fitful attempts to achieve some rest.

"EUREKA!"

Johannes jumped up at the sound of Erasmus's excited scream in the distance. The boy was jumping in the air, the stones he had been playing with now discarded as he lifted a familiar looking stone up to the sunlight.

"He found it!" Johannes croaked, as he sat up and wriggled into an upright position against the tree.

It was a funny feeling, seeing Erasmus holding the same stone he and Elna had found together a year ago. It hurt and healed, all at once.

So that was the way it was, a succession of things no more: his mother and father, both gone; Elna and what might have been; and now, a diamond that could have belonged to them too. What could be left for his journey to reveal? How many more mistakes could he make?

He watched Erasmus and friends as they ran away from the river, no doubt to share their good fortune. Johannes was happy for him. He only hoped the boy would hold onto the treasure, and not let anyone else reap the rewards of his find.

Settling himself into a comfortable position again, he smoothed his hands over the bark and dried grass that surrounded it.

If this tree could talk!

How many afternoons had he sat here, brooding about his losses to the barks and leaves? Had it absorbed his tears, like the roots that entwined underneath him, draining the moisture from sky to earth?

There was something strangely comforting about the idea that his pain could provide some nourishment. That life continues and grows, even when others are taken away. His mother used to say that the roots of a tree were like a family's bonds, each one intertwined with another, lending strength to the twists and turns of our individual journeys.

What a lady, his mother had been. So many dreams yet to live out as a writer, a poet, a grand-mother. How could it be, that she was no more? There were so many possibilities she had wanted to explore. There were so many questions he had never had the chance to ask.

Would you have understood? Would you have still loved me if you knew how I treated Elna. How I made her feel rejected so many times, just because I felt there was something more that I could find?

He liked to think his mother would have held him close to her chest and whispered that, yes, she understood how love can find you in the most unexpected places. That our timing may not always suit our surroundings, but love knows no boundaries, and will always prevail.

"What do you think tree?" he whispered.

Foolish thoughts young man.

It always seemed to whisper such admonishments to him. He imagined that it had an old, smoke-filled voice, this tree.

"Elna was right! I really am...*finally*...going mad!" he said out-loud.

His eyes felt drunk-heavy again, despite it being a good few hours since his last drink. All these memories, discoveries, revelations and resolutions had drained him.

He closed his eyes, letting his need for sleep push him off into a fast-fall towards heavy slumber. He had hardly reached it before the sound of breaking twigs and rapid, heavy breathing nearby, jolted him back to alertness. Something, an instinct, prevented him from opening his eyes. A voice, a sweet one, belonging to a girl, spoke nearby:

"Did you...call my name? Was that you?"

He knew it was a dream. It had to be. This voice was familiar. It was also wrong. She was not supposed to be here. You couldn't really wish somebody, or something, back into your life. He wasn't that deluded, was he?

"Hello? Can you hear me? Understand me?"

She was still here: the voice... the voice that sounded *exactly* like his mother, just higher pitched, and softer.

Johannes gripped clumps of dried mud at the side of him, steeling himself to open his eyes and face whoever this talking vision was.

He opened them. It wasn't his mother; of course not.

"You! You're back? How...? How did you get here?"

The girl from the pink bubble, she was here; real, solid, a body standing on these dry, muddy banks. She was beautiful. She was *naked*!

Johannes jumped up. But it was too quick. He fell backwards, narrowly missing the trunk of the tree. Damn, useless, foolish tree! It should have broken his fall. Instead, he twisted awkwardly, landing on his side before bouncing off towards the water. He tried to grab a water branch that bridged between the bank and the river, but he was too weak for his mind and body to come together in any order.

The girl – the *naked* girl – did not hesitate. She jumped in straight after him.

Johannes couldn't help himself. He laughed: big, loud, hacking laughs. This had to be the most bizarre dream he had ever had. The girl waded towards him, frowning. And that's when he noticed her eyes, the flickering, pulsating lights. He stopped laughing. His mouth gaped wide open.

"Who are you? What kind of dream is this?" he managed, pulling himself to a standing position, that water lapping at his waist.

"I am not a dream. I am Tiegal...Tiegal Eureka. Was it you? The one who called out my name?"

15. MIRROR

The mirror was positioned at just the right angle for him to catch a good eye of her as she dressed. He had not placed it in that way on purpose, but it was impossible not to notice how it reflected the shine of her body behind the dressing screen. Johannes tried to avert his eyes, but he couldn't tear them away. Her body was a perfect hourglass in shape and her strange, amber-coloured skin glistened with an iridescent glow.

His heart beat so fast he found it hard to breathe. And his mind raced with every possible scenario to explain how this could be happening.

Who was she? And how did she get here?

He caught her watching him and their eyes locked in the mirror. She flashed her eye-light at him in rapid flickers. The shock of it caused him to stumble back into the wooden frame of his parent's bed that he now called his own.

Determined to regain some composure, he seated himself on the edge of the mattress, mindful of the obvious tremor of his legs.

"Why do you keep falling? Do I frighten you?" the girl called out to him. She walked around the screen and moved herself close to him.

He coughed and averted his eyes to the floor, focusing on the edges of the long dark grey skirt she had chosen from the bundle he had given her to try on.

He noted, with relief, that the skirt she had chosen to wear belonged to Annarita. Thank goodness she had not picked one that had belonged to his mother. That would have been too much! Still, he couldn't help wishing she had also chosen a blouse to wear too. Anything to cover up the upper part of her body. As arousing as seeing her like this was, he knew his body would soon betray him, and make it obvious just *how* aroused he was. He lowered his eyes to the floor and crossed his fingers.

"Do my eyes scare you?"

He could sense her moving towards him and could hear how she was struggling to breathe properly, occasionally taking in big gulps of air as though she had been close to drowning and had only just reached the surface.

Finally, he dared to raise his eyes a fraction higher, enough that he could see her folded arms parallel to his head. The thought of looking higher up was tempting, but also unnerving. He knew being so close to the dark red tight buds on her naked breasts would push him too far. Instead, he buried his hands underneath his bottom to restrain himself from making any inappropriate moves to touch her body.

"No, I'm just...I'm not used to seeing girls in this way," he stammered, focusing on the light brown hairs on her arms in front of him. She was so human and yet, so not.

"Oh, my body? You do not like to see skin? Do I not look the same as the other females here?" she asked, stepping back from him.

Not knowing how to answer such a bold question, he took a deep breath, and then sat up straight, forcing himself to really look at her.

If he was going to survive any attempt to converse with her, without making a complete fool of himself, he needed to adjust to her extraordinary optics.

As they looked at each other, he realised that she seemed uncertain where to place herself in the room. Her hands kept folding under her breasts and then falling to her side again. She appeared to be waiting for him to speak.

Forcing himself to focus on her radiant eye-light, rather than the more tempting parts of her body, he quickly adapted to the strangeness of her eyes, noting that it was calming rather than threatening. Alluring rather than grotesque.

Finally, she broke the silence. "Who is this Elna you are thinking of so much? Is she the girl I saw you with? The first time?" the girl asked.

Unable to keep his eyes from darting to her breasts any longer he handed her his mother's woollen kaross to cover herself with. And then instantly cringed as he watched how she leaned her face into the wool and breathed in its scent, wrapping it around her shoulders like a shawl. Even after all these years, it still contained the memory of his mother's scent.

Annoyed with his intrusive thoughts, he pushed it out of his mind, aware that it was her mention of Elna that was the true cause of his rapid heart rate.

"How do you know her name? Elna?" he grunted, clenching his hands over the bed sheets at the side of him. It was close to a growl, a version of his voice that he did not even recognise. The girl must have sensed his unease as she backed away, hiding herself behind the dressing screen once more.

"I can still see you, in the mirror," he admitted.

The girl looked at him through the reflection in the mirror.

"I can hear you, in your mind," she conceded.

Before he had a chance to let this revelation sink in, the girl started to shake violently. Despite inwardly screaming at himself to 'get off the damn bed,' to catch her before she fell, or hurt herself, he found himself unable to move from his position.

"What the..." he managed to squeak as he watched, in disbelief, as her skin visibly changed before him, rapidly transforming from her rich amber tone to the shocking colour of egg white.

"Help me!" she trembled, pressing her fingers to the mirror as though reaching for him through her reflection.

Her plea was enough to break his trance. He darted over to her, catching her in his arms, only just in time

---

Johannes watched her chest heaving up and down as she slept on his bed. Her mouth was parted ever-so-slightly, and her nose flared with each sleepy inhale she took. She was, quite simply, breathtaking to behold. She was, also, an absolute enigma. Where on earth had she come from? In fact, was she even from this Earth? It made his head hurt just thinking about this possibility.

You have finally gone crazy Johannes!

Once again, Elna's venomous words rang in his head.

This is what happens when you do bad things. You lose your mind!

Elna hadn't actually said that part to him. He was sure of it. But it was all too easy to imagine she *would* say such things, if she were here, now, watching him curled up in a chair, waiting for this strange creature to emerge from her deep slumber. Waiting for her to give him some answers. To explain how she had found herself, naked, on the section of the Orange River nearest to his house.

But, then, what was it Kagiso always said to him? Be careful what you wish for! Well, hadn't he wished for this? For this girl in the bubble to come back.

All this time, he had been willing her to appear to him again, and yet now she was here, he was starting to wonder if Elna had been right. He *was* losing his mind.

"Wake up! *Please!*"

His spluttered out his words on instinct, not certain if he was begging for the 'girl' on his bed to wake up, or for himself!

He pulled out his right foot from under his bottom, where he had been sitting on it for too long, massaged his toes to encourage the blood flow to return to them, and then finally gave into the temptation to touch her arm once again. As before, her skin felt searing hot to his touch. And he loved it. It was like a scorching heat that didn't burn. A pain that didn't hurt. If anything, he felt a burning need to hold on to her.

This was not a dream. This was something extraordinary. *She* was extraordinary. The alluring diamond-shaped pupils that pulsated a magnificent light; her sensual body that radiated an alluring heat; and her chameleon skin, like none he had ever seen before. The skin tone that had already regained its glorious colour; a magnificent combination of soft peach, yellow, pink, and woody hues, that seemed to alternate preference for each tone every few minutes, as though designed to depict the various stages of an African sunset.

He glanced around the room, silently thanking whatever part of his useless brain had finally triggered him into action so that he had caught her before she had smashed her head on any of the furniture in his overcrowded bedroom. He had been meaning to clear out some of the unnecessary side-boards and cupboards his father had made, and his mother had treasured, for a long time now.

"I'm not letting you go! It's a miracle you are here at all!" he whispered out loud, stroking her cheek with the back of his hand.

He couldn't seem to stop finding reasons for making sin to skin contact with her as she slept. A quick move of her hand from under her back so she wouldn't wake up to a dead feeling in her arm. A little readjustment of her splayed out hair. A gentle, reassuring pressure on her arm every time her body jerked or stirred.

This was so unlike him. He had never been one for offering physical affection, certainly not to complete strangers. Even Elna, who he had known almost all his life, had practically had to beg for a hold of his hand on their walks.

This radiant girl who was now lying on his bed, was like a magnet that had been especially designed - just for him. And her scent. It smelled like coming home again. Not the familiar, damp air he breathed in this farmhouse, but in a deep, instinctive sense; the smell of a home that he had been longing to find in his mind.

"Magnets repel you know," the girl grunted with her eyes still closed.

"Hello? Are you awake? Can you hear me?"

The sound of her voice gave him such a start that he accidentally gave her arm a hard squeeze.

"Oh, sorry!" He jerked back from the bed, shifting his body back into the chair. The last thing he wanted was to frighten her. Who knew what she felt about being touched by a complete stranger? Let alone, whilst she was sleeping on his bed!

"You don't need to withdraw from me. I liked the feel of your touch. It did not frighten me at all."

He gasped, torn between relief that he had not offended her, and fear that she had been serious about her ability to hear his thoughts.

"Did...did you actually hear what I was thinking, just then?" he dared.

The girl let out a deep exhale. She appeared relaxed, almost content, as she reached her hands up to her eyes, rubbing at them hard with her fists.

"Ugh! My head feels like it is in a windstorm! And my eyes are stinging like crazy. I don't even know if I dare open them again. The light is so different here."

"Oh, yes, sorry. I can make it darker for you if that helps?"

He reached over to the small window behind him and pulled down the brown felt material that Annarita had pinned up for him to act as a curtain a few months before, back when his tendency for early morning rises had become a menace to the whole household.

"Thank you." The girl sounded out-of-breath.

"You can look at me now," she assured.

He didn't need any more encouragement. He spun back around to face her, only to be rewarded with a blinding flash of her eye-light. His hands flew up to protect his own eyes.

"Am I too bright? Are you frightened of me?"

He was about to say 'no', but his instinctive thoughts entered his mind before he could think to block them.

I am terrified of you!

As soon as he heard her reaction - a sorrowful whimpering sound - he let his hands fall from his face. He had no choice but to squint as he allowed his eyes to adjust to her phenomenal optics, although, thankfully, within seconds he found he could focus on her face with ease.

"I am captivated by you," he blurted out.

Her instant smile lit up her face as much as her eyes.

"Really? Because, I think I was meant to find you! I have been dreaming of this for a long time now."

With a little groan, she pushed her hands down on the mattress beside her hips and pulled herself up so that she sat upright, resting her head against the wall.

He watched her, transfixed by this confusing combination of her normal human body movements and her entirely non-human eyes and changing skin tone.

"I am really hungry, yes."

He frowned, trying to remember if he had just asked her this or whether he had merely thought of asking her.

"You were thinking of asking me if I was hungry, so I just answered your question before you asked it."

She yawned and stretched, instantly releasing an intoxicating scent of warm breath and sweet sweat. Johannes had never before been aware that he even had a strong sense of smell.

It's like she has released a new part of me. Like everything now makes sense! Even though it shouldn't.

"Ooh, you like how I smell? I make sense to you!" The girl clapped her hands in front of her face, clearly delighted. "You make sense to me too. You smell of baked goods and maple syrup and comfort and excitement."

Johannes stared at her. Unsure how he could possibly respond.

She was so forthright with her feelings. He had never heard anyone talk in such a way.

His heart was pounding so hard he was sure it had increased in size.

"What is your name?" he finally asked her, lowering himself down into the chair with the uncertainty of a much older man, who no longer trusted his bones and muscles to support him.

"Tiegal Eureka."

"*Eureka?* Oh!"

"Yes!" She shuffled her bottom to the left, edging herself nearer to him. He could feel the heat from her skin radiating towards him. "I heard a male voice call it out, when I arrived here earlier. Was that you?"

"No, no, not at all! I didn't even see you arrive this time. That was one of my neighbours you heard, Erasmus Jacobs"

He paused, trying to think how he could explain.

"He found a diamond. That was what made him cry out my name?" she asked.

He sighed, realising once again too late, that her ability to access his mind meant she was one step ahead of him.

"Well, yes. Eureka is what you shout out when you have discovered something. I guess it is a strange coincidence that it is also part of your name."

The girl, he now knew was named Tiegal, let out a peal of giggles. A sound so soft and child-like compared to her speaking voice it made him shiver. Being this close to her, watching and listening to her, was almost overwhelming. She really was a delightfully confusing, yet exciting, bundle of contradictions.

"I don't believe in coincidences. Anything like that should make you stop and think: what is the message I am supposed to be picking up on here?"

Johannes didn't know what he could say to this. What was the message behind all of this? His mother's voice popped into his head, as it so often did when he felt disconnected from how he was feeling.

What is worth having is never easy to obtain.

He thought of these words as he watched this marvellous discovery before him. How her eye-light dimmed as she yawned again.

"Agh! You must think I am so rude. You said you were hungry."

He reached into his pocket to pull out a few strips of biltong that Mrs Francis had shoved in his hands before he had left her hotel.

"Here, try this for now. I will get you some proper food of course but this will help keep your energy up in the meantime."

He held out the dry strips of meat to her.

"Ugh! What is that smell?"

She recoiled from his hand, scrambling away to the other side of the bed. And then, to his horror, her skin colour transformed from its amber tone to an olive green.

He pulled his hand back and shoved the biltong back into his pocket.

"It's erm, dried meat."

On hearing his answer, she reacted again: her nostrils flared and her shoulders shook.

"Meat? From what? Please tell me not an elephant. Not one like my Namnum."

Her face had crumpled into a frown and a tremble of lips. He had to fight the urge to run over to her side of the bed and pull her into his arms, so that he could apologise for whatever foolish mistake he had just made.

"No, it's made from a cow, definitely not an elephant," he reassured her, holding his hands up in the air and letting them hover at the side of his face.

She took one look at his hands, sniffed the air around her and then began to retch. Not hesitating, he swung round, yanked open the window, withdrew the rest of the dried meat strips from his pocket and threw them out.

"It's okay. Look! All gone now. No more meat. I promise. I will get you some bread and fruit."

Tiegal's face lit up. Her skin instantly returned to a peachier colour.

"Fruit. Yes please!"

His shoulders relaxed immediately, but almost instantly then stiffened as the sound of Kagiso's voice filtered up through the open window.

"Oi! Johannes Smit! What do yer think you are doing throwing food out of yer window like that. Show yourself young man."

"Oh no! Kagiso! She can't see you here."

He needed to think - and fast.

"Ka-gi-so? Hmm..." Tiegal squinted her eyes as she focused on him. Her expression made him wonder if she was trying to listen to his thoughts.

"She is one of your family? Why don't you tell her I am Elna? The female you were thinking about earlier?" Tiegal suggested, her voice a careful whisper. She was clearly letting him know that she agreed with his silent plans.

Despite registering the calmness in her voice, he squirmed at how intrusive her power to access his mind was.

"Johannes! Who have you got in there with you?" Kagiso sounded more than her usual exasperated. She sounded positively angry.

He leaned his head out of the window.

"Hi Kagiso!" He gave her one of his cheeky smiles and waved at her in a deliberately young, child-like fashion. It usually worked like a charm where Kagiso was concerned. But, clearly not today.

"Who do you think you are? You go out all afternoon getting all angry with Frederick after a few too many whiskeys. And then, you have the nerve to just not turn up for the supper that I spent all day making for yer."

Her words stung. Kagiso did not deserve such ill-treatment. But, how could he possibly explain how his life had just been transformed in a matter of only a few blissful hours?

"Hey, hey, Kagiso. Please don't be mad. I'm sorry. And you are right! That was all very unthoughtful of me," he placated.

"*And,* not to mention that you then sneaked into the house and took some girl up to your bedroom! I can hear you talking to someone in there. It is not proper Johannes!"

He raked his hand through his hair as he contemplated his next move. He could hear Tiegal shifting back down the sheets behind him and could still smell her intoxicating smell, but he knew he could not reveal her to Kagiso, or to anyone else in his family just yet.

"It's not what it looks like Kagiso. Elna was just making sure I got home safely. You know we have been friends for a while. I will make sure she also gets home safely, now that I am feeling better," he lied.

Kagiso tutted at him and threw her arms into the air.

"You must think I was born yesterday Johannes. I would have heard if Elna was back in town."

"Damn," he muttered under his breath, as he realised how obvious a lie that must have sounded. Elna had been gone for a year now. How could he have been so stupid?

He watched Kagiso trudge away, her head hung low to show her clear disapproval.

"Maybe you could find a place for me to hide, for now? The one you just thought of then?"

Her suggestion made him flinch.

The cabin? No! I never go near that place. It's too full of bad memories.

Tiegal flashed her eyes at him and then shook her head.

"A *place* does not contain memories. They only exist inside here." She pointed to her forehead. "And here," she whispered, directing her finger towards her chest.

"Yes, but not the cabin. It is tiny and damp, and cold, and dirty..." he protested.

"I have lived in a tiny cabin before and that one was not something I did out of choice. This is different. I am making the choice to be in your cabin. Dirty or not. I think you should take me there, Johannes."

Hearing her speak his name made him feel dizzy and confused. He was sure he had not actually introduced himself by name yet.

"I heard the female outside address you in that way," she explained, before he could ask.

"Please, let us go now. Something tells me we can change this troubled connection you have with this place. And... keep me safe whilst we do."

16. THE CABIN

Tiegal shivered in the darkness, pulling at the sheets to cover her body. The bed was unfamiliar to her and the room was full of conflicting smells that she was struggling to identify. She rubbed at her eyes and tried flashing them around her. But no matter how many times she tried widening her vision, no light would come. It was as if she were blind.

"What's the matter Tiegal? Is your light dimming by any chance? Are you losing some of your powers now?"

Tiegal flinched at the sound of a female's voice somewhere nearby. It resonated in the blackness of this cold room she had awoken in. And it filled her with dread. She knew this voice. And she also knew that it was not human.

"Oh, now come on, Tiegal. Surely you must remember me? My powers are not that much stronger than yours, are they?"

The taunting words rippled across to her. The threatening undercurrent they carried was palpable.

"Where am I?" Tiegal pleaded.

Please say Earth, please say Earth!

"In your cabin of course, where else?" the voice answered.

Hearing this made Tiegal gasp. She couldn't have found herself back here again, in her Tandro prison? That awful tiny cabin Atla had contained her in? Hadn't she just fallen asleep listening to Johannes reading to her. Wasn't it his warm, sweet breath near her cheeks that she had felt before she had fallen asleep?

Just as she was about to plead with the voice, to stop playing games in the dark, the unmistakable scent of mint wafted across to her.

Hold on, I know this smell too!

A fog-like memory of being in a hot, dry field filled her mind. Of carrying a bucket full of bananas and figs for Namnum, her beautiful elephant. And of the grumbling sound, the animal's warning - to back away from the strange female that had approached them.

Tiegal sat up bolt-right and blinked in rapid succession. Her eyes reacted instantly, finally allowing her light to fill the room and reveal the female before her. She was standing with her arms crossed at the foot of her bed. The way she was smiling at her was anything but warm.

The moment she saw her, it all became clear. She was the same mysterious female who had appeared to her in that gust of wind, and who had then disappeared in a burst of turquoise colour energy.

"You! The one who told me to release all my deepest thoughts in the Erasmati Pyramid. The one Namnum reacted so strangely to."

The female moved towards the bed, her eyes beaming a brilliant reflection that flashed out in alluring steps of light towards her.

"I knew you would remember me. But I wonder... do you remember everything?"

The female's name was on the tip of her tongue, but she couldn't seem to pull the letters together...pa...do... or?

"Parador!" the female answered for her. "And no, you are not in your Tandro cabin. Look again!"

Tiegal flashed her eyes around the space. Once she saw where she really was, she breathed out deeply.

"Johannes' cabin!" she almost cried with relief, just as another realisation hit her. "But...if that is the case, then, why are you here? I mean, how?"

Parador pressed her fingers to the Derado she wore close to her throat and smiled. A gust of turquoise mist burst around her.

"You should know better than this by now Tiegal. You haven't been in this other world for long enough to forget everything have you?"

Tiegal rolled her eyes. Her light created a rainbow of reflections over Parador's colourful mist.

"Of course! I'm in one of my dreams!"

Parador sauntered around the bed, as though she were tiptoeing, and then sat down on the part of the mattress close to Tiegals' feet. Her distinctive scent made Tiegal shiver with trepidation. Her every instinct told her that this female was dangerous, even if she still could not quite remember why.

"Hmm...glad to know you are catching on! Although, it is a shame that you can't quite recall how we are connected." Parador licked her lips and flicked her raven black hair. Her Tandroan style bob shifted back and forth before resting back under her chin.

Tiegal found herself shaking her head with vigour, unable to know how else she could respond. There was something else about this female. It wasn't just her smell or her taunting voice.

"Hold on! You have something inside your eyes. I remember that part now."

As she said this, she squinted her eyes to focus on Parador's strange pulsating reflection.

"That's it! Your eye-light contains a hidden image. It's something powerful and strong...an animal of some kind..."

"A horse-tail. The very symbol of power," Parador filled in for her, yawning loudly as she glanced around the cabin. "Interesting that you have found yourself in another cabin again, don't you think? Shame your fantasy male couldn't find you somewhere cleaner ."

An immediate urge to defend Johannes made Tiegal launch herself towards her and give her a sharp prod on her arm.

"Hey! It was my choice to be here. And we have made it cosy together, and clean!"

Parador smiled and shook her head.

"Ah, I think you and I both know that it is anything but clean in here. I am not the only one who has something hidden inside of them, just as you do. And, as you well know, so does this male you dreamed yourself over to!"

Tiegal squirmed. There was something about Parador's words that made her feel sick. What did she have hidden inside of her? And more importantly, what was she suggesting that Johannes had hidden inside of him?

Parador stood up. As she smacked both her hands on her mint green trousers a cloud of black dust burst around her.

"So much dirt in here Tiegal. Perhaps you should take more care with your choices? Have you considered that choosing to stay here means choosing to die?"

Before Tiegal could respond Parador vanished, taking her beaming light and glowing energy colour with her, and leaving Tiegal alone and afraid.

There was never any escape from these dreams. If she tried to trick herself into awakening she could encourage them to return. Instead, she curled into a ball and closed her eyes, crossing her fingers as she begged whatever universe she was in to not let this dream prophecy come true.

———

Johannes bent down to check that the newborn calf was happily nursing. Once satisfied all was well, he closed the gate and ran down to the dense area of bush land behind his house in search of Tiegal. He was desperate to hear her voice again, although he knew he had to be careful. It would be foolish of him to frighten her with his deepest thoughts, this powerful attraction he felt towards her. Yet, he just couldn't help himself.Those eyes of hers! They really were a portal to another world. He just wanted to get closer to her, to see where they would take him. These were crazy thoughts, he knew this, but she really had enchanted him. She was just so deliciously different, so beautifully out-of-the ordinary.

By the time he reached her, sitting patiently by the old tree swing his father had built for him as a child, she was already smiling and nodding, as though she were amused by what she could hear.

"Oh dear! Why do I get the feeling you are one step ahead of me again?" he teased as he pulled on the rope to give her swing some momentum. "So, tell me again how this works. You sometimes choose to hear what I am thinking and other times you turn it off?"

He knew what her answer would be, but he enjoyed teasing her. It always made her skin radiate more heat and her eyes flash just that much brighter. It even allowed his imagination to stretch that much further. He could almost picture her fire – the energy that she had told him about – dancing its flames under her skin.

"Here we go again," she groaned. "Johannes, I keep telling you. I don't have any control over here. I *used* to be able to access the minds of others in my other world, but I can't do this so easily with you. It's only *sometimes* ...mainly when you are more tired, like now for example. Then, I seem to catch a bit more of what you feel," she explained as she stretched herself out into the shape of an angel lying on her back in the long silvery grass.

Without hesitating he lay down next to her, turning onto his side to face her, and resting his head on the palm of his hand. He was more than tired, exhausted even. The prospect of keeping the farm running in this way - balancing his chores whilst sneaking out to see Tiegal - was unthinkable. He had hardly slept in weeks. But then, it didn't help that he was so worried about anyone finding Tiegal. And he would do anything he could to keep her hidden.

"Has Annarita asked you any more questions?"

Tiegal had her eyes closed. He knew she loved to catch the last rays of sun before it settled, so that she could prepare herself for the darkness and the big reveal of the African star lit sky she always found so magical. She said it reminded her of earlier days, and a girl called Zeno who she used to make dreams with.

It was the reason they always met at this time, here in this open space, in the bush at the back of his family farm. Well, one of the reasons. It helped that it was also close to the cabin; an area no one ever ventured near anymore. Not since the day the cabin became such a dark place.

He shook head, determined to banish these thoughts from his mind. This area was the perfect spot for her to hide out during the day and the cabin was the most obvious place for her to sleep, for now.

"I told you Tiegal. Don't worry about my sister. She is too exhausted looking after her baby and helping me run the farm to worry about what I am doing all the time! She probably assumes I am sneaking around and being improper with some local girl anyway."

A waft of heat from her body hit his face. It made him gasp.

"You did it again!" he cried.

"I did what?" Tiegal whispered. Her eyes were open now, flickering more rapidly than usual.

Something he had said must have alarmed her in some way; or excited her. He was never sure which.

"You made a morning sunrise," he suggested. Poetic metaphors had never been his strength, as much as he had tried when he was with Elna, but he was getting better at them now he was spending time with Tiegal, the bubble girl.

"You called me bubble girl!" She teased him.

"I *knew* you could hear me."

"Just a few words and thoughts. It's an intermittent connection," she clarified. "And your comparison to my sudden body heat being like a sunrise is beautiful Johannes. I understand what you mean. Do you remember how I told you about our morning mantra on Tandro?"

He nodded. Everything she told him about her world fascinated him. And there were many things he thought were truly wonderful about it. He had even begged for her to find a way for them to transport over there together. But that request always made her skin turn cold. He knew that it terrified her to think that she may wake up and find herself back there again.

"I am an island. I am fire! Yes, I even chant it myself now," he admitted.

"Well, don't Johannes! I didn't tell you that because it is a good thing. I told you because I wanted you to understand why it was so hard for me to live there. I am not an island, and neither are you. Do you even understand what chanting such things turns you into?" She stood up and started gathering sticks into the folds of her skirt. She always did this, in readiness for a sunset fire

Johannes rubbed his eyes. He didn't have the energy for such philosophizing between worlds right now, and he always found watching her build a fire unnerving. It made him feel ashamed. It reminded him of Elna and the day they had first kissed, when he had suggested collecting sticks for a fire on her birthday. And, of another fire. One he had been helpless to control.

Tiegal stopped in her tracks and turned to glare at him.

"I sometimes wonder if you feel guilty when it rains? You can't take responsibility for everything," she bristled. "It's when you think of her that I hear you the most you know."

Her voice was a whisper. It reminded him of the smoke of the fire soon to be made; a dance of carbon particles suspended in the air, and of the nightmares that plagued him. Of a mother that had left this earth. And another nightmare, even worse, where Tiegal and her bubble vanished before him.

"What do you mean Tiegal?" he finally dared to ask.

She let the sticks fall into a pile near his feet and then slumped down in front of him, her legs curled underneath her dirty skirt. He sat up to face her, making a mental note to remind himself that he needed to find her some more clothes.

"I mean that you still think of her Johannes. You feel some kind of shame that we are friends like this. That you think of me in such...ways."

"Because it makes me feel guilty."

He could not bring himself to look at her. The way her eyes flashed would give away her emotions. They always did. Her eyes always revealed her feelings that he could somehow read, more than any human eyes he had ever connected with.

He had thought about this a lot recently; that he may not have the power to access her thoughts, but he could feel things about her emotions he had never thought possible.

"I know it makes you feel guilty." She placed her hot hand on his cheek. "You think I smell more familiar than she did. And that I would probably kiss like her too, but perhaps even better? And that makes you feel bad. It makes you want to put a boundary between us?" She challenged.

He could feel the heat of the blush in his cheeks.

"So, you see Johannes, that thinking of yourself as an island like my world people do, is not so good."

He frowned.

"Now you've lost me," he said.

She reached her hands out to close around his.

"I mean that we are all full of energy and yes we have to protect this, like it is a fire that needs fuel, but to think of ourselves as a place that no one can enter...it is not right Johannes. It means we do not burn the way we really should. I want people to enter my island and enjoy my fire. I don't want to travel on the edge of other islands, only exchanging fuel when I need to, like cargo boats that float around the boundaries between guarded lands. Because what is the point in that? Then we all just return to our individual islands on our own again. We are just lonely beings with only flickers of flames to keep us warm."

Johannes stared at her and then leaned back, his body rigid, letting himself fall into the grass in a deliberately dramatic fashion. Luckily, she laughed at him.

"Oh please don't think I am so crazy. I was hoping you understood me, perhaps a little?" she pleaded. He watched with fascination as she crossed her hands together, as though she were praying. Her gesture surprised him. Their recent talks about the concept of a higher being - a God- had left her utterly confused, if not amused. It made him wonder, for a moment, if Tiegal had taken to exploring the area beyond these bushes. He *had* warned her of the dangers such venturing could entail, but he suspected she was far too curious by nature to obey all his instructions. Something told him she was naturally rebellious. It was easy to picture her peeking through the church windows in the town, observing the religious statues in the early hours when no one else was awake.

"It's not easy to understand any girl when you are just a simple farmer boy like me Tiegal, but *you* take it to a whole other level," he teased.

The blank look she gave him made him feel strange in a way he could not place. There was something different about her today. It took a few seconds for him to clock that it was her eyes. They were no longer flashing as brightly as they had when she had first arrived. What had it been now? Just over a month. Not a long time and yet, it seemed she was already adapting to her surroundings. Tiegal was looking more and more human every day.

Still, as incredible as this was, he knew that she must still be feeling very lost and alone, hiding out here, waiting for stolen moments with him.

He beckoned for her to lie next to him on the grass. This was the deepest conversation they had shared. Something was already changing between them, he could feel it. It was like she had described to him. The energies between people flow in a positive way when they are open to the experience.

"You can feel it can't you?" she asked him as she lay down, parallel to him. Her breath smelled so sweet and pure. He wasn't even sure how she was surviving on the small parcels of food he had managed to sneak away from Annarita and Kagiso's watchful eyes, but yet she carried a scent of ocean breeze and warm honey, sweet and sweaty after being left out in the midday sun. In fact, it was anything but stale or dehydrated as you might expect.

"I can feel something very strong, very real and very right about us, yes, Tiegal," he answered.

"Then maybe we should see where that connection could take us?" She reached out to stroke his cheek with the back of her hand.

"Why did you tell me you know I think about kissing you? Were you testing my reaction?" he dared.

"I *said* you thought I would kiss like Elna did."

Johannes sat up and turned away from her.

"Why do you keep bringing her up? She's gone! I can't see how this energy you talk of will flow between us if it gets mixed up with things that are no longer relevant."

"Because, Johannes, you are still broken by something. And whatever it is, you've hidden it so deeply that even I can't reach it!"

She ran her hand through his hair and then held her hot palm under his chin.

"You need to let it go Johannes. Because, whatever it is, it is hurting you more than you realise."

Sensing she had more to say, he waited, listening to her ragged breathing. It sounded as if she were close to tears.

"And it's stopping you from...from connecting with me!" she finished.

The tear that ran down her cheek confirmed what he had suspected. That once again, he was in danger of losing something precious, someone more valuable than anything he could have ever wished to find.

17. SHIVERS

The loud bang on the door made her jump with fright. Her heart pounding, she ran to the corner of the cabin and huddled herself into a ball on the floor.

Go away! Whoever you are, please just go away.

There was a treacherous storm blowing outside and she knew it was long past the normal bedtime for the people who lived in this area. Johannes had already been and gone earlier this evening, apologizing that he had farm chores to attend and that he would return in the morning. Whoever was standing outside her door now must be a stranger. She was in serious trouble.

It was only a matter of time before the fragile wooden door would give way and, when it did, she had no idea how she could defend herself. There was nothing in here other than the bed, a wooden crate, a small chair and the few items of clothing that Johannes had given her.

Closing her eyes tight she gripped the hem of her nightdress and steeled herself for whatever would happen next.

"Tiegal! OPEN the door!"

"Johannes?" she dared, not sure if her ears had betrayed her. It made no sense for him to be here now, in the middle of the night and during the worst kind of weather she had ever experienced. Plus, they had a code for his knock: four, short little raps – tat, ta, ta, tat. They had agreed on it, so that she would know it was him and not a random stranger wandering through the bush.

"*Yes,* it's me! Can you open the door? I'm freezing out here. I got caught in this storm whilst fishing. Foolish, I know, but...*please* can you let me in."

Tiegal shook her head in disbelief. He really was here! There was no mistaking that husky voice of his.

"Oh, I'm so sorry. I'm coming right now."

Unclenching her fists, she let her nightdress fall and ran over to let him in.

As soon as she saw him standing there, his hair and clothes soaking wet and his skin a terrifying shade of creamy blue, she knew it was not her life she had to fear, it was *his.*

Alarmed, she pulled him towards her and closed the door behind them, quickly pushing some spare sheets against the bottom of the door frame.

"You look terrible Johannes. And you scared me turning up like this," she started and then stopped. He really did look desperately ill.

Johannes did not say anything, he just stumbled over to the chair and slumped down into it. A part of her wanted to scream at him, to demand that he explain why he had exposed his body to such awful weather conditions, but she bit down on her lip instead. There would be time for explanations later. Right now, he needed her help.

"You need to warm up! Your body is shaking Johannes. You look like a tree trying to withstand a storm. Let me give you some of my heat." She could smell the threat of death on his skin.

Johannes didn't look as though he had heard her. Or if he had, he was being stubborn.

"I'm not going to ask you again. I'm telling you to get into this bed with me now so that I can warm you up," she demanded.

He squeezed his eyes shut, wincing in obvious discomfort. He looked close to drifting into a deep sleep, one she feared he may not emerge from. Not unless she did something.

She waited for a few seconds, to see if he would move from the chair. But when he curled his knees under his chin, wrapping his shaking arms around his legs, she knew she was going to have to do something drastic.

"I am not going to lose you Johannes. I will do whatever it takes."

She pulled her nightdress over her head and slipped under the bed sheets. Careful to ensure he was still unaware of her movements, she then reached underneath the bed in search for the box he had given her not long after she had arrived here, the one that contained her Derado.

Connecting with this part of her other world was a risky strategy. She had no way of knowing whether activating it with her body and energy again would take her away from this world. It was quite possible that it could catapult her back to Tandro, and towards a danger of her own. Yet there was no choice. Her heat from her energy release was the only way to save him. Yes, it ran the risk of transporting her away again, but this was Johannes' life at stake. A young, beautiful, strong life that she absolutely must ensure survived.

Casting her fears aside she placed it around her neck. At first, the metal of her Derado felt cold on her skin but it warmed up as soon as she pressed the pink diamond. Her colour energy released instantly and the white bed sheets that covered her naked frame glowed with luminous pink.

The reaction was quicker than she had anticipated. There were two things she needed to check as a first response: if she were still solid in body, and whether Johannes had noticed her colourful light display coming from the bed.

She squeezed the flesh around her legs to check that they were still firm and intact.

Okay, that's a good sign. I'm not disappearing, not yet!

Her sigh of relief revealed itself as a mist in the space above her bed. There was a cold draught in this cabin that no amount of sheets stuffed under the door could withhold, an even more compelling reason for her to find a quick way to warm Johannes up.

She looked over to the chair. Johannes was no longer there. He was now standing by the side of her bed.

"Wh...wh... what are doing now?" his voice trembled.

She could hear the confusion in his thoughts. His mind was racing with theories.

"No, you're not hallucinating. It's my colour release. I'm heating myself up for you. You *need* my energy Johannes. Now get in the bed. I'm not going to hurt you."

She pulled out her hand from under the cover to take hold of his and encourage him to make a move.

"You sh...sh ...shouldn't play with that necklace T...T...Tiegal. We ttt...talked about this. It's how you tttransport."

"Get in the bed now Johannes! You can hardly stand, never mind walk." She sat up on her knees and fixed her hands under his armpits, in the shape of a handshake, and then pulled him gently onto the mattress next to her. He groaned as his body hit the hardness of the wooden planks of the make-shift bed they had put together in the cabin Tiegal now called her home.

"Are you naked Tiegal?" he managed.

"Yes, I *am*. It's the best way for me to conduct the heat to your body."

His eyelids flickered. She couldn't resist smiling at the hint of desire in his trembling voice. It was obvious he was desperate to see the details of her body up close. But she also knew that he was too weak to keep his eyes open for long enough. It was dark in here. There was only one candle still burning inside her tiny cabin and it flickered wildly, providing them with a limited light source, alongside the dim light from Tiegal's eyes.

She placed the back of her hand on his forehead. He was clammy, cold, and had begun muttering things from his blue lips that didn't make sense. His thoughts, on the other hand, were loud and clear:

Ma...why did you leave me? I need you...

Elna... I'm sorry. I know I treated you unfairly. I know that you felt you had to leave the place you called home. Because of me!

Tiegal flinched at hearing the words of loss inside his head. It was impossible to control the sweep of pain that engulfed her. It made her angry with herself. She didn't want to feel jealousy towards his grief. It was wrong. It was selfish. The bond he shared with his mother sounded magical to her. The way Johannes had described her tenderness and warmth towards him, and towards his sister, had touched Tiegal so much that she had cried in his arms a few nights ago, never having experienced such familial love.

But Johannes' grief for his mother was not what hurt her. It was Elna. This obvious heartache and guilt at losing her had wrenched, so that she shivered at the sight of her changing energy release from her Derado. The colours that were now muddied with dark green and brown mists.

This was not going to help Johannes at all. She was supposed to be saving him, not letting her stupid emotions reduce the power in her energy. She scolded herself for it, digging her overgrown nails into her palms.

"Come on now Johannes. You have to let me get you warm. I can smell the threat of death on you. You're scaring me. Let me help you."

At last, he succumbed, nodding at her.

Breathing a deep sigh of relief, she shifted her body towards him, wrapped her arms around his shoulders, and then clamped her chest and hips to his back. Her right leg coiled around his. They fit together like a jigsaw.

"Ouch!" he managed to protest between his raspy attempts to breathe.

"Oh, I'm sorry. It's the Derado. It gets extremely hot. Let me move a little higher."

She shimmied her body higher up the bed so that the burning hot pendant would sit parallel to the back of his head, hoping she could arch herself back enough to avoid scalding him.

"That should be better now. You're starting to warm up already," she whispered into his ear. Her leg was now wrapped around his waist and she could reach her fingers around to the top of his chest. His breathing was already settling.

"I can't believe you attempted fishing in this temperature Johannes," she scolded in a gentle hush. He was already falling into a deep sleep, but she felt reassured by the smell on his skin that he was safe enough to rest now.

Her body still felt strong and firm as she clenched her thighs against his hips. It seemed that, she too, was out of the danger zone. The Derado had managed to do its job without sending her away from him. Still, just to be sure, she reached across to release it from around her neck.

Once they were settled together in a comfortable and warm position, she closed her eyes and rested her cheek against his skin. He was starting to smell like him again: baked bread and sweet pastry with a hint of maple syrup. It made her stomach growl with hunger just thinking about it.

This was what she had yearned for all these years. This enormous sense of satisfaction that came with holding him like this. She had dreamed of such closeness all her life. It was her fire blending with his, and it was so much more powerful than any release that Tandro had promised her, just as she had always believed it would be.

There was just one barrier she still had to overcome, they both did.

If only you could you relieve yourself from the burden of this guilt you carry. If you were not so broken, so damp inside? Then you could enjoy your fire. We could enjoy it together!

She knew Johannes would awake feeling shocked at how they were lying here together like this, but she would explain it all to him tomorrow. It was clear how much he desired her. It was also abundantly clear that something he had buried deep inside of him was preventing him from letting himself go.

Still, she couldn't think about that right now. Her body was starting to feel the effects of her energy release. Her eyelids dropped down, shutting out her eye-light so that they soon lay wrapped together, in complete darkness.

Elna, like a pebble: solid and familiar and of this earth.

Tiegal, like a bubble: unstable and unpredictable, and from some-where unknown

Elna, a pebble, too easily kicked and displaced

Tiegal, my bubble, too easily consuming me and colouring all that I know

Johannes' thoughts were loud and clear. He was constructing a poem of some kind that was on repeat in his head.

Tiegal removed her hand from where it stuck to the hairs on his sweat ridden chest. The sun had already risen, now seeping easily through the thin sheet that Johannes had pinned to the square window he had fashioned from wood. She slid out from the covers in a backwards motion, quickly retrieving her clothes.

Her Derado lay upside down on the floor. It must have fallen off the bed during their fitful sleep together, when Johannes had awoken with more shivers.

She looked it at now, turning it over so she could run her fingers over the details. It was a stunning piece of jewellery. The niobium metal that made up the collar section of the neckpiece reflected a luminous pink shine, and the rose gold triangles that fitted over it complimented the colour perfectly. She had tried to explain to Johannes how the mechanics from her world had discovered that this metal would change colour when charged with different amounts of electricity. He thought she had been talking about magic people, alchemists who could change stone into metals. She had laughed with him about that. Of all the things he could have called magic about her stories of Tandro, he had picked up on this!

It was impossible to deny that the Derado *was* alluring. Even she felt drawn to it whenever she held it.

It even made her feel a small sense of loss for her old world, a familiar loneliness rearing once more. She had made it all the way over here, to a whole new world, one that had already changed her, and yet, there were some things that would always stay the same.

"Erm...morning!"

She turned her back towards the sheepish voice coming from the bed. Johannes was blinking at her, frowning in confusion. Reacting quickly, she hid the Derado behind her back, mindful that she had promised him she would never activate it again.

"Do you remember anything of last night?" she dared.

"Well, I know I knocked on the door and kind of fell into you?"

"Yes, you did, because you were shivering like crazy after trying to wade into the river and catch some fish! I dried you off and you fell asleep in the bed. You look much better now. Your lips were blue last night!"

"I'm, well, I'm so sorry Tiegal. But, really, you didn't have to give up your bed for me."

"I didn't."

"Oh, I see." He looked hopeful, unsure, and concerned, all at the same time.

Tiegal couldn't help herself. She had to laugh. She needed to release something easier, and lighter, from inside of her.

"You were extremely cold Johannes. Your body was running on a dangerously low temperature. I needed to warm you with my body heat."

He didn't need to remember the colour glow, or the Derado. It would only frighten him more. Johannes widened his eyes at her. She could see he was feeling under the covers, no doubt checking if he were still wearing his trousers.

"I took them off because they were soaking wet," she explained, not daring to look him in the eye.

"Of course, yes...erm, thank you."

Tiegal groaned. She hated this awkwardness between them. They had been so peaceful and easy together, from the moment she first jumped into the river with him on her first day here. It felt strange to think that this night had confused things between them. Crawling on to the bed she sat herself next to him. His complexion was still pale after his near-death experience but there was enough colour in his cheeks that she felt satisfied he could manage a small conversation before she set off in search of breakfast for them both. There were some apple trees at the edge of the wood that no one seemed too interested in. She had been using these as her main source of food energy for the last few days.

"Can I ask you something Johannes?"

He turned his body so that he could face her more easily in the bed.

"Did you and Elna ever do intimate things together? I mean, connect in the way that animals do? I know you kissed her. But, I wondered, anything else?" Her words were rushed. She had practiced saying them many times in her head, but now she was allowing them to come out, she couldn't stop herself.

Johannes sucked in his breath. It was an odd action, one that Tiegal found hard to place.

"I thought you could hear my thoughts?" he questioned.

"I told you...only some of them...when you are very tired," she explained, careful to reassure him that she was not constantly invading his every thought. He averted his eyes from her gaze.

"So, I guess you must have been listening to me last night then? If I was so drained of energy?" He sounded cross.

"Why are you so angry?"

"I'm not angry Tiegal. I'm scared!'

"Of what? I don't understand. Please tell me what you really think. It is all so disjointed in your thoughts and I know you don't like me digging into your head too much," she pleaded.

"It probably sounds disjointed because I *am* disjointed! I don't know what to do! To make sure I don't..."

"You *don't* what?"

She could hardly breathe as she waited for his answer.

"I don't want to break something again."

She shook her head at him, determined to let him see her frustration.

"*I* am not going to break. Is that what you mean?"

"No! I mean that whenever I have something of value, I lose it, or break it. At least, that was how my life was going until you appeared, and, well, everything changed again."

"Was that a good thing though?"

"How could you even question that Tiegal?"

"Because you never, well, *touch* me!" She turned her shoulders away from him, embarrassed by her own honesty. "Yet I can hear your thoughts about this Johannes, and how you want to. That is what I don't understand. You have the choice to kiss *me* too now! Just like you did with her, when I saw you together that time, from across the river. The first time I appeared."

Johannes shook his head and then swivelled his legs over the edge of his side of the bed. He nearly fell over as he stood up, but just managed to catch his fall on the wooden crate by the door.

"Elna and I never did anything intimate other than that kissing. And only that one time! Her family kept her under tight control. She was never allowed to go very far, or to meet me for very long either."

Tiegal nodded, determined to display some empathy:

"Being under tight control. Now, that I can understand. Poor Elna!"

"Well, yes, but never mind her now. Look, I want nothing more than to kiss you Tiegal. I'm just scared to let myself get too close. My relationship with Elna was complicated. It was burdened by other people's expectations. And my love for you would be complicated too – if anyone discovered us together."

Her entire body reacted to his words: goosebumps appeared on her arms, her stomach did a strange flipping movement, and her knees banged together uncontrollably.

He said 'my love for you!'

"It's just that I know how easy it is to lose people in this world. What if I lost you too, either in this world, or to the one you came from?"

Ignoring his objections, she jumped up onto the bed and bounced up and down.

"Tiegal! Did you understand what I just said? I'm scared of falling for you and then losing you!" Johannes asked.

Laughing, she stopped bouncing and jumped onto the floor into the space in front of him, reaching her arms up to wrap around his broad shoulders.

"I hear you loud and clear. You are ready to feel love again. That's all that matters."

But even as she said these words, so full of hope and excitement, she could hear his doubts. And as she looked into his eyes, she couldn't help wondering what secrets lay hidden inside. This burden he had buried so deep inside, that even she could not access it.

18. PROMISES

Tiegal giggled, bursting with unrestrained delight as Johannes ruffled her hair. She loved rolling around in the bush with him like this, tumbling over each other in turn, collecting haphazard patterns of dry grass on their backs. She clung onto him as tightly as she could, determined to keep their momentum going, not wanting their game to end. Johannes seemed especially happy and playful today. He was full of a special kind of contagious, exuberant energy, the type she had rarely detected before. Perhaps only from the younger Tandroans - the kimberlings - in her previous life.

It was impossible to get enough of him when he was like this. And better still, his happiness was so easy to absorb. Who needed to wear a diamond necklace to exchange your energies when you were having this much fun together? Johannes was exuding joy in her arms, she never wanted to let him go. And why should she? They were clearly good together. This was the first time she had heard his laughter – his full, unequivocal pleasure.

It had to mean a turning point had been reached, she was sure of it. It was as though they had overcome something momentous together in these last few minutes. Amazing as it was to think, it seemed something magical had just occurred between them. A new spark, elicited from the simplicity of carefree play!

It was almost as if they had set him free, together, and released him from the chains of the grief and guilt he had tangled himself up in. Perhaps they had opened a new door, one that allowed them the freedom to finally explore their connection, fully, and let the feelings they had for each other, flow without obstructions?

Johannes was the first to slow down their roll, holding his body over hers, his feet jutting into the ground at the side of her ankles

"You are one very complicated girl Tiegal Eureka. But you are *my* complicated girl," he declared, in between fits of laughter that he seemed powerless to stop, now that he had finally let himself go.

She twisted her hips allowing her to maneuver them both over again, so this time *she* was on top.

"What do you mean?" she asked, letting herself rest on top of him as their rolling reached the barrier of some thorn trees.

"I mean, you keep talking about finding your complete circle, and fires on islands, like this is something we all understand," he replied, giving her a wink to assure her that his words were full of affection, an action that gave him a temporary lopsided expression.

"Is it really that confusing? The way I talk?" she panted, breathing in his intoxicating smell, which was even more delicious when he was joyful like this.

"You talk in a *beautiful* way Tiegal! I don't mean to offend you. I'm teasing you. In an affectionate way, I promise. I just have to play catch up when you talk about your worlds and the philosophy of your people."

"Tandroans!" she corrected him.

"Ah, yes, of course." He rolled his eyes and smiled at her again. She gave him an exaggerated frown and then sat up, straddling her legs either side of his hips.

"Ooh no you can't do that Tiegal. That's pushing my human willpower too much." He put his hands under her armpits and gently moved her on to the grass beside him.

Tiegal made a popping sound with her lips in response. It was her little joke sign to him when she was frustrated by his over-gentlemanly manner towards her. He always looked confused when she did this, but it made him laugh again all the same.

"I still don't understand the bubble thing. I know you appeared to me inside one, but please remind me again how it relates to a type of food?"

He stroked the side of her cheek with the back of his hand, before taking a strand of her hair and wrapping it around his index finger. He seemed to love touching her hair. She often wondered if it was his safety net, a way to distract him from the urge to touch her anywhere else.

"Okay, let me try again. It's like a stretchy sweety-gum? You chew it and it releases sugary tastes and then you can put your tongue through it and blow air at the same time – to make a bubble out of your lips!"

She puckered her lips into an 'o' and pretended to pop something in mid-air near her face.

"No! Still can't imagine that at all! But it sounds like fun! Actually, talking of sweet things...you know you said my skin had a smell that reminded you of sweet pastry and maple syrup?" He raised his eyebrows at her, not waiting for an answer

"Well...I might be able to offer you something more than just a smell because over there..."

Tiegal squealed before he had a chance to finish his sentence.

"You brought some more food?" She clasped her hands together in anticipation of some much-needed fuel. It was getting harder to keep her energy going on the long days when Johannes was on the farm, when she was left to occupy her time on her own.

She watched as Johannes walked over to a shady area under some trees and reached into a brown basket. He must have hidden it there before she had arrived to meet him at their special place - an area close to the river, but still hidden from view of his farm.

"Wait until you taste these Tiegal," he called to her, as he ran over to where she had positioned herself by the edge of the riverbank.

"Now this is what you can call a treat. These were my mother's favourites," he explained as he unwrapped a white towel to reveal two sugar-glazed doughnuts that had been braided into a plait.

"These are called Koeksisters. I believe the recipe has evolved over time from when our Dutch ancestors introduced them here, and now everyone loves them. Annarita has been trying to match my mother's recipe for weeks! I think she is trying to get them ready for a church gathering or something of that nature. Anyway, I managed to sneak a few into my basket before she saw me," Johannes admitted. He handed one of the braided pastries to her.

Tiegal took one bite and immediately started choking. Without hesitating, Johannes rushed to her side, slapping her on her back.

"Tiegal! Breathe!" he shouted, utter terror flashing over his face. She shook her head at him, waving her hands up and down.

"I'm fine!" she reassured him, as she picked him the pastry to take another bite. "Hmmm. That is just delicious." She laughed at him as his shocked expression instantly transitioned to confusion.

"I wasn't choking from the taste. It was a surprise that's all."

Johannes shook his head.

"Of course! Gosh, I'm sooo sorry. You must be starving hungry. I do keep trying to get more food to you but it's just difficult with Annarita. She watches me like a hawk these days. I don't know if it's because she thinks I'm going mad. She said something the other day about people in the town talking about me again. It seems some folk have noticed that I wander into this area after dark and now they're speculating that I'm mixing with dangerous black magic type of people. Or that is the latest theory anyway. It's amazing what people can come up with when there is enough space for their imaginations to run wild!" he explained.

Tiegal tried to respond, but her mouth was still filled with koeksister and she was enjoying it too much to stop.

"Keep eating. I want you to eat as much as you can," he urged, giving her a gentle, reassuring squeeze on her arms. "In fact, eat both of them. I brought two for you and I have some fruit in the basket too."

He ran back over to the basket again and returned with two oranges and a bunch of red grapes. Tiegal's stomach grumbled loudly at the sight of the additional food he placed at her feet. She wiped her lips clear of the sticky sugar and quickly picked up an orange to hold in her hands. She relished the feel of the texture. It was just another reminder of how similar this world she now inhabited with Johannes was to her own.

"The koeksister is exactly like a pastry we have on Kimberrago Island. We call it a Plassimer where I am from, but it tastes exactly the same. I used to serve these to the kimberlings when I was teaching. That's if I could get permission for an end of week treat. And the fruit is the same too. I would collect oranges when I was younger, for the banquets they held at the Estate Hall, and then later, when I was in charge of Namnum, my elephant, I would bring her bananas and figs, exactly the same as you have here too, and mostly called the same names, with the exception of a few."

The sound of a deliberately loud intake of breath, followed by his lips smacking together, surprised her.

"We have not really talked too much about this have we? About where you came from and what it all means."

"No, we haven't," she agreed. "I think we should."

"You must think I am rude Tiegal. You've heard everything about my life, and my family, but I only know bits about this world you came from."

"Hey, Johannes, you know the bits I have told you. The parts I wanted to tell you, or I was ready to share. I am grateful for how much space you have given me."

The way he shifted his bottom deeper into the hard ground beneath him indicated how this turn in the conversation was making him feel uneasy.

"Johannes, I wasn't ready to talk about it with you, because I could hear how muddied your head was. So much has happened to you with your parents leaving this world. Your mind has been darkened with pain from all your hurts. But your thoughts sound clearer now so..."

"So much has happened to *me*! You have found yourself in a whole new world and you are worried about *me*!"

Despite her efforts to appear serious but calm – to set the scene for him for a more complicated conversation ahead - she allowed herself a little giggle.

"It wasn't as shocking as you might think. I *had* dreamed it was going to happen remember?"

"But that's just it! Most people dream about things, but they don't actually happen! You have all these powers Tiegal and I don't understand any of them, but they are just normal to you. And you keep mentioning how you also have this on Tandro, and that this is very similar to where you grew up, but I just can't imagine how, or what? You must be more advanced in some way. You looked so human and talk just like we do and yet your eyes are like magic lights and you can hear what I am thinking!"

He sounded exasperated, but she knew it was more about his fear of what she could tell him – of how it could separate them even more – than a reluctance to learn of things beyond his world. His mind was surprisingly advanced. They had spent enough time together for her to know that he possessed an ability to think outside the confines of the small world view he had lived until now.

"You know, I was thinking about this yesterday, about how similar and yet different our worlds are, when I had nothing else to do but wait for you."

"I know, I'm sorry you are so on your own..."

"Don't be! It can't be helped. You have things you need to do, and I have things I can think about here, and try to work out."

"What are you trying to work out? How you got here?"

"Well, yes, that part of course, but also, how connected the worlds are too. So, why do we have these similar things and yet your world is so much simpler? Your technology is almost non-existent compared to Tandro. And you are only *just* discovering diamonds, and you haven't even really understood their true powers yet."

"We sound simple, *here?* You told me you grew up living on floating decked tents on the edge of islands. It doesn't even sound like a whole planet, more of a little section of one."

"'That's because it is! It's..." Her words became lost in the wave of a yawn. Just the prospect of explaining everything – at least, everything she understood – was exhausting. She needed more fuel. Luckily, her fingers were still sticky from the sugary pastry he had given her. She licked them all over, keen to absorb any extra source of energy available, ignoring his frustrated but amused gaze, or how she knew it was making his thoughts drift to ideas of what other things her tongue could do.

She raised her eyebrows at him, enjoying this extra bit of power she had over him. His cheeks burned red.

Guiltily, she wiped her fingers on her skirt and mouthed a silent sorry to him. Twisting her body at an angle, she fell onto her back with a thud, resting her head on the softer patch of grass next to where he sat with his legs crossed and elbows resting on his knees, waiting patiently for her to speak.

"What I know about what Tandro is, and what I *think* Tandro might be, are two very different stories. And neither are quick picnic ones either."

The sound of Johannes' chuckle – an affectionate response to her words – made her body shiver with pleasure.

"Your stories are the best ones I have heard Tiegal. But short? They never are!" he teased her. His fingers tickled her scalp, running between the strands of her hair.

"I love the way you always touch me," she whispered.

"Good! But don't get distracted. I only have so long here."

"I know. So, I will have to talk fast then. Okay?"

Without waiting for a response from him, she lay one hand on his knee at the side of her, and the other on the grass, and then closed her eyes, enjoying the feel of the afternoon breeze. When she felt settled enough, she opened her mouth to start her story and tell everything about Tandro that she was ready to impart.

"Before I describe the world I used to live in, I need you need to open your mind, even more than ever, because when I said your world is simpler, I meant that it is much more primitive. And there is a good reason for why I think this. Because..." she stalled, waiting for the sudden breeze to pass over them, before she launched into her theory.

"It is 1866 here right now? Yes?" she checked, without really needing to. She had lost count of the times she had asked him the year they were in.

Johannes nodded patiently.

"Okay, well, where I came from, in Tandro, it is... 2066."

She paused and waited, listening to the change in his breathing as he absorbed this information. When she was satisfied that he was ready to hear more, she continued.

"So, of course, this must mean that not only did I come over here from another world, that looks very similar to yours, but I also came from a place in time, two hundred years from now."

She waited a few more seconds, listening to his silent reaction, noting how he was trying to remember things she had said to him these last few weeks, all her references to Tandro that could verify what she was now telling him. When she was satisfied that *he* was satisfied by the possibilities in her theory, she carried on.

"From what I have been told, or at least what they want me and the others to think, we did used to live across all the land spaces on the planet, as you do here. There were lots of countries spread out all over, where people spoke different languages, and looked quite different in their skin colour, and what they wore and how they appeared. But, that all came to an end over a century ago. That was when the war ended. The worst one we had ever had. This was the war without winners. Well, I say that, but impatience and fear won, I guess. That's the only reason I can think of to explain why someone would be stupid and selfish enough to release a gas they knew would destroy everything - and everyone. Well, almost. And before you ask me, no one knows for certain how this happened. I mean, no one like me anyway. The elders do of course, because they lived through it, but the new species, like me, are just told the story they want us to hear - when we are kimberlings."

"kimberlings?" he interjected.

"Sorry, what you refer to as children. We don't have families like you do here Johannes, remember. We are raised as single islands, to protect our own fire, like the morning mantra I told you about?"

"Oh, yes, of c- c- c course," he stammered above her head.

She could hear his mind struggling to piece together what she was relaying, trying to imagine such a scenario, at a time that had not even happened in his world yet.

"So, you see, when all is gone and ended, there has to be a new beginning. And that is the world I was created into."

The word 'created' was deliberate – and important. Again, she waited to hear his reaction. Strangely, he was quiet.

"Atla, and his team of scientists were the only ones who survived the ending. The story goes that they had foreseen the destruction ahead and decided to build a hideaway to survive in until the air was clear enough again. And when they came out, they sailed to the safety zone that remained, what was left of our world, the archipelago of habitable islands, that we now know as Tandro."

She paused to gather her thoughts, her head all of a sudden feeling foggy, as it always did when she tried to fit the pieces of this story together.

"And that is when Atla ordered the scientists to experiment with their ideas to make a new species of people, in a new way..."

The rest of her words - what formed the crux of her story - were in her head, but for some reason she couldn't get them out of her mouth. A strange buzzing sound was darting in between her left and right ear and she felt herself drift into a different state of consciousness – a foggy in-between place - as she described the world she had come from.

"Tiegal! You are moving!" Johannes shouted out. He pulled on her shoulders to pin her down. Even though she knew her body had moved position and was now elevated slightly from above the ground, she couldn't bring herself to open her eyes.

"I'm serious Tiegal. Wake up from wherever you are going right now."

She blinked her eyes open in reaction to his fingers clicking in front of her face.

"What happened then?" She searched the grass around her, digging her fingers into the dry mud to confirm she was once again on solid ground.

"I have no idea Tiegal. You're not even wearing that neckpiece of yours, but you looked like you were going somewhere. Away from here! Do you think you were connecting with Tandro maybe? Because you were talking about it?" he suggested.

"I don't know Johannes. I didn't feel like I was losing my body again, or disappearing, it was more that I just had some sort of extra energy as I was talking. It's almost like I was connecting with something."

She made her bubble sound with her lips again in an attempt to lighten the mood, or at least, relieve the pressure of the strangeness of it all. Johannes ignored it. His forehead was burrowed into a deep frown.

"What do you think you were connecting with?"

He placed his hands over hers, as he so often did when they talked in this way. It instantly calmed her.

"I can't explain it really. It's just this feeling I have that, you and I have connected to something much bigger than we realise, perhaps even connected to a link between our two worlds?"

She paused for a moment, taking her time to peel the skin off an orange, enjoying the smell of the citrus juice as it ran between her fingers. It was so tempting to tell him more – about her dreams of what will happen the first time they kiss, *and* when they eventually dare to take their mutual desire for intimacy even further – but something told her to hold back, to let this prophecy unfold more naturally. She knew it would happen soon. Patience was the key.

"Now what are you thinking about? You look like you are drifting away. Do I need to pin you down again?"

"I wish you would!" she teased him. Catching his blush, she winked to show it was another of her jokes.

"I was thinking about a theory I have."

Johannes laughed. "Not another one. This was supposed to be a relaxing picnic and so far I've heard how we all need to make our islands complete before we can connect with another one. *And* that thing you said earlier, about me being like your mirror in your dreams."

"You *were* a mirror in a way, yes! Like I said, I dreamed about you when I was in my loneliest and darkest moments and it was your image that gave me the strength to follow my true desires, over here. You woke me up to who I really am!"

It was starting to feel like a struggle to hold back all her thoughts with him. She knew she was pushing him with her ideas. That, as a human, he could not possibly be ready to accept.

"You're my soulmate Johannes." She spoke in a whisper.

"I think you are too Tiegal...no, I *know* you are!" he answered just as softly. "And I *do* understand your island and mirror ideas. Well, just about anyway. But, please, do tell me more," he urged her, still holding her hands.

Tiegal nodded. "Let's just move into the shade first. I can see your light skin is burning in this midday sunshine. It is not healthy for you."

They both picked up the food around them and walked hand in hand to the shade under a group of thorn trees where they could comfortably sit next to each other and look out on to the river.

"So, I have been having some dreams recently about the first time

I appeared, and it felt like it was trying to explain something to me... something that I needed to share with you."

When he didn't answer her, she waited and listened to his breathing, ensuring he was in a receptive state. This was going to push him even harder.

"You may remember I told you that there was a lot of excitement around my Derado initiation ceremony because they had discovered an enormous blue diamond which was abundant with energy."

Johannes nodded. She leaned into him and willed herself to carry on.

"Okay, so from what you have said, you and Elna also found a diamond too, at exactly the same time that I released my energy from my Derado?"

She watched his expression as he clocked together her words in an attempt to follow where she was going.

"So, I think we both connected to a diamond find at exactly the same time. I stood in diamond water on my world and you were standing right next to water with your diamond discovery. Perhaps, with these parallel conditions, we created a kind of magnetic link between our two worlds?"

Johannes turned to face her. He looked excited.

"Okay, well there are a lot of coincidences here, yes. But what about the water? I don't see the link there."

"Water amplifies energy. That's why we stand in a pool of diamond water when we first connect our Derados on our Release Day. It's supposed to increase the release."

As she finished her sentence, she dared to steal a look at Johannes, wary of how far she had taken her theory. He was gazing out at the river ahead of them. She moved herself closer to his body, hoping she could pick up on his thoughts:

But there is also another key part to this. My first ever kiss... with Elna!

Tiegal jumped back from him, not wanting to hear any more of his private debate. She moved herself over to the riverbanks and leaned over so her tears could drop into the water. They made little ripples. It was something she used to do when she was younger, when the others were asleep in the camp – even Zeno – and she felt her loneliness would consume her.

Nothing had really changed. This new life was different, but somehow just the same. She was still the same girl.

"Tiegal! What's wrong? Why are you crying? Did my silence upset you?" She could sense Johannes' unease from behind her.

She turned away from him, feeling both guilt and shame. She had promised not to keep reading his thoughts, but she couldn't believe that was how he had decided to interpret her theory.

"You were listening to me again, weren't you?"

She flinched at the anger in his voice. He was furious.

"I didn't mean to Johannes...well, I did, but I just wanted to make sure you didn't think I was completely crazy. And then, I heard you thinking about your kiss with Elna! That it was this that brought me over to you! I can't believe that was your first thought! Why would you think such conflicting energies would flow like that? Didn't you say that my appearance upset Elna so much that she left you?"

She hated the sound of her voice. This was pain she had brought upon herself! There was no Atla here playing with her emotions now; this was all *her* creation, her inability to cope with these human feelings she was having to now contend with. And her stupid dreams! She slumped down onto the grass.

"Rinzal!" she whispered. It was his voice that filled her mind at this moment. How he had said that too much choice, too much connection with another, can bring pain.

"Who is Rinzal?" Johannes asked, his tone still full of fury.

"A male I used to know. One who understood me."

She gasped at the abrupt way Johannes pulled on her shoulders to lift her to a standing position. He twisted her around to face him, still holding her firmly in his arms.

"*I* understand you Tiegal. I can see you more than you think I can. I may not be as highly evolved as your Tandroan people are. I can't hear the words you think or smell. Nor can I *see* your energy, but I can *feel* you. I can recognise you too. You're like a mix of every part of everyone I ever cared for – all of them - my mother, my sister, Kagiso, and yes, perhaps even Elna a little. So, no, I don't think you are crazy. I think you're right. Something did happen when those coincidences between our worlds collided to catapult you over to me. And I think it was *meant* to happen."

Tiegal pulled away from his grasp.

"Then why did I hear you questioning whether it was your first kiss with another female that connected us?" she argued back at him through her sobs.

"Did you listen to all of it?"

She shook her head.

"Exactly! That's why I asked you not to do it. You never wait to hear the full story. I was playing with ideas, that's all! Like, perhaps there are three components to your theory of what connected you over here: one, the diamond discoveries; two, the water, on both sides; and a third one..."

She shrugged at him, not wanting to hear him say any more words that could hurt her again.

"Release! That has to be the key to this?" He gripped both her shoulders firmly in his hands.

"Look, *you* released all this powerful emotion you had built up inside you on your Release Day and I..."

"Don't say it again Johannes, please! I've not been trained for this kind of human emotional warfare. I'm just not armoured."

"No! You need to hear it Tiegal. You are in my world now. It's not always easy being human, trust me I know, but if you want to enjoy the benefits of connection, everything you have told me you were not permitted on Tandro, then you have to take on all the hard stuff too." He paused and then leaned into her so that his cheek rested on hers and his breath blew across her ear.

"What I was going to say was this: the moment you released your energy on your Release Day in your world must have coincided with the same moment that I finally released my biggest fear!"

"Which was?"

"Connection!" he blurted out, turning away from her with a heavy sigh. "Tiegal, look, you need to understand. Unlike you, I have always struggled with the idea of letting myself really connect with anyone, ever since my mother died. It used to drive Elna crazy. But something made me take the plunge that day, just before you appeared. I think my kiss with her was my rite of passage, just like your Release Day was yours. It's just that mine was like a human Release Day!

"I know that was bad luck for Elna and trust me there is not a day goes by that I don't feel guilty about that, but I also know this: you and me, how we were pulled together, it is bigger than us. It is incredible and as your dreams predicted, it was inevitable!"

He stopped and bent his upper body forward, out of breath from his hurried speech. Tiegal stood still, unsure of what to do or what to say. It was Johannes who made the first move. Taking two confident strides towards her he lifted her up from under her bottom so that her head paralleled his.

"And now I am going to kiss *you*, here, by this river, and hope that when I am finished you are still here, in my arms. Is that okay?" he asked, his voice thick with emotion.

She nodded.

"I'm not going anywhere," she managed to respond.

"Good! Because once I have finished kissing you here, I am going to carry you back to that cabin and we are both going to discover what making a *real* connection is all about."

And with that promise, Tiegal let herself fall into his embrace, holding on to him as tightly as she could. Feeling breathless and unprepared, she leaned into him, so that their lips could finally meet, hoping she could enjoy the feeling she had so longed for, and still contain her energy on this earth, where she now knew, more than ever, that her heart and soul truly belonged.

19. FACETS

"Your body keeps changing temperature. Are you sure you are ready for this?" he asked her. Her chest felt burning hot, but her legs were cold and had just started to shake violently.

"I'm fine. I think it's just an overload of things happening all at once," she answered him between his urgent kisses.

The cabin felt colder this evening. This was their fault. They hadn't bothered to border up the draughts under the wooden doors when they had entered earlier. There had been other things on their mind at the time.

Hoping her temperature would even out once she settled her breathing, she willed herself to relax, and to enjoy this feeling of his tongue moving inside her mouth. He tasted incredible. From what she could hear, he was thoroughly enjoying being with her.

In some ways she was grateful that the bottom part of her body was regulating her body heat for her. For as excited as she felt by Johannes' sudden display of desire for her, she was still terrified that she would be transported away from him. It was a fear she could not entirely ignore. They had no precedent on which to base the outcome of making a physical connection with each other, and no experience on which to ensure they both did what each other wanted.

Although, she did have an advantage in her ability to hear what he desired, and she wasn't going to switch this off. It was like owning a treasure map to his body.

They kissed and swayed together whilst standing near the bed. It was a position that made it easier for her to detect what he wanted. There was no question about where he desired her touch; the male part of his body that she could feel growing and pushing between her hips.

Despite this knowledge, she couldn't quite bring herself to move her hands in that direction. For some reason, Atla's booming voice kept entering her head. How he had admonished the animalistic and dirty practices of the older age. The way he had ridiculed those who contemplated entering the personal islands of others. Disgusting primeval acts, he had always called them. And yet, here she was now, ready to rebel against all she had been told since her creation day.

"Go away," she hissed out loud, without thinking.

Johannes broke away from her, clearly startled by her words.

"Oh, Tiegal, I'm so sorry. Did I take it too far?" he stammered as he backed further away from her.

"No, no, sorry Johannes, it's just me, thinking out loud, I was talking to my old self. My Tandro way of thinking; the kind that finds all this connection so wrong!" she assured him, reaching her arms out to encourage him to come back to her. He turned his body away. The candles burned in front of him, creating a warm orange glow around his frame.

"Johannes! Look at me. Please," she urged. As he turned around to face her again, he gasped in surprise.

"Your eyes!" he gasped. "How are you making them do that?"

"It's not *me*, it's you, and the way you're making me feel. This is my light. This is how bright you are making me reflect it back to you. I can feel it pouring out of me. Like you have cut me, already, just by giving me my first kiss."

She spoke fast, keen for him to understand just how important his effect on her was. The pulsations from her diamond-shaped pupils bounced reflective light off his face as she faced him. He looked beautiful standing in front of her, candle and eye lights in front and behind him.

"I cut you?" he questioned. He still seemed unsure whether to rejoin her. His hands covered the area under his waist where she knew he had responded to her so quickly.

She laughed. "Sorry, I mean that you polished me! With your kisses. Like a brillianteer polishes a diamond! You brought out my light!"

She stopped herself when she realised how much she was rambling at him, and no doubt confusing him by comparing him to a diamond polisher. She still hadn't explained how she had been made to him. Even now, she was reluctant to reveal this part of herself.

"Are you trying to stall things Tiegal? I do like your theory, it's kind of flattering in a strange way and your eyes look magnificent right now, but I'm not sure philosophy works well in the bedroom, not at times like this."

They both erupted into fits of uncontrollable laughter.

"This is so crazy!" she cried, still laughing as he swung her around in his arms, nearly bumping her head into the low-lying ceiling.

"So, are we doing this or not?" he dared. He didn't wait for an answer this time. Instead, he cupped her cheeks with both hands, murmuring something about lights and facets, but she had turned off all her audio by then; and any distracting thoughts of her world before.

This was their moment. The wind was picking up a storm outside, but she was earth-bound with him now. They could protect each other from any elements that threatened them.

"Let's get under the covers Johannes. You're shivering."

They undressed each other without taking their eyes off each other's.

"Is it not blinding you, looking into my eyes?" she whispered, aware of the feel of a cold breeze on her bottom as he removed her skirt from her waist. He shook his head in response.

"I think you changed how I see things a long time ago Tiegal."

He winked at her and then lifted her onto the bed.

"Lay back and relax. I want to try something I think you will enjoy but hold on to the bed sheets whatever you do. I don't want you going anywhere!"

She did as he asked, clutching at the sheets, her heart beating loudly in her ears. Her entire body was now burning; a dry heat that made her skin buzz. Johannes was hot too, but his skin gleaned with a cooler sweat, that she used to trace circles on his back. He reached over to kiss her mouth one more time and then bent down on the floor by the bed to bury himself between her legs.

She cried out in surprise at the feeling of his mouth exploring in a place no one, other than she had before. It felt terrifying and exhilarating, all at once. It was also, surprisingly, a very similar sensation to the first time she had released her energy, on her Release Day. The feeling of a rush of pent-up emotion deep inside, culminating in one big release.

She bit her lip as the feeling became more intense, something she knew she could not control. It scared her that she could be made to feel this way so quickly by him, without the need for diamonds or water. Arching her back, a new feeling washed over her. Daring to look down at him she grasped his hair with her right hand.

The room was now alight with her pink glow. She cried out suddenly. It was a noise she had never heard from herself before. Before she had time to recover, he pulled her body further down the bed towards him. She watched in awe, so determined about what he wanted to happen, and somehow so gentle and reassuring in his smile, so clearly full of desire.

"I'm completely in your control Johannes. And I'm not going anywhere I promise," she assured him, knowing he was battling an internal dialogue, weighing up the risk of over-exciting her – and potentially losing her – and how much he wanted to prove to her that he could bring her the deeper pleasure he knew she had dreamed about.

"*You* might be in control Tiegal. I'm not sure I am!"

His breath was hot and laboured. It tickled the skin around her thighs and hips where he rested his head, recovering.

"Do you think we could create something really dangerous if we took this further?" he asked her.

She knew what he was leading towards. Her body was starting to feel lighter, weightless. They *were* in danger of taking things too far.

"Can you feel underneath me?" she managed. Something wasn't right.

Johannes slipped his hand to the space underneath her hips. He jumped up and backed away from the bed.

She heard the surprise in his head before he even spoke the words.

"I'm hovering, aren't I?" she asked.

Even though her hands still grasped the sheets she knew her arms had changed angle, that she had risen higher. For some reason, she dared not move an inch, afraid to disturb her current physical state.

Johannes ran his fingers through his wet, sweat ridden hair, pacing the room back and forth. He shoved both his legs into his trousers in two quick movements and let out a frustrated growl noise.

"You look like you are transforming again Tiegal. I went too far! What was I thinking? I mean, I've never done anything like that before...with anyone...but trust me to just dive in."

Despite how strange and detached her body felt – and how unnerving Johanne's frantic pacing was – Tiegal started to giggle.

"What's so funny?" He frowned at her, standing with his hands buried in his pockets.

"Everything Johannes! Your choice of words... *dive in* ...and how I can hear you doubting yourself and your inexperience, with *me* of all people. It *is* amusing. It has to be. Look at me! I can't even move after what you just did with your mouth. You're like a magician."

The smile he returned in response to her words was all it took. Her colours dimmed from their intense pink glow to a softer pink hue and slowed their rhythmic dance around her.

This had to be a positive sign. As she twitched her arms, and wriggled her back and bottom on the mattress, feeling the hard wood of the bed underneath her, she knew she was moving out of the danger zone.

"There! Look, you see, I'm back again. All solid and in one piece."

She reached her hand out to him, urging him to lie down next to her, desperate to feel his touch again. To feel reassured that she was safe, on Earth, and still with him.

That *had* been close. The colours around her had been forming into something more substantial than just mists of her energy. It had started to feel as though the bubble was forming around her again, and that she could soon lose control of her body. That she would be taken away.

Johannes fell onto the thin mattress next to her and buried his face into her cheek.

"I thought I was going to lose you!" he whispered. She shivered in response. He wrapped his arms around her to help control her tremors.

"You were burning hot and now you are shaking! My extreme girl, that's what you are."

She turned over so that she could curve herself into his body, to feel all of him wrapped around her, keeping her grounded and balanced.

If only you knew, my love, just how extreme that moment nearly was!

She was grateful he could not access her mind. Thankful that they had been able to make a human connection with each other and still hold on.

The thought of sleep scared her. The idea of letting herself fall into another place, where she had no control of her journey, made her shake even more.

Johannes' breathing indicated he had already succumbed to a peaceful slumber. She listened for a few minutes, happy that his mind was quiet and settled and then she finally let her eye-lids droop, shutting out the remaining light from the cabin.

20. TEARS

"What have you done Tiegal? Did you really think you could take things this far and still get all you desire?"

Atla's angry words filled the small space of her tent.

She stuck out her tongue at him, determined to make a dramatic play of putting her hands on her hips. In this dream, she was a young kimberling again, no more than six years old.

Looking around the space she had inhabited as a young one, she quickly familiarised, surprised at how detailed this dream was presenting itself to her. She remembered this scene now. This had happened! The day when she had been so disobedient that Atla had been forced to make an appearance on the kimberling camp.

His presence had alarmed everyone. Atla never visited the kimberlings, but she was different. She, Tiegal Eureka, had caught his attention.

She caught a glance of herself in the mirror, her young kimberling self. So defiant. So unafraid of being scolded by the most powerful Tandroan of them all.

She laughed at her own reflection then, amused by this memory, when she had shocked so many around her, and still managed to avoid receiving any punishment.

"You're not six-years old though are you?" Atla was the one who was amused now. "Look again Tiegal!" His sardonic tone grated on her – it always had – but she did as he instructed, regardless.

As she looked at her reflection again, it made her recoil in horror. She was old, her face a pattern of rippled, sagging skin. Her body appeared frail, and fragile, bent over as though about to break in half.

Atla laughed. "You can't have it both ways Tiegal. You want all this love you think you deserve? Well, go on and get it then. And if you do, you *will* get what you deserve! You will get old very quickly, and then you will die, alone, with no human to look after you."

Aware of him staring at her, eager to see how she would react to his damning prophecy, she knew she was not hiding her confusion well. It must be written all over her face.

Atla laughed again.

"Your man human won't live very long. They never do. Enjoy it whilst it lasts!"

Now he had taken it too far – dream or not – she had to react. Roaring seemed the most appropriate release in this instance. She ran at him, punching at the satin fabric of his cloak, banging her fists into his arms, in a chopping style action, similar to the way she had observed Johannes attacking tree logs before their fires together.

"I can make my own fires now. I don't need to listen to this nonsense. You're the one who rains down on everyone's fires...everyone's chance of pursuing a dream!" she screamed at him.

But Atla just laughed. He leaned down to her ear and whispered ever so softly,

"Look in the mirror, one more time Tiegal!"

She looked in the mirror, and then she saw herself, her midsection and hands covered in blood. And then she screamed.

"Tiegal! Stop! Calm down."

She could hear Johannes' voice, trying to wake her, but she just kept kicking, willing herself to stay in the dream for just a few more moments so that she could alter the vision and override the reflection of painful lies Atla had shown her in the mirror.

It was only when Johannes' hold on her wrists became painful enough to jolt her into reality again that she opened her eyes, now aware that he was lying on top of her, pinning her down.

"There!" He hushed her. "Are you going to stay with me? Or am I going to have to keep lying on top of you like this? Because you know that could lead to other things...and the way you have just woken up... I'm not sure that's a safe thing to do."

Tiegal squeezed her eyes shut to clear away the tears. That was the worst nightmare so far. It was too real!

"Hey, why are you crying? You just had a bad dream that's all." He rolled off her body, positioning himself at her side. "I can't lie on you like that for too long!" He explained with his side-slanted smile that always made her want to inhale him even more.

"How do you always smell so good?" She leaned into the space under his ear, where she could pick up his scent the most easily, and breathed him in.

"You know that tickles."

"You know you love it!" she replied.

"And, *you* know that I can tell when you are trying to distract me from what just happened!" He raised his left eyebrow.

"Hey, how do you do that Johannes?"

Doing her best to mimic his control over one eyebrow, she wriggled her forehead up and down, knowing full well it would make him laugh – and distract him further. At least, that was her intention.

"Tiegal! What happened in your dream this time?" he tried again.

"It's nothing to worry about. Just strange memories of a life I lived before, that's all. No different than you dreaming about your mother," she tried, instantly regretting mentioning the person she knew he still missed so badly. His nightmares were hard to ignore. They moaned of his pain and his loss. At least, they had done when they first started sleeping together. Recently, she sensed they were becoming more peaceful. Particularly the ones where his mother held him and talked to him about the roots of trees. Those dreams always brought him a more settled sleep.

"*And* the Elna dreams you still sometimes have," she added, surprising herself. It was a naughty ruse. She knew her night terrors had disturbed him more than normal this time. Raising Elna's memory was the only way she could think of diverting his attention from it. But it still didn't make it right. Johannes shook his head at her.

"No way! I am not falling for that trick again. You can't keep using her name to send a conversation where you want it to. I don't even know why you would want to keep bringing her up either. We have moved beyond that now. Haven't we?"

She nodded. "Sorry."

"Are you going to tell me why you woke up trying to beat me up? I've got to go soon you know. It's almost sunrise and Annarita needs me back at the farm. So, come on now, tell me what bothered you so much or I am going to worry about you all day. I don't want you to leave you here feeling all lonely."

You will die, alone...

Atla's words repeated over and over in her head, mocking her with their truth.

"I will always be alone here, won't I?"

Johannes' looked startled at her words, as though she had hit him once more, this time with her breath and her thoughts.

"I will *never* leave you Tiegal. You are my everything. I just need to get the farm through this next harvest with Annarita and Frederick and then we can start making plans, for you and me, to be together properly."

She sighed heavily. This was not the first time he had promised a future of idyllic togetherness. It was all he thought about. That, and how and when, they could risk taking their physical connection even further.

"Johannes, my love, you do know that just because we want something really badly doesn't mean we can have it," she dared, whilst pinching at the skin around her fingernails, not feeling quite daring enough to look him in the eye.

"Tiegal! That's not like you. What happened to your light? And how I make you reflect it more brilliantly? Didn't we agree that something much bigger than us connected us?" His voice quavered along with his shaking hands that were still trying to settle her, rubbing up and down her arm as they faced each other.

"I know what we said Johannes but..."

"But your dreams don't predict we can stay together?" he interrupted, rubbing his eyes to clear the sleep. And then, with his big calloused hand, covering up his mouth as he yawned.

"Don't be mad, please! It's not that my dreams have told me anything like that, it's just that I can't see through this fog that exists between us sometimes. I mean, you have responsibilities to other people, your sister for example, and the rest of the farm workers. And I can't do anything helpful here, hiding out in this cabin all day. I don't have any purpose."

Johannes made a loud groan.

"We will sort that out Tiegal. I told you, the diamond Erasmus found - the day you re-appeared again - has created a huge stir among the people here in Hopetown. It's like a big rush has started and more and more people from all over are moving to the area to see if there are more diamonds. There could be some real opportunities for us further afield, beyond the farm. I have already spoken to Annarita and I've told her I plan to search for some diamond opportunities, and she agrees with me. She thinks she can keep the farm going with her husband and the rest of the neighbours joining together. It's all going to work, I promise!"

There was something so intoxicating about the smell he emanated when he spoke of his dreams and their future together. His excitement seeped out of him. It was even sweeter than normal. She breathed it in again, willing it to override the darker scent of danger that still lingered in her nostrils from her dreams.

"*You* found the diamond *first*, Johannes, remember, you and Elna!"

The words left her mouth before she had time to think of the implications, that she could break something that would not be so easy to fix.

"Why do you keep bringing it up?" He growled, edging his body away from hers.

It was too late for her to take it back. She may as well have placed a mirror in front of him and then expected him to un-see what she had finally shown him: that *she* was the one who had interrupted his fortune. It was their connection that had interfered with his journey for a normal married life with Elna, and the diamond.

"I'm so sorry, my love, I think I was the one to burst your bubble... not the other way around!"

It hurt to say it out loud. Her throat constricted in sympathy. But it *was* the truth. And now she had to set him free!

21. BLOOD

He awoke just in time. There were only a few minutes left before the sun would rise and he wanted to be in the right spot to see it. He threw the bed covers away from him and pulled on his trousers and shirt as quickly as he could, careful not to make too much noise and risk alerting his sister to his movements. Annarita's impatience towards his regular disappearances was growing by the day.

He tiptoed down the stairs of his family farmhouse covering his mouth to avoid breathing in the relentless dust that Kagiso struggled to rid, on a daily basis, and broke out of the front door in a fast run. He knew exactly where he wanted to position himself and he was already pushed for time.

Last night he had come to a decision: to make the next sunrise *his* Release Day – *his* decision day.

It pained him to think of Tiegal all on her own, also rising to watch the dawn of a new day – a Tandro habit she had yet to break - but he needed to see this one on his own.

They couldn't keep having the same conversations. They were hurting each other with their fears. Tiegal had been the first to admit this.

"We are not exchanging our energies in balance anymore. We are in a battle for power, which is never good," she'd said.

It was probably why she was losing her light too. Neither of them had vocalized the recent changes to her optical features. How her diamond pupils no longer pulsated radiant light or how the dark hollows had become light grey. There was even a hint of a green colour in the centre. There was no doubt about it. She was starting to appear more human, just as he had prayed for. A way to bring her out into the light of Earth, so that he could share her beauty and his love for her with others. There was nothing more wrenching than having to leave her for so many hours on her own.

The nights had become colder in the last few weeks and although he had worked hard to adapt the old cabin into something more sustainable for Tiegal to keep warm in, he knew it was not enough to keep her radiating her light in the way she deserved. She was like a hidden gem. One that only *he* was getting the momentary pleasure of seeing.

It made him feel guilty – and wrong. This couldn't be what the stars, or dare he even consider...God...could have intended, by bringing them together like this?

He just knew they were missing something about their connection, and he couldn't let his desire for her blind him to the message he knew he needed to see.

Yes, there was a part of him that got excited when he thought of the potential her transformation into being more human could mean. They could perhaps be together in every way possible, without the fear of her being taken away to her other world. Yet, he also feared this change would mean the end of what made her *who* she was: so special, unique, and just so unbelievably radiant.

She must have been tuning into his thoughts too. For it was Tiegal who had suggested they spend a couple of days apart, "I think we need to seek wholeness within ourselves again Johannes. We can come back together soon, when we are complete individuals again, with more clarity. Go spend some time with your sister and the farm people. I will be fine here. You have given me plenty of food supplies, which is far more than I survived on when I was alone like this before. Remember, I told you how I spent a year in a tiny cabin before I came here? This is a luxurious palace compared to that! I can get some sleep, and who knows, I may even dream a dream to help us understand what is planned ahead of us?"

There had been no point reasoning with her. He may not be able to read her thoughts, but he was attuned to her enough to know she meant what she said: she really did want some time to gather herself.

Even so, he hated leaving her on her own. She may appear more human to him now, but to anyone else she was still an extraordinary sight. What if someone found her? They could react. Hurt her in some way, out of fear. It was unthinkable.

Two days was too long, too much of a risk. It wouldn't take long for him to find the answer he sought and then he would go back to her and tell her what they needed to do.

Tiegal had come to his world. She was a stranger and it was his job to make sure that she could find a way to live here happily – or, as strangling as this idea was, to go back to where she came from.

Even the thought of suggesting she return to Tandro made him shudder. It was not what she would want – the opposite of what *he* wanted too – but if it was the right thing for her, and her life, then he would hurt himself to make sure it happened.

There! You see, you can make a decision!

He told himself, as he reached his destination: his favourite tree on the riverbank.

Wriggling his bottom into the dry, hard ground, he closed his eyes and began counting slowly, inside his head, allowing his breathing to regulate as Tiegal had taught him to.

As he paid attention to how his chest raised and lowered, he felt himself relax. Before long, his mind shifted to an image of Tiegal doing the same thing as he was now; sitting legs crossed, as she always did, on the dry grass in the clearing near her cabin, waiting for the dawn of a new day.

"Grrr!" he growled, shaking his head to clear his mind. It was important that he focus on what he had come here to do.

In less than a minute, he felt a welcoming shift in temperature. It compelled him to open his eyes; to witness the stunning glow of orange and pinks as they emerged from the horizon ahead. Aware that the farm workers would soon be heading this way, he glanced around to check his surroundings were clear and then he spoke the words he had practiced for this very moment.

"I am fire. I am light. No one can douse my fire. No one can dim my light."

He deliberately left out the part about no one entering his island. He knew how much Tiegal despised that part of the chant from her old life. And he felt he owed it to her to respect this much of her experience. But the rest of the Tandro morning mantra, he chanted in a quiet but determined voice, enjoying the spectacular movement of the rising sun ahead of him as he did.

A long, peaceful, but uneventful minute passed – he counted it in his head – and then nothing. No answers. Not a single sign, or feeling, that he could grasp onto.

"What was I thinking? Stupid, stupid idea." He berated himself, with only the orange glow of the sun-filled landscape before him. Frustrated, he dug his fingernails into the dry mud at the side of him.

"What am I going to do? I thought being here would give me the answers. It did the last time I was here..." He stopped, mid-sentence, re-playing his last words.

The last time...when Tiegal appeared before me!

There was the answer!

"Eureka!" he whispered.

And now he could make his decision.

Both the clearing and the cabin were silent. There was no sign of her anywhere. The bed had been made and her shoes – the ones he had found for her at the church shelter – were lined up neatly by the door. His rapid breathing disturbed the soundless room. It added to the eeriness, exacerbated by how wrong this space suddenly seemed. It still smelled of her, but something told him, just by the way things had been positioned, that it was a scene she had created, that it was meant to signal her goodbye.

Clenching his fists tight in order to steady himself, he lowered himself down to the floor. He needed to check the box underneath the bed. Tiegal had done her best to convince him that she had buried her Derado neckpiece deep down under the mud near the trees outside, but he knew she had kept it closer at hand. He remembered – despite being in a delirious state at the time – how she had worn it when he was sick and needed warming from the spell of hypothermia he had brought upon himself.

It had always concerned him that the powerful neckpiece was so close to her, but something had prevented him from raising it to her; aware that they needed to respect at least some of the private parts of their worlds from each other – just as he had kept her from Annarita and the rest of the neighbours here.

"Tiegal! No!" he groaned, as he pulled open the box. The diamond collared neckpiece had gone, which had to mean so had she.

Even though he was already kneeling, he felt himself sink further into the floor, rolling on to his side in a ball, still holding on to the lid of the box. This was his fault. Her Derado was the only link to her previous life. Who was he to demand that she bury it, the way he had hidden her? And what stupid arrogance had led him to think he could storm out on her and leave her for more than twenty-four hours, on her own, with no reason or belief that there was anything worth staying here for?

He knew she was scared of what would await her if she were to return to Tandro. She had never verbalised the things that had disturbed her there, but her nightmares had demonstrated the lingering hurts she still suffered from.

Perhaps that was why he had so foolishly believed he could

contain her here, with him, living this secret life, devoid of all purpose, other than to love him. Because he knew there was nothing worth returning to on the other side.

He squeezed his eyes shut, fighting back the tears that threatened to flood from the well of despair inside him. After his mother died, he had sworn he would never let himself cry again. Enough tears had been shed in one man's lifetime. But this was different. Tiegal was part of a thousand lifetimes and possibilities – and he had let her go.

"Fool! Idiot! Complete, arrogant, imbecile," he scolded himself, banging his fist on his knee.

A screeching noise sounded out from outside the cabin, making him jump up to his feet. He let the box fall to the floor and ran in the direction of the tormented screams that he knew belonged to her. The sounds were coming from somewhere near the river - the spot where he knew she sometimes bathed in the morning twilight – and it was getting louder by the second.

"Tiegal! I'm coming! Wait for me! I'm coming for you," he shouted in a repetitive roar, bashing and beating the branches of the trees in his way, determined to reach her before she disappeared, whether from this life, or the one belonging to another world!

As he swiftly navigated around obstructions in the bush, he clocked the broken tree house ahead, the one he had made with his sister as a child, and knew he was near. Tiegal loved to hide in there. She said it made her feel more connected to him and his human play-fulness. But her terrified screams where coming from further afield.

"Johannes! Help me! I'm bleeding."

Her reference to the word 'blood' urged him to pick up his pace. He slowed only to make an awkward jump over a fallen swing, one from his youth that no one had bothered to mend. He could hardly breathe, due to both exhaustion and fear, as he darted through the space between two thorn trees, scrambling to get to the small pool of water from where her desperate cries resounded.

"Tiegal!" he shouted when he finally saw her. Her face was frightened and child-like. The water around her only reached her waist. The sight of her made a sob form in his throat. He forced it back, determined to conceal the terror he felt at what he saw. Ripples of red-coloured water circled around her. She was naked, her hair, now grown longer, only just covered her breasts, and she shivered violently. But it was her eyes that made his body stiffen. They were sparkling, emerald-green circle pools, and surrounded by brilliant white. She looked like a beautiful, human girl. One who was swimming in a pool of her own blood.

The only thing that betrayed her new earthly look was the diamond neckpiece she wore around her neck. Her Derado that was now radiating pink light and emitting bursts of colour mists in response to each sway her body made.

Not hesitating, he slid his bottom down the muddy bank to reach the water. As he waded towards her, she calmed her cries, reducing them to small sobs and whimpers.

"Come on now, it's all okay. You probably just cut yourself on a stone or a branch under the water that's all."

These were words intended to soothe her, and they seemed to be working, but inside, he felt waves of utter fear rush through him. His heart raced like a tribal drum on a new moon eve.

"Wh...wh...why are you thinking about a river monster?" she stammered as he reached her side. Without stopping to answer her question, he turned around to offer her his back.

"Jump on Tiegal. We need to get you out of here," he ordered, splashing his hands against the surface of the water in the direction of the riverbank. The moment he felt her slippery skin glide over his shirt and her weight fully positioned over the arch of his spine, he set off wading them both back to the river edge. He counted each stride he made in silence, conscious that her ability to access his thoughts was clearly still active, even if her face had become less Tandroan in the last twenty-four hours.

With every ounce of energy left inside him he pulled them both up the sandy bank and lowered her down into a softer patch of grass. He didn't dare glance at her body. He was too afraid of where the blood could be coming from. Instead, he yanked at some river leaves and placed them over her legs and focused his gaze on the mesmerising green of her new emerald-coloured irises.

"Thank you," he heard. It was such a small sound he was not sure whether it came from her mouth, or the whisper of the trees behind them. She didn't seem to be in any pain. If anything, she appeared content, sitting with her legs splayed forward and her arms arched back, hands fanned out behind her. But then, just under her knee a trickle of deep ruby-red blood appeared, meandering its way into a river across the sand towards him.

He stiffened, unable to breathe as he watched the bloody scene before him. Tiegal didn't scream this time. In contrast to her earlier cries, she seemed resigned – fascinated even – by the liquid.

"It's not a river monster Johannes. I heard your fear that it was. Although I can't imagine why you would believe such stories of things."

He couldn't bring himself to respond to her. His voice was stuck somewhere in a strangled knot that had formed in his throat.

"Even if something like that did exist, I would smell it a mile away. Danger is my easiest scent," she continued, as she scooped up a pile of sand and let it trickle through her fingers to cover the blood around her. "I'm sorry I scared you. I don't know why I screamed like I did."

"Tiegal, you are bleeding from somewhere. Of course, you were going to scream. I just don't know what to think could have happened or why?" he trailed off, turning away from her as he rummaged his hands through his thick coarse hair.

"Where does it hurt? Did you do something to yourself?" he dared to ask, not courageous enough to face her. He knew he should check for the site of the bleeding but something instinctive stopped him from doing so.

Her disappointment in his choice of words was obvious.

"No! Of course not. I would never do that to you," she said.

"Sorry...I just don't, or can't imagine what could have happened out here and I'm damned scared to even ask you right now. I thought you had left me Tiegal, your clothes and shoes are all in the cabin, neatly folded away as though ready to be returned to my house, and then I hear your screaming out here in the water like this, with blood all around you! Someone, *anyone* could have heard you and discovered you out here like this. Naked and so fragile and..."

"Human?" she answered for him.

He let out a cry, a deep guttural moan

"I thought I'd lost you!" he wept. It was his release. It came from somewhere caged, and now free, from deep inside him.

The soft fleshy pads of her fingertips pressed down on his forehead, playing invisible piano keys on his skin. Slowly, but deliberately, her hands moved down to wipe away his tears, cupping his cheeks with her warmth. He knew then that she was okay. Whatever had caused her to bleed was not something he had to fear.

"I dreamed that this would happen. I'm bleeding like a girl, a human girl, Johannes. I think my body has made a decision to be of this Earth." It was an announcement, a decision. He could sense her smile without needing to turn his face to her. He was enjoying the feeling of her hands on his face too much.

He nodded, eyes still closed, twisting his lips to kiss her wrist as she caressed his face. A part of him knew it was dangerous for them to stay here like this, her with no clothes and bleeding from her private area, but he sensed she was not afraid.

"So, your eyes are green like a human girl, and you bleed as one who can now breed, but yet you can still hear the crazy words in my head?"

The sound of her laughter startled him into opening his eyes. Her face was now inches from his, both of them shadowing each other for the first time now that her Tandro eye-light had disappeared.

"I didn't read your mind this time, my love, you strode into the river shouting about a monster. I think it was you who can no longer hear the difference between what you think and what you say."

The moisture on her lips glistened in the low sunlight as he pulled his face back enough to survey the new combination of her features. He decided then that he was going to kiss her, hard, and with the passion he had been holding back until now.

"You're going to kiss me?"

"I thought you couldn't read my mind?"

"I think I can still do that. It's not all gone away, but I didn't need to Johannes."

It was his turn to cup her cheeks in his hands.

"I don't want it all to go away – what makes you so *you* - but I am glad you feel more grounded here now. Maybe we can have the best of both worlds after all?"

Not waiting for a response, he took off his shirt and placed it under her bottom, signalling her to wrap it around herself where necessary. When she was happily tied up in her makeshift covering, he cleared the leaves away from her and scooped her into his arms.

"I can walk Johannes," she protested, giving him a playful punch on his arm.

"Tiegal you walked over here all by yourself. You must have been full of fear and sadness. But that's all gone now. And I'm going to carry you away from it all, like a man should carry his girl, his very human girl. And take her back to where she belongs," he determined, in a voice hoarse with emotion.

"Back to bed - with you," she agreed.

22. MEMORIES

"Are you sure you want to do this?" Johannes asked. His warm breath tickled the inside of her ear, making her entire body shudder against his.

"I'm *very* sure." Tiegal answered. She nodded, a little too enthusiastically, causing an awkward collision as their foreheads knocked against each other's. They both laughed, holding each other tighter in response to the nervous energy between them. She could hear the rush of excitable thoughts running through Johannes' mind: his desire for her, every part of who she was, and where she had come from. Just hearing these thoughts made her feel a strange aching inside, a desperate urge to answer his need.

She blinked in surprise at the new sounds she was making in anticipation of their physical intentions. A sigh, a gasp, hints of pleasurable moans that must have been restrained inside her all this time. She even let out a tiny squeal when he rolled them both over from a side-ways embrace, to one where she fit perfectly underneath him.

"And are you sure you are not going to go anywhere?" he asked, for the second time since they had taken their clothes off and climbed under the sheets together.

"I am sure! And *you* are stalling." she breathed. "I told you. I have been dreaming about this every night since.... well, you know..."

She stammered, unsure whether to use the obvious word to explain what she was referring to. Johannes raised his eyebrows to her.

"You mean since the day when you tried to leave me?" he suggested.

"No, silly, I mean since the day I started being more human, when I started to bleed!"

She coughed, allowing them both a nervous pause to absorb this reminder of that shocking day.

"*And...* I wasn't really trying to leave you. I just didn't know what was happening to me," she reminded him.

She wriggled her hips to move her body slightly lower down the mattress, to where she sensed their bodies would fit together more naturally. They were *both* stalling now, but she wasn't worried about that. She had seen how making this connection together would play out in her dreams. It was one of the most useful dream prophecies she had ever experienced. Neither of them had done anything like this before, nor had any idea of what doing such things was supposed to look, or *feel* like, in practice. She knew that Johannes' family had been conservative in their talk of such things. Even his friends and his sister had shied away from revealing what occurred in the marital bedroom after the lights were turned off.

And she was just as ignorant. Growing up in Tandro, the idea of letting someone enter your body – your *island* – was considered barbaric. Her entire upbringing had been one long attempt to indoctrinate a belief system in her that 'making love' was a fairy tale ideal from a destructive time. Viewing it as a natural act of desire was akin to calling yourself an animal, with no respect for your own body.

It was such a false philosophy. Even as a young kimberling she knew serious errors, *lies*, underlay Atla's teachings. This knowledge had been as instinctive to her as believing her dreams really could come true, and even, that she would one day find herself in the world she truly belonged to.

Nothing was going to stop her now. She was prepared for what they were about to do together. It was a gift, this foresight of hers. She knew how different this was than the animalistic way her fellow Tandroans had always objected to. Even Johannes had finally accepted that she was human enough now, that she could separate herself from what she had been told to believe.

As she had reasoned with him, "It's so stupid this comparison to animal procreation and how we desire each other. How we want to connect because of how it *feels*. We are more evolved than that now. We can attach ourselves to each other and still look into each other's eyes. How could that be wrong? What could be more energizing than that? In a truly deep way?"

This was her argument. She knew this way of talking shocked Johannes, but he liked it really, and he seemed to understand why she needed to dissect her philosophies between her two worlds. That's why they had agreed that it was time. They were both ready to be truly human, together.

There were no doubts in her mind about this. Now, she just had to make sure they enacted version one from her dreams, the safe one, and not the one where they took it too far. There were too many dangerous versions of what happened if that scenario occurred. She just wanted to make this about the two of them, together, as far as they could take it.

"It's all going to be fine. Just remember what I said about reaching the peak. That's when you need to..." she started to warn him, but his hand covered her mouth in a gentle brush to stop her from ending the sentence.

"Tiegal! *Please*. Just stop talking. It's excruciating breaking it down like this."

"Sorry! I'm just excited...and scared too," she admitted.

"And please don't listen to my thoughts during this either," he begged her as he moved his hand from her lips so that he could trace the outline of her eyebrows with his finger and down to her jaw line in a circular motion. She knew he was concentrating on maintaining his self-control.

"I'll try," she answered. It was as good a promise as she could give him. His desire for her was almost screaming out of him. It was almost impossible to shut it out, even if she *had* evolved to a more human-like state. She only wished he could hear how much *she* wanted him too, but she had learnt her lesson. Thinking out loud always created distractions in these tender moments together, and she knew he preferred to kiss and touch her, rather than discuss every detail as it happened.

You can do this Tiegal. Show him how you feel in your touch and let it happen.

She urged her body to relax into the moment. To feel the kissing, exploring, and the pressure between his hips that he tentatively pushed towards her. Her hands moved down to his solid abdomen. His muscles tensed in anticipation of her touch. She tried to follow the sequence she had practiced in her dreams, *and* the voice from somewhere inside her that reminded her it was his first time too – only, he didn't have the benefit of foresight that she did.

Closing her eyes, she pushed her tongue further inside his mouth in a bid to convince him she was feeling as thrilled as she knew he was by what they were doing together.

They kissed like this, their bodies moving against each other's in a gentle rhythm, for as long as they could both control themselves, and then, when she could tell he was getting anxious, she pushed her hips into him, using her hand to guide him. It was easier, and more natural than she had imagined. They fit perfectly together, as though they had connected in this way together, many times and moons before.

Once they realised what they had achieved, they both released their unrestrained pleasure at the same time, a harmony of uninhibited sounds, instantly muffled by tongues and lips, urgently dancing together.

"Tiegal. I'm inside you. And... you're still here."

She heard him say the words in her ear, but she didn't respond. It didn't warrant a verbal response. She just held him tighter, letting him know she was indeed still here, all intact, strong, and still in his world - their world now, together - even if her old magic still burned inside her.

As their movement became faster, she became aware of a dance of electric currents jolting from her fingertips. This was not a surprise. She had seen this part too, how the remnants of her Tandroan elements would make their appearance in this moment. Fortunately, she had also had the foresight to pre-warn him.

"Hey, you're sparking, like you said you would!" she heard him grunt, and not with displeasure.

"Am I hurting you?"

"Shh...no...it feels good I'm just..."

She could see he was struggling to control what his body would do next, as their rhythm became even faster, but she didn't want him to stop, not just yet.

"Look at me!" she whispered. She arched her hips upwards then, urging him to raise them both higher, feeling the need to position her body into the shape of a crescent, so only her shoulders and head still touched the bed.

"That's making it even stronger," he protested.

"Look at me!" she tried again, biting her lip, aware that there was not much time before this scenario would revert to the second version of her dream prophecy.

When his eyes finally met hers, she breathed a sigh of relief. Her colours were all around her now. It was only a faint mist, but it was enough to stall the explosion. Johannes' shoulders instantly relaxed as he watched her glow dancing between them. He was still connected to her, but she could see he was now able to find a pace he could control. She heard his relief and knew they were back to the version she had been wishing for.

"Can you feel that?" she dared to ask.

"I think I feel a bit of everything" he finally managed to respond.

"I *mean*, can you feel my energy, mixing with yours now?"

She fanned out her fingers in the space between them, relishing the pleasurable wave of the movement. He matched his fingertips to hers and in the moment their skin met, a flash of light sparked between them, quickly followed by a burst of colours glowing in-between. Pinks and amethyst from her, and a faint green and blue emanating from him.

"That's me?" he marvelled.

"It's you, my love. Pull me up, so I can sit on you. I want to try something else."

Without hesitating he reached underneath her, where her skin was soft and fleshy, and pulled her up and on top of him. She quickly wrapped her legs around him.

"How are you doing this so well?"

She placed her finger on his lips, gently shushing him.

"Just move with me slowly and look into my eyes. I know what's coming next and it's even better," she promised.

This was the part where she knew she must watch her breathing. Her dreams had promised that being in this position with him would feel even more exquisite – and it was. But she just didn't want to let herself go too soon, knowing she would have to extricate herself from him as soon as she did.

Aware that her fingers were still active with the hot coloured sparks, she moved them around his back in a bid to keep herself balanced whilst ensuring she did not burn him at the same time. It seemed to add to his pleasure, his body responded in muscle spasms wherever she touched it.

They were both burning hot now, but somehow their skin was still dry. And the smell in the air was almost overwhelming. Still, she inhaled in their combined scents and then lowered her mouth into the soft skin on his shoulders, sinking her teeth in as gently as she could. She didn't want to hurt him, but she knew she needed to channel this rush of surplus energy that being connected to him had conjured.

"Tiegal...I'm not sure I can..."

She heard the plea in his tone, but she wasn't ready to detach herself from him, not just yet, not when she was so close. There was a way she could slow him down, just for a little longer. Her fingers pressed harder into the base of his spine. His body flinched at first but then went rigid. She counted five seconds, her mouth still buried in him, and then she finally released the intense rush that he had built inside of her, letting herself ride the wave of emotion it conjured.

When she could bear it no longer, she opened her eyes to see the intense glow of colour that surrounded them both, encapsulating them into one spectacular bubble.

Their eyes locked into each other's, both pupils enlarged and open with pure amazement, allowing every possible particle of light to enter into them.

And then, just when she knew it was time for him to experience the feeling of pure liberation too, she moved her fingers around to the front of his chest, pushed him down onto his back and rolled herself off him. He immediately responded by turning on his side, his body jolting in relief as she held him in her arms. She waited for as long as she could bear it before she finally said the words that she had been desperate to say all her life, at the right time, and to the right person, "I love you."

Still turned away from her, curled now into a ball on his side, completely exhausted by the effort of restraint and escape, she didn't need to hear his response out loud. The smell of pure contentment that emanated from him, and the sight of his colours ever so faint around him were all she needed as confirmation that, he too, knew that he had finally come home.

.

23. REVELATIONS

Waking up with Tiegal on a morning after a full moon was always an interesting experience. Johannes had noticed how she always seemed more restless after one of these nights. He had tried broaching the subject with her before, but she always said the extra light from the moon made her sleep talking more intense. This morning was no exception. But then, full moon aside, last night had provided more than just a night-time light spectacle; it had marked a new awakening in them both, *and* in their abilities to reveal their light when they connected together.

"Nam num...num...nam..." Tiegal's body jerked in fits. A layer of sweat glistened across her furrowed brow as she narrated her early morning sleep journey, her eyes still clenched shut. He watched her, noticing how her expression suggested she was frustrated by something, as though she was trying to get past an obstruction.

"Shhh...bubble. Wake up, my love. Come on now." He rocked her shoulders from side to side as gently as he dared, not wishing to startle her into consciousness too quickly. He had made this mistake before. She mumbled a few more incoherent words, but she did not seem eager to join him in a wakeful state just yet.

"Okay, get some more sleep then. I can stay a little while longer," he hushed, using a clean rag to wipe her forehead. Her body relaxed in his arms in response to his comforting words and he listened to her breathing settle again.

It amazed him that she perspired like this when she was feeling so troubled by something as unreal as a dream. When they had indulged in their lovemaking together, her entire body had burned dry against him, glowing from a controlled heat inside her, rather than glistening with surface moisture. But then, he was not sure his body had reacted to what they had done in a typical manner either. It certainly wasn't how he had imagined his first time. It was beyond and above his expectations; it was transformative!

"I'm a bit green and blue then," he mused into her hair which was splayed out onto the pillow. He sensed she was awakening. He heard her giggle; it was his cue.

"Tickle fight!" he warned, before reaching under the sheets to find one of her most sensitive areas, the sides of her waist, that he knew would send her into a crazy fit of laughter.

"This will wake you up," he teased. "Tell me you want me to stop!"

"Never!" she declared, twisting her body away from his searching fingers with admirable dexterity.

"You won't get away from me that easily."

Without waiting for a reply, he dived under the sheets, grabbed her hips to pin her down and clamped his mouth on her stomach so he could blow his air into her skin. To his shock, instead of more wriggling and laughter, her body stiffened in his hands and turned icy cold to his touch. Without hesitating, he let her go and then quickly pulled his head out from under the sheets so that he could see her concerned face.

"Are you okay? Sorry if I hurt you. It's just a little game I play with my nephew, Henri, it always makes him laugh. I thought that you'd erm..." he stumbled across his words, suddenly self-conscious of how to talk to her. They had fallen asleep in each other's arms almost immediately after they had finally made their physical connection. There had been no need for words, only happy murmurings and kisses, full of content and completeness.

Now, though, her eyes seemed a darker green and they suggested a faint flicker of pulsating light behind them. It seemed to send a warning to him.

"Tiegal, are you okay? Say something," he tried again. Her face relaxed and the richer emerald colour glowed from her irises, as though returning from a dark trance.

"I'm good. Sorry, I don't know what happened then." she looked as confused as he felt.

"You were fine, apart from your sleep talking, but other than that I thought we were just having fun, like we always do. I thought it would break the ice too, after such a hot experience," he said, instantly regretting his choice of words.

The last thing he wanted to do was push her too far, but she put her arms out to rest on his shoulders before he had chance to worry any further.

"There is no need to break any ice or whatever that expression means. I guess you mean, make things chilled?"

He shrugged, not knowing which of their chosen expressions were more appropriate for this first exchange between them after what they had just done together!

"Then why did you go all rigid like that?"

His question was not meant to be an accusation. He willed her to understand this from his thoughts, hoping he could avoid explaining himself further, and possibly wind up confusing things even more. To his relief, her expression showed him she was tuning into his mind. The way she stared straight at him sometimes, without blinking, was always a clear sign.

"It was not an intentional reaction. I didn't mean to upset you in anyway, *never*, I mean, I love it when you touch me, in all the ways you do. It's just *where* you were touching me that bothered me," she explained, breaking up the spaces between her words with care.

The way she lowered her eyes, and then pulled the sheet further up towards her neck, made him wonder if she was embarrassed by something.

"Did you really just say *where* I touched you?"

He watched her, as she nodded at him, her head still bowed, as though she felt great shame. He laughed, in spite of himself. Not just a little chuckle either, a deep, hearty laugh, that he knew he should hold back but just escaped from him in an instinctual response.

"You do know how absurd that sounds Tiegal? After all the ways we touched each other last night! That was just a belly tickle."

Her eyes flickered up to meet his incredulous gaze, frightened and wild with fear.

"It is my *star* Johannes."

Her rigid, defiant pose was back again.

"Your star? I don't understand. Is that what you call your stomach?"

He reached his hand out to her, but she folded hers against her chest.

"The part where you were attached to your mother, before you were born. You call it, whatever you call it, but mine is called my star. It has eight points. I don't like it to be touched, that's all."

He tried to let out his breath, he was starting to feel dizzy from the lack of oxygen, but he couldn't seem to let allow himself to exhale again.

"Breathe!" she finally ordered him.

Tiegal you're scaring me! I hope you can hear this, but I really don't understand what is going on or what you are saying right now. Did I hurt you last night or make you feel something about your other world again? Why are you only telling me NOW where you don't like me to touch you?

He knew she could hear what he was conveying to her in his mind and he let himself breathe out a sigh of relief when she finally nodded her understanding. She uncrossed her arms from her chest and placed her hands in his.

"Sorry, my love. I didn't mean to frighten you. I had some strange dreams again last night. They seemed to be telling me that I had to tell you some things about me that I really didn't want to, and then you woke me up and went straight for the area I had been trying to avoid you touching," she explained, rushing her words out in a tremble, her body shaking as she stifled a yawn.

"Okay, so I didn't hurt you physically then? Either before when we, y'know, or just now?"

"No, no, not at all Johannes. What we did together was beautiful, in every way possible. It was truly magic."

Her answer brought him some warmth, but her hands still felt cold in his. It was an unusual temperature for her and didn't match the warmth of the morning sunrise that had already filled the room. He rubbed them together and reached down to blow his breath into the space between where she had cupped them together in the position of a prayer.

"I feel cold because I'm scared about what I have to tell you."

Her admission made him feel sick with trepidation, to the point that his body actually trembled. He couldn't imagine where this could be leading. Their coming together had finally happened, he had controlled himself at the end, as he had promised he would, and she hadn't disappeared. Why would she think that anything else could shock him about her?

"Because you don't know how I was made," she explained further.

It was obvious she had heard his frustration.

"You said you are like a diamond, made of carbon and star stuff, just as we humans are. I liked how you explained how we are all made of star explosions, and how you understand the science of the universe, in a way we have not come to understand yet," he interjected.

"But you didn't ask how *I* was made. How it was possible for me to be *born*, if I don't have a mother or father. You never asked me how a Tandroan could become a physical being, one that looks so similar to a human."

He could detect her words were heavy with sadness, not quite fear, but still, he knew he had failed her in some way.

"I did think about asking you," he admitted, still rubbing her ice-cold fingers together.

"I know you did. I heard it bursting to come out of you many times. And I know why you stopped yourself, because you thought the moment had passed. When you saw my eyes had changed and that I could bleed like a human woman, you told yourself it didn't matter anymore. Am I right?" she asked him, her fingers entwining into his, willing for reassurance.

He nodded in agreement.

"So why does it matter then?" he finally asked her, vaguely aware of the sounds of a wagon being dragged by an ox at the other side of the trees. Annarita had mentioned something about a delivery this morning. She would be waiting for him to return, no doubt angry once again that he refused to tell her where he had spent the night away from the house. He couldn't let himself think about that now.

"It matters because I am not human, and I am not Tandroan either anymore. I am somehow both now. And you are the only one who knows that I exist, as I am now, in this form that I am in. So, I need you to understand me, as I was, as I am, and therefore what I may even become. Does that make sense?"

It pained him to hear the agony in her questioning. It surprised him that she could even question that he would contemplate leaving her at any of these stages, despite what it meant she was or would become.

"Tiegal, I *do* want to know you, in every form or place you are in, or have been. But can I ask you a question too?"

She nodded her head in a frantic motion, so he cleared his throat, desperately trying to ignore the moaning sound of the distressed ox near the farmhouse.

"Did you dream something about your future just now? Something that you fear will affect whether we can be together? I heard you mention Namnum again. The elephant you talked to me about."

The hint of a smile on her anxious, pale face, indicated that he had turned his attention in the right direction.

"Yes!" She squeezed his hands. "Namnum sometimes communicates to me through dreams. She told me that I have to tell you *everything* because you need to be prepared for how it could change, when I become two."

"When you what?" he stammered.

"I mean, sorry, I forget that I don't say things in the right way sometimes. I mean when I become Tiegal, the Human Tandroan girl... who carries your child inside of me."

Johannes gasped. His mind raced as it struggled to adjust to this bombshell of a revelation that she had just dropped on him.

"Tiegal, are you saying what I think you're saying?"

He shouted his question, his voice high-pitched with adrenaline.

Tiegal nodded at him, her face passive and confident as she pulled back the sheets from where it had covered both their naked frames. She then climbed on top of him, so that her legs straddled his hips and her chest lay on top of his. He responded to her in an instant.

"Hmmm...how much time do you have left to stay here with me?" she mumbled into his ear.

Johannes groaned. "Not long at all. And now you're distracting me away from what you just announced! A baby! Really? When?" he demanded in a voice that broke between each question. The pressure of her weight and the sensation of her wetness between his hips was already driving him crazy.

"I don't know for sure, and I'm not sure it's a good idea anyway, not since I have to hideaway like this. And yet, in all my dreams I am with you and we have a little girl," she answered. Her breath was hot and tickled the hairs on his chest.

Johannes could feel his heart beating. The urgent, excited beats distracting him from all the sounds both inside and outside the cabin.

His mind raced as it scrambled to conjure up images of a future baby.

And it was these thoughts – along with the burning desire to make another connection with Tiegal – that so consumed him, and to such an extent, that he failed to detect the obvious danger approaching: the sound of two sets of footsteps approaching their door.

"What the...JOHANNES!"

Johannes flinched at the sound of his sister's shocked cry.

"Annarita! Get out!" he bellowed back, quickly rolling over so that Tiegal was underneath him. He would rather bare his naked body to his sister than expose Tiegals' naked form to her.

"Go back! There's nothing to see here," Annarita screeched. She looked like she was trying to push someone backwards from behind her.

"Hey! What's going on? I heard you shout his name? Let me in."

Johannes froze at the sound of the other voice behind his sister.

"Who's there?" Tiegal whispered. He could feel her shaking underneath him. He reached his hand down the bed to pull the sheet back over them both, even though he knew it was too late. It was impossible to protect Tiegal from the truth. Elna was already in the room.

The screams of his former girlfriend filled the tiny space. Johannes squeezed his eyes shut and then whispered into Tiegals' ear, "I'm so sorry. I've got to go."

As Johannes ran after Elna, he yanked on the cord tie of this trousers so he could tighten them around his waist. The wrenching sounds of her sobbing ahead of him were impossible to ignore. And yet, as much as her sounds of anguish pulled him towards her, they also repelled him. He willed himself to put more effort into his run, but his legs felt heavy, unwilling.

Annarita's voice bellowed behind him, urging him to catch her up. He pushed his legs further, albeit reluctantly. What he really wanted to do was turn back. Tiegal was the one he was most concerned for.

How will she understand me running after Elna like this? She has never experienced relationships. And here I am, leaving her naked, and alone, after she has just given her body to me!

This thought stopped him in his tracks.

She might leave! The last time she saw me with Elna she disappeared.

He stamped his foot in frustration, glancing around in a panic. He had no idea what to do.

"Johannes, go after her!" Annarita exclaimed. She was gasping for breath as she ran up to him. Her face was red and sweaty. Her expression was furious.

"Annarita! Please, calm down! It's not what it looks like. And you shouldn't run like that. Your body is still fragile after Henri," he reprimanded, now bending his head down to his knees to counteract the dizziness. Looking his sister straight in the eye was too painful. He knew she was disappointed with him.

"It is exactly what it looks like brother. You were engaging in *activity* with some other girl in a hideaway cabin and your ex-girlfriend walked in on you. So now go catch her up and talk to her."

Annarita pulled on his shoulders to encourage him to stand back up and face her.

Johannes shook his head.

"But which her? Why do you assume that it is Elna that I should go to in this moment? She left *me* remember," he argued.

"Look at me! You have to face this. And you know Elna left because you pushed her away," Annarita demanded.

Slowly, Johannes raised his body, wiping away tears as he did.

"Sister, Elna left because *she* wanted to. And the *strange* girl you just saw me with means the world to me. She is everything I have ever dreamed of. And I love her," he cried.

Without stopping to wait for Annarita's response he broke into a run, this time faster and more determined. He knew where he needed to be – with the girl who needed him the most. The one who was still in the cabin

24. FINDINGS

Elna's scent was easy to follow. It was strong, distinctive, and fortunately not too offensive to her olfactory senses. There was cucumber, juniper berry, and lemon, mixed with an earthier, grassy aroma. A pleasant, almost heady scent that Tiegal could easily imagine would mix well with Johannes' smell of coconut and orange, fire and matches.

"Stop it!" Tiegal muttered under her breath. Her jealousy towards this girl was almost frightening, even to herself. She had to keep calm and controlled – and quiet.

It was vital that she did not take Elna by surprise when she approached her. Enough damage had been done in the past few hours already. It was now time to heal things, *not* to make the girl's pain even worse.

As she rounded the edge of the bush and headed east following Elna's scent, she stopped in her tracks as soon as the thatched-roofed stone farmhouse came into view.

This had to be the house where Elna had grown up. It was small and cosy-looking. Nothing like the grand estate that Atla enjoyed, nor the decked tented camp on the water where she had been raised on

Tandro. But it was in keeping with the area. A very similar style of residence to Johannes', although the carefully planted flowers at the front, and the neat wooden fencing, suggested there was an order to the house which the Smits did not place as much importance on.

Focusing her attention on the front door, she waited. But after several long minutes had passed she started to waver, unsure whether it would ever open.

"At last!" she breathed, when eventually Elna appeared from behind it. Tiegal started to make a move towards her, but quickly stepped back again into the shadows, alarmed by what she saw. Elna appeared to be carrying something in her arms. A small bundle of white fabric, that she was cradling with great care - even snuffling her face into it - in a manner that suggested it was the most precious thing she had ever possessed.

She had witnessed this kind of human behaviour before, when she had observed Annarita playing with her baby, from afar. It had a smell to it this human mannerism. It carried a particular type of love scent, a protective one.

Before she could stop herself, Tiegal let out a little wail, which she quickly muffled into her fist.

A baby? No! Please tell me it's not true. Is that really why Elna left? Because she was carrying a child? Johannes' child?

A sensation of burning attacked the back of her throat. Confused, she pulled her hand out of her mouth, jerking back in fright as she saw the reason for the heat on her tongue, her hands had caught on fire!

"Stop it!" she ordered them, her voice, a hoarse, terrified splutter. She fanned her hands out in front of her, both fascinated and terrified by their fiery display. Each of her fingertips burned blue flames that flickered and sparked as she wiggled them.

Why is this happening now? I'm not even wearing my Derado.

Taking a deep breath, she exhaled in small, controlled bursts, blowing on each finger in turn. Yet no matter how much she tried she could not extinguish the flames.

"I knew you were not from this world."

Tiegal cried out in surprise at the sound of Elna's voice. She was standing in front of her now, still holding her bundle, her eyes wide and alarmed.

"I...I... wasn't spying on you. I wanted to see you. To apologise," Tiegal rushed to explain, shoving her hands behind her back.

"Careful there. You don't want to set your skirt on fire with those hands of yours! Fires can be dangerous you know. Once you get them started, you don't always have control over them," Elna commented. She swayed her body from side-ways as though rocking the bundle she carried to sleep.

Tiegal swung her head round to check the back of her dress.

"Oh no!" she cried again, shaking her hips from side to side in an attempt to put out the flames, realising too late that she was only fanning them into an even livelier dance.

"Use the tree," Elna suggested. Her voice, although shaky, sounded calm and poised. Strangely, she did not appear shocked, or in any rush to help Tiegal put out the fire on her clothes.

Without hesitating further, Tiegal threw her back against the tree and rubbed herself up and down, finally succeeding in taking control of the burning before she caused any serious damage to her skin.

As black smoke whispered around her frame, she threw Elna a look, one she hoped conveyed a sense of gratitude.

"Good idea. Amazing how you panic in a crisis," Tiegal joked. Now that her hands had calmed, and resumed into a natural, non-fiery state, she clasped her fingers into a fist and let herself fall down the trunk of the tree, crouching at the defined base of its trunk, her hands in-between her knees.

"I don't think I want to know where you have come from, but, wherever it is, it does not look like being you is very easy!"

Elna's words made Tiegal chuckle. A sense of absurdity finally bringing her back to a more stable place of reasoning.

"That has never happened before. I'm not sure what is

happening to me," Tiegal responded, her head still faced towards her skirt-covered knees.

Maybe you absorbed some of that darkness in that area of the bush you were messing about in?

Tiegal gasped at the sound of Elna's voice inside her head.

"What did you just say?" Tiegal demanded.

Elna frowned at her, stepping back in alarm.

"I didn't say anything."

"Sorry, I mean, what did you just think...just then?" Tiegal insisted.

Elna's voice filled her head again.

Has he told you what he did to his father in there?

Tiegal stepped towards her.

"What are you talking about? What did Johannes do?"

Tiegal shook her hands again, to check they were still safe, and then ran them through her hair. Frustrated, she pulled her hair into two bunches that she tied together with dried grass, and then yanked on them hard. Already, this was not going well.

"I didn't say *anything!* And I'm leaving. You're scaring me!" Elna announced, turning away from Tiegal, the bundle in her arms now clasped even tighter to her chest.

Just as she swung around, a strange high-pitched moaning noise sounded out from the white blanket that Elna held close. The sound caused Tiegal's ear to prick up and her nostrils to flare in response.

"Hold on! What *is* that in there?" Tiegal asked, reaching her hand out in Elna's direction. When Elna continued walking ahead, Tiegal cried out again:

"Please! Wait! That's not a baby in there is it?"

This made Elna stop in her tracks.

Tiegal was almost laughing as she now realized just how wrong her first assumption had been.

"Is that a small animal you are carrying, Elna?"

Slowly, Elna swung round. Her arms loosened, allowing a section of the blanket to fall down. At first, it was not clear what squirmed inside Elna's arms. A few black strands of wiry hair poked out and then retreated back. Unable to contain herself any longer, Tiegal moved herself closer, craning her neck to get a better view of what was still hidden from her curious eyes.

"Oh my! Just beautiful!" Tiegal squealed as soon as she reached them and absorbed the unmistakable sight of a beautiful, silver-grey, feline animal with long black whiskers and huge emerald green eyes. It turned its furry face towards Tiegal and gave her a wink.

"Ha ha! I'm not sure what you are. But, you're beautiful!" Tiegal clapped her hands, both delighted and relieved by what she saw.

Forgetting all that had occurred in the last few hours, and the frightening thoughts she had just heard, she ran over to where Elna stood holding the animal and threw her arms around both of them with unrestrained delight.

"I am truly sorry for any pain I have brought you Elna," she cried into Elna's stiff shoulders.

"You actually thought I was carrying Johannes' baby?" Elna hissed.

Tiegal pulled back from their embrace, immediately feeling ashamed. She couldn't believe she was behaving so foolishly, or so disloyally. What would Johannes think if he knew she had jumped to such a conclusion?

"I...I...I just saw the way you were holding it and...well, I wondered if that's why you left."

Elna's shoulders began to shake. A forced, robotic laughter erupted from her as she squinted her eyes at Tiegal.

"Is that what kind of girl you think I am? Someone like you? The kind of girl who would give her body to a man who killed his own father!"

At that moment, everything around them froze: the feline creature stilled its frantic paw-licking; the leaves no longer moved in time to the strong afternoon breeze; and Tiegal's lungs stopped heaving.

"I c...c...can't b...b...breathe," she gasped.

Elna didn't move an inch.

But her frantic thoughts shot through Tiegal's mind in snippets:

Accident...

Too many bottles...

The other woman...

Not really his fault...

Tiegal almost cried in relief. Although not a complete exoneration, it was enough for her to know that Johannes' terrifying secret was not as dark as she had feared.

With this confirmation, she managed to find both her breath and her strength. And as if on cue, the world around her un-paused once more.

The feline creature gave its paw a long lick and then broke out of Elna's embrace. It sauntered over to Tiegal's feet and began to circle her ankles. The tree branches burst back into their rhythmic dance with the dust-filled wind. And then Elna threw her hands into the air and let herself drop to the ground in a defeated heap.

"What a mess!" she muttered.

"You may think I am even stranger when I tell you this Elna, but... I can hear your thoughts. So, I know you didn't really mean what you just said." Tiegal bent down to stroke the furry creature by her feet.

"I didn't mean it. Johannes didn't kill his father. It was an accident."

Elna's confession was barely a whisper.

"Tell me the truth Elna. Please. Whatever did happen, I know it has been hurting Johannes for a long time. And I know you care about him deep down. That you would want to help him, if you could."

Elna slowly raised her head. Her upper lip was smeared with a thick liquid that had run down from her nose. She wiped it away on her sleeve and then attempted to clear it from the cotton material with a nearby leaf.

"Please, Elna..." Tiegal tried again.

Elna looked up at her and nodded. Her eyes looked like two pools of clear liquid that shimmered in the sunlight, revealing just hints of her blue-coloured irises underneath them.

"His mother, Cezanne, had only just passed away. It was an awful time for him, and for Annarita. Their father took straight to the drink after she died and would sometimes leave the house, and the farm, for days at a time. The entire neighbourhood had to help to keep things going. Kagiso was the only one who held it altogether. I don't know what Johannes and Annarita would have done if not for her."

Tiegal shuddered. She had watched Kagiso from afar, on the days when she had nothing else to do but observe the daily comings and goings of the people Johannes lived with. Even from a distance, it was clear what a strong, loving energy the older lady possessed. Tiegal was very much looking forward to meeting her, when the time was right.

"He talks about Kagiso a lot. I know she is very important."

Elna nodded.

"Yes, she is. And, she is the only other person who knows about what happened."

"Which was..."

"It was about two weeks after Cezanne's death. His mother had been sick for a long time and her passing was long and painful. I called round to his house and had to *order* him to come out for a walk with me. He was so sad about his Ma, and so angry that his father had deserted them, that I knew he needed to get out of the house and vent. My mother told me he'd not been eating, so I brought him some meat strips and bread to eat on the way so that he could get some energy and...are you okay? Your skin has turned a green colour."

Tiegal shuddered. The cat had now curled up into her lap and her stomach was rumbling from hunger and lurching in nauseating waves at Elna's mention of Johannes eating meat.

"Sorry, please go on," she urged, annoyed with herself that she had stopped Elna in the middle of such an important story.

"Johannes and I were both twelve, you know that strange age

between being a child and a young adult?" Elna raised her eyebrows in an expectant manner. Her lips curled in a way that suggested she was attempting a smile, and her fair hair glowed from the dappled sunlight that had broken through the tree canopy above. For a strange moment, she reminded Tiegal of Zeno in the way she presented herself. An ally - perhaps, even, as a friend.

"I, well, I never experienced such age transitions. I think you have already gathered that I don't come from around here...."

Tiegal pulled the feline creature up from her lap and gave her a gentle push towards Elna. She felt a sudden need to offer her something in return for disclosing all this vital information.

Without hesitating, Elna picked up the creature in a way that allowed its paws to rest over her shoulder. She looked confused as she considered Tiegal's response.

"Oh, well, being twelve can be tricky. And, of course, losing his mother at this age was not good timing. Not that it could ever be. Annarita was seventeen and was already courting Frederick so she had more support. But Johannes really needed his father. Anyway, on this particular day, when I called for him, Kagiso suggested we headed out to the bush behind his house. She had spotted his father earlier that morning. Said he'd gone wandering off in that direction looking a bit lost."

"The area behind the bushes being where..."

"Yes" Elna, lowered her eyelids. "Near your cabin!"

At the mention of the cabin, Tiegal felt the rush of a familiar heat in her cheeks.

"Go on," she urged her.

"When we got there the cabin looked empty. So, I suggested we eat our picnic in there, even though there was nothing but a very beaten up bed, but then we heard voices approaching and for some reason we decided to hide under it."

"A young woman with all this long reddish-coloured hair came crashing in and landed on the bed above us. She was laughing and had clearly been drinking. I had never seen her before. Nor had Johannes. She kept calling out for Anton to join her."

"Anton?"

"That was his name. Johannes' father."

"Oh!" Tiegal felt a strange scrunching up feeling. Her shoulders squeezed into each other, as though her body was attempting to make itself smaller. It was all too easy to imagine what must have happened next. She wasn't sure she wanted to hear it.

"No wonder Johannes was so afraid to do anything intimate. He didn't want to be like his father," she managed.

Elna made a snorting noise in response.

"Trust me strange one, you got a lot more than I did! But, you're right. Johannes has been afraid of getting close to anyone ever since that day. Certainly, of allowing himself to feel anything like desire anyway."

"What did happen? I heard your thoughts just before, about how Johannes killed him. Why would you even think that?"

She was torn between curiosity and fear. The feline creature turned its head around and gave her another wink.

"Well, as you can imagine, he was furious that his father would do such a thing with some woman so soon after his mother had passed. We hid for long enough to hear what was going on, but then it all became too much. Johannes screamed at him, pulled him off the woman and then hit him hard across the jaw. He... he called him some very bad things. This, of course, made Anton go a bit crazy too. Ugh! It was just awful. Anton hit Johannes hard across the back of his head and shouted some truly awful things back to him."

Elna shuddered, took a deep breath and then continued:

"He actually said that his mother had always loved her first born the most, the baby boy who died. That she never really bonded with Johannes. Which was complete rubbish of course."

Tiegal's fingertips started to burn as she imagined the scene Elna was portraying.

"What did Johannes do? When he heard his father say that?"

Elna shook her head sadly.

"He screamed at him to go burn in hell!"

"Hell?"

Even though she knew of this bizarre, old-world concept, it was still strange to hear of a young Johannes using such terminology as a genuine threat. Elna didn't appear to have registered Tiegal's question.

"As fate had it, his father did burn that night. But it wasn't Johannes' fault. After Anton had hurtled all his abuse, we fled the cabin and ran back to his house. I told Kagiso everything and then left her to console Johannes. But... Anton never came back. All I know is that he got so drunk he stayed up all night and must have decided to make a fire nearby. He probably carried on drinking and at some point, somehow, fell, or accidentally rolled into it. Some of the farmers found his body the next morning."

"Everyone knew how much Anton loved Cezanne but obviously his grief made him crazy. Johannes has never stopped blaming himself for it though. And I never once brought it up with him again. That is, until you appeared."

Tiegal flinched at the mention of her involvement.

"Why? What did my arrival have to do with it?"

Elan closed her eyes and sighed.

"When we found the diamond by the river Johannes seemed to change in that moment. It was as if he took it as a sign of good fortune, that he could finally move on, and let himself live fully at last. I had been waiting for him to kiss me ever since we were children. And then he did..."

"Oh...I..." Tiegal interrupted without meaning to.

"No, no, it's okay don't worry, I won't go into detail. It was just a kiss, but it meant everything to me. I was so happy. But then..."

"I turned up!"

"You just appeared! And that was it! That was the *real* moment he changed. He became absolutely transfixed by you. I was so hurt. So jealous. I didn't even really care how shocking it was because I was so consumed by his reaction to you. I threw it in his face - this awful secret about his dad - before I left, because I knew it would be the worst thing that I could say to him."

"Oh, I see! That's why you left," Tiegal whispered.

Elna wiped her cheeks with the back of her hand. Her tears seemed to fall in a never-ending stream down her face.

"Yes, that's why I left. It was too painful to see how obsessed he had become with you. But when word reached me that he had started drinking heavily, I came back to see how he was. That's why I suggested to Annarita that we look for him near the cabin. I thought maybe he was torturing himself with his demons and bad memories. *But...* clearly he was ridding them, or should I say exorcising them, in a very different way."

Elna blushed, averting her eyes from Tiegal's stunned expression.

"I see."

Standing up slowly, she raised her hand out to Elna.

"Can I come sit with you?"

As soon as Elna nodded her agreement, Tiegal walked over and sat down close to her side. Not wanting to overthink it, she then wrapped her arms around both Elna and the furry creature. Much to her relief, Elna relaxed into her embrace.

"What do you call this animal? The name is lost on me."

"Oh! It's a cat. I found her near the river. She was starving hungry and looked lost and afraid."

Tiegal buried her nose into the cat's fur and inhaled. Animal scents always comforted her.

"Thank you for telling me this Elna. You said earlier that you need to be careful starting fires, and I can see why you said that now. But, where I come from, we see fires very differently. In my world, we look to the fire inside of us as the very thing we must control. That we must not let anyone dampen it because it is our power."

And with that she held out her hand to the girl she now understood.

"You have a beautiful fire inside of you Elna. And you helped Johannes keep his fire burning all those years, when he couldn't."

Once again, Elna burst into tears. Tiegal pulled her close. Their heads knocked together as they found their awkward embrace. Although inexperienced in such emotional displays between almost strangers, it felt like the natural thing to do. Enough thoughts and words had been exchanged. Tiegal felt confident that a truce had been reached.

But as she held onto Elna's shaking body and waited for a sense of peace to reach her, she had to gulp back her own tears as the all-too familiar feeling of fear and dread overwhelmed her instead. A new danger brimmed now. Her body was screaming at her – attacking her with violent nausea and dizziness - to get away from Elna and her emotional distress. Her own fire was struggling. All these human emotions and experiences – jealousy, grief, anger and loss – were draining her emotional resources. It seemed that the more she exchanged such powerful human emotions, the more she was in danger of losing her own strength, and her potential to survive here in this world.

25. ENDINGS

Johannes slowed his walk down to match his pace with Kagiso. It had been a while since they had enjoyed evening walks around the river together like this, but it still surprised him how much slower she had become since then. He had forgotten how old she actually was.

"When you were smaller, I used to say to your Ma, 'let me take him down to the river and see if I can burn some of that energy outta him'. You always needed a good run around when you had too much going on in your head," Kagiso chuckled, in-between her raspy breaths.

"You okay Kagiso? You sound tired," Johannes checked, linking his arm into the crook of hers.

"And *you* sound confused. Is Annarita still giving you grief about Elna?"

"She won't even look at me!"

"I've told her to try being more understanding, but you know what a romantic that sister of yours is. She's only ever loved Frederick. I think she assumed it would be the same for you with Elna. I think it's hard for her to accept that even when we love someone we can hurt them, even if we don't mean to."

Her voice wavered, an uncertainty that did not match her usual conviction. It made him feel strange.

"I think I *have* always loved Elna - but as a friend. I realise now that I wasn't *in* love with her, but still, I never wanted to hurt her."

Kagiso sighed. "Who does? Love someone or not, you don't want to hurt them with your choices, but sometimes you do! Just as I didn't intend to hurt you."

"Hey, stop there, what's all this about? You have never hurt me. Let me see your face!" he demanded, pulling her back gently with his arm. As soon as he clocked her sad, mournful expression, he reeled back, almost pulling her over as he did. He had seen this kind of look before, and it terrified him.

"You look like... like..." he struggled to get his words out.

"Like your Ma did? Before she passed?" Kagiso offered helpfully.

"Don't say that Kagiso! I didn't mean to sound like I was comparing you to what happened to Ma..." he faltered, giving her one of his apologetic shrugs.

They had now reached Johannes' favourite thorn tree and he could see she needed somewhere to perch. He motioned for her to sit on the low-lying branch, quickly checking that it was still strong enough to support her weight. Kagiso lowered herself down carefully, wincing as she supported her back with her left hand.

"Bones are quick to age but my mind still feels so young. And as old as I may be, I still remember how all these choices can make a young heart so confused. Your Ma was the same when she met your Pa y'know!" she mused, batting her apron together with her hands, as though she were applauding herself.

Johannes twisted his hips as he settled himself into his usual spot, under the shade provided by the looming branches of the thorn tree.

"I can't see why Ma would have struggled with her decision to marry Pa! They were childhood friends, weren't they? It was set in stone that they would be together."

Kagiso laughed, a hearty chuckle, that quickly transformed into a nasty-sounding, chesty cough. Johannes jumped to his knees, leaning over her and gently patting her back. He offered her his handkerchief so that she could spit the phlegm into it without any need for embarrassment. He knew she was a proud woman; just as his mother had been.

Just like Ma! She used to cough just like this before she left us...

He quickly shook his head to rid his mind of such foreboding. Losing Kagiso was unthinkable, even if it was seeming more likely with every desperate bid for air that he heard her take.

"Breathe. Breathe now," he encouraged, "no wonder you are so out of breath like this, laughing at every little thing that I say," he teased, hoping his jovial and familiar banter would lift her spirits. Or somehow mend her tired lungs.

Maybe Tiegal will know what to do? She might have some advanced ideas about medicinal plants from her world or something?

He trembled as he thought about her now, waiting for him to return to her in their cabin. And all at once he felt that all-too familiar conflict within him: torn between running over to fetch her; and simultaneously, feeling ashamed that he could even contemplate leaving Kagiso on her own here like this. He always felt the burden of choice. He never felt he had made the right one.

"I was laughing at how blind you have become Johannes," Kagiso finally spoke, as her breathing steadied. She held onto his arm as she twisted herself on the uncomfortable branch and then smiled at him.

"You said it was set in stone that your Ma and Pa would marry. Can you not see the irony there?" she asked him.

Johannes squinted as he poured over his own words that she had echoed back to him.

Set in stone...like Elna and I had been. By our fathers. Only it all changed when we found a stone, well a diamond...and then Tiegal arrived. A girl who really was made of diamond.

He shook his head in amazement as the parallel pieces of his life and those of his parents' came together in his mind.

"Did they both want to be together though? Even if their

destinies had been pre-determined for them?" His question was a whisper.

Kagiso shook her head.

"It's never simple where matters of the heart are concerned. I think your Pa was enthralled with the idea from the start. But, your Ma? Well, she was like you. A dreamer. There were hidden desires she was forbidden from exploring. And she never did of course. But you see, that's why I think she would have wanted different for you. And even for Elna too."

Johannes flinched at the sound of her name. He still hadn't been over to her house to see her since she had fled the cabin scene.

"Is that why he betrayed her the way he did? Even when her body was still warm? Because he felt unsure of her feelings for him?" He spat out his anger. It had never truly left him.

Kagiso reached out her hand to squeeze Johannes' arm. At least she tried. Her attempt only highlighted just how weak she had become.

"I promise you Johannes. Your parents shared a great love. Your father made some bad choices and said some hurtful things after she died. But that was because he was grieving. It wasn't your fault. You were a child. If anyone should feel any regret it is me. I should never have let you go after him. It was my job to protect you. I promised your mother I would!"

Her head lolled to the side a little as she spoke, her words slurring with each utterance.

Shocked by the sound of her breaking voice, Johannes reached up from his kneeling position and pulled her into his arms.

"You have always protected me Kagiso. I would have ended up finding him anyway. Please don't blame yourself," he whispered into her ear.

"Thank you, my sweet, sweet boy. I guess sometimes we find things we wish we hadn't. And others, well, we must hold on to those finds and never, ever, let them go."

As always, she spoke the truth.

"Did Annarita tell you? About the girl I found? The one I have been hiding?"

Kagiso chuckled.

"She didn't need to. I knew all along that it wasn't Elna I heard you talking to her in your bedroom. I could see it in your eyes and the way you were smiling again that you had found what you have been waiting for. What your mother had been promising you would, in your visions, hey?"

"Unbelievable!" he whispered, staring ahead to the space in the river, where Tiegal had first appeared.

"Please Johannnn..." Kagiso started, the rest of her words lost in a fitful of hacking coughs.

"Please what?" Johannes rubbed her back gently but with several firm strokes. A surge of panic filled his body with adrenaline. His mind raced with the possibility that what Kagiso was asking him would be the last thing she ever asked of him. How could he possibly save her if she really was nearing her last breath?

"Don't let this new girl think me leaving is her fault. It's just a coincidence that I have to go..." Kagiso said, jerking her head up to him, as though wanting to say more. Her mouth moved as though speaking but only her breath exhaled in front of him.

"Kagiso!" he cried, over and over, rocking her in his arms as he felt her slip away.

Tiegal waved goodbye to Elna and then broke into a run, darting through the trees as quickly as she could. Her body was out of control and she needed to get back to the cabin. Something was bubbling inside of her. She felt as though her energy was seeping out of her, or perhaps, bursting in sparks. She couldn't be sure. But the way her fingers were heating up again she knew there was trouble ahead.

Her Derado was calling for her. She could feel its power from all this distance. Calling for her to re-energise, to get her fire burning inside her again.

Just as she reached the parting of trees where the old swing announced the pathway to her cabin, she stopped in her tracks. The unmistakable scent of grief and despair had suddenly wafted under her nose. Something was very wrong.

Instinctively she jerked her head up to check where the scent was coming from.

"Tiegal! Where are you?"

The sound of Johannes' desperate cries approaching made her turn. He burst out of an entangled branch of trees to her left and fell into her arms. His face was wet and his shoulders were shaking.

"What is it?" Tiegal demanded. Her body went rigid as she clamped her arms around him. Taking a deep breath, she lifted his chin upwards from where he had buried it into her chest.

As soon as their eyes met his face crumpled.

"Annarita said she saw you heading this way, after you had been talking to Elna," he managed to respond.

"Hey, Johannes, I'm sorry, okay. I didn't mean to frighten you. I just wanted to make things right again. It's not worth this kind of upset!" she reasoned with him, pulling him closer to her chest.

Johannes' body continued to shake as he let out his anguish into her tight embrace.

Someone has left this world.

It was an ominous, undeniable scent that oozed from his pores. It triggered a sharp, lightning pain to shoot from between the back of her eyes. Annoyed, she shook the thoughts away. She had never been near death, or such grief before. How could she possibly determine its scent?

Although, something else - a feeling deep inside her stomach- warned her that her instinct was correct. The way Johannes was unleashing such distress could surely only mean one thing: that a tragedy had once again befallen his family.

There was nothing she could do but wait – allow him all the time he needed to cry his heart out. His heart-breaking sobs filled the air, the only sound in the otherwise sleepy, dusty, pathway between the bush and the house.

It was only after Johannes' had fully exhausted himself, to the extent that his cries became choking splutters, that he finally lifted his head and faced her. Wiping the tears from his eyes, he announced, "It's Kagiso! She's gone!"

26. CONFUSION

"Oh dear, Tiegal, are you running out of fuel again?"

She could hear Parador's mocking voice but she refused to respond to it. This was just another dream. The darkness wasn't really here. What she could see was not real, just a scene made from her fears: a cold, soundless night; the clearing near the cabin; and an older man who was stumbling around a furious fire.

Stamping her foot down hard she turned her back to the scene before her and closed her eyes.

"Do you think he needs help, perhaps? You wouldn't really want to watch him burn would you now? Surely not my sister? The one with the heart inside her eyes?"

Tiegal couldn't help herself. She swung around to face the pulsating eye-light of her nemesis.

"What did you say? Sister? What are you talking about?" she demanded. A disturbing moaning sound filled her ears. It made her squirm. Out of the corner of her eye, she could see that the man was getting closer to the fire. He was mumbling words that sounded like 'wife' and 'baby' as he waved a half-empty glass bottle around his head. Tiegal put her hands over her ears to shut out the agonising sound of his human pain.

If Parador was going to torture her like this in her dreams then she would force her to converse in the Tandroan way:

What did you just call yourself? We don't have sisters.

Parador made a shrieking sound that sounded like a trapped animal. But then she clapped her hands in front of her face, several times. Tiegal gave her a little growl, letting her know she recognised it as a deliberate, mocking impression of one of her many over-enthusiastic habits.

Parador moved closer to her and flashed her golden eye-light towards her. Tiegal clenched her fists as the menacing voice channelled through to her:

You really are losing all your power out here. To think my magic has stayed with you for so long that you still can't remember. Look at you! Playing this pretend game of being human and so happy and in love!

You are weak now Tiegal Eureka! And you are only going to get weaker. Your fire, your light, it is barely even in existence anymore. You are smoke!

Tiegal smacked both her hands on Parador's chest and pushed her away. She didn't even flinch. Instead, she flickered her eyes to the side and mouthed: "Watch!"

Unable to resist the temptation, she turned her attention to where Parador had indicated and screamed at what she saw.

The man was getting too close to the fire. Waving his hands around and dropping brown liquid over it. The fire was getting stronger, and out of control but he just kept moving closer to it until he lost his balance completely tumbling...falling... and then consumed by it, until all she could see through her tears was a blurred vision of Johannes' father writhing around in flames.

Tiegal awoke to the sensation of heavy pressure. It only took a few seconds for her to realise the feeling was connected to Johannes. His hands were clamped over her mouth. His eyes were inches from hers. And he was sweating profusely.

"Shh...sweetheart. It's just a dream."

He released his hands from her lips and then kissed her, ever-so-gently. His breath smelled of wonderful contrasts; of happy, safe and desire, all at the same time.

"Did I wake up Henri?"

"I think you woke up the whole house." He grinned at her. "Which is a shame as I was hoping we could enjoy a little bit of early morning playtime."

"I am sure that is not allowed. Not when you are supposed to be getting up for your early chores."

Johannes groaned.

"You were supposed to be my early chore!"

Normally she would find such temptation irresistible but not this morning. The horrifying dream experience still lingered. Forcing a giggle, she gave him a playful slap on his upper arm. She could feel his arousal as he pressed his body against hers, but she managed to wriggle her hips from underneath him. Annarita and Frederick's voices could be heard outside the door as they took it in turns to soothe the cries of their little boy.

"Oh, no, I really did wake Henri. They will hate me!"

"They love you Tiegal. And Henri has been awake for hours. You were just so lost in your nightmare you didn't hear it."

Please don't ask me, please don't ask me.

Johannes sighed as he rolled over onto his back.

"I heard you mumbling something about fire again. Is that something from your old world?"

His concern was etched all over his face.

"Oh, it's nothing. Just memories of that ridiculous mantra they used to make us chant. Nothing for you to worry about!"

She watched him get dressed in silence. His thoughts were all over the place; worries, past hurts and fears deeply embedded within him.

She squeezed her eyes shut to turn it off. The more she absorbed these emotions the weaker she was becoming. Just as Parador kept warning in her dreams.

"Johannes! Stop worrying. Everything is okay," she assured him.

He nodded at her. "Okay, well, get some more sleep now. You don't need to get up just yet. You've been very tired recently."

"I'm fine. It's just the silly dreams."

He kissed her once more and then flung open the door, shouting out to Frederick that he was ready to go as he bounded down the stairs.

If only it were just dreams!

The heat from her fingers was burning the skin on her back where she had hidden them. She pulled them out from underneath her to let them cool as she held them above her head.

Please stop burning! Please let me keep my fire and stay here with him!

She pleaded to whoever might hear her silent pleas.

"You have a beautiful voice. I've never heard anything like it before."

Tiegal watched how Annarita reacted to her praise, a bashful shrug followed by a careful smile. The compliment must have confused her.

"Tiegal, I was just humming that's all. But, thank you. You do say the nicest things." Annarita muttered her words in an absent-minded fashion, busying herself with moving the baby from one hip to the other as she cleared the table of breakfast items.

It was proving hard to hide how much affection Tiegal felt towards this hard-working young mother now they had spent some time together, but even Johannes had advised her to take it slowly with her.

"Remember, she cannot know all about you. It would be too much. Try to keep a part of yourself, and your emotions, hidden. I think it's lovely that you are so fond of her, but your eagerness may frighten her a little. You can release it all to me when we are on our own again tonight," he had promised her that morning, before leaving the house to tend the neglected fields.

His advice was - as always - on point, but still, it jarred. It had been his idea to introduce her to Annarita, properly this time, and to move her into the farmhouse with him. It was supposed to be the beginning of her new human life, learning to be part of a family, in readiness for when they started one of their own.

"Do you want to hold Henri?" Annarita asked, unable to hide the pleading nature in her tone. The dark circles under her eyes had become more pronounced in the last few days and Tiegal could smell the exhaustion on the girl's skin.

"Of course, I will Annarita! I would love to," she cried out in response. In her eagerness to help, she jumped up too quickly from the table, failing to remember how loud the chairs sounded when they scraped on the floor. The noise startled baby Henri, prompting him to raise his head from where it rested on his mother's shoulders and let out a frustrated sleep-disturbed wail.

"Oh, I'm sorry. I..."

"It's okay Tiegal. He's just really tired. Why don't you sit back down, and I will hand him over to you? He'll soon settle when he is in your arms. He likes you! Frederick noticed that straightaway! We all do."

"I'm so glad. You have a wonderful husband. I'm so grateful to be here with you all."

"And...Kagiso would have *adored* you too. I'm sure Johannes has told you that already, but...I just thought you should know that."

Tiegal clenched her fists behind her. It still hurt to think that she had been so close to meeting Kagiso just before she left this world. Even now, her fingers would flicker little flames from their tips whenever she thought about it. Only Johannes knew she was still struggling to control it.

"Thank you. It means a lot. I wish so much that I could have met her properly." Tiegal's voice faltered as she darted her eyes around the kitchen, mentally ticking off all the objects she knew had once belonged to their beloved adopted mother.

It was the cream apron that reminded of Kagiso's absence the most. It had been four weeks since Kagiso had passed, but the apron still hung from a nail in the wall. Her memories wafted their scents whenever anyone walked past it - milk, vanilla, and sugar. The greying kaross shawl she had worn around her shoulders, almost religiously even in the heat of summer, still graced the back of the old, worn, chair where Kagiso had apparently always rested on an evening. The wool still contained her floral smell within its threads: lily bush, chamomile and bay leaf.

"You are all so strong. The way you have come together after another loss," Tiegal added, squirming inwardly as soon as the words had left her mouth. Despite the warmth Annarita and Frederick had extended towards her since she had joined their household, it was still impossible to gauge if her tendency to speak her emotions so openly was the appropriate manner to adopt.

Much to her relief, Annarita gave her a reassuring smile, whilst moving her ears away from the loud cries of the now distraught Henri and then lowering him down into the cradle of Tiegal's waiting arms.

"Is this right? Tell me if it's not!" Tiegal insisted, suddenly fearful of taking on the responsibility of holding such a fragile being.

"You are doing fine! Have you never been near babies before? You did mention you dreamed of being a mother yourself one day." Annarita asked.

No! Tiegal wanted to cry out in response. She had never been near a baby before meeting Henri, Johannes' nephew. In her old world, the baby kimberlings were kept separate from the main camps until they were five. She had no recollection of her own life before that age either. One day she just realised she was alive.

The temptation to share – to reveal her strange past – to this new sister of hers was almost painful to resist, but she stopped herself, remembering Johannes' warning.

"I am sure I did. I just can't remember." She finally replied in a whisper.

"Oh, yes, of course, the accident. Well, you are doing a fine job with Henri. Look, he's already snuggling into you."

Annarita gave her another reassuring smile, before slumping down into one of the softer chairs at her side.

Tiegal returned the smile, keen to experience the intoxicating smell of Henri's skin now she had him so close to her. Careful not to alarm Annarita, she buried her face into Henri's hair, so she could plant a gentle kiss on his forehead.

"Hmmm..." she let a satisfied murmur without thinking.

"He smells yummy doesn't he?" Annarita looked delighted by Tiegal's reaction.

Still, her words made Tiegal stiffen, momentarily wondering if she had underestimated human abilities.

"You can smell him too? His scent: chocolate strawberries?"

Annarita's eyes widen with curiosity.

"Well, I hadn't thought of it like that exactly, but yes, I guess it does smell sweet and satisfying." She laughed then, a tired, croaky chuckle; a sound that made Tiegal feel warm inside. Somehow, she knew their conversation had already given Annarita a much-needed energy boost.

"You are something special Tiegal. I can see why my brother has fallen so hopelessly in love with you."

The way Annarita looked at her, with such grateful contentment, confirmed to Tiegal what she had secretly been hoping, that Johannes had been right about bringing the two of them together. They both needed this special female companionship. Annarita had lost her mother and Tiegal had been deprived of the experience of being loved by one. She only wished they had not been forced to lie to

Annarita about why she had ended up near their farm, all on her own, in the first place.

"I love your brother too, *so* much. He is all I have ever wanted."

Tiegal rocked Henri from side to side, enjoying the sounds of his baby lips smacking against his thumb as he sucked at it intermittently.

She knew Annarita wanted to say more, to seek clearer answers to the reasons behind Tiegal's presence, all these things that didn't make sense to her. The questions that Tiegal could hear running through her new friend's tired, mind that were probably driving her crazy.

It didn't seem fair to keep lying to her with stories of a boat accident on the river that had left Tiegal confused and unsure of where she had come from. And yet, equally she knew it was not reasonable to burden a girl who had already suffered enough shocks in her young life, with the futuristic phenomena that had both created her and had led to her journey over here.

"Does it upset you that we hid away in secret at first?" she dared, at last, unable to bear listening to the anguished concerns in Annarita's head.

"I don't know. I think it did at first, if I'm being honest, because I know how much Johannes hates people lying. It was just so unlike him to be so secretive."

"He didn't want to burden you," Tiegal protested, quick as ever to defend him.

"I know that, and I do understand that now, but I still find it hard to believe he hid you away for so long. Does he really think I am so untrustworthy?"

Tiegal shifted her arm to the left to rest it on the arm of the chair. Henri was heavier to hold than she had imagined.

"He thinks the world of you. He just wants to protect you."

"And protect you too," Annarita added.

She knew it wasn't an objection, nor a competition for Johannes' love, that made Annarita's voice sound so strange. Yet there was something in her tone - an unusual tremble - that Tiegal struggled to place along her limited knowledge of the human emotional spectrum.

"Is there something you are afraid of Annarita?"

The awkwardness in the silence that followed this question was palpable. And yet the clarity in the words inside Annarita's mind was like crystal chiming in Tiegal's ears. Annarita didn't believe their story. She *knew* that Tiegal had somehow come here from another world.

An impulse to run away burned inside her but she bit her lip down hard to stop herself from standing up and waking Henri. It seemed they had all been playing a game with each other; pretending to hear and accept stories that didn't make sense.

"Tiegal you look pale all of a sudden. Do you want me to take Henri from you?" Annarita offered.

"No, no, I'm fine. I like having him here. But you didn't answer my question."

"Which was what again?" Annarita responded, her eyes looked vacant and lost as she tried to find a way to stall answering Tiegal's question.

"I asked you if there was something you were afraid of?" She tried again.

Five long seconds of silent contemplation passed between them before Annarita finally stood up from her chair, her arms folded.

"Okay, yes there is something. I am *terrified* that you will vanish again. And that if you do, it will break my brother's heart."

If there was one thing Tiegal had learned since being in this world, it was that being around people all the time was exhausting. It had been easier when it was just two of them in the cabin, or even, when she was on her own during the day. But now they had moved into the farmhouse, she felt exhausted by the constant emotional exchanges between everyone living here. There were only four of them, five if she included the baby. Annarita, her husband Frederick, their baby Henri, Johannes and her - all individuals constantly filling the house with highly charged voices.

The current exchange she could hear between Johannes and Annarita downstairs was making her feel sick, knowing that it was her presence that was causing such discontent between them.

If she had been braver, she would have waited outside for Johannes to come home this afternoon. She could have warned him about Annarita's revelations, that their plan to conceal her true identity had failed. But instead, she had buried herself under the comfort of the bed covers for the afternoon, refusing to face this new exposure.

Hiding herself in their bedroom had seemed the safest option – to give Johannes time to talk to his sister on his own - but now she wondered if that had been a cowardly move on her part.

There was no point avoiding the fact that Annarita and Frederick knew she was from a foreign world. A fact that made it hard to process that they had still let her move in with him despite this secret knowledge. Now, she just hoped Johannes would not let his emotions get the better of him, like suggesting they do something outrageous such as running away. He certainly sounded exasperated with the news that they had been outed. It was obvious by the way he was stamping his feet downstairs.

Careful not to make her movements known, she forced herself to move off the bed. Luckily, she had detected the floor's weak points on her first night here. She knew how to move across it in silence. Her heart pounded in her chest as she opened the door. It was Johannes' voice that boomed out the loudest and she could hear the anguish all the way up the stairs.

Go to him!

She willed herself. Her right foot moved forward, ready to take the first step downstairs, to where the rest of the household was engaged in a heated discussion. But she stopped in her tracks at the sound of fury coming from Johannes.

"You did what? You asked Elna if she thought we were lying about where Tiegal came from? Why would you do that? Where is your loyalty?" Johannes shouted.

"Oh Johannes. Come on now, you know that Elna wouldn't have wanted to cause trouble intentionally. We all knew there had to be more to this story," Annarita reasoned.

"What? Why are you defending Elna now? You didn't even like her that much when we were together!"

"I *did* like her Johannes. I just didn't want you to be held down by some stupid pact our father had made all those years ago. But then when Elna came back here, I could see she was in obvious pain. And then there was that awful day in the bush. She was so upset, as you know, so I spent some time with her afterwards, to make sure she was okay. I wanted to know what was going on with you.

"But I *did* think she was crazy at first. She told me how you had seen a girl in a bubble across the river, who somehow *appeared* and then just *disappeared*, and that it was your reaction to seeing her that made her leave Hopetown."

Tiegal heard Johannes' growl and then Frederick's heavier footsteps walking across the kitchen, his deep, gentle voice pleading for them both to calm down.

"Hey, keep your voices down. You are going to upset Henri. Let's just talk about this clearly, and start afresh, from the beginning. No more secrets!"

But it was too late for the moment to be taken back. Hearing Annarita's words had sent a shock wave of pain up and down Tiegal's body. It hadn't occurred to her that Annarita and Elna had become closer, or that they had since become *friends*. This changed everything. How could she and Annarita share a bond if Elna had told her that she and Johannes had lied about where she came from?

It's my fault! She reprimanded herself, pressing her right foot down hard on her left in frustration.

I should have tried harder to be Elna's friend. I promised I would!

"But you didn't try hard enough!" Tiegal whispered angrily, reprimanding herself both silently and audibly.

No wonder Elna exposed us and our lies. How could I blame her for that? She hasn't seen me since the day Kagiso died. She wouldn't know that I have tried to get close to her many times but every time I did, my fire started burning out of me again.

A solid lump lodged in her throat making it harder for Tiegal to breathe. Her body seemed to be reacting to her emotional distress in a dangerous way. The skin under her fingernails burned pulsations of angry fire. The suddenness of it made her flinch. She shoved both her hands into the caves of her armpits, clamping her arms down over them, already aware of the smell of smoke emanating from them. This was the other extreme of her emotional energy, where all her fears and loneliness threatened to escape in an excruciatingly visible display. She had to hide this. Even Johannes may reject her if he saw she contained a darker energy inside her.

Calm down! Breathe!

She scolded herself inwardly, desperately inhaling the air around her in a bid to control her breathing again. The sound of Johannes' footsteps pounding up the stairs towards her made her heart beat even faster. Squeezing her eyes shut, she silently pleaded for him to retreat back to the sanity of a normal, human, family argument. It had to be preferable to him getting any closer to the strangeness of her body.

"Tiegal! What are you doing here like this?" Johannes' hands clamped over the tops of her arms. She shrugged him away, scared that he would feel the heat coming out of her or that he would see the wisps of black mist swirling inside the huddle of her frame.

"Please..." she managed. "Just leave me for a bit. I want to be alone."

"What? Don't be silly. You hate being alone. It's all a misunderstanding that's all."

"Johannes. She knows who I am. Annarita knows we lied to her."

"No, no, you must not think like that," he whispered in her ear, leaning into her. It was getting hard to keep her hands tucked away. The heat was becoming unbearable. But she did not dare to unfold them, not while she was releasing some part of herself, that she had not known existed before now.

"Look, Tiegal, come on, she just heard a story that no one would ever believe, and she connected the two together, thinking it was you and..."

"She knows it is true Johannes. Elna knows it too!" She managed to interrupt in between her gulps for air. Even though her eyes were still closed she could imagine his expression clearly, and the deep frustrated frown he wore when his search for the right words to say to her failed him.

"Why do you always think the worst?" she heard him mutter in front of her.

This response *did* surprise her. It was unlike him to be so blatant in his criticism of her. Pulling her hands out to rest on her lap she breathed a sigh of relief as the burning sensation under her arms subsided.

"Are you okay? You've got a strange colour around you and your face is pure *white*!"

She could hear how laboured his breathing was, how the panic was setting in.

"Annarita! Come! *Now!*" He screamed his order for his sister's help. She tried to protest but she couldn't find her voice. The last thing she wanted right now was for Annarita to see her like this, how she was revealing the worst parts of both her worlds, this magnified jealousy emotion that seemed to have manifested itself since becoming human, and the residue of her original make-up.

But her new sister was at her side before she had a chance to object to her presence.

"Tiegal! You look terrible. We need to get you back to bed," Annarita insisted. Hearing the warmth and acceptance in her voice instantly settled her. She managed to flicker her eyes upwards to meet Annarita's concerned gaze and nodded her head to show her grateful assent. The sensation of hands holding her arms and of being lifted off the ground, then moved through to the bedroom and gently lowered onto the bed, felt surreal in its swiftness.

"I don't feel too good," she managed to whisper, searching for Johannes despite her limited visibility. She was so weak she didn't even have the strength to open her eyes fully. His warm hands were on her cheeks before she could say anything else, the things she needed to let them know. She was in danger, and her body was losing its energy.

27.VIBRATIONS

Her need for a deeper energy reserve was like a thirst she could not quench. For two days now her body had vibrated at a constant and visible high frequency. It was impossible to move from the bed. She had tried many times, but she would simply fall to the floor, laying in a helpless, shuddering trance.

Both Johannes and Annarita – and even Frederick – had brought her food of every variety they could think of, but nothing offered her the rejuvenation she needed.

There were a number of reasons she could attribute to the change in her physical state. None of them she was prepared to share with her family. How could she tell them that she would not survive with them for much longer? That she would soon have to choose between love and emptiness, between life and death.

"Hey, are you awake? Can I come in?"

It was Annarita. She was never far away. Although she did not have the strength to project her voice, she managed to make a noise that sounded welcoming enough. She heard Annarita's soft footsteps approach the bed.

"I've just bathed Henri and he is having his afternoon nap, so I wanted to see what I could bring you. You still haven't eaten anything today." Annarita's voice was a sing-song chirrup. An ill-disguised attempt to sound cheerful despite how terrifying the scene before her must appear.

"What colour am I now?" Tiegal stammered.

"Erm...you look good actually. Not as dark as before." Annarita's response was too quick.

"Tell me the truth. Please."

Before Johannes had removed the dressing mirror from the room, she had managed to catch a glance at her reflection a few times. That's how she knew that what was left of her colour energy had risen to the surface as a constant vapour that circled her fragile body. The last time she had seen her reflection she was surrounded by a dark, grey mist. The sight had made her scream, a release of emotion that had so exhausted her that she had not been able to wake up for hours.

"Oh, Tiegal, sweetheart. You are still looking a bit grey, but don't you worry. Johannes has taken a trip over to see someone he thinks will be able to help you."

This news made her flinch. She knew where he had gone. As much as he tried to hide what he was thinking when he was near her, it was impossible for him to break the connection she shared with him in this way, low energy or not. She had never been able to access someone's thoughts, *and* their intentions, the way she could with him.

"Why does he think *she* can help?" she managed to ask, closing her eyes to preserve the little reserves she had so she could talk to Annarita.

"Erm, Johannes thinks she is the cause of it all."

Annarita was being careful with her words. Tiegal could detect her reticence, how she feared upsetting her new sister again by mentioning any connection to Elna.

Just hearing how tortured Annarita was about the part she believed she had played in Tiegal's breakdown was torturous in itself.

As tired and frightened as she was, she owed it to this beautiful soul, who rarely left her side, to help rid her of this unfairly imposed guilt.

"This is not your fault Annarita. You have given me more energy than you can ever know by being my sister and by welcoming me into your family."

"Oh, but it *is* my fault dear Tiegal. I never should have said those things to Johannes about you driving Elna away when you arrived here. That wasn't my concern at all. But I can imagine it would have sounded like I was angry. I just wanted to know the truth, to make sure that you were both safe. I want you to believe that. You are a gift that came to us, and especially to my brother, at a time when he needed light more than ever."

The heartbreak in Annarita's voice was enough to force whatever human energy Tiegal had absorbed to rejuvenate, just enough that she could turn her head to her sister and reach her right arm up from its dangled position over the side of the bed. It was time for her to explain herself, whilst she still could.

"Don't overexert yourself Tiegal!" Annarita warned.

"Sister, please, let me talk while I have enough strength. I want you to know something about me. Where I have come from, who I am, and what I may become." She paused to catch her breath and then, when she felt her breathing was steady enough, she continued her carefully rehearsed speech.

"The world I came from did not allow its people to connect, to form bonds, or to love one another. You do not have family in Tandro. Your purpose is to protect your own self, your own island, and not to let anyone else enter it. My ruler, Atla, was part of a group of scientists who made a decision to start a new society; a new world, within a world that had been destroyed. This all happened at a time in my past, before I was even created, but at a time in, well, I imagine a parallel version of your future."

"Sorry, I'm confused? So, you are from the future on here, on Earth, or from somewhere else?"

"I'm not sure. I *feel* that my world is not this one in the past but that it is a *version* of this world, but in the future somehow, two hundred years from now."

"Okaaaay, well..."

"I know Annarita. It stretches beyond anyone's imagination."

"But I still believe you Tiegal. I can see you and all your colours. That in itself is enough for me to know that I have to also let myself believe in the things I *cannot* see too."

Tiegal exhaled her relief. "You have no idea how much that means to me. Do you want me to tell you more?"

"Yes, please, I want to know everything there is to know about you," Annarita pleaded, holding tightly on her hand.

Tiegal nodded and took a deep breath. It was a long, complicated story but she had to make it concise and somehow believable to Annarita. Even *she* found her own story implausible if she thought about it too much.

"There was a time, long before I was created, when a catastrophic war finally ended on our world. That's when everything was destroyed. Only the ones who had the means to hide and survive did. And only they could choose how to start it all again. And that's what they did. They designed Tandro out of the only habitable archipelago of islands on the planet. And from there, they made the new creation process: the children of diamonds. Which is what I am!" She paused, only continuing when Annarita squeezed her hand again.

"No one made me out of love the way your parents did Annarita. I may have developed in a creation pod, a cocoon suspended in water, not too dissimilar to a womb in a mother's fluid, but I am really just a whole bunch of energies from many others. From Tandroans who competed and won a series of challenges we call a Jarm Match. It's the greatest honour on Tandro, to be one who contributes parts of their carbon to further the evolution of our species."

She waited to see if Annarita would walk out of the room in disgust at hearing such lies, but instead she was met with an expression that conveyed a quiet acceptance.

"You know how Johannes told you I could hear your thoughts?" she dared.

Annarita nodded.

"He did tell me that. I have to say that one *did* scare me - and Frederick - quite a lot!"

"Well, don't worry too much. Those powers have diminished considerably since I have been here. It's only Johannes that I can still hear as if it is my own thoughts in my head."

"That must be because you are so connected to each other! And maybe that's why you didn't realise that I already knew you had made up the story about an accident? I wondered why you had not already worked that part out when Johannes told me about this gift. If you could read my thoughts?" Annarita suggested.

"I didn't even try to read your thoughts too much when I first met you. I was enjoying how human I thought I was becoming. I was so excited to think we could be sisters and friends. Companionship like that is not encouraged where I am from."

"But why? This is the part that I just can't understand. You are an abundance of love! It pours out of you. I can't imagine how you could have come from such a world. You have must have felt so lonely."

Annarita's hands felt warm to touch. Her words, even more so.

"How wise you are, and so very like your brother. It still amazes me how open your hearts and minds are – both of you. Your mother must have been a special lady."

Annarita's eyes glistened with pools of tears.

"She was. You remind me of her. I can't explain why."

"Johannes said the same thing. He also thought, at one time, that I reminded him of Elna," Tiegal dared.

"Okay, well, now I am glad you have mentioned that." Annarita rolled her eyes at her.

"The elephant in the room?"

"Sorry? I don't know what that means?"

"It means, at least in my world, the mistake everyone fails to notice. Well, that is what it is supposed to mean but I prefer to think of it as the obvious truth that no one wants to acknowledge." She waited to see if Annarita would object to her placement of this expression in their conversation. When she saw how confused Annarita looked she quickly clarified:

"I don't think of Johannes and Elna as a mistake. Please don't think of me like that. Even though I know I must appear to be jealous about her to the point of destruction."

Annarita let out a sad sounding chuckle.

"I don't think of you like that and I don't think of Elna as a mistake either. I just know that the people you meet in your life have a message to share with you and you should embrace that."

Tiegal twisted her head to get a better look at her new sister.

"Where did you get such ideas from?"

Annarita shrugged her shoulders.

"You! It's like ever since I met you, I have this whole new way of thinking. It's like you and this energy of yours is so compelling that I have absorbed it too and I just *think* differently. Frederick has noticed it too and he loves it. He says I am like the old me again. Before all the tragedies. But an even better me, lighter, happier and more open. It's like you are my friend soul mate!"

"Your mirror?"

"Yes! You made me see myself differently and what I was capable of thinking and seeing," Annarita exclaimed, blinking excitedly as she rushed her words out.

"But that's not what we were talking about Tiegal. Now, I am going to point to this elephant in the room idea you talk about because I want you to stop feeling guilty about Elna. I know it's not jealousy that is making you so sad about her. It is what you still believe *you* caused by appearing in front of them when they kissed that day. That you feel responsible for their break-up and even for Kagiso's death. And even crazier, you feel guilty that you love Johannes and that he loves you, but Elna is the one who is suffering because of it. Am I right?"

"Every word," Tiegal admitted, no longer able to keep her gaze on Annarita's. All these revelations and confessions were making her feel dizzy again. Luckily, Annarita was full of enthusiasm and happy to lead their conversation.

"Okay, good, so now I can tell you the truth. Will that help relieve you from this burden you have placed on yourself? Will it set you free?"

Tiegal nodded. She could not believe how similar their thinking had become. It was almost as if Annarita had absorbed some of her own thoughts – was looking after her energy for her while she recovered – and was now holding a mirror to her through her words.

She was not even speaking in her usual way or using words that were common to her area and experience. It was like she had become her echo!

"Here it goes. So, Elna and Johannes shared an early, first love. Not even that, but perhaps more of a familiar, easy, connection. Is that something you can understand at all? I know it may be difficult if your world did not allow connections at all," Annarita asked carefully.

"No, I do understand that. My friend Rinzal and I shared an easy connection. I used to worry that he felt things for me in a deeper way, which was also forbidden, but I held back from it because I knew it would hurt him if my dream prophecy came true. That I would eventually find the male I had been dreaming about – your brother as it turns out!"

She gave Annarita a shy smile, which quickly turned into a yawn. It made her think of Rinzal even more. It was easy to conjure an image of him rolling his eyes at her, and to imagine what he would say to her if he could be part of this conversation now. No doubt something on the lines of:

"And you thought it was difficult being a Tandroan! Look at you now then! You have almost extinguished yourself by burning all your energy with these human emotions."

"I did always like Rinzal's smell," she explained to Annarita, "which to me, is so important. But...there is a good scent and there is an intoxicating scent – and that is what Johannes is. I can't get enough of him."

Annarita clapped her hands in delight.

"Exactly! So, you see, perhaps then these earlier experiences have shaped you and made you ready and prepared to meet your *perfect* connection - which you have!"

Her words sounded like a hum of a memory, of sunbirds vibrating their wings outside the windows of her prison cabin on Tandro. What Annarita spoke of lay at the heart of her personal philosophy and yet she had not even spoken these words herself. It had taken meeting both her soul lover in Johannes and her soul best friend in Rinzal, for it all to connect together.

Tiegal felt ready to take over now.

"So, maybe the people who come into our lives shape us. Like a diamond cutter shapes a rough stone and transforms it into a multi-faceted light reflector. One that sparkles with brilliance. In the same way, our love interactions will shape us too! And even if some of these connections are broken, like Johannes and Elna, or me and Rinzal, as our paths diverge, their influence on us will never leave us? It is as though they have given us a memory that transforms us into who we are – human or Tandroan!" she declared.

"Well, I don't know anything about how diamonds are shaped or cut Tiegal, but somehow, I can see what you are saying. You were made from the energy of diamonds, and the connections you made both in your world, and here, have shaped you into this amazing light in our lives."

Annarita shook her head as if she were surprised to hear the words coming out of her own mouth.

"I am not so bright now! I am grey, and black, and weak," Tiegal pointed out.

"But maybe that's because you lost something when you heard Johannes and I arguing. Perhaps that kind of talking between people frightened you because it is so different from how you lived amongst your people before? You said you were supposed to protect your fire and your island and not let anyone enter it? Well, trust me, when you live in a family, as we do, it is impossible not to cross each other's islands and, yes perhaps we do pour water on each other's fires when we get angry with them. But, you see, we just as soon hand them some more logs and we help them light it up again when we show them our love."

They both turned their heads at the sound of footsteps outside the door.

Johannes beamed at them both from where he stood at the entrance to the bedroom.

"My two beautiful girls! What have you turned each other into? I can't tell who is teaching their diamond philosophy to whom? But it's beautiful all round. And, Tiegal! You are getting your pinker colours back," he enthused, clearly delighted by the scene that he had returned to.

Tiegal watched as Annarita held her hand out to him, beckoning for him to join her at the bedside.

"I think she is getting her energy back. We just have to keep showing her how much we want her here."

Johannes frowned at that. "You don't need to tell me that Sis. Tiegal knows she is the world to me."

Tiegal widened her eyes, feeling strong enough to keep them open for long enough to maintain her blurry gaze over them both.

"You two are funny. I sometimes think it would be easier if you could both hear what the other really thinks. Annarita didn't mean it as a criticism," she pointed out.

The sound of startled awakening resounded from the hallway where Annarita had placed the crib. Henri was awake and ready for attention.

"There is my calling! It's time for you both to have some privacy anyway. I will start making us some supper once I get Henri settled," Annarita promised as she lent down to give Tiegal a kiss on her forehead.

"You feel warmer again now. Everything is going to be okay sister."

Annarita winked and then scurried out of the room to tend to the insistent cries of her baby, leaving Tiegal and Johannes alone, both unable to tear their eyes away from each other.

"I missed you," she whispered.

"You have no idea how much I missed *you!* And seeing your true colours. It's pink again now. Only faint, but that horrible dark colour has gone at last. You look like you again."

He sighed. She could smell the relief on him, the muskiness of his sweat from the insufferable heat he endured on his journey to the fields, mixed with the release of endorphins from the pleasure of seeing her nearly restored to full health.

"Did you find what you were looking for?" she dared to ask.

"I guess you heard my plan. That I went to see Elna? To see if she could give me any answers, to help you, of course! Are you mad?" he asked her, his fingers running up and down her arms as he shuffled himself closer to her on the bed.

"Lie next to me. I want to breathe you in now that I have more strength again. And, no, of course I'm not mad," she answered.

He placed both hands on her hips to slide her body to the edge of the bed so that she fitted into the wall, making enough space for him to lay down next to her. As soon as his head rested on the pillow next to hers, they turned to face each other, their lips finding each other's in an instant.

"You still smell delicious, even when you have not eaten or drunk properly for days," he mused. "I think you have extra water inside of you, which is why you are so fresh all the time. A good theory hey?"

Without answering him, she nuzzled her nose next to his, rubbing the tips against each others, relishing the feeling of having him so close to her again.

"Thank you for trying to find the answer for me. I know how hot it is out there and how much work you need to do. Did you make your peace with her, with Elna?"

Johannes nodded. "I did, yes, and you were right. She admitted that she had told you about what happened on the day my father died."

"Oh no. Oh Johannes. It doesn't bother me! That's not why I've been so grey. You must not think that. You were only a child. How could you know he would react the way he did?" She started to protest.

"Shh...I know that now. Elna explained that you talked it out between you and that you were very understanding. She was very apologetic about it all."

Her heart raced as she watched him run his hands through his hair. But then he gave her a reassuring smile, that somehow reached his eyes despite how tired she could sense he was, and her shoulders relaxed.

"At first, I was angry with her. I didn't want to think that you had heard something I felt so ashamed about from someone else, but then I realised that was unkind of me. And that I was the one who should apologise to her!

"Anyway, when she had dried her tears, she went on to explain the rest of it. About why she really went away. Something about the day we first saw you in that bubble of yours and how the experience consumed her with strange thoughts that she just couldn't shake off. She said it made her feel that her being with me, on that day, had disrupted my destiny somehow! She cried her eyes out as she told me this, terrified that she sounded crazy. Of course, I told her not to worry about *that*! Not after everything that has happened!"

Johannes shook his head, clearly dismayed and exhausted by the energy he had exerted trying to unravel it all.

"And she also said to tell you that she would like, one day, when she is ready...to be your friend. Now that she has accepted our remarkable connection with each other, it seems she has found some peace in herself too."

Tiegal, using all the strength she had, pulled him to her. As soon as she was strong enough, she would venture near Elna's house again.

"I am so relieved you made peace with her. And I am also sorry that I scared you these last few days Johannes," she breathed, enjoying how their hips rubbed together, their bodies so quick to gravitate to each others. It didn't surprise her when his body reacted to her so quickly. Giving him a little nudge, she managed a little chuckle into his shoulders.

"I don't think I have enough energy for anything like that Johannes, but we can still hold each other. I'm feeling better by the second now that you are here," she assured him, knowing how the fear for her safety was still raging inside of him. It hurt her to think of him filled with so much worry.

"And hey, you can rest with ease now. I am not going anywhere. Annarita and I had an epiphany in our talk just now. I think I am beginning to understand what being human entails. My body has just needed some time to adapt, that's all," she explained, hoping her theory would settle him, for now.

"You mean having emotions? Being sad, angry, hurt and upset, like we all were the other day?" He yawned his question into her hair.

"Exactly! But I'm all yours now. No more guilt about the past or misunderstandings. I'm ready to be part of this family now."

"That's my girl. And don't forget your dreams too. That they would tell you when the time was right. When we can finally release ourselves, together, to make our own family at last?"

She nodded, burying her face into his hair.

"I was just thinking about that. Maybe we don't need to wait for a dream anymore? I mean, if I am going to let myself embrace being human, I think we should just follow the dreams we *feel* In our hearts?" she resolved. Her voice rose and fell in the wave of a yawn, matching his own.

"Hmm... Only if I get to play the main role in this dream reality."

"Always! Never question that! You're a part of me now Johannes. You transformed me into someone who can love and be loved. I feel you with me even when you're not here."

She exhaled her words in a rush, now out of breath, but unable to resist the urge to pull him even closer to her. She could tell by the way he was holding her how much he wanted her.

"I'm always with you. You should never question that either. You let me enter your island and now I'm staying there for good!"

Her laughter was muffled by his kisses, urgent caresses that he planted all over her cheeks and lips, intent on filling her with his relief and love.

"Now, you, get some sleep. It's my job to keep your fire going but it needs some fuel. Any more kisses like that and I think we both burn ourselves out too soon."

"Hmm...okay. Maybe tomorrow then..." she managed to whisper. Closing her eyes, she felt herself drifting into sleep, finally believing that things were falling into place.

28. VISIONS

The dream kept stopping and starting. She could only make out snippets and flashes. It had captured her in complete darkness. And no matter how many times she blinked she couldn't get her eye-lights to reactivate. It seemed her transformation to human had transcended into her dreams.

All she knew was that she was in great pain. That she was in danger. And that she needed Johannes to rescue her. But he was nowhere to be found.

A flash of light illuminated the scene.

There was blood all around her, on her clothes, on the floor...

Flash.

Dark again. Only the sound of a female screaming in pain. It sounded like her voice.

And then another flash.

Her hands reaching for something, under the bed...

Darkness once more.

A final flash.

It was Parador, watching from the corner of the room. She was making a tutting noise and shaking her head. Her lips were moving, silently forming words. They were easy to read:

"Tiegal, you have to make the choice...love ...or death?"

That she would soon bear a child was not breaking news. They had all had months to get used to the excitement. Still, all three of them stared at her, equally transfixed by her swollen stomach.

Tiegal smiled, both amused and slightly irritated by their obsessive fascination with her body. Leaning back in this arch position made the urge to go to the toilet even stronger, and although she wanted to shift her body further back into the chair, she decided to let her baby perform her acrobatics inside her stomach for them a little while longer.

"I have never seen such an active pregnancy! She never stops moving. It must be exhausting Tiegal!" Annarita frowned, unable to hide her obvious worry. It was Frederick who rolled his eyes first, swiftly followed by Johannes.

"Stop worrying!" both men chimed at the same time.

"I'm just being a good sister! Henri hardly moved at all inside me. I just want to know that she is comfortable that's all," Annarita argued. She always got defensive when anyone questioned her protective nature towards Tiegal.

"Are you still insisting it is a girl then?" Frederick teased. He also knew how adamant his wife was about this, but it amused him to question her about her conviction.

Annarita just groaned and gave him a playful slap.

Tiegal smiled and let herself fall back into the chair again. Before she had a chance to ask, Johannes was up on his feet, already rubbing his hands together to warm them up. He was the only one who knew how to massage her back in a way that quickly eased the pain. He was also the only one who could lull their growing baby into a sleep - if they were lucky.

"Thank you, Jo Jo," she grunted.

"Jo Jo?" Annarita squeaked. "Since when have you started calling him that?"

"Since she started mumbling it in her sleep. I did ask her if she had found another handsome farmer around here that I didn't know about." Johannes grinned at his sister, who returned her almost identical, slightly crooked smile back at him.

"Well, I kind of like it. Pa always hated it when we tried to shorten our names. He used to say that we should respect the full names we were given. But then, Frederick still tries to call me Nita sometimes, even though I've told him to stop," she reprimanded her husband, landing a playful thump on his good arm.

"Anna then?" Frederick tried.

Annarita ignored him. She still wore her troubled frown.

"What's bothering you so much today lovely?" Tiegal asked her eventually. She squeezed her eyes shut, slowly inhaling and exhaling as Annarita had taught her, to help relieve the discomfort of the baby's weight bearing down on her internal organs.

A part of her didn't really want to know why Annarita was so stressed by her growing pregnancy, she didn't see how these anxieties were helping any of them. The baby was going to be big. She would just have to manage it. There was no way she was going to let anything happen to her. This new life growing inside her was the reason for her dreams, her desires and this remarkable love connection she shared with Johannes that had drawn her over to him.

"I'm not bothered as such. I just had another bad night's sleep that's all," Annarita lied.

They all knew how excellent Henri's sleep patterns had become since he had started walking. The little boy spent all day on his feet, exerting every ounce of his energy during his waking hours. By the time sunset came, he was in the land of slumber before anyone had the chance to read him a story.

No one challenged Annarita's reasoning though. There was a time, not so long ago, when Tiegal could have uncovered the truth behind a thinly veiled lie with just a look. But, not anymore. Those powers had long gone. Now, she had to rely on her intuition and body language as much as anyone else. And she couldn't be happier that she had transformed in this way. It was a blessing to live this relative life of silence. It was only Johannes' internal dialogue she occasionally picked up on. Their connection was much harder to break, transformed or not.

Feeling uncomfortable again, she jerked her hips from side to side to encourage Johannes to take a break from massaging her. She still hated tearing herself away from him, in any capacity, but her back was now starting to get sore from his hands repetitively rubbing on her skin.

"As much as I love your touch Jo Jo, I'm okay now thank you. I think Cezanne has finally decided to give me some rest!"

The moment she said the words she realised she had revealed more than she had intended.

"Oops!" she sent an apologetic look to Johannes who just smiled and shrugged at her.

"Well you've said it now!" he teased.

Annarita was already crying.

"Really? You are going to call her Cezanne," she spluttered between her sobs.

Tiegal nodded at her, blinded by the sudden appearance of her own tears.

"You both always say how much I remind you of your mother. It wasn't even a debate. We knew we would name our baby after her."

Johannes bent down to tie his shoelaces. She suspected he was crying too.

It was only Frederick who looked confused, rather than emotionally distraught as the rest of them did.

"So, you *all* assume she will be a girl then?" Frederick asked.

Johannes answered this time:

"Tiegal may be ninety percent human these days, but she still dreams predictions for the future sometimes. Rest assured we will have a baby girl we will call Cezanne joining us shortly," he announced in a loud, proud voice.

Annarita gasped, hands on her hips, tears still running down her freckled cheeks.

"So, you have dreamed her? You know what she looks like as well?"

Tiegal leaned forward, reaching her hand out to her sister.

"I would say she looks a lot like the wonderful lady she is named after."

This couldn't happen now, not yet. Johannes was not due home for another two hours and Annarita and Frederick had taken Henri for his afternoon walk.

The pain was getting stronger, the tightness forcing her to bend over. Sheer terror engulfed her. Just the thought of what could happen, if the baby tried to make an appearance before her family returned, made her shudder with violent tremors. It was unthinkable! It was dangerous. And she had no idea what to do, or *how* it should happen.

For some reason, an image of Namnum flashed in her mind, a memory of the day the animal had given birth. How calm she had been as she had transitioned, hardly making a sound. It seemed strange – or fortuitous even – that such a memory would appear to her at this time. And yet the vision was almost in front of her, surrounding her even.

The sun was blazing hot that day, when Namnum gave birth. Tiegal could recall clearly how serene the majestic elephant had looked, as her baby slipped from her body; she could detect the distinct odour in the animal birth scene: primal, earthy, bloody.

It was such a bizarre feeling to think of that life now, and yet it was exactly the right memory to bring her the resilience she needed. Her baby was moving downwards, inside her. This was not a practice. Cezanne was on her way.

Without making a sound, Tiegal got down on all fours, and let out the loudest noise she could summon. It came from somewhere deep inside her. It was a release. One that urged the pain to leave her, and one, she suddenly realised, that threatened to change her – again.

She heard the clock chime in the hallway outside her bedroom. Four o'clock! The baby would surely arrive before the others returned.

Tiegal looked down at her hands, stretched out like fans on the wooden floor. They were already starting to fade. She let her elbows drop down, her bottom arched upwards towards the ceiling. It was a relieving position, both for her weight balance and to counteract the pain of the contractions. Her baby had already made it into the birth canal, bearing down with force. Cezanne was getting impatient.

Tiegal cried out again, terrified by her own ignorance of what could happen – or more importantly, what could go wrong. Her memory of an animal giving birth was no help for her now. If only she had seen another human, or even a Tandroan do this, then she could find comfort in knowing that her body was capable of doing this.

"Come on now baby girl. It's all going to be okay. Take it easy. Let me breathe a bit more."

As the pain engulfed her, she let out one long, horrific scream. It rose in a wave from her bottom, shooting up to the back of her ribs, before finally releasing from her throat. Her screech made her cough, followed by the sensation of liquid filling her mouth. It was a metallic taste, and one she did not recognise. Without thinking, she spat it out onto the floor. Droplets of blood splattered in front of her. This time she didn't scream. Instead, the bloody scene before her, stunned her into silence.

Stupid girl Tiegal! How could you have blocked this one? The most important dream warning of your life and you didn't listen to it!

"No! Cezanne, no!" she wailed in a broken whisper.

She must have blocked out this traumatic nightmare. It was only just coming back to her now – the ominous dream that had prophesized the dangers around Cezanne's birth. The warning of the hideous choice that she would be forced to make.

Visions of the dream now crashed all around her, in flashes of horrific scenes. Her desperate screams, her blood, so much of it, spilling out of her body, and...something else...

"There were two versions!" she spluttered, sinking her teeth into her arm to deter the pain away from her groin.

It was all coming back. She could recall that there was a juncture in this dream prophecy; a decisive point in which she would have to choose how this part of her story – and her baby's – would play out.

"I'm not going to let you die," she grunted her promise, bent-over and rocking on her knees. If she stayed in this position for much longer, and did nothing else, her baby girl would not survive. That scenario - version one of her dream - was not an option.

"But I'm not going to leave you either! I can't do that to you. I need to be with..." she wept, unable to finish her promise.

Both versions of her dream prophecy had delivered horrific, final results. But, even so, the second version - the one where she engaged the help of her Derado - was the only one that offered her daughter a fighting chance.

Pulling herself into an up-right position, she grabbed the side of the bed to steady herself.

"Think Tiegal!" she growled, grasping at the bed sheets with one hand and squeezing the upper part of her thigh with the other. The pain was too intense for her mind to make rational decisions. A parlayzing spasm flared all around her stomach and her back; a compression that felt like a thousand daggers stabbing at the middle of her body.

Despite the terrifying sensation of helplessness that shuddered through her, and the gripping tightening of her abdomen, she forced herself to lift up her head and focus on the objects that surrounded her. There had to be something in here that would provide an answer to keep them both alive, and together.

Faded, lace-fringed curtains billowed in the fresh spring breeze through the slightly jarred window. A ceramic washing bowl lay on its side, that she had dropped and left abandoned in the shock of her first contraction. One of Johannes' felt brown hats hung on the back of the dark wooden chair she had taken to reading in. And next to it lay a neatly folded woollen kaross. That was it! The sign she had been searching for.

"Ka...gi...so!" Tiegal whispered, barely able to form any words between her desperate gasps for air. She remembered Johannes saying the kaross had belonged to Kagiso. It was drenched in her scent, and it appeared to be releasing her vapour, an intoxicating, but pleasant smell, that was so strong it overrode the sweet, musky odour of Tiegal's birthing water, that had gushed out between her legs only moments before.

Come on, Tiegal. Why can you smell Kagiso so vividly now!

Squeezing her eyes shut she breathed in the strong scent, determined to empty her mind from the distraction of her physical pain. There had to be a connection.

An image of Johannes holding the kaross to his face filled her mind. In this vision, he was younger, perhaps of an age between childhood and early adulthood? And he appeared to be burying himself into the wool, whispering tearful words into the soft texture, in a voice that had not quite broken into the lower tone she was so familiar with.

"You promised you would never leave me! You promised me you would always be here. Even if I can't see you. But you're *not* here, are you? You're dead! How can you be here if you're not even in this world anymore!" the younger Johannes wailed.

His anguished cries made her body spasm in sympathy, only to be followed by another contraction across her front and back; a sharp reminder of Cezanne's imminent arrival.

Despite the double onslaught of jolting pain, she opened her eyes, navigating her way over to the chair in a stumbling, awkward crawl.

Johannes' desperate cries for his mother in her vision had given her the clarity she had been vying for. The kaross must have belonged to his mother, before Kagiso had worn it. It carried the scents of them both. And it represented a connection between the two women who had cared for Johannes, before she had come into his life.

Ignoring the extreme tightening of her stomach, and the discomfort of Cezanne's foot pushing outwards against her skin as she moved further down towards the birth canal, Tiegal grabbed the kaross and rubbed it all over her arms, neck and under her breasts – anywhere where her scent would be absorbed most easily.

A plan had started to form in her mind. The chance of it working was slim, but she had to try, for Cezanne's sake – and Johannes.

And, if it didn't work, at least she could leave them both a part of her, for them to hold on to, until she could find a way to get back to them again.

"Right then, where are you," she groaned, crawling back over to the bed. "Because this really is the only way we can do this."

Although her dream version two had shown her that by wearing her Derado she could generate enough energy inside her to deliver her baby safely, it had also shown her that this energy release would take her away.

"Okay, think!" she ordered herself. "If I locate the Derado now, I could save Cezanne and still have enough energy to keep us both alive without overdoing the release. I just need to take it off before it gets too much!" she reasoned out loud.

The key was to time it right. She knew that if she didn't remove the neckpiece from around her throat before it released too much of her colour energy, she risked being transported away. The prospect of that happening made her body shake violently. She couldn't bear the thought of her baby being born and then left on her own.

But even if that did happen, she knew Annarita and Frederick would be back soon and that they would engulf her baby with their love, as her beautiful father would when he returned too.

And if that *did* happen, then she would just have to endure whatever journey was laid out in front of her. Whatever that was, she would find a way to get back to them again, as soon as was humanly - and Tandroanly - possible.

Another contraction sent a searing pain across her lower back. It knocked her sideways, but she managed to steady herself straight again. She could feel herself building up. If she was going to do this, she had to make it happen now.

The box containing her Derado was under the bed. She knew she had to crawl over to it; she only hoped there was still enough time.

It took every ounce of her willpower to shuffle herself back across the floor. The dusty rug scratched her knees. The wooden slats cut splinters into her arms. She didn't care. Nothing could distract her from her mission. She was full of determination now. The nearer Cezanne came to releasing out of her, the more convinced Tiegal was that she needed to borrow some of her previous energy supply in order to survive the ordeal to bring her daughter safely into this human world.

At last, she rounded the corner to where the bed she shared with Johannes loomed above her twisting, bloody body. She grabbed the cotton sheets in a bid to relieve some of the pain from her right arm and used her left hand to pull out the box which lay dusty and abandoned under the bed. The Derado was inside it. It was their only chance.

It took every last bit of strength she had to maneuver her body into an upright position, so that she could lean against the bed and push the collar around her neck. It felt cold at first, so long rejected and out of use. Yet she knew what she had to do.

It was all happening so fast. Cezanne's head crowned and tore at her bright pink, wet opening as she spread her legs further apart. Tiegal screamed in agony, reaching her hand down to feel in between her legs. Then she cried out in relief as she felt her daughter's hair, full and remarkably long atop new skin and bone. Her daughter was ready to arrive.

But where would she, her mother, be when she did? Here on Earth? Or, back on Tandro?

PART THREE

Tandro
2066 - 2067

Earth 1867 - 1869

29. SACRIFICE

The conditions in the cave were perfect. The air was that delicious balance of both frigid and humid and the lagoon water lapped around her skin in an icy, teasing dance. Her entire body was tingling with excitement.

Parador had waited an entire year to return here. Twelve wasted months spent enduring the obligatory pilgrimage to the rest of the islands, the journey that all Tandroans must take once they receive their Derado. But now she was finally back on Kimberaggo. She was back where she was meant to be. In her birthplace. This secret lagoon, where it all began.

And, she was finally getting close to becoming who she was meant to be, the most powerful Tandroan that had ever been made.

Submerging herself below the surface of the water, she allowed her hands to explore her body. The delicious sensations it conjured through her made her moan and exhale little bubbles around her face.

This was exactly how she had imagined returning to her lagoon, an exquisite few hours where she could honour her precious body on her own again - *her* precious island.

And, even more importantly, where she could absorb the power of the diamonds that lived within it; the precious stones that still contained the memory of her three secret sisters - along with their incredible powers.

"And they don't even remember a thing about it?"

Her laughter exploded around her as she twirled around in circles, absorbing the energy from the diamonds that illuminated the lagoon. Her body vibrated as the memories of her sisters' powers transferred from the luminescent light of the diamonds and filled her Derado. She could feel the magic rushing through her veins.

"Hmmm..." she moaned loudly. Feeling dizzy, she reached out to the stony edge of the lagoon to steady herself. The power that now raged inside her was almost too much to bear.

She growled in frustration. The energy was building up too fast. She needed to release some of it before she hurt herself.

Her Derado burned around her neck, warning her of the risk she was posing to her body. With great reluctance, she pulled herself out of the water and pressed down hard on the turquoise diamond in her pendant. Within seconds, her energy mist released in a thick burst of colour around her.

"There you are!" she breathed out in relief and then smiled as she saw the colour spectacle that danced around her. The unusual combination of her colour energy now gloriously tinged with the energies of her sisters. The tangerine orange from Indramia, the chocolate brown from Ochrani and that deep, rich pink of Tiegal.

"Okay, then, show me what you have."

Leaning back on the cave flooring with her hands stretched out flat behind her she watched in amazement as the colours became stronger and faster in their swirling frenzy.

"Show me what you can do!" Her impatient demand echoed around her.

A picture was already forming from the colour release. Leaning further back, she squinted her eyes.

"There you are!"

Delighted by the euphoric feeling conjured by this new power, she stared, transfixed by the scene before her as it transformed into an image of Tiegal, in her bubble, hovering over a river. The image entranced her to such an extent, that she failed to detect the heavy breathing nearby.

"What have you done?"

The angry male voice that boomed behind her made her jump in alarm. She swung around to face him, her naked frame still dripping wet from her dip in the lagoon.

"Jovil! What are you doing here?"

The lagoon master's eyes were ablaze with fury. His eye-lights pulsated so brightly she could see tinges of blue around the reflections.

"I could ask you the same thing Parador!"

She scowled at him and then swung back round to check if the image was still visible. When she saw it was now merely a faint vapour whispering over the water she walked over to him and pushed him hard in the chest.

"You ruined it!"

"I wouldn't do that if I were you Parador." His voice was calm and even.

"How did you know to come here?"

"You mean, how did I get my memory back?" he hissed.

His calm composure unnerved her. There was something about his anger that was too controlled for her liking. It made her breathing feel laboured and her nose twitch from irritation. All the power she had gained before had already drained.

"What's the matter? You don't look so good." He crouched down in front of her and beckoned for her to mirror his action. "Really... you look like you may faint. And, you really should put on some clothes."

Her legs wobbled, as though responding to his words. Everything was wrong about this. Why was the lagoon master here now? He was supposed to be getting things ready for the forthcoming Jarm Match.

And, how had he regained his memory from the last time they were here?

Sighing, Jovil stood up and took two strides towards her. She could smell his warm breath. It wasn't unpleasant, just too close, too overpowering. She needed some of her mint, but she had left her clothes at the other side of the lagoon.

"I think I have what you need to feel better." He flipped his black cloak out of the way and then reached into the pocket of his dark grey silk trousers and pulled out two large sprigs of mint.

Without thinking, she grabbed it from him and shoved it into her mouth, chewed on the softer leaves, and then spat out the twigs on the floor.

Jovil's eyes widened as he watched her.

"Well, now you really do need to sit down."

As soon as she swallowed, she realised her mistake. Her body was already going into shock. Her throat was so tight she could hardly catch her breath and her heart banged so violently against her chest she felt the need to press her hands against it to hold it in.

"What have you done?" she stammered. Her hands flung out in what she imagined was the direction of his head. She yelped with pain as he caught her wrists in his hands and then yanked her down onto the floor.

Her body immediately started to shake. Already delirious, she was only vaguely aware of his cloak being wrapped around her arms and of being pulled onto his lap so that her back was against his chest.

"Calm down. I have the antidote. You're not going to die. Or, at least you don't have to. I just need you to tell me what you saw just now. In that vision you summoned."

She heard his words, but she couldn't bring herself to register that he had actually used the word 'die'. No one died on Tandro!

But she didn't have the strength to protest, or even to speak. Instead, she let her eyelids drop and her thoughts flow.

You poisoned me! Why would you do that? Do I mean that little to you? Are you only interested in the other daughters you made in this lagoon?

Jovil pulled her tight to his chest. She could sense he was still angry, still dangerous, but she knew he could hear her thoughts. And she could hear his.

Parador. We don't have time for debating which of your sisters I prefer. It's not a game, even though you seem to think it is. You all possess incredible powers, but you have to be careful how you use them. And right now, time is of essence for you. So, if you want that antidote just tell me what you saw in that vision.

She tried to twist her hipbone into his lap, to hurt him in any way she could think of, but whatever he had used to lace that mint had rendered her completely useless.

"It's not a nice feeling being paralysed, is it?" he said into her ear.

Shut up! None of the others can do what I can. Even you have to use chemicals to overpower me. I can do it with my mind, over all of you! And how do you remember what happened in here? You were supposed to forget it all, forever.

"You used the energy you manifested from all of them to manipulate our minds. But what you failed to realise is that it only works when we are all near enough to this lagoon. You have all been on pilgrimages this last year. Tiegal has too, even if hers was somewhere much further away. Your magic will eventually wear off on them, as it did on me. So, now tell me what you saw before your body gets into real trouble!"

With every bone in her body she tried to muster the energy to fight him off her. She was too weak. Her throat was now so tightly closed she was rapidly losing consciousness.

"Okay...I saw her..." she managed to splutter. "She's coming back. And soon..."

"I knew it! I knew she would come back. When?" Jovil cried. "When? Where?"

"The Pyramid... on Release..." She choked, grabbing at his arm.

"Release Day? But...that's tomorrow!"

It was the last thing Parador heard before a honey tasting liquid filled her mouth and she let herself fall asleep.

———————

The hand of a male broke through the sac, her bubble, and grabbed at Tiegal's arm. His fingers slipped through her body, wiggling like he was trying to tickle her. It seemed her body had not yet transported enough for him to take hold. Although she had identifiable limbs her body was still only a buzz of vibrating atoms bonding together to bring her back to her existence in this world, the one where she had been made, but had never truly belonged.

Tiegal knew she had returned to Tandro again. Every essence of her old world engulfed her with one intake of breath. But this return was different. This time she sensed there was a much larger audience waiting for her. She stilled her struggle to allow the sound of muffled voices to reach her:

"Quite extraordinary! My hands travel right through her. It's as though she is rebuilding herself, in front of us!"

"I was just thinking the exact same thing Atla. Quite magical!"

"Magical it is Jovil. When you see it up close, it really is! But then, so is this incredible magic you've been hiding from me all this time. This ability of yours to foresee when something great will happen."

"Ah, it wasn't magic on my part Atla. I just had an intuition that she would return here today. You see, I think Tiegal's ability to transport is linked to two key conditions."

"Which are?"

"Well, looking at the history, I think she has to connect to powerful energy releases. Either from her own release, or a release coming from wherever she transports to. And if I'm right about this, then a Release Day provides the most ideal conditions for this to happen."

"Spoken like a true Lagoon master! You have always had a knack for understanding energies Jovil. That's why I consider you such a valuable asset to my Team."

"Well it's nothing special where Tiegal is concerned. Everyone can see and feel the energy she has conjured in here. Look at how all the Derados are lighting up on everyone. They all seem to be gaining more energy! Which... makes me wonder...if, well, perhaps Parador was mistaken in how she advised you, Atla? The last time she returned you ordered the prison cabin and the experiments. All worth trying, of course, but I now wonder if such confinement was too oppositional to Tiegal's energy."

"What exactly are you proposing Jovil? And where is Parador anyway?"

"Ah, yes, I asked Parador to help with the preparations for the next Jarm Match. She sends her apologies. And, I guess what I am proposing is that we change our approach this time. That we place Tiegal in more agreeable conditions. That we make sure she is happy being back here in Tandro. That we make sure she doesn't leave us again."

Although Jovil's words filtered through to her they did nothing to calm her frantic struggle. Nor did they convince her that what Jovil was proposing could possibly come true.

How could they ever make her feel happy being back here? Not when she had left her newborn baby, gasping for air on the wooden floor of her bedroom on Earth. Alone and helpless, abandoned by her own mother. And worst still, abandoned in another world and another time.

She squeezed her eyes together to shut out the painful vision of her baby girl slipping out of her body, and out of her hands, before she had no choice but to let her rest on the floor without her. Just remembering her first gasps of air, the first wail as her tiny hands flailed out in front of her, sent a burning heat searing through her rapidly transforming body. The pain was so strong she felt as though she could combust.

"My baby!" She wailed inside the bubble that still contained her, twirling herself around in a circle so she could direct her anguish towards each and every one of the blurred figures that surrounded her.

A phrase popped into her head.

What's in a name?

It was Johannes' voice she could hear. A memory of evenings spent together, reading by candlelight. Tiegal would always reply, "Everything is in a name. It was why I willed myself to you from the river the second time, when I heard my name being called".

He would laugh at her then, always with affection.

"But it was not me, my love, as you know. You heard the cry of a *find*, of an answer, from Erasmus, who found the diamond I lost there."

And she would tousle his hair and shake her head, reveling in their game-play and familiar banter.

"It does not matter who said it. It matters that it was said, at the right time. And, that it led me to you," Tiegal would say.

A desperate urge to say her daughter's name out loud burned inside her. There was power in identification. The boldness to declare one's self, their uniqueness, and their truth.

Tiegal roared out her daughter's name into the space of her bubble.

"*Cezanne Eureka Smit!*" She screamed.

The hands that reached out to her immediately withdrew from their attack.

She shouted it again, and again. They would hear her daughter's name. They would know her beautiful child existed.

30. POMELO

The smell of buttery popcorn wafted under her nose, reviving her from the coma that had retained her in the same horizontal bed-ridden state for the last three months.

"Hey, Tiegal, can you hear me? It's me, Rinzal."

After this long period of darkness and silence, the sound of his familiar voice was music to her ears. It sounded as though it chimed in waves around her. The hushing noise he kept making, whenever she attempted to speak - her eyes still closed despite how much she willed them to open - reminded her of the winds rushing through the trees outside the bedroom she and Johannes had shared for all those blissful months as their baby grew inside her.

"You have been asleep for a long time Tiegal, but that is a good thing. You are much stronger now. Don't open your eyes if it is too much for you. Just keep squeezing my hand to let me know you can hear me," Rinzal reassured her.

Squeezing his hand with as much strength as she could muster, she inhaled his smell and then sighed with relief.

"Popcorn," she whispered.

His laughter filled the atmosphere around her. The welcoming sound engaged her natural curiosity and the desperate urge to open her eyes and discover where she now was. She *hoped* it was one of the floating tents, like the one she had shared with Zeno as a kimberling. But, deep down, she knew this was wishful thinking. It was much more likely they had contained her inside a prison cabin again, like the last time she had vanished in front of them.

"Yes, I have brought you popcorn, two big pots of it. Lots of melted butter," Rinzal explained. He sounded excited to hear her voice.

His words made her frown, an action that felt strange and uncomfortable, as though she was *forcing* her facial muscles to respond to her emotions.

"How long have I been here?" she managed. Her eyelids flickered, allowing intermittent shafts of light to reach her. It made her entire body jerk in response. Something felt different, and yet, familiar. Slowly, she dared to let her lids raise up higher. The lights and shapes around her were blurry. Maintaining a steady focus seemed impossible. And yet, strangely, this was not the most shocking part of this awakening experience. Much more disconcerting was how she felt about the visions in front of her, slowly reforming into decipherable shapes that she was seeing deeper again. Like when she was a Tandroan.

She started to cry. Loud, hacking sobs that propelled her knees to reach up to her chest in defence of this pain inside her.

"Oh, Tiegal, please don't cry. It's not as bad as you are imagining. I can hear you clearly. I have been listening to you all this time, watching over you. Both Zeno and I have. She will be back here very soon. And look, I know you have lots of questions, and there is a lot you are missing from where you have come from but it's all going to be okay. I heard your thoughts just then. You were asking if you were back in the prison cabin again, and I can assure you that you are not. Atla learned from his mistake last time.

"He was delighted when you reappeared. Even if you were naked... *and* covered in blood! "

Rinzal hardly stopped to take a breath. His voice contained an intriguing mix of both anxious and excitable energy.

"So, you are in Atla's Estate now. He asked both me and Zeno to keep watch over you as he knows we shared a connection with you, and all he wants right now is to keep you on Tandro, but happier this time, so you don't disappear from us again."

Finally, Rinzal took a break from his long speech. She waited, letting him access her mind, knowing it would enable faster communication this way, and also preserve whatever energy she had. It was obvious that whatever transformation she had been though, that had pulled her back here - even reignited the sparks in her Tandroan eyes - had not recovered all her original abilities. This fact was slowly becoming clearer as she realised that the smell of buttery popcorn was a *real* food scent - not her interpretation of Rinzals' skin or the taste of his name. As hard as she tried, she could not hear a single utterance of Rinzals' thoughts. She let her lungs fall and rise in a deep, gentle rhythm as her thoughts flowed through her mind. Tiegal was determined for Rinzal to hear the pain that tore through her from losing her family. She could sense him listening to her.

After a few minutes of their one-sided silent communication, Rinzal cleared his throat and spoke up again. His voice was much deeper this time, and much quieter.

"You have more friends here than I think you realise and we are all going to help you," he consoled, wrapping his arms around her coiled-up frame.

"My baby..." she started to cry out again.

Rinzal hushed her once again.

"Shh...I know all about her. It's all you have been thinking about during your long sleep. Your daughter *and* her father."

"Jo Jo," she whispered.

"That's right. And it's okay. We *will* get you back to them again. You might just have to be patient, that's all. Just like the name you gave to your baby girl, Cezanne. I can see why you may have chosen this for her. After the lotus, the flower that roots in mud and pushes up through water to bloom."

"And you will find her again this way. It may just take some time to find the right environment. Your roots are entrenched and entwined with hers. But, there *is* some good news Tiegal. You were still holding the cord that attached her to you when you appeared to us again. So we have this - your root connection to her - and now we just have to find the perfect water source that will enable you to propel your way back to her, and to her father, again."

Both Zeno and Rinzal beamed identical, expectant grins as they handed her the plassimer pastry she had asked for. Their matching expressions clearly revealed what they were hoping for in return for their food offering: to see a genuine smile on Tiegal's face. A sign that she was even close to feeling any sense of joy again.

She tried to force her lips to pull back over her teeth, but then quickly gave up, suspecting her attempt would appear more like a grimace than the twinkle they were looking for. There was nothing to feel sparkly about. The taste of sugary pastry was just inciting her sense of longing for her human family even more. It tasted like plastic in her mouth. Annarita's koeksisters were so much tastier.

"So, we have news for you," Zeno declared.

Tiegal raised her eyebrows at her. It was not the first time Zeno had promised a positive development in their plans to get her back home. So far, they had tried sneaking her into the Erasmati Pyramid in a bid to see if the diamond water would help her summon a vision of Johannes and Cezanne; a plan that had failed miserably. Any diamond energy in the water had been absorbed by the last Derado initiation ceremony that had taken place there, which she had interrupted with her bloody reappearance.

All they had achieved was an afternoon of cold feet and disappointments.

"What are you thinking?" she asked Zeno, desperately trying to conceal her negative thoughts from her friend. The last thing she wanted was to sound ungrateful. Rinzal and Zeno were her lifeline here, and the only ones who knew her true intentions – to return back to the Orange River, as she had left her family, in 1867.

It was her only desire. It was all she could hold on to. And yet, the longer she stayed here, in this other world the more she feared she was losing her connection with them.

Over the last few weeks her Tandroan abilities had slowly begun to return to her. Once again, she could hear the thoughts of others, detect their distinct scents, and sometimes even taste their names. Her sensory powers had renewed with the same intensity as before – the strength of which she had only ever experienced as a Tandroan. Gone were the faint whisperings of thoughts, or the gentle, easier, scents that she had become accustomed to on Earth. The subtle hint of blueberry and apple that greeted her whenever Annarita had entered the room, or the waft of sweet bread and syrup that woke her every time Johannes pulled her into his arms for a morning embrace. Now she was back to sensory overload, a constant assault of sounds and smells that just made her want to switch off from everyone around her, even those who had her best interests at heart.

At least Rinzal had taught her how to practice mind concealing again, something he had been determined to do. As he had pointed out on many occasions, relearning how to do this was an absolute priority if she were to stand any chance of getting back to Johannes and Cezanne again. And, as always, she had known he was right.

Zeno glanced at Rinzal, clearly checking permission from him to reveal their plan. When he nodded at her Zeno clapped her hands with excitement.

"Okay, in a few minutes you are going to hear a knock on the door," she started.

"Is this supposed to be one of your jokes?" Tiegal interrupted. She really wasn't in the mood for their games today. Action was what she needed.

"No, of course not, I mean literally, there will be a knock at the door. I don't know why I started explaining it like that."

Rinzal chuckled, giving Zeno a friendly nudge.

"I imagine because you are nervous?" he challenged.

Zeno rolled her eyes at him in exasperation.

"I am *not nervous*. I am just trying to find the right words. I don't want Tiegal using up any of her energy trying to access my mind right now either. She is going to need to hold on to all the reserves she has."

"Okaaay, well this sounds ominous," Tiegal joined in. She had deliberately closed her mind from listening to them as soon as she started hearing the sounds again. Her experience as a human had taught her how exhausting and unnecessary it was to have access to such intrusion. And they were right about preserving her energy too. She knew the fire inside her was a dim flicker at the moment. Her pain and misery at being separated from her loves was like being extinguished by dark rain every day she woke up here.

"No, it's nothing to feel caution about Tiegal. You know you can trust us. The ones we have asked to come here have some vital information to share with you, to help you," Zeno reassured.

Her eyes darted in the direction of the large metal door of Tiegals' assigned bedroom on Atla's Estate. The sound of footsteps approaching made them all turn towards it.

"Who are they? Quick! Give me some warning at least," Tiegal hissed.

She was beginning to feel uneasy at the lack of knowledge she possessed about the visitors approaching them. It was one of the rare times that she wished she *had* opened her mind up to internal voices again. The door creaked open before Zeno had a chance to respond.

Rinzal jumped up from his chair to greet the two female figures who stood next to each other in the doorway. Both of them had adopted identical, rigid, straight-backed poses.

"Ah! Welcome! Thank you for your prompt arrival. We were just about to prepare Tiegal for your appearance, but alas, our timing was not as expeditious as yours." Rinzal exclaimed. Tiegal sucked in her breath. If it were not for the shock of seeing the two females at the door, she would have struggled to contain her laughter at how Rinzal was speaking. Why he was using words like 'alas' and 'expeditious' she had no idea. It seemed he was keen to impress.

"I think I know you already," Tiegal announced, standing up to face them, mirroring the confident soldier-like stance of the figures at her door.

The one on the left, slightly taller, who wore an unusual chocolate coloured diamond in her Derado, was the first to answer.

"We hoped you would recognise us."

The female nodded at her, leaning forward in a suggestion of a courteous bow.

"Ochrani? Indramia?" Tiegal whispered, not knowing where the thought of their names had come from.

"That's right! I am Ochrani and this is Indramia. Do you really remember us? Everything?" Ochrani clapped her hands in front of her face. The sound, along with her excitable mannerism, triggered a flash of a memory. A lagoon that glowed with colourful diamonds, and of a feeling, a powerful yearning to touch and connect with them.

"Yes! Oh my! I *do* remember you both. We held hands in the lagoon. The secret one. The one where we were all made. And Jovil! He was there too. The lagoon master!" Tiegal exclaimed.

The other one, Indramia, appeared to shudder at the recollection.

"I'm so sorry about everything that happened after that. That we failed to rescue you Tiegal. We think our memories of you were wiped from us. This memory has only just come back to us in the last two days, since we returned here to Kimberrago Island. We've been away for the last year on our pilgrimage."

"Me too! I have also been away. And I had forgotten about you too, until just now," Tiegal said, without a hint of restraint. She rocked on her heels, and suddenly giddy with excitement, she became aware of a feeling that she had feared was impossible for her to experience on Tandro ever again.

These two females, her sisters, had unlocked something inside her and opened a door to a deeper part of her memory.

Ochrani cocked her head to the left, and twisted her lips together to the right, as though in deep contemplation.

"And do you remember the other one? The one with the image of a horse's tail in her eye-light?"

Ochrani's statement made Tiegal flinch. There was something dark and ominous about the word 'horse tail' that stilled her, quickly locking her body into a state of shocked paralysis. Zeno shook her arm at the side of her, but she was frozen stiff.

She sensed that both Rinzal and Zeno were pleading with her to do or say something, but she cut them off in her mind. The sound of Ochrani's voice had filled her head, blocking out the voices and thoughts of everyone else around her.

That's right Tiegal! She is the one who paralysed us all in the cave. The one who cleared our memories of each other and then tricked Jovil into turning against you. She made him betray you. That's why you were imprisoned all that time. Because Jovil and Parador told Atla that you needed to be contained.

Tiegal could feel her heartbeat slowing down. Her breathing calmed and a feeling of control washed over her. She closed her eyes to allow the jumbled flashes of memories come together and form a coherent picture.

"Parador? That's her name isn't it? The one who has been taunting my dreams."

Tiegal frowned in frustration as she realized this part was present and yet somehow still blocked from her memory bank. Ochrani and Indramia nodded in unison.

"That sounds like her," they chimed together.

Rinzal and Zeno looked at each other, as though both taken aback by this instant recognition between Tiegal and their visitors.

"I met Ochrani and Indramia when I returned the last time. It's just that we all seem to have lost our memory of it. Until now."

"And who is Parador?" Zeno asked.

Ochrani and Indramia stepped forward. They knocked their shoulders against the narrow walls of the corridor outside the stark grey-coloured room. Rinzal beckoned them.

"Please, do come in," he urged.

Ochrani made the first move into the centre of the sparsely decorated attic room that Tiegal now had no choice but to call her own. Indramia followed, swiftly closing the door behind them both.

"Parador is one of us. By this, I mean she was made from the same batch of carbon contributions that both I, Indramia, *and* Tiegal, were all made from," Ochrani explained.

Indramia leaned forward. She said, "We all seemed to have been granted advanced sensory abilities from this batch. But Parador's *powers* are ones that we are not sure would be too helpful to Tiegal right now. So, we didn't ask her to join us."

Ochrani placed a hand on Indramia's shoulder and stared at her in a way that suggested she was communicating something to Indramia privately.

A few awkward seconds passed before Indramia turned back to face Tiegal and the others.

"Ochrani has just reminded me that not everyone in the room is aware of the similarities and differences between us, or how these could be used productively in these circumstances," she stated in a monotone.

Tiegal could feel her heart race faster and with more purpose than it had done since she had arrived here, however long that time had been: weeks, months? She had lost track during this abyss of despair she had been hovering in. But now these females had arrived she sensed a better prospect for the future – hope.

"Sisters!" she blurted out without thinking.

It was Rinzal who reacted first, moving himself nearer to her in a protective stance.

"You know we don't think of each other like that here Tiegal," he reminded her gently.

"Yes, I *know* that Rinzal. But I have had a lot of time to think about this and I think we could be classified in this way," she grunted, flashing him a look she hoped signalled her annoyance.

Indramia moved nearer to her, brushing her shoulders against Rinzal as she did. It was a subtle maneuver, but one clearly meant to indicate that he should step aside.

"I don't think we should be too quick to brush aside the language or emotional understanding that Tiegal absorbed as a human. After all, it was her ability to connect and bond to these humans that has made her so powerful. If she wishes to view our shared creation period as a form of sisterhood then perhaps this could be explored?" Indramia suggested.

Ochrani nodded her agreement.

"As Indramia was trying to say, there are similarities and differences between the four of us - the *sisters* created from the same carbon contributions. Each one of us has developed unusual abilities that, as far as we know, has not evolved through any Tandroan before us. And although very distinct from each other's, they can prove complimentary."

"Apart from Parador's that is!" Indramia corrected. "We really need to keep Tiegal away from her. Her gift is arguably the most powerful of them all. And the most dangerous."

Rinzal clapped his hand on his forehead.

"Of course! I knew she was up to something. I warned Tiegal about Parador during her confinement period. Am I right in thinking she can manipulate minds?"

Indramia flashed her eye-light at them all with one swoop of her head from left to right.

"It seems she can. But what she didn't realise was that her powers have limitations. It seems it wears off if we are too far away from each other for any length of time. Which, as it turns out, has worked in our favour since we were both placed on pilgrimages to different islands than her for the last year! And Tiegal, well...she placed herself in a different world entirely!"

Tiegal shuddered at the feeling of Indramia's arms around her shoulders and again when she whispered into her ear. "Do you remember what we told you about our gifts?"

She squeezed her eyes shut as the memory of their lagoon reunion filled her mind in snippets.

She could smell lilies and basil. Ochrani!

And the sound of water splashing.

A second combination of scents filled her - orange blossom and peony: Indramia!

"It's coming back to me," she enthused, aware of the others breathing heavily as they waited.

Another snippet of a memory flashed before her.

Ochrani said she had the ability to create a location perfume. A way of pinpointing someone's location by making a perfume oil to replicate their scent.

And, Indramia possesses the gift of sight.

Tiegal opened her eyes and surveyed them all one by one. Her mind raced with the possibilities these combined gifts could bring to her mission. There had to be a reason Rinzal and Zeno had brought them to her. Surely, they must believe they could use them to help her return to her real family on Earth? She started to ask the question that was bursting to get out of her, but it was Zeno who asked it for her.

"And, you did tell Rinzal that you thought there was a way to use your abilities to help Tiegal connect to her baby?" Zeno urged, now standing close to Tiegal, as though keen to ensure her relationship was relevant too.

Ochrani took three large steps forward, towards Tiegal, only stopping when her feet touched hers. Their noses were now only inches apart. Ochrani inhaled the air all around Tiegal's face, hair and neck.

"Your smell really is exquisite. I think I can still detect a bit of her on you," Ochrani mused.

"Her? You mean Cezanne? My baby? You can *smell* her?" Tiegal exclaimed.

Her knees wobbled in shock. Zeno grabbed her shoulders to

prevent her fall, whispering in her ear, "It's a lot to process but Rinzal has the cord, the one that connected you to her when she was growing inside you. He recovered it from the evidence room to show Ochrani, so she could smell the scent you share together, your connection with her."

Tiegal tried to speak but the lump in her throat made it hard to breathe.

Ochrani took a pace back from her.

"I think I can make the perfume we need now. It's mainly floral with some cocoa, basil, lime and something else I cannot quite place."

"Pomelo?" Tiegal managed to squeak.

This was the strongest of the smells she had imagined when she thought of her daughter, even whilst she was growing inside her. Some nights when Cezanne had kicked and elbowed her way around the bubble inside her stomach, Tiegal had actually tasted the citrus fruit in her mouth.

Ochrani smiled a wide, perfect, white-teethed grin.

"Yes!" she enthused.

She then swung around on her toes, in a perfect ballerina pivot, clapped her hands and then declared:

"One, Cezanne Eureka Smit perfume coming up!"

31. PERFUME

Tiegal refused to join the others in the sunrise ritual anymore. The last time she attended she had turned into a howling mess. Just hearing them chant the words, 'no one can enter my island' had made her scream at them all.

"You stupid ignorant beings. You have no idea how powerful it is when you make a *real* connection. There is more energy created in that kind of exchange than anything you lot have ever experienced!"

It still amazed her that she was not punished more severely for this outcry. In fact, she had not been punished at all. Instead, she had received an invitation for afternoon tea in the rose gardens with Atla himself. An afternoon that she now realised had been a carefully designed ruse to play with her emotions *and* her energy, once again.

Every time she recalled their conversation, she found herself shuddering at the memory.

"Tiegal Eureka, you are really are abundant with surprises. You must tell me more of what you speak by your recent experiences. How this human exchange created a more powerful energy," Atla had asked her, pouring them both green tea under the shade of his favourite gazebo, in the tiniest cups she had ever seen.

In hindsight, telling Atla to mind his own business was not the most intelligent thing she had ever said, as she knew he had the power to place huge obstacles in her way. And obstructions were the last thing she needed, not when they were so close to forming a workable plan to get her back to Johannes and Cezanne.

And yet, to her surprise, Atla had ignored her rude response. Instead, he had offered her some more plassimer pastries and had then walked her through his gardens to show her his latest fountain feature. One that he had commissioned with *her* in mind. A stunning design of a tree, and not just any tree, a thorn tree with glass-cut bubbles and stars hanging from its branches.

"Johannes!" she had stupidly blurted out, realizing too late her reaction was exactly what Atla had hoped for. No wonder he had let her wear her Derado for a short period, clapping his hands when a burst of her vibrant colour filled the space around them from her pink diamond.

Just recalling this made her stamp her feet as she dressed in front of the mirror in her room, running her hands over the star on her stomach.

"He didn't see me cry," she consoled her reflection.

But that afternoon with Atla still unnerved her, because her every instinct screamed at her to heed the veiled warning in his kindness.

As Rinzal had said, "There is no doubt the fountain was a test to see your reaction. He may not have locked you up in a cabin, as he did before, but he showed you that tree fountain to see if you would release some of that magic emotional energy of yours."

Rinzal had a point, but it still confused her. As if on cue, he knocked on her door. His warm, buttery smell wafted to her through the keyhole.

"Just who I wanted to see!" she cried out, pulling him into her arms for a tight embrace.

"Have they stopped that moronic chanting yet?" She asked.

Rinzal burst into a loud guffaw. One so loud and out of character that it implied he was deliberately trying to drown out her words. But then, he had always found her turn of phrase amusing, even when she said things no one else in their world would dare. Yet, there *was* something odd about the way he was reacting now.

"Careful you! We have no way of knowing how long this shield of yours can protect you," he warned as he closed the door behind him, letting her know she had failed to hide her thoughts from him yet again.

His twitchy movements and repetitive tugging on the longer strands of his hair immediately made the hair on *her* arms stand to attention.

"What do you mean shield? And why are you so jumpy?" she asked, careful to keep her voice low in case there were others nearby who were making Rinzal nervous.

Rinzal shook his head and gripped his hands together, stretched out in front of his chest, as though he were offering himself a handshake. Another very odd gesture for him.

"Rinzal! What is wrong with you? Answer please, and now!" she demanded.

"Okay, okay. Calm down. There is just a lot to put into place that's all."

He beckoned for her to sit with him on her bed, shifting himself backwards so he could rest against wall, as he always did when they exchanged conversations in this way.

"Before I explain anything further, I just need to ask you something about that fountain experience with Atla the other day," he whispered.

"Not the love or death dilemma again Rinzal. I don't care what Atla says, or anyone else. I have made my choice. I would rather live a short life that is filled with love than a never-ending one with no love. Johannes and Cezanne *are* my life."

Rinzal kicked his foot on the wooden leg of her bed. She knew he was still struggling with her choice.

"Okay Tieg. As long as you are sure about *that* part."

"I am Rinzal! It doesn't scare me. Not at all. And you can tell that to the others too. Zeno and my sisters. I'm more scared of being stuck here, regardless of the longer or even endless life span, because that would mean not being with my loves," she shuddered. That version of her possible destiny was unthinkable. "I really don't want to talk about it again."

Discussing life, love and death with her Tandroan family was exhausting. They were all fascinated by her stories of her life on Earth and the people she had connected with. Indramia seemed intrigued by her sisterly relationship with Annarita. Zeno was almost obsessed by the drama caused by Elna's return. And Ochrani adored hearing the more intimate details of her experiences with Johannes. But it was Rinzal who the most difficult to placate. He seemed traumatized by the story of Kagiso and how she had died. He couldn't comprehend that Tiegal was not afraid of death. Or that she had been to a spiritual building with her Earth family to pay her respects to Kagiso. And that she now believed that it was only fair that she kept an open mind to the things they believed in on Earth, the things you cannot always see.

Rinzal was the only one that had not accepted her resolution. That she chose love over a much longer life. Even now, as sat with him on her bed, an awkward silence hung between them.

"Hello in there!" she tried.

Knowing it would irritate him, she pulled on a strand of his dark brown hair.

"Ow!" He nudged her with his shoulders. "Okay, I won't go on about that again."

He wasn't finished. There was another question brimming, she could sense it.

"But...going back to your tea date with Atla."

Tiegal groaned.

"Rinzal! We have been through this, countless times! It was creepy, and weird, and I would even say it was exploitative of him. He knew I would get upset by how his Team accessed my thoughts when I first got back here, about my time with Johannes. And then he made a huge fountain scene out of it, just to taunt me!"

She hissed back her answer, frustrated now that Rinzal was still obsessing over this afternoon. They were supposed to be getting ready to make the location perfume with Ochrani and Indramia to get her back to where she belonged.

"Yes, but it's important we understand it fully. There has to be more to it than we are seeing. Tell me the part about him giving you your Derado back again. How long did he let you wear it?" Rinzal urged.

"Not long at all. I would say no more than ten minutes," she answered carefully, still unsure what Rinzal was connecting together.

"And did you see if there was any water in the fountain?" he asked.

"Water? No, that was the bit I did ask him about. When would they be turning the water on?"

Rinzal smiled.

"That was what I hoped you would say. They worked it out before we did!" he enthused, shaking her arms with his warm hands.

Tiegal pulled away from him, needing her physical space to gather her senses and work out where he was leading with this theory. She counted to ten, inhaling and exhaling, before clarity finally reached her.

"The water! You think *water* is the key to getting me back?" she suggested.

Rinzal nodded, waving his hand back and forth to urge her to expand on her thinking.

"And, that's why he didn't let me near it. Why the fountain was dry. And why they keep offering me that weird milk mixture to bathe in. They think the water encourages my transportation!"

It was all starting to fit together as her words filled the room.

"Exactly! Well, that's part of it. You need to be wearing your Derado too. Just as you did on your first Release Day, *and* when you transported back again the second time, and finally when you came back here after giving birth to your baby. You can release your colours yourself but that's not strong enough on its own. You must need to be wearing it."

He said the last words in a barely audible whisper.

"But I wasn't standing in water when I transported the second time, when Atla tried to upset me. *Or* when I gave birth..." She choked on the last part. It was too painful to say those words out loud.

"Ah, but you were *near* water and you were pulled over to water, both times. You said you lived near a river with Johannes and that's where you arrived when you were pulled over there to him again, *both* times. And when you returned you either appeared in the lagoon or the pyramid pool. I think there is a connection there, whether it's on this side or the other one," he reasoned.

"But then why doesn't everyone do that when they wear their Derado on their initiation day?"

Rinzal flashed her a look, *the* look. The 'why are you asking me things you already know the answer to' look.

"Okay, sure, so that's to do with me and my extra deep emotions."

"It's that, and your ability to have made this remarkable connection with Johannes, and now Cezanne too, that has made all of this possible, despite how exceptional it is. It's like a gravitational pull that exists between you two. He is your moon. I think you need to be near water, so he can pull you towards him." Rinzal looked on the verge of tears.

"Hey, don't you get emotional on me now," she teased.

She was about to reach her hand out to him, but he jumped up off the bed before she could offer him her reassuring touch.

"I'm just going to miss you when you go again, that's all. But I know you have to do this. Are you ready? You *sisters* are waiting for you. We need to get you to the Iris to make that perfume."

Tiegal clapped her hands in glee.

"I will miss you all too. But, you're right. I can almost feel them pulling for me to come back to them. I'm ready!"

Entering the Iris - a dark circular tomb underneath the unused gardens of Atla's Estate - was like assaulting the olfactory senses with every scent that had ever existed. And for someone like Tiegal, this was almost unbearable. Not only could she smell a myriad of scents, bombarding her all at once, she could taste of many of them too. Her mouth filled with saliva as soon as she entered the circular room. She gagged to relieve herself of the taste of manure, quickly followed by coriander, the herb she detested the most.

"Ah, Tiegal, I forgot about these extra senses of yours. I used to get this when I was younger too. It can be really annoying. I remember it well."

It was Ochrani, loud and even more excitable than she had been the last time they had met. Indramia was there too, nodding companionably at her side.

"I did too," she contributed handing Tiegal a piece of thin, satin material.

Tiegal took the red handkerchief from her quieter Tandroan sister and wrapped it around her nose and mouth.

"How did you learn to control it?" Tiegal asked them, her voice muffled by the handkerchief material.

"Allergies!" they both replied in unison.

"Sorry? You have allergies? I thought they had been eradicated?" she questioned. Their twin-like responses were so intriguing she was temporarily distracted from the impending mission before them.

It was Ochrani who answered for both of them:

"Long story. We realised that if we made a plate full of all the foods we despised - and some of the other disgusting non-food tastes like vomit for example - we could override this connection with hearing words and tasting them."

Tiegal gagged again. The word 'vomit' tasted of vomit.

"You eat what's on the plate?" she managed to splutter.

"Of course. That's the whole point. And you have to keep doing it every few months but it's worth it, trust me!" she explained.

Tiegal watched how Indramia wrinkled her nose, clearly recalling the offensive experience. It made her think of Annarita, her human sister, and she realised how much she had missed her too.

"Well, I'm grateful you haven't overridden your smell ability Ochrani. Have you had any success with the perfume? For finding Cezanne?" she dared.

Ochrani and Indramia looked at each other, a silent communication passing between them. Tiegal could hear her legs knocking together as she started to shake. It was excruciating even waiting a few seconds for the answer to this. But then, much to her relief, her sisters' colours began to seep out of their Derados. Ochrani's chocolate submerged with the alluring orange of Indramia's, forming a spectacular glow that illuminated the vaulted room. A room adorned with an array of glass bottles, all lined up on shelves than ran around the room in an onion peel circle.

Indramia stepped forward.

"Ochrani has made a perfume oil to match the scent she detected on Cezanne's umbilical cord, which Rinzal gave her. Do you want to smell it first before we diffuse the vapour from it?"

Tiegal let out a squeak, unable to stop herself from stamping her foot with impatience.

"Yes, now!" she demanded.

Ochrani, her face serious, almost deadpan, gestured for her to follow her over to the rectangular steel table which dominated the circular room.

Tiegal gasped when she saw the umbilical cord lying in a plastic case on the table, surrounded by hundreds of flacons all filled with liquids of different colours.

"Don't even think about touching that! I know it used to be attached to you, but we cannot risk contamination from anyone!" Ochrani instructed.

Tiegal didn't respond, but as her heart pounded inside her she had an urge to call out for Rinzal. She needed to feel his reassuring touch on her arms. But it was far more important that he and Zeno kept watch above ground, as they had promised.

Indramia pulled open a drawer on the other side of the table, paused to consider the contents inside it, and then lifted out a silver handkerchief. It was similar to the one she had handed Tiegal before. Ochrani took it from her without uttering a word, unfolded it and then picked up the flacon nearest to her.

"Now, pinch your nose together. I am going to take the stopper off first, to release the alcohol. Keep your nose closed whilst I do that. You don't want to override your smell sense with it," Ochrani ordered.

Tiegal did as instructed, also holding her breath to stop herself from asking any more questions. Rinzal had explained that Ochrani liked to work in relative silence in the Iris. She watched as Ochrani released the stopper from the top of the flacon, sprinkled a few drops of the light tea-coloured liquid onto a handkerchief, and then waved it in the air. Then, without warning, she thrust the material under Tiegal's nose.

"Smell it now!" Ochrani commanded.

Tiegal released her hold on her nose and breathed in the scent in one deep inhale. It took only seconds for Cezanne's face to appear in front of her. The many different visions of her daughter that she had seen in her dreams: first, as a baby, all chubby faced, white blonde hair, giggling as her daddy blowed bubbles on her soft, fleshy, tummy. Then, a bit older, sitting in front of a birthday cake dressed with just one candle, mesmerised by the flickering flame in front of her. This image was swiftly followed by one more vision of Cezanne, rolling around in the grass by the river bank, before stopping to stand up and point at something she could see ahead, that made her beam a toddler, toothy grin.

"I saw her!" Tiegal cried. " I saw my baby girl. And she saw me!" she added, before her legs finally gave way and then she fainted on the hard, cold floor of the Iris.

32. VAPOUR

"Tiegal! Wake up!"

She could hear Rinzals' voice. He sounded terrified. But she couldn't bear the thought of opening her eyes for him. For in her mind, she was hovering across the river. She was close to her family again. It was a pull that was too strong to resist, even if it was just a sensation.

"Shouldn't the smelling salts be working by now? She isn't coming around!"

Rinzal's anxiety was almost tangible.

Ochrani's commanding voice boomed out, "She will come around soon. It's probably good she can't see the vapour release anyway. We don't want her to distract Indramia when she is trying to locate the baby."

That was all Tiegal needed to hear to rouse her from her daydream.

"Locate her? Yes! Please! I need to get to her now!"

She tried to stand but her head whirled. Rinzal's hands were under her head to catch her before she banged it again.

"You need to stay lying down Tiegal! What did you see to make you react like that?" he urged.

She was about to explain the vision of Cezanne and what looked like her baby's first year, or maybe even two years. How happy and healthy she looked. But the sight of a pink and silver vapour mist swirling in front of Indramia stunned her into silence. From where she was lying on the floor, she could watch the swirls above her.

"Is that her again?" she whispered.

Neither sister answered her, nor did Rinzal. They all stared at the dance of perfumed vapour mist that filled the room with an ethereal silvery pink light above them.

"What a scent!" Rinzal breathed.

It *was* an intoxicating smell, deep, intense and mysterious. It was also somehow light, deliciously floral and harmonious. The scent evoked a feeling of peace and purity, of unbridled child-like happiness.

And then it was gone, lost amongst the abyss of the Iris's previously released odours. Tiegal's arms lurched into the air towards the dome like ceiling above her, reaching out for the pinky silver mist of her daughter's memory. Just as she was about to cry out again Indramia's voice alarmed them all.

"I know the location now! It's called the Orange River. And it's near a place called Hopetown? A town situated... in the northern territory of a country called South Africa!" she declared.

Tiegal frowned, a waterfall of disappointment cascading over her as she absorbed Indramia's words. She had expected something more compelling than this. Something new!

Boosted by the energy from her daughter's scent she managed to find the strength in her arms to pull herself into a sitting position first and then make the final reach upwards by grabbing the side of the metal table. She leaned so that she was positioned directly opposite Indramia.

"Is that it? You released my daughter's scent to tell me what I already know?" she trembled.

Tiegal's angry accusation seemed to bounce off Indramia.

"I confirmed what you suspected and hoped. Cezanne was alive and well in the same area you left her. But what you *didn't* know, and what I *do* know, is the timeline. I can now tell you exactly *when* you can connect back to her, and Johannes," she delivered.

Rinzal shifted. Ochrani started moving the flacons around aimlessly and Indramia yawned. Everyone besides Tiegal seemed unalarmed by this information.

"What do you mean by the timeline? I want to get back to when she was born. When I was taken away from her!" Her voice strained by the effort it took to restrain herself from screaming. Indramia yawned again, clearly exhausted by the energy she had expended in using her ability to read the vapour scent.

"That would have been ideal, of course, but it is not possible. You will have to wait for all the conditions to be in place," Indramia stated.

"Wait? For how long?"

"Don't worry sister Tiegal. It's not too long into your daughter's life journey. I placed it as 1869."

Just hearing the date, the wrongness of it, released a taste of metallic blood in her mouth.

"But...that's two years since I gave birth to her. She will be two by then. I would miss her first years. And Johannes! He won't know where I have gone. No. I need to get back to 1867, to the time when I vanished!" she insisted, struggling to hold back her tears.

Rinzal planted his hands on her shoulders. Ochrani stopped moving the glass perfume bottles, and Indramia finally stopped yawning. No one seemed to want to respond.

"Why can't I go back to then?" she tried again.

Indramia leaned forward to rest her upper body across the table so she could place her hands over Tiegal's.

"Because you need to wait for the next diamond to be found there," she answered.

Tiegal climbed up the winding stairs that led out of the Iris and pushed the door with such force she nearly sent Zeno crashing to the ground.

"Hey there! Steady on Tiegal. What's wrong?" Zeno cried out as she grabbed the side of the door to reclaim her balance.

"Sorry, Zeno. I forgot you were waiting out here for us."

"I was keeping guard, like we agreed! I *thought* the idea was to keep our mission on the stealth side of things. I wasn't expecting you to burst out like that. You looked like you were trying to escape a monster or something equally terrifying. Not exactly an inconspicuous departure Tiegal," Zeno complained.

Tiegal slumped, instantly digging her fingers into the soft ground and then grabbing handfuls of grass at either side of her. Filled with rage, she threw two big muddy clumps out in front of her and then unleashed a deep roar. The noise she made sent Zeno crashing down next to her and clamping her hands over her mouth.

"Shush! Keep it down Tiegal. We don't want to draw attention. What are you trying to do?"

Zeno kept her hands firmly over Tiegal's until she was happy that her friend's breathing had returned to a safer pace.

"Now...tell me what happened in there," she whispered.

"I *was* trying to escape from monsters. The ones in there who now say I can't get back to my family until 1869! When my baby will be two years old!" she cried.

Rinzal joined them first.

"How did you get up those stairs so quickly?" he panted, plonking himself down next to Tiegal and only narrowly missing a spray of mud debris from hitting his face.

"Taking out your frustration on the grass is not a good idea Tiegal! You know Atla hates his gardens looking anything but perfect," he warned

"And I prefer to keep the Iris hidden too! Atla only let me have this space for mixing scents to emulate energies. I'm not supposed to let anyone know about it," Ochrani hissed from the doorway where she now stood, with Indramia just behind her.

Tiegal looked at them all, one by one: her friends on Tandro, her allies. They were risking everything for her, and this was how she was repaying them, by throwing a tantrum. It was inexcusable behaviour. They were her family too. Not in the same way Johannes and Cezanne were, but she was connected to them. She hung her head in shame.

"I'm sorry. You're trying to help me and I'm just throwing it back in your faces. I'm the worst example of a Tandroan there ever was. *I'm* an energy vampire. I make Atla look like an angel!"

Zeno laughed first, then Rinzal, closely followed by her beautiful, and she now realised truly gifted sisters. Indramia knelt in front of her and offered her hand.

"You have given us *new* energy Tiegal," she said. "My abilities have enhanced since you returned. I never dreamed I could connect with the past or future of another world. I feel abundant with energy whenever I'm near you!"

Ochrani knelt down next to Indramia. She wore her infectious grin again. The wide, sparkling toothy smile. It always helped to exude her extreme happiness.

"I'm the same Tiegal. The first time we met I could just feel something change inside me when I was near you. And then you returned and what I was capable of became clear. What I was made for!"

Tiegal could hardly breathe. She couldn't believe what they were telling her.

"Are you saying you become more powerful when you are near me?" she asked.

As her sisters nodded at her, a rush of warmth and love flooded through her. Johannes had been right about his theory. She may not have been born from the love of two people, but she was connected by her creation journey to others like her. Ones who also had advanced powers.

"Connected!" she whispered. The word resounded, pounding its three-syllable rhythm as a high shrill in her ears, taunting her into recognizing its significance.

"Jovil!" she hissed, turning away from her crowd of sisters and friends to steady herself. Memories of her pre-release day flooded her mind. The secret cave, the shimmering lagoon filled with glowing diamonds, and the smell of coconut, orange and bonfire that had seeped out of the skin of the lagoon master. The one she had thought of as her creator, her father figure. Slowing her breathing she counted her heart beats carefully, determined to assess these confusing thoughts, without the intrusion of the others nearby.

"If we are more powerful together then...why are we not including Parador in this mission? Maybe she is the missing piece? The extra source of power to get me back to the right time, in 1867?"

Even as she said the words, she knew she sounded self-absorbed in her fixation on getting back to her Earth family. She only hoped they could somehow understand the pull of love that drew her to her child, that they would *feel* the tug on her heart, how it was driving her selfish purpose. Indramia knelt down in front of her and took both her hands in hers.

"We have never experienced a life growing inside us as you have Tiegal. Nor have we felt a bond towards another the way you do to Johannes, but we *can* feel your pain, and this pull towards your other family when we are near you. It's like gravity. It makes you – *and us* – more powerful," she explained, whilst pointing to her forehead to indicate that she was accessing her thoughts.

"But Parador cannot join us," Ochrani added. "Her ability to manipulate minds is extremely powerful. And it is also dangerous. You would probably only magnify it by being near her, and that is the last thing you want to do."

Tiegal nodded, but then shook her head. There was too much at stake.

"Okay, I *can* understand your argument. But surely Parador's power could help us? Perhaps she could anticipate and manipulate what Atla will do next?"

Ochrani and Indramia looked at each other before answering her question.

"Because she does not want you here!" they whispered.

Tiegal frowned at them, clenching her fingers into the material of her coral coloured jumpsuit to keep her frustration in check.

"Please understand that I do not mean any unkindness when I say this, but I do *not* want to be here! Isn't that the whole point? If Parador wants me gone from Tandro, then why can't we let her help me to *be* gone!" she finally responded.

It was Rinzal who stepped forward with the answer.

"Because that kind of power is too unpredictable. There is no way of telling if she would help or hinder you. I think Parador is jealous of you and your powers. In fact, she is probably jealous of all three of you sisters. Of how Jovil protected and watched over you all and not her. Can you not see the problem this could present Tiegal?"

Her first reaction was to shrug her shoulders at him.

"Well, I'm not sure what she has to be so jealous about. Where is Jovil now then? Why is he not here protecting and helping us?"

Rinzal groaned.

"I told you already, Tiegal. Jovil is doing his bit by staying close to Atla to ensure he does not see what we are doing. *And*, by making sure Parador stays well away too." He paused to rub his eyes. His hands were shaking. "Look, we need to get ourselves away from here. If anyone from the team saw us talking in this way, it would be obvious that we're breaking the rules. We look far too close to each other and Atla doesn't know about Ochrani and Indramia's enhanced abilities. We need to keep it that way."

Rizal shoved his hands in his pockets as he surveyed the area around them, before bending down to whisper, "Look, I know you don't want to communicate in silence Tiegal. Even though it would be safer if you did, and useful, since you can access the hidden thoughts too. But I hear your reasoning.

"However, you do need to work on controlling your own thoughts, like I taught you before. We could all hear your deeper thoughts just then. You absolutely *must* work on your thought barrier. It's the only way we are going to make the plan work."

Tiegal reached out to grab his arms. Her hands seemed to have a need to reach out to anything around her at the moment.

"Is there a plan? I mean, even if I have to go back two years ahead. If it means I *do* get back, then I'll do anything you ask me to. Whatever you say, all of you," she promised, forcing herself to smile at them all. The idea of missing Cezanne's first two years, *and* leaving Johannes' for so long still ached, burned even, but it was nothing compared to the pain of never seeing them at all.

Rinzal took a deep breath and in a barely audible voice, one that required them all to enable their lip-reading skills, explained what they had to do next.

"The next stage of the Jarm Match will take place on Saturday. It is an ideal one for us because it is the animal energy section. And, this quarter, they have decided to hold an elephant painting competition. It is something one of the elders remembers from the older age. I don't know all the details yet, but from what I can gather they are looking to see who can generate the most creative energy from their elephant.

"Now, as we all know, one of your gifts Tiegal is your ability to connect with animals. You certainly shared a strong connection with your elephant, Namnum. In fact, all animals seem drawn to you. They always have."

Tiegal shook her head, letting her memories of Elna's cat come to the forefront of her mind. Rinzal squinted his eyes at her, closely monitoring her expression.

"Ah, so you did connect with another animal on this Earth place? A feline creature you say? Well...you never fail to astound me Tiegal!" Rinzal nodded in approval.

"They call them cats there. I think we used to have similar kinds before the destruction of the older world," she clarified. Rinzal waved his hand back and forth in front of her, as though brushing these inconsequential words away.

"Okay, well, if you still maintained that ability over there, then you will surely still possess it now. And the good news is..." he paused for effect.

Zeno gave him a light punch on his arm, a clear reminder that he should temper his natural tendency to add drama to any announcement.

"Get on with it!" Zeno hissed, looking behind her to check for any unwanted observers.

Rinzal grunted an apology, lowering his tone as he explained the significance of his news.

"Namnum has been selected to take part in the competition. And, even better, I happen to know that Atla is planning on testing how Tiegal, and her energy, reacts to being with Namnum again.

"I suspect he is counting on Tiegal being motherly and protective towards Namnum when they force her to work too hard with a paint brush in her snout and exhaust her. This of course means Tiegal will almost certainly release her special energy in response, which is what Atla is sure to be hoping for.

"Now, this scenario creates two ideal ingredients for our plan. First, they will have to let Tiegal wear her Derado during the match. It is the only way they can extract her energy. And second, they will have to let her near some water. They won't sacrifice the essential needs of the animals, particularly not elephants."

Rinzal paused, eyeing them all in turn to check they followed his reasoning.

"There really could not be a better time, or place, to make this happen, and Atla has set it all up for us. First, he will wind her up emotionally for us. Sorry Tiegal but it's just part of the process. Then she will be given her Derado to wear. And, even better, there will be water all around her! I couldn't have written a better script.

"Now, the only thing we all have to do is make sure we are there, ready to release Cezanne's vapour, and at just the right time. Can you have it ready Ochrani? And are you absolutely sure of the date Indramia?" he urged them.

Ochrani nodded her head three times.

"Yes! I have Cezanne's scent in the perfume oil I just made, and I will make sure I have placed it in a small enough dispenser that I can hide somewhere close to her," she said.

Indramia waited for Ochrani to finish and then focused her eyes on Tiegal's. Her pupils pulsated more frantically than normal, as though she were willing Tiegal to accept the location she had identified for her.

"I am one hundred percent certain of the time for you to get back to them," Indramia began. "In 1869 another rough diamond will be found near the river where your family live. A 47.69 carat diamond they will call the Star of Africa. It could have been named for you. A shepherd boy will find it and will then sell it to one of Johanne's neighbours. I saw it all happen when Cezanne's scent swirled around the ceiling in the Iris. It was quite magical to behold!

"I assure you, it's the perfect timing to get you back. And, Tiegal, it really is the only way. It seems that you cannot connect to a diamond discovery more than once. You managed to find your way via the Eureka diamond both times it was discovered, first in 1865 by Johannes, and then again, the following year by the other boy you told me about, Erasmus.

"If you think about it, you're incredibly lucky that another diamond will be found on Earth so soon after this, *and* in the area that you wish to go to."

Tiegal didn't hesitate in her response, nodding at them all through her smile and tears. She understood it all now. The reason why she had to be patient. It was just as Johannes had suggested, that they had connected to something bigger in their discoveries of each other.

You can be hard work sometimes, but you're worth it!

That's what he had told her. It was not the first time he had prophesised far and beyond his age and experience. Johannes, as always, was right, more now than ever. It *was* going to be hard work getting herself back to him, and to their daughter. Everything had to be aligned, all the conditions had to be just perfect.

And yet, despite all the obstacles – and the magic they would need to conjure - she knew it would all come together, as incredible as that seemed. It had to. And it would, because it was *all* worth it if she could be with them both again.

33. PAIN

Pain had become his friend. Johannes invited it into his life now. It was easier, safer, than trying to avoid its inevitability. He had left himself vulnerable to life's blindsides too many times before. Not anymore. Now, he *expected* life to hurt him. He waited for it to arrive at his door.

As he thought about this new philosophy - his conscious resolve to prepare for disaster - he dug his nails further into the palm of his hands. It did not take long for his blood to seep out between the creases of his clenched fists. At the sight of it he let out a long, slow, sigh.

"Release! That's what you are!"

The mirror in front of him, the same one in which he had first stolen a glance at Tiegal's naked body all that time ago, now taunted him with his sorry reflection. A sallow-faced shell of a man stared back at him, who wore clothes that hung off a dangerously fragile frame.

"What do you think Tiegal? Do you think I'm right? Is this another way of releasing your inner colour!" he asked the man in the mirror, even though the question was meant for her, his love, who he had not seen for over a year.

"What are you asking the ghost of Tiegal now then?" Annarita challenged.

He didn't even flinch at the sound of his sister's voice, nor at her words. Having heard her approaching the bedroom, he had already anticipated her attack. The heaviness in her footsteps was always an easy tell; the warning that she was ready for a fight.

"She is not a ghost! Tiegal is alive. Just not in this world, or this timeline," he argued, in his practiced monotone. It was the same response he always gave Annarita.

"I don't know why you keep trying the same tactic either. I'm not wasting my energy by raging, or crying, or thrashing out any other emotion you keep trying to draw out of me!" he persisted.

"So you keep saying," Annarita sighed. "But as I do keep reminding you brother. *I* miss her too. *Every* day!"

His body stiffened at the sound of her sobs, muffled by the arm that he knew without looking at her she had placed over her mouth.

"Cry if you must," he grunted in response. "But tears won't bring her back. You're just draining yourself of energy."

He shot her a look he hoped would encourage her to leave. It didn't surprise him when she stared back at him. And by the way she stood at his doorway, her hands on her hips, he knew she had no intention of moving.

"Crying is better than deliberately hurting yourself! I can see your bloody hands you know!"

"Leave me alone!" he shouted back at her, hiding his hands behind his back.

"I don't want to cry anymore. It doesn't change anything. It won't bring her back! She vanished, okay. It happened. Again! Just as we knew it could. We took it too far thinking we could be a normal couple. A human couple, who do normal things. It was stupid and dangerous, and we paid the price!"

Annarita threw her hands up in the air.

"No! That is such a wrong way of seeing this. You didn't pay the price at all. You have a baby! A miracle. No, correction, she's more than a miracle. Cezanne is a gifted, beautiful, little girl who *needs* her daddy."

Annarita moved herself from the door to stand in front of him, blocking his view of the mirror, her hands gripped on the fleshy handles of her hips.

"Do you hear that noise Johannes? Can you hear that sound of your daughter giggling downstairs? You are missing all these moments. You should see the things she can do already! It is amazing. She doesn't just walk now. She *runs* around the farm. She is even faster and more coordinated than Henri! And he's more than twice her age!

"And she can dance too, Johannes. You need to see it, it's simply magical! The other day she was watching me in the kitchen and she just walked over and said, 'I can make a beat!'

"Before I could ask what she meant by that she picked up Ma's old saucepan and a wooden spoon and began drumming away. I thought it was sweet at first, and not so shocking for a one-year old, but then she got a towel and wrapped the saucepan around her waist and started dancing along to the beats. Her timing, the rhythm, and the way she moved her hips and shuffled her feet. It was perfect! I'm not sure you could teach that kind of instinct to anyone. It was just coming from somewhere inside her!"

Annarita's voice trembled with emotion.

"Tiegal was just like that," Johannes managed to respond. He couldn't bring himself to look up to her.

"Another tooth came through this morning and she is talking in full sentences already, saying words that I don't even understand, but Frederick looked them up and they are real words! She is a little genius and you don't even know her. I'm going to say it again, Cezanne needs her daddy!" Annarita shouted.

"Another tooth hey? That's nice!"

It was all he could manage. The shame was too heavy for him to clear his mind adequately, to form a more acceptable response. Instead, he just stared at the triangular shape Annarita had made with her arms, hands resting around her waist at either side of her.

It reminded him of a conversation he had once shared with Tiegal on one of those nights when they had woken restless with desire, unable to resist the opportunity to explore their bodies' mutual hunger to connect together again.

"You know what it feels like when we make love?" she had breathed her question into the hairs on his chest.

"Well, I hope it feels amazing? It does for me!" he had replied, nervous all of a sudden, momentarily afraid that he had scared her by taking it all the way this time, finally releasing himself into her.

"It's more than amazing. It's like the perfect alignment. I'm not in a bubble when we do this. I am like a triangle, the pavilion of a diamond. And, you are my crown. We just fit perfectly! You make me disperse my fire when you connect with me. When we come together it feels like our two journeys – the roads we have both travelled before meeting each other, and the experiences that have cut and shaped us – have finally aligned, like the perfect cut of a diamond."

He had laughed at her then.

"You and your diamond philosophy. It always comes back to diamonds."

He remembered her frustration at his response. It had flashed across her perfectly symmetrical face. But it hadn't taken long for him to understand what she was trying to say. She had been made for him. She had been made to love him, and he her.

"I hoped you would understand," she had complained. "But then you don't know how diamonds, and people, can be shaped so they shine more brilliantly, so they can release their light. It hasn't happened yet on your world. Well, not fully. You are yet to experience that kind of star light. It's only just being discovered."

He had pulled her into his arms and squeezed her tight, alarmed by a ripple of fear that had shuddered across him. A foreboding memory of how easy it can be to find something and then lose it all too easily.

"I think I do understand Tiegal. It's like you said. We connected to something bigger when we found each other. I think I may be the first man on Earth to have discovered the light you are talking about. Which, makes me wonder if perhaps we should keep making this perfect connection over and over again?" he had suggested hopefully, his fear of losing her driving his desire for her even further.

"I think we already made it! Just now!" she had answered him in her soft whispery voice.

"What? Does that mean no more? One time only?"

"I wasn't just talking about perfect love making symmetry... I mean it was perfect...but I think we just made a beginning. A new, perfect creation. Something that has never existed on your world, or mine, before."

She had touched her stomach then, circling the area around her star and whispering something about the light that we cannot see.

Recalling her beautiful face, Johannes blinked away his tears, pushing the heart-wrenching memory of her sweet voice from his mind.

"Brother, please, look at me. You're scaring me! You look like you've gone into a trance again. Did you hear what I just said? About going for a walk with Cezanne?" Annarita shook his shoulders but he shrugged her away.

"Cezanne *is* perfect. Too perfect. I can't even look at her."

"What? Are you going to say it's too painful to spend time with your own daughter? I thought you liked pain! You must do, or why else would you make your hands bleed? For what other reason would you starve yourself the way you are? Anyone would think *you* are trying to vanish now too! But, you can't!

"Listen, Johannes, you don't get to just sign out when you're a parent. Don't you think I wanted to wither away and die after Ma and Pa died? But it wasn't an option. Henri needed me!"

She sounded close to tears as she paused to tap her bottom lip with her index finger. He could almost hear her debate with each tap she made, how she was questioning how far she could push him.

"What would Tiegal think if she saw you now? How devastated she would be if she saw you like this Johannes!" she finally cried out.

He closed his eyes and growled, preparing himself to order her out of his room, but was stopped by the sound of a little voice that sounded out from the hallway.

"She will come back soon."

"Cezanne! How did you get up here? I bordered up the bottom of the stairs. Sorry, Johannes. I didn't organize this or anything..."

Johannes placed his hand gently on her sister's arm to quiet her. His eyes were locked on the tiny little girl standing in front of him. Her emerald green eyes that stared at him expectantly.

It was the first time he had allowed himself to look into them, to fully focus on the intensity of their colour. And now that he finally was, he could hardly breathe. They were identical to her mother's, the human version.

"What do you mean?" he dared to ask his daughter.

"I see her sometimes. I think she wants to get back to us, but she has to wait for the next star to shine," Cezanne replied.

Johannes gasped.

"Annarita!" he managed, barely able to speak. He tightened his grip on his sister's arm.

"How can she talk like this? She is only one year old?"

His sister sniffed above him. She cried so easily these days.

"It's what I've been trying to tell you Johannes. She is gifted. Tiegal left you a miracle."

He put his arms out to his daughter. Cezanne took two steps back from him, her tiny chest heaved up and down.

"Oh! S-s-sorry. You don't really know me. I..." he stumbled, awkwardly folding his arms around his chest.

"Your hands Johannes! *Think!*" Annarita hissed at him. Coughing away his embarrassment, he scrambled to find a handkerchief in the pocket of his jacket that lay wrinkled in a heap on his bed.

The pain he had been expecting had now arrived in full force. This sudden unveiling of his shameful behaviour, how he had abandoned his daughter to the care of his sister, felt like being pounded by a flurry of punches. He had to hold his breath to prevent the screams he could feel fighting to release from inside him. Everything about her reminded him of Tiegal. The way she cocked her head to one side as though listening to his thoughts. The little smile that twisted to one side. Even the kaross shawl that she wore attached to the back of her little dress like a cape, the same kaross she had been found wrapped in on the day she was born, reminded him of Tiegal. The last time he had seen it, it had been covered in blood -Tiegal's blood. Now, it was gleaming white!

The memory of her birthday, the horrific bloody scene and the screams that had filled the house, made his body shudder in awkward jolts. But then, his little girl made a move forward, towards him. Her tiny hands covered the ragged cloth he was still trying to wrap around his cut skin.

"I don't mind the blood. But I don't want you to hurt your hands."

He gasped at the sound of her voice, now so close. It was soft, yet deep, like a cello. The kind of voice that belonged to a wise, experienced woman. It made no sense coming from the tiny, baby lips that glistened in front of him.

"That's the voice she uses when she is explaining her emotions. It changes," Annarita explained in a whisper. Johannes nodded, as though this were a normal thing to hear about your child of only one year.

"Cezanne. I'm sorry."

He didn't know what else to say. There were so many things he *wanted* to say, to ask her. What did she know about her mother? Had she really connected with her in some way? Was she happy? Was she lonely?

More than anything, he felt an overwhelming urge to pull his little girl into his arms.

"I'm so sorry Cezanne. I should have been protecting you. I've just been so sad!" he blurted out, realizing too late how absurd his excuse must sound. How his explanation would confuse a child of such a young age.

"I am happy," Cezanne replied. "And I can wait for her. And so can you. It won't be long now."

Her smile was wide, full of perfect little white teeth. She looked straight at him, her gaze intense, but relaxed. Her shoulders bobbed up and down as though she were laughing inside. He watched her in fascination, waiting for a hint of a sound to erupt from her. A few seconds passed before it finally did - a flurry of musical giggles, tiny bell chimes that were filled with innocent wonder.

He glanced at his sister and nodded. Annarita was right. His little girl's voice was an instrument she could tune to the song she wanted to play. Her own emotional song sheet.

Her laughter was so infectious he felt compelled to join in.

"There you go! I told you she was magical." Annarita laughed along with them.

Johannes jumped up from the bed, finished tying up the handkerchief around his palms and held his hands out to his daughter.

"Would you like to go for a walk?" he asked her.

Cezanne clapped her hands and then placed them both in his. Her warm skin radiated through the bloody cloth and he breathed a sigh of relief. Just feeling her touch was healing.

"Don't be sad anymore. It's my birthday," she pleaded, her voice older and more instructive again.

Not holding back this time, he pulled her into his arms and lifted her up so she could sit on his hip. Without hesitating, Cezanne rested her head onto his shoulder. Her breathing changed in an instant and he glanced down to see her eyes were closed and she was already in a peaceful sleep.

"Happy Birthday baby girl," he whispered into her soft blonde hair.

Annarita held her thumb up to him and then took a step to the side.

"Now you can look in the mirror," she said.

"That's the man, the father, who Tiegal can come back to."

34. PLAYERS

What happened at a Jarm Match was never revealed to those outside it. Only those who attended knew what occurred. During Tiegal's teaching days she had lost count of the times the kimberlings had asked her what kind of competitions took place. It was one of those Tandro secrets that had everyone fascinated and intrigued from their earliest memory. In her role as a teacher she had answered them then, as she would still do now. She had no idea.

Today was different. Today, she *would* find out what happened at a Jarm Match, because today she was taking part in one.

Last night, two hydro-cities had arrived at the main harbours on Kimberrago Island – one at the North end and one at the South – both depositing the selected Jarm Match competitors before setting off again to their designated Island stops.

Tiegal had watched the competitors arrive on Atla's Estate from her bedroom window, each eager and determined. They wore silk jumpsuits and swinging cloaks in the colour of their energy. They also wore their Derados, each adorned with their allocated coloured diamond to match.

Much to her relief, her own pink jumpsuit and cloak had arrived this morning. To her disappointment, her Derado had not. She was not too worried about this, not yet. She had faith in Rinzal's instincts. He had always been adept at tuning into someone's next move and he had assured her that Atla would let her wear her Derado, when the time was right.

"You can do this!" she muttered, fastening her cloak to the shoulder clips on her jumpsuit.

A bell chime rang out from the atrium of the Estate Hall.

It was time.

Turning to face the mirror she gave her Tandroan reflection a nod and a final wave goodbye and then made for the door. Rinzal was already standing on the other side of it, waiting.

"You look beautiful Tiegal!" Rinzal enthused.

"Well, thank you! It is the most luxurious piece of clothing I've ever worn. It's almost a shame I won't transport over wearing it. I would love for Johannes to see me looking like this," she whispered. She was about to add that Johannes would probably be just as happy to see her naked, but she thought better of it at the last minute. She had seen how Rizal enjoyed the Tandroan method of release, exchanging his energy colour via his Derado with others around him, when, and as he liked. It was difficult to gauge if he truly understood her preference for the human style of intimate exchange.

"I can hear you Tiegal. I thought you were going to work on hiding these thoughts of yours for today. None of this will work unless you do!"

Rinzal pushed her gently back into her bedroom and closed the door behind them.

"First of all, I can very much appreciate the human ways of connecting with each other. You should know that more than anyone! We were the ones who used to talk about the possibility of it together. But I take what exchange I can get here...and it's not so bad. It's easy, and simple at least."

"It's not so difficult the human way, believe me!" she chuckled.

"Well, that's not something I will ever find out." He scratched his chin and coughed, unable to look her in the eyes.

"By easy, I meant in an emotional sense. You can't deny you are more emotionally intense since you experienced human life. But that's you Tiegal! That's your destiny, and we are going to help you get back on that journey, okay?" he rushed.

"Thank you Rinzal. I can't even begin to say how grateful I am for all..."

"I know you are grateful, but we haven't got time for this chat now. Look, you *need* to hide your thoughts. If Atla hears what you are planning then it will just end in disaster for you, for all of us. So, quickly, put your fingers on my chest and find my beats like you did all that time ago. Can you still create some sparks? Without your Derado?" he urged.

"Yes, I can! I have been working on this to make sure I have some control over it," she answered, placing her hand near to his heart. One cue, her pink energy sparks jolted out of her fingertips, following the beat of his rhythm. Her mind instantly filled with blissful memories of all the comfort he had given her. It surprised her how easily she had forgotten it.

"Okay, good! Now, think of something you don't want me to hear," Rinzal demanded. His chest burned under her touch and she knew she couldn't risk pushing him any further. Removing her hands from his skin, she concentrated on thinking about how she was feeling:

I love you Johannes. I'm coming back for you baby Cezanne! *And...I love you too Rinzal, for all you have done for me. For being my friend.*

"Good! I didn't catch any of that. Now don't forget. Keep your mind, your island and all its thoughts and desires, barricaded off from everyone, just for today, until you get back to your family."

Although his voice sounded gruff, she could sense his excitement for her – and how much he believed they could all pull this off. Just feeling this positivity from him gave her the boost she needed.

"Let's do this!"

She clapped her hands and pointed in the direction of the door.

The Atlatheatre was an impressive, open-air, circular-shaped stadium that she had only ever seen from a distance. But now that she was standing in the centre of the stage she couldn't help thinking about how absurd the design was.

Why would they build an exposed theatre in such a tropical climate? And even more ridiculous, to dress us all up in silk suits.

Her under arms were already itching from where the thin material had stuck to her sweat. The oppressive heat bounced off the thin layer of gritty sand beneath her feet. It created an illusion of colourless, ethereal waves that shimmered and danced around her. An impression that was enhanced by the circular flashing of over a thousand pairs of Tandroan eyes that beamed out at her from the stadium benches.

As if the skies had heard her complaints, a welcoming breeze greeted her, simultaneously billowing the material of her silk shirt. It wafted the alarming scent of expectation that permeated the humid air. It was this smell, seeping out from the spectators who had already filled the stadium, that caused her breathing to become ragged and further agitated Tiegal's already fretful state of mind.

It didn't help that the other participants in today's Jarm Match appeared to be studying her with great amusement. There were thirty of them in total, including her, each of them standing by their respective elephants, waiting for their next instructions.

Never before had she been so grateful for Namnum's calming presence at her side. And for Rinzal's company too, particularly as he seemed much more composed than her.

"Tell me again how this Jarm Match works. I still don't understand how they assess the winners. And please don't look so exasperated with me Rinzal. It just seems really um..." she stammered.

"Really what? Really Atla?" Rinzal guessed.

"Well, yes! If by that, you mean, frustrating, nonsensical, and downright disappointing, then yes! All these years that we dreamed up ideas of exciting adventures in this theatre and now we're finally here, it turns out to be a painting competition! Seriously! Of all the great competition they could have designed to determine whose energies should contribute to the next generation!

"And look at this crowd! Hundreds of them! What do they think they are coming to see, *really*?"

With her right hand outstretched, palm-faced upwards, she swung it out in front of her and made a 360 degree turn on her heel to demonstrate the crowd of Tandroans dotted around the entire circumference of the Atlatheatre. The spectator benches were already nearing maximum capacity. There was a palpable excitement in the atmosphere.

"I mean, why are they so excited about watching such a ridiculous event? It's not like we are being asked to race or anything remotely physical, competitive, or entertaining. No! They have committed themselves to sitting in exposed sunlight for hours on end whilst foolish participants like me manipulate our poor elephants into painting pictures from our thoughts!"

With too much force, she jutted her blush pink sandals into the sandy flooring. "Ouch!" She cried out, realizing, too late, that the thin layer of sand provided little protection for her toe against the hard travertine flooring underneath.

Rinzal tugged on the elbow of her sleeve reminding her that she was allowing her fear and anger to override her rational thinking.

"Tiegal! Try and find some calm, *please*. I told you last night that it works in your favour that Atla has chosen this type of challenge. The matches are normally much more thrilling, in a physical sense, but I am convinced he has deliberately avoided going down that route this time...because of you! And that's where he has completely misunderstood you. Designing a match in which the emphasis is on emotional energy is exactly what we wanted. It's quite shocking that he has made such a misguided decision. You have *got* this! All you need to do is channel your thoughts on what you most desire and Namnum will do the rest. Atla is judging the winners of the match based on how the crowds interpret the paintings the elephants produce as a result."

Rinzals' voice was a confident hush, like a pleasant flutter in her ear, reminding her that everything was going to be okay, that she had the upper hand.

With an agile movement, he then reached his arm behind him so that he could give Namnum a pat and turned to face Tiegal, treating her to one of his most charming of smiles.

"There are no complicated rules here. Even if there were... you... Tiegal Eureka, will not be around by the time any judgments are passed!"

———

Atla looked surprisingly handsome in his purple Jarm Match outfit. He always stood out from a crowd, not only because of his old-world features – eyes with strikingly blue irises and circular black pupils, and a short side-parted hair-style – today he stood tall amongst his Tandroans as both their ruler and as one of them. It helped that he was also wearing the uniform today; a silk jumpsuit and cloak, like the rest of the participants and trainers in the Atlatheatre, and that his non-diamond eyes were covered by dark, silver-rimmed sunglasses. But, even so, there was something very un-Tandroan about him.

From her position, sitting on Namnum's back, Tiegal watched him as he strolled around the circular enclosure, stopping to greet each of the elephant riders on his way. He wore his Derado fitted firmly around his neck. The violet-coloured diamond in the pendant gleamed in the sunlight. The Tandroan ruler appeared relaxed, strong, and full of conviction. And yet, Tiegal sensed he was missing something. She could smell it on him, a longing.

Her own voice, from somewhere deep inside of her, sent her a warning.

He wants to live forever! That's why he is so obsessed with harvesting my energy. He may not have my sensory abilities, but he does have power around him.

It was this instinctual caution that made her entire body shiver with trepidation. For just as Atla turned and made his way towards her, she saw the female her friends and sisters had warned her about. The one who posed the greatest threat to their plans, Parador.

"Ah, Tiegal Eureka. What a pleasure to see you looking so radiant today. And your first Jarm Match too. You must be excited to see how this all works?" Atla clicked his fingers in front of her and then smoothed the longer side of his parted, slick-backed hair. Tiegal growled inwardly. The sound of fingers clicking together was one of the most grating traits anyone could adopt. Atla always did it when he approached her. He must know that it set her nerves on edge. A piece of information about herself that she had no doubt revealed in the past, back when she had been unable to hide her secret thoughts.

"I am most honoured to be here Atla. Thank you for inviting me to participate. I only hope I can prove a worthy competitor."

Atla seemed amused by her choice of words.

"Very good! And of course, you must wear your Derado. We all have high expectations of the surge of energy you may release today! Just no disappearing this time of course."

His laughter sang out with a nervous tremor.

Parador stepped forward then, holding a black box in her arms.

"Your Derado is in here! You have permission to wear it for now, but it will be taken from you as soon as the first painting is completed."

Parador's voice was brisk, her expression hard, almost vacant. She raised her arms up to allow Tiegal to reach for the neckpiece from the opened box.

Caught off guard, Tiegal leaned down towards her, much further than was necessary.

Namnum's reaction was immediate. The elephant's body rumbled underneath her, a vibration that so startled her she almost flew off the saddle.

"Woah, there, now do we need to change your elephant? I was told you work well with this one?" Atla looked amused now. He smoothed his hair again.

Tiegal straightened herself upright, shook her head at him and then flashed him her best forced smile.

"Not at all! Namnum is just excited to get started that's all."

She patted the covered section of her elephant's skin under the saddle, silently thanking her for the warning. Parador shot her a slightly mocking, amused look.

Stay focused Tiegal!

She scolded herself.

There was something powerful and dangerous emanating from Parador, a magnetism she sensed was designed to pull Tiegal in so that she could assume control.

Careful not to make eye contact with Parador again, she managed to reach down and extract her Derado from the box without further interruption. There was an awkward silence as Atla and Parador waited for her to attach the neckpiece around her throat. Atla looked as though he were about to say something else but the appearance of another figure approaching from behind made him swing himself around in a dramatic turn.

"Is everything in order?" Atla boomed to the male. Tiegal craned her neck to catch a glimpse of the male, but the absurd ruffled white collar that was attached to the neckline of Atla's cloak obscured her view of him.

"Atla, sorry to interrupt but we need to make a start before the animals become too hungry. And I have checked the colour energies from amongst the participants, as you requested, and the mix is ideal. We should create an excellent batch of creation pods from the donations of the winners here today," the male stated firmly.

"Jovil!" she cried out.

Atla raised his eyebrows in an overly dramatic expression of amusement.

"Ah yes, you may have encountered the lagoon master on your pre-release day! Interesting to hear you are on first name terms," he mused, rubbing his chin with the back of his hand. Atla's excitement was palpable.

Jovil turned his back to Tiegal, addressing only Atla. It was a clear rebuke, one that made her shudder with rage.

Why are you working with Atla? I thought of you as a father.

Even as she channeled her anger towards him, she sensed a conflict in her own reasoning. Jovil had barely crossed her mind since she had returned to Tandro. Her focus had been steadfast in its direction towards Johannes, and yet now she felt a deep disappointment that he had not even acknowledged her presence.

Almost as soon as the thoughts entered her head, she brushed them aside. Rinzal had explained Jovil was deliberately keeping Atla close by. She had to believe that Jovil was ignoring her to protect her.

She sat back on the saddle, to observe how Atla and Jovil conversed. Parador was still close by, boring her steely eyes into her. The sense of her, so near, made her feel strange. When a gust of wind wafted Parador's scent in her direction, the distinct mint odour, she pinched her nose to prevent it from overwhelming her.

Tiegal clenched her hands over the lip of the saddle. Something was very wrong. The air around her reeked of danger that she now feared her allies had failed to anticipate.

Biting down on her bottom lip, she deliberately made it bleed. For once, she relished the metallic taste in her mouth. It was a welcome, albeit distasteful, distraction. Or perhaps a punishment to herself for not assessing the players in the game more carefully.

It had been stupid of her to shut off her abilities. If ever there was a time to use her powers to dig deeper into the minds of others, it was today!

Clarity was the key. She focused on a bunch of bananas on the table ahead of her, clearing her mind from all the distractions around her, and then mentally tallied the abilities of those around her.

The obvious opponent was Atla, the puppet master in this operation. What did he really want? What was his true motivation? Her every instinct screamed at her.

Your superior energy! He wants immortality. He thinks you can give him this.

This made sense. Atla was more like a human in origin than Tandroan. There was only so much power he could derive from his Derado. He needed her. This was a good starting point. At least she had pinpointed his desire. But what was his flaw? She paused for a few seconds and then felt a smile return to her face as the answer came to her. Atla wanted to play games with her emotions, to extract what he could from her.

But this posed a great threat to his hold on the situation. It was what he *didn't* know that gave her an advantage, because he had no idea how to control her emotional release. There was no cage he could place around her to stop her from transporting away from him again, if things went too far. That was a big risk for him to take, particularly when he was testing her in such a public domain, which had to mean, someone had fed his ego, made him believe he was capable of winning the game.

Without moving her head, she darted her eyes to the side to glance at Parador again. What was her strategy?

From the way she had spoken to her, just now, with what sounded like utter hatred in her voice, there was no chance of finding an ally in her. She was more enemy *and* the most likely candidate for convincing Atla that *she* was the one who could control Tiegal.

Just as the thought entered her mind Jovil made a strange noise. The sound made Tiegal smile. To anyone else, it would sound like an innocent clearing of the back of his throat, but to her the sound echoed of an encouragement.

Remember where you have come from, what you can do.

Both she and her sisters, even Parador, had been created together.

And, it had come out of something with good intentions, Jovil's thoughts. Which meant, like she and her other sisters, Parador must contain goodness inside her too. She *had* to!

"Are you ready Tiegal Eureka?" Atla bellowed at her, as he clicked his fingers four times in front of her, as though trying to mark the shape of a diamond in the air.

"Oh yes, ready and armed!" she replied through clenched teeth. The rules of the match had still not been fully explained to her, but the bag containing her allocated paint brushes and paints dug into her knee from where it hung from the saddle. She moved her leg sideways to gaze across the rest of the contents inside. It was only when she felt the shape of the bottle resting at the edge of the bag against her thigh that she let out a huge exhalation of pent-up breath. She could do this.

35. PAINT

Tiegal counted over a hundred easels, all lined up around the arena. The thick, white-rolled papers that hung over them gleaned in the stifling midday sun. Namnum did not seem stressed as they approached the easel allocated for them, but Tiegal could smell dehydration on the animals all around her already. Each of them reeked of distress. Rinzal had been right about the water. There were water hoses positioned at regular spots between the easels but none of them had been turned on yet and the animals had already been left for too long without being hosed down.

Her Derado burned against her skin and not just from the heat of the air around them, but as a direct reaction to how she felt. She was bubbling with rage. Just the thought of the elephants being exploited made her want to jump off Namnum, run to the gates, throw them open and shout at them all to escape. But she knew better. It was exactly what Atla had intended. It was exactly what her friends had predicted.

A female competitor, to her left, reached into her saddle bag and withdrew a large paintbrush, which she then dipped into a jar of black paint attached to the side of her saddle. Tiegal watched her carefully. The female removed the brush from the jar and then hovered it in the space below her nose, as though to check the paint had adequately covered the hairs on the end of the paintbrush.

"Unbelievable!" Tiegal hissed.

Now she had a better view of the design of the paintbrush, a rage of anger coursed through her. The paintbrush had a dividing bar placed across the bottom of the handle. Tiegal's stomach heaved as she realized what this was for, to place on the end of the elephant's trunk, to stop it from sliding up the snout.

"Namnum! I can't put that on you. It will hurt you. I know how sensitive your trunk is," she hissed.

Her elephant flapped her ears backwards. The left one smacked Tiegal right across the face, Namnum's way of urging her to get on with it.

"Okay then, here goes nothing," she sighed. "Let's see what you can paint with your trunk shall we? Such a natural thing for you to do of course. I mean, how could we have missed this evolutionary design for your vital and most sensitive body part!"

Namnum wafted her trunk behind her so that the snout swung in front of her face.

"Okay, okay, I get the message Namnum."

The saddle was weighed down by a dozen different jars of paint that were attached to it by a thick rope strap and arranged in a neat row at the side of her right leg. It reminded Tiegal of the bullet strap Johannes had worn around his waist before a hunting trip with Frederick, one of the few times they had argued, when she had called him an animal killer and he had pointed at the empty table before slamming the door in her face.

Brushing this painful thought away, she reached into her saddle bag, found a paintbrush, and then dipped it into a jar filled with green paint. Reluctantly, she then attached the bar at the end of the brush handle and fixed it across the width of the tip of Namnum's trunk.

Whispering a tearful apology, she leaned back into the saddle to see what would happen next.

Namnum didn't hesitate. Her magnificent elephant pressed the brush across the white art paper, starting from the top right, and then let it flow in a swirl downwards. She repeated this action eight times, alternating her starting point and angles, and then twirled her trunk backwards again, before stopping just in front of Tiegal's face.

Through her tears, Tiegal managed to detach the brush from Namnum's snout and replace it with a blue-dipped brush.

Before she could stop her, Namnum flicked her trunk over again and proceeded to add more colour to the painting with this second brush. This time she started on the bottom left side of the paper. Without moving the brush off the page she painted waves across the paper to the other side.

Tiegal grinned as her Derado began to release her pink mist in response to what the painting was already starting to reveal.

"His tree. The river!" she breathed. It was impossible to contain her excitement. She didn't even notice the crowd that had gathered around her as she reached into the bag again to replace the brush and colour for the third time. Without needing to think, she dipped this brush in orange.

As the clear shape of a rising sun appeared on the paper, the crowd around her muttered noises of approval. Tiegal glanced around her to see if any of her trusted allies were nearby, but it was Atla's face that caught her attention as the crowd parted to make way for him.

"Quite a talent your elephant has there I see. Would she like a break? Some water perhaps? It *is* rather hot here today."

Tiegal frowned. Namnum *did* need hosing down. All the elephants did, but there was something about the smile on Atla's face that confused her. It seemed he was trying to play with her again and she wasn't sure what his strategy could possibly be. Rinzal had said he would not sacrifice the welfare of the elephants in front of a crowd. Animal neglect went against everything Tandroans were taught to believe. And yet, her instincts told her he was offering her something he did not intend to deliver.

Still, she answered him.

"Water is *exactly* what Namnum needs."

Without waiting for further instruction, she swung her right leg over to the other side of the saddle and made to jump down. In her haste she misjudged her foot placement, narrowly missing the stirrup, and fell down onto the sandy floor in an awkward heap. The crowd burst into laughter. Ignoring them, she pushed past two tall males who were standing in front of Namnum's painting and strode over to the tap by the wall to turn on the hose pipe. Not a drip of water appeared.

"There is no water! Nothing is coming out!" she shouted, but Atla had already retreated back into the crowd. She could see the back of his shoulders shaking with laughter as he walked away from her.

"So, this is the master plan! Wind me up but turn off the water," she growled under her breath.

"Do you always need water?"

The sound of Jovil's quiet voice behind her made her jump.

"Nice of you to finally speak to me great lagoon master! And what do you mean by that question anyway?" she snapped back at him.

The last thing she needed was someone creeping up on her, asking her cryptic questions.

"I think you *know* what I mean." Jovil didn't look at her as he spoke. In fact, he didn't even appear to be moving his mouth.

Tiegal could hardly breathe. Too much was happening all at once. Her Derado was burning hot now and the pink energy mist was getting thicker.

"Tiegal! You need to act quickly. You're already releasing too much colour. They will only let you build up so long before they take it away from you. And you still haven't answered my question. Do you always need water?" he insisted.

Instinctively, she put her hand up to cover her Derado, desperate to keep her colour release contained. Indramia had insisted that for their plan to work the timing and the conditions of her full release had to be just right.

"No! I don't think I need to be *in* water, just near it. I was in my house the last time I transported, when I gave birth, but I *was* near a river," she whispered. The crowd were still watching her, waiting for her to return to Namnum, so that the painting could be completed.

Jovil nodded his head slowly.

"That's what I suspected. So, now you need to carry out your plan - and quickly," he urged.

"But they've turned the water off! I'm nowhere near water now. And I'm already raging inside. The elephants *need* water. I can't believe the crowd is not reacting to this. We don't allow this treatment of animals. It's like the old era all over again!"

Her body was shaking as she tried turning the tap on again.

"Listen! Really listen. It is only Namnum who can't access water. The other elephants in the arena are being hosed as we speak. Look!"

Tiegal frowned, stepping up to the next level of the spectator seats behind her to get a better view of the area. Sure enough, Jovil was right. The other competitors had moved their easels away from their elephants, free from the bustling crowds, and were hosing down their elephants from pipes on the walls. A loud growl of frustration roared from within her. A thick burst of colour vapour released from her pink diamond and she stamped her right foot three times.

"But, how come the crowd around Namnum are okay with this? Surely someone should be helping me to get water to her. Not laughing at me!" she complained.

"Look again! *Who* is near them?" Jovil cocked his head towards the right side of the crowd gathered around Namnum.

She gasped when she saw who he was referring to.

"Parador! Of course! Wow, she really does hate me!"

"Don't be so quick to assume things Tiegal. Who do you think convinced Atla he could pull off such a stunt? To risk enraging you like this when you are wearing your Derado? To press your buttons by isolating you and your elephant and depriving her of water? And who else could then work with a crowd to ensure they played the parts she needed them to? What kind of power would that entail?" he asked.

"Mind power!" She clapped her forehead with the back of her hand. "Of course! So, are you saying Parador *is* on my side?"

Jovil's long dark hair swayed around his shoulders as he turned to face her.

"I don't know if I would use the words on your *side*. But, put it this way, if Parador's ultimate desire is power, *helping* the more powerful sister to escape would make a lot of sense," he reasoned, stroking the bristly hair on his chin. "Can you listen to my deeper thoughts, just for a few seconds, like you did before?" he asked.

She nodded. Now was not the time to hold on to stubborn resolutions. Taking a deep breath, she focused her gaze on Jovil's eyes, letting her mind channel deeper into his.

Okay, before you returned the last time, Parador and I had a rather interesting confrontation. I suspected she had been manifesting more powers in the lagoon, whilst your other sisters were away, and so I tricked her into revealing her vision of your next return. Let's just say, I resorted to methods I would not normally use!

Of course, Parador was furious and I feared she would do something stupid, or even dangerous, in revenge. But, fortunately, we have made a truce. She doesn't want Atla to know about her powers, just as I don't want him to know about the lagoon and how the four of you are connected.

So she is here, today, on my terms. I'm not a hundred percent sure what she plans to do but I know what she wants. She wants you out of the way. Away from Tandro and away from Atla. Trust me on this. I have made sure that she will help you get back to your family. We will ALL make sure you get there.

He paused and bowed his head. Just as she thought he had finished his transmission he returned his focus to her.

And, I want you to know this Tiegal...I will always think of you. You have transformed everything. Do you understand just how much?

Tiegal had to hold her hands under her armpits to stop herself from throwing her arms around him to show him her gratitude. There was something so sad about the burden she could see he wore across his face; a beautiful face, almost *too* perfect – even on Tandro.

"Yes, yes, I do," she nodded, blinking back tears. "Thank you Jovil! For everything. For the powers that made me like this. Without them I never would have found Johannes and could never have made Cezanne. Whatever you thought about all those nights you sat by the lagoon whilst my sisters and I were forming, it ended up creating a remarkable connection between two worlds. Please, do not feel any guilt about the part you played in that," she assured him, touching his arm gently.

An unmistakable cry of pain sounded out from the arena. It startled them both into a momentary freeze.

"It's your elephant! You need to go to her! Now!" Jovil urged.

Tiegal nodded and then ran towards Namnum, pushing aside anyone who stood in her way. Heart hammering in her chest, she reached her elephant and buried her face into the folds of her grey, rubbery skin. The smell that filled her nostrils made her retch.

She could smell blood. Elephant blood. Namnum's blood!

Without stopping to think, she grabbed hold of Parador's clenched hand and prised her fingers loose. A bloody nail wobbled back and forth in Parador's sweaty palm.

"You *stabbed* Namnum's ear!" Tiegal hollered.

Parador stared back at her, not a trace of an apology registering on her impossibly perfect face.

"The painting is not finished yet. I was *helping* it along, that's all! And you!" Parador answered.

Tiegal turned her back on her, desperately trying to clear her mind.

She must be trying to rile me. To build me up! But you need to calm down!

She warned herself, aware she was at risk of releasing too much energy if she lost any more control over her emotions.

Namnum made another noise, a softer call this time.

"I'm sorry, so sorry she hurt you. I think she's trying to anger me on purpose. To build me up for a big release," Tiegal whispered to her, looking deep into her eyes.

Give me a pink brush! Namnum seemed to say.

Reaching into the saddle bag, Tiegal grabbed another paint brush, along with the glass bottle spray Ochrani had hidden in there earlier. They couldn't afford to waste any more time putting their plan into action.

Ignoring Parador, she dipped a brush into the pot filled with pink paint and fixed it to Namnum's trunk. Her elephant took a step towards the easel and with one circular brush stroke added a pink object to the painting.

"A ball! The elephant painted a ball!" A female kimberling cried out from the crowd.

But Tiegal shook her head, still staring at the painting.

"No, she painted a bubble. *My* bubble!" she breathed.

After that, it all happened so fast, like a crucial scene in her life that Tiegal was helpless to direct. Each character appeared at her side in turn. Each, ready to play their part to ensure all the conditions were in place, some planned, some unexpected.

First, Rinzal and Zeno ran up to her and pulled her Derado from her neck. Together they plunged the neckpiece into a bucket of water and then quickly reattached it to her again.

Then, Ochrani and Indramia arrived. As soon as they saw Parador standing next to Namnum, blood still dripping from her hands, they both stepped back in horror. Tiegal had less than a minute to reassure them that she was not an enemy, at least only half of one, and that Namnum would be okay.

Then, Atla.

Tiegal could barely breathe as she watched the next part unfold before her. Atla clicking his fingers, then grabbing one of his Team members and pushing him to the floor for no apparent reason. His face an ugly distortion of contorted features. His words a flurry of protests.

"Who brought this water over here? Who defied my orders? Why is Tiegal Eureka being given extra help?"

With each outrage Atla's face reddened. No one made a move. No one attempted to appease him. It appeared they had reached a stalemate.

But there was one key player who had yet to finish her part in the scene. For just as Atla launched himself at Tiegal, his hands grasping around her Derado, Parador pulled on his arm and yanked him back. This was the moment she had not predicted. It was also the moment when Tiegal realized all was not lost.

Parador, the maverick and unpredictable sister, was taking control. Tiegal watched in awe as this sister of hers fixed Atla with a blinding glare. How her spectacular eye-light dispersed its golden feathery glow around Atla's face and had him entranced within seconds.

"Do it now Tiegal!" Parador ordered, her voice a low rumble. "Do whatever you need to do in order to leave Tandro. And this time... make sure it's for good."

With this instruction, Parador took hold of Atla's arm and led him away. The rest of the crowd and the members of Atla's Team followed, equally transfixed by the power of Parador's unusual light.

"Thank you, sister," Tiegal whispered.

It was time. The conditions were back in place. The bottle containing her daughter's scent was still in her hand. The cooled-down Derado was around her neck and she was finally ready to return home.

"Release Cezanne's scent now, Tiegal! You're ready. Just close your eyes, breathe in her smell, and think of where you want to go and who you want to see," Indramia urged her.

Tiegal could barely see the lid of the bottle, her tears were blinding her, but eventually she managed to twist it off in one harsh pull. Closing her eyes, she let her mind drift hearing Indramia's sweet, melodic voice around her, urging her to find her way to 1869. To return to Hopetown, to the draw of a new diamond find, and to a man and a little girl who were waiting for her by a river.

It was strong at first, the senses she reached for. The smell of her baby, cocoa, basil, lime and pomelo. Then the heat increasing around her, followed by the exquisite release of desire from within her, and the sound of Indramia's words repeating the date, 1869 over and over again.

Then there was nothing, no smell, sound or burning heat, just white space, a sensation of floating. A feeling of peace and a sense of knowing that patience was all she needed now, for soon the fog would clear and she would see them again. Finally, she would return, back to where she belonged.

36. CANDLES

Two candles flickered in front of Cezanne's face. The reflection of the flames created an illusion of flickering fire in her stunning green eyes.

"Are you going to make a wish?" Johannes asked, moving in front of his daughter so he could catch her answer. Annarita, Frederick and Henri were creating so much noise around them, singing and clapping, that he almost wished they would leave. He wanted to treasure this precious moment with this daughter. Her second birthday. He had missed too many of her milestones in her first year. It still tortured him no matter how many times his sister reminded him that Cezanne was exceptional, that no normal child could develop as quickly as she had done, and that he had more than made up for his initial neglect by how close they now were.

"I'm wishing for a discovery!" Cezanne declared. Her voice was excitable and determined, like a frantic drum, beating to announce an arrival.

Frederick banged his fist on the table, shocking them all into stunned silence. The candles both flickered and wavered from the tremble of the table.

"Sorry! Didn't mean to alarm you but Cezanne has just reminded me of something. I can't believe I forgot to tell you all," Frederick enthused.

Johannes frowned at his brother-in-law. It was unusual for him to command attention like this. He was the one who usually shied away from holding court in a group conversation.

"What is it Frederick? I think Cezanne was about to tell us her wish!" He pointed out, darting his eyes between his brother-in-law and daughter.

"Ah yes, forgive me little one," Frederick winked at Cezanne. "But I think our little star wisher will like what I have to tell you all! *Because* I just heard from our neighbours that there has been another diamond find! Apparently, one of the griqua shepherds found it on the banks of the river. It's a big one too. Everyone was talking about it this morning when I went over to the fields. Of course, Schalk van Niekerk has already made a move. Bought it from the boy for five hundred sheep, ten oxen and a horse! And now it sounds like we are going to be seeing a lot more people around here, all looking for more diamonds! Interesting times hey!"

Frederick's voice was filled with excitement as he leant over to ruffle Cezanne's hair.

"So, maybe your wish has already come true? More discoveries," he added.

Cezanne banged both her little fists down on the table, clearly copying what she had seen her Uncle Frederick do just before. The cake rocked from the force of her hands landing on the table. Everybody stopped what they were doing, each them stunned by the strength she had just exerted from her two-year old body, all of them waiting to see what she would do next. Even Henri stopped whining for his mother to give him another koeksister.

Then, just as Johannes was about to scoop her up into his arms – he hated it when they all stared at her like this, almost as if they were afraid of her – Cezanne's concerned expression transformed into one of pure, utter, joy.

"This means she will be here very soon!" she announced.

He held her hands as tightly as he dared, not wanting to crush her little bones but equally terrified of letting her go. Ever since Frederick had revealed the news that another diamond had been discovered on the banks of the river, Cezanne had become obsessed with being near it, and at all times. It was hard to get her to come back inside the house and even more difficult to encourage her to take a nap. It was like she was bursting with relentless excitement, a boundless energy that no longer desired sleep or food. It frightened him. He didn't know how to keep her safe. How to protect her when she was like this. And it didn't help the mission either, the one that he, Annarita, and Frederick had all agreed upon: to keep Cezanne away from the farm workers and neighbours before they asked too many questions about her remarkable development.

"A few more minutes little one and then we need to go in for supper," he warned her. Cezanne looked at him and smiled.

"Too early. Must not miss opportunities."

Despite himself, he smiled at her as he twirled a finger around the one black curl that had recently emerged amongst her blonde ringlets.

"How can you only be two years old? You should not know such ways of talking, or thinking, yet," he whispered, bending down to pick up five small pebbles so they could play their game together.

Cezanne shrugged her shoulders at him, took the five stones from his hand and then placed each one on top of the other so they stood tall in an upright pile.

"This could help! Maybe?" Cezanne frowned. "Or do you think a fire too, this time?" she added.

Johannes sighed as he bent down to crouch next to where his daughter was sitting in the dry grass. The sun would soon set across the river and although he had promised his daughter that they would watch it tonight he had also assured Annarita that he would get her back to the house in time for supper.

"I know you see things my little love, things that you wish to appear to you, but sometimes we have to look around and enjoy what we have all around us. What we *can* see. You know Henri really wants to play with you, but you always want it to be just you and me, here, by the river."

"It has to be this way," Cezanne answered, not looking at him, her little legs splayed out at either side of her at an awkward angle.

"You really must not sit like that either. It will hurt your hips," He scolded her. It was his softest version of a reprimand

Tiegal used to sit just like that too, he reminded himself. He used to wonder if it was her way of trying to imprint her body more firmly into the ground, as though she wanted to secure herself to the earth beneath her.

He reached his hand out in a beckoning wave near to her face.

"Come on now little one. If we are not going to play five stones, then I think it's time we get you in for some food and bed."

Cezanne moved her head around the obstruction of his hand so that her nose just touched the highest stone on the pile she had made.

"It should be six!" she announced.

Johannes shook his head at her even though he knew he didn't have her attention.

"No, it's always five stones, not six."

But with her tiny index finger Cezanne touched each of the stones in turn:

"Johannes, Annarita, Frederick, Henri and Cezanne," she counted, allocating names to each of the stones. He knew what was coming next. To speed things up he reached behind him and picked out another small pebble from a collection he always kept for her in his pocket. Just as he made to offer it to her, he stopped as he caught a good look at the stone. It was the most stunning looking pebble he had ever seen.

"Pink!" Cezanne clapped her hands in delight.

"Yes, you're right little one. This does look pink - how unusual."

"It's hers!" Cezanne grabbed the stone from his hand and placed it on top of the pile.

As soon as it was in position Johannes scooped his little girl in his arms. He could feel his tears welling up. His precious baby girl – so much older and wiser than her years – always had a way of turning something so ordinary into something truly magical. She had a way of moving him, just as her mother had done not so long ago. He flipped his right arm downwards, where her head rested near the crook of his elbow, to tease her into thinking he may drop her. On cue, Cezanne giggled her cello chime. He blew bubbles into her neck. She roared her delight. And then he swung her around in a dizzying roundabout before he stopped and hugged her close.

"This looks fun! Can I join in?"

He laughed at the sound of Cezanne's newest voice. How was she now impersonating her mother's voice so perfectly? His daughter's abilities never ceased to amaze him.

"Why did you say that? You're already joining in!" His voice was lost in the muffle of her hair.

"Wishes do come true." It was Cezanne's higher, more baby-like voice that responded this time. Her little hands reached around his neck pulling him in the direction of the voice he had wrongly assumed belonged to her.

"Look! Open your eyes Daddy. She came back."

His entire body stiffened. His heart pounded in his ears and his legs wobbled. Without opening his eyes, he managed to lower Cezanne down to the ground. He heard the sound of her little feet run away from him, her happiest voice squealing in delight as she shouted out, over and over, "You're here, you're here."

And then he lifted his head, finally daring to let himself leave the darkness so he could embrace the light of her diamond eyes once more.

"Tiegal?" he whispered.

"Yes, it's me!" she cried. Her body was naked and glowing as she held their beautiful daughter in her arms. He stared at them awe-struck, their bodies were locked tightly together in an embrace by the river. Rippling waves lapped behind them, suggesting a recent distur-bance had sent the current in the opposite direction. He found his way over to them in quick, urgent, strides, throwing his arms around them with such force they almost fell into the water together.

"Look what we made," he heard Tiegal whisper into his ear.

Between their desperate kisses – mainly ones that landed on their lips, cheeks, necks and the top of Cezanne's head – they struggled to get their breath back. It was their daughter who finally broke them apart, giggling as her little hands found both their chins and sepa-rated them.

"You made me?" she asked them with a deep frown on her face, and in a voice more suited for her age than any he had heard from her before.

"We did make you Cezanne. The perfect miracle," he answered his daughter.

Tiegal buried her face into his cheek then, inhaling his scent as she always had whenever they greeted each other.

"Hmmm...I missed this," she mumbled. And then it was Cezanne's turn to receive her mother's devotion. First, she kissed her forehead, then the tip of her nose, before reaching down to the soft skin behind her ear, breathing her in loudly and urgently.

"You were made from love Cezanne. You were made from one remarkable love story. And something tells me...that you are going to transform everything."

EPILOGUE

Parador and Atla walked together in silence. They had already circled the rose garden, at least ten times. One of them needed to start the conversation. They both knew who that someone had to be. He would decide when *he* was ready to talk.

Finally, Atla stopped in front of his favourite glass sculptured fountain.

"Ah, the Bellesortium of Stars!" he boomed, nudging at some of the glass stars that hung from the sculpted branches of the tree-shaped fountain. At his touch, they bounced together, chiming musical excitement as they danced in the light evening breeze.

"Do you know why I commissioned this particular design?" he asked, unable to hide the slight tremor in both his voice and in his hands.

Standing statue-like still at the side of him, Parador smiled, aware that her expression would be reflected in the glass in front of them.

"I believe it is intended to pay homage to our celestial provenance, is it not? To remind us of all of our carbon connection with the diamonds?"

Her answer was quick, delivered with the obedient tone she

knew Atla preferred her to adopt, an expectation that grated on her. And yet, equally, always reminded her of his stark ignorance.

It was a game, after all. He was too ego-driven and foolish to understand that she was more in control. Atla's mind, and his lack of abilities, made him particularly easy for her to both read *and* to manipulate.

Without taking his eyes away from the twinkling glass stars, Atla reached out to his side and clapped her on her back three times. It was an unusual gesture for him to make towards her, but as irritating as such physical contact was, she knew better than to enrage him in anyway. Not now, not when she was so close to leading this old horse to water.

"That is correct, my dear Parador. We should never forget our origins, and how fortunate we are to have discovered the powerful energy of diamonds before we almost lost this world for good. How we salvaged this planet and started a new, superior species of Tandroans, like you."

"It *is* a spectacular design," Parador agreed.

Careful not to offend, she took a stealth step to the side, moving herself to a more comfortable distance, and away from him. Now that he was finally talking, Atla had begun to release a particularly unpleasant odour, a scent of intense fear. She watched him as he stretched his arms up in the air and then proceeded to hold them there, as though reaching to the burning star in the sky to give him more power.

I'm not surprised you are so full of terror! Or that you feel so weak. You are losing control now. Tiegal showed everyone the weakness in your philosophy. This idea of individual islands and fires. Her emotional energy release carried more power than anything you ever anticipated.

Parador allowed her ruler a few more moments of quiet contemplation before she dared to push him any further.

"Atla, we need to find a new source of energy. After Tiegal transported at the Jarm Match there has been a noticeable loss of confidence in your rule. I am sure you have been made aware of the increasing numbers who have begun to experiment. There are too many who are rejecting the traditional energy exchange in *preference* for physical intimacy again," Parador announced.

Her statement was dramatic, and intentionally so. She wanted him to be frightened. She was deliberately sending him to the edge. This strategy always worked. She would make him feel vulnerable and then, when the time was right, *she* would be the one to pull him back to safety again.

Atla placed his arms back down to his side, inhaling audibly.

"The Tandro philosophy *works*! If we want to experience supreme energy and health, to live longer lives than ever before, then we must protect our *own* islands and learn to light our *own* fires. It is the reason we have order, and peace, and such an abundance of energy amongst us. The old ways of connection *didn't* work!"

He spat out his words, creating bubbles of saliva that collected and remained at the corners of his mouth. Parador had to glance away, repulsed by the physical sight of his rage.

"But Tiegal Eureka never understood that, did she? Her obsession with making a deep connection, all these destructive old-world ideas about being in *love*! It was her downfall." He smashed his fist into a branch of stars in front of him, an action that created a ringing of frantic, high-pitched chimes. The sudden, pealing sound attacked Parador's hearing, making her flinch.

"It was her power!" Parador responded through gritted teeth.

Atla swung round to face her, his hands still clenched into fists.

She really has riled you, hasn't she? Parador thought smugly.

"Her *power*! Surely your fellow Tandroans must realise that she will not have survived for long on this other world, and in whatever timeline she continued to exist in? They must see that?" he implored.

Parador managed to suppress the satisfied smile that quivered behind her lips.

You really can't see it, can you? That Tiegal has transformed everything you have tried to create?

"Atla! I am sure *you* realise that Tiegal's release, *and* the power it gave her, is only part of the problem. The diamond supply has almost depleted. Our energy resources are drained. Any species would look to another source in such circumstances," she reasoned.

"Then we will just have to keep making more synthetic diamonds. Just as I ordered." Atla bellowed back.

"It's not the same."

Parador lowered her voice, willing his calmer energy to return. She knew from experience that Atla was more malleable when he was just the right balance of afraid. Too much anger made him deaf to any reasoning.

"The energy inside a synthetic rock is minimal. It just cannot match the energy inside a real diamond. How can it compare to a rock that took billions of years to form?"

As she said this, she flickered one of the resting stars on the tree with her elbow, knowing her celestial nudge would provide the perfect emphasis to her point.

She took a step closer to him, and inhaled the air surrounding him.

Oh Atla, you really are terrified. And, you are exactly where I want you!

"Maybe the diamonds were the starting point for your new world? Perhaps now, we need to look to another solution? Even if it does not exist in this world?" she declared.

Atal turned to face her, his eyes wild with confusion and terror. It was clear that he was preparing for a fall now. He was exactly where she wanted him to be.

"And I know where to find it."

She waited for five carefully timed seconds, before continuing:

"It starts with a dream," she whispered, waiting again, before adding, "It ends with a resolution."

Atla gasped as her words registered.

"Tiegal? You think she will come back again?"

His desperation smelled delicious. She could even taste it!

Parador shook her head, finally allowing the smile that had been dancing on her lips to emerge.

"No, Atla! But one of her descendants will. One who is even more powerful."

Parador shivered with delight as she said these last words. She had offered him the branch to hold onto and now she had him exactly where she wanted him.

This was going to be fun!

End of Book One.
To be continued...

THE TRANSFORMATION

Extended Epilogue

NAOMI E LLOYD

1885, Cezanne's eighteenth birthday, and all appears well in the Smit family. That is, until the Derado calls for them to connect with Tandro once again.

It is impossible to destroy and Tiegal knows that the only way to protect her daughter and any future descendants from opening a door to her other world again is to find a way to transform it.

The question is, how long can this transformation last?

To receive your FREE copy use this link:

https://www.tandro.co.uk/the-transformation

PLEASE LEAVE A REVIEW

If you've enjoyed this book, it would be tremendous if you could leave a review (it can be as short as you like) on the book's Amazon page.

I am reaching out to my readers to ask this favour as reviews help me gain visibility and they can bring my books to the attention of other readers who may enjoy them.

Thank you so much!

JOIN TEAM TANDRO

Intrigued by how the future descendant of Tiegal and Johannes will re-connect with Tandro again? You don't have too long to wait.

EXCHANGE is the second book in the Tandro Series. See overleaf for more details.

In the meantime, there is so much to discover in the exclusive password protected area on my website: **The Tandro Energy Cave.**

In the Tandro Energy Cave you can also find fun diamond energy quizzes, character profiles as well as book and diamond treasure hunt competitions.

Sign up to my reader community and become a Tandro Team member at:

https://www.tandro.co.uk/jointeamtandro.

I am so looking forward to connecting with you.

ALSO BY NAOMI E LLOYD

COMING SOON - BOOK TWO - THE TANDRO SERIES

Love. The most precious currency there is.

Sexual energy. It's most dangerous opponent?

Stefanie's connection with Adam is like a diamond, unbreakable. But then

Tandro comes into her life, another world she had no idea she was connected to. A world that is hell bent on breaking them apart.

Life on Tandro has fallen into chaos. The diamonds are running out and sexual energy exchanges are no longer fulfilling the Tandroan's desires. They need to source a superior energy and Parador knows how she can get it: by playing an exciting game with human emotions.

A prophetic vision reveals to Parador the target for this game: Stefanie Barrett, a beautiful woman, living on Earth, in 2015. A happily married young woman, mother and a descendent of an incredible love affair between a Tandroan female and a human man back in 1865.

Exchange is the second book in an irresistible series of paranormal time travel romance novels: The Tandro Series.

One Choice Can Transform Everything

Follow Naomi on the following platforms to be one of the first to know when it is released:

https://www.bookbub.com/profile/naomi-e-lloyd

https://www.facebook.com/naomielloydauthor

ABOUT THE AUTHOR

Naomi E Lloyd is the author of the Tandro series, a fantasy time travel romance series that transports readers to another time and place.

Naomi is a passionate reader and has an avid interest in sci-fi/fantasy stories, love journeys and diamonds!

Her diamond world is an internationally connected one. She works as a photographer, a diamond philosopher, and a charitable ambassador for YouCanFree.Us, which focuses on rescuing trafficked women.

As part of her charity, photography, and research work, Naomi has been lucky enough to travel around the world, meeting and inter-viewing fellow like-minded science romantics of the world.

Naomi's diamond passion is about connection—the journeys that shape rather than break us—although her characters do face extremely tumultuous experiences along the way! It is their resilience and determination that makes their journeys so transformative.

Naomi has woven in her diamond philosophy—along with her romantic imagination—to combine her passion for time travel, parallel worlds, and love stories into an unforgettable journey across time and space.

Although born in Yorkshire and a northern girl at heart, Naomi now lives by the historical beaches of Portsmouth, where she can often be found in a café, tapping away on her laptop, or walking along the sunny promenade with her camera in hand.

Find out more about Naomi E Lloyd at www.naomielloyd.com, where you can sign up to join her reader community and gain access to her exclusive Diamond Energy Cave on her website, where fun quizzes, character profiles, and treasure hunts are waiting to be explored.

ACKNOWLEDGMENTS

Writing this book series has taken me on an incredible journey around the world and introduced me to some truly sparkling characters along the way: the diamond people who have inspired many of the themes inside this story. I am, and will be forever grateful, for the time given to me and the expertise shown from each of these wonderful people.

A special thanks goes to the incredible jewellery designer, Johan Louw, of Uwe Koetter in Cape Town. From the moment we met to discuss the design of the Derado we were on the same page. Your patience and warm hospitality extended to my family on our visits to South Africa provided a much-needed boost when the mountain looked too big to climb. Much love to your beautiful wife, Annarita Louw. I will always remember waking up to feel the energy from Table Mountain as we set off to explore it from the gardens of your beautiful home.

Huge thanks to the brilliant *Diamond Cutter*, Mr Brian Gavin of Brian Gavin Diamonds. Thank you for showing me the beauty of a fluorescent diamond when it glows in reaction to a new energy source, and for not calling me crazy when I then applied this to love connections and the energies between people.

To my good friend, Denis Bellesorte, of Bonds of Union in London. The most romantic diamond philosopher of them all! I wrote the Bellessortium Fountain for you and I owe you a huge gratitude for being the most excellent physics teacher. I only wish you had taught me science at school.

To Clemence Merat and Edward Johnson, both wonderfully fascinating people and expert gemmologists. If it were not for you both, I never would have known of the secrets hidden inside diamonds and how perfect these inclusions or "imperfections" really are.

To Kako Komatsu, for enlightening me to the things we cannot see, the power inside our thoughts and how diamonds magnify the energies around us.

To Vida Allen, of McGregor Museum in Kimberley. Your advice on the landscape and people living in this area of South Africa in the 1800s was truly invaluable.

To Jo Malone, for leaving me both inspired and speechless when hearing you talk of the beauty within a scent and how advanced sensory abilities are, in fact, glorious powers. Every one of my characters was inspired by your incredible journey.

To Eddie the Eagle for accepting my invitation for tea and thus granting me at least a million extra mum points. More importantly, for leaving me with a timely reminder that a dream can always be reached, even if you have to take the long way around.

To the indomitable and highly inspiring author, Kathy Lette and her brilliant actor son Jules Robertson, for welcoming me into your home. The tight bonds you share is visible and one of my all-time favourite photo shoots.

To Clarissa Anderson, Sujo John, Sunita Shroff and all the team who make YouCanFree.Us such a wonderful charity to be a part of. Your tireless fight to end human trafficking is a beautiful example of how people will always light up when exposed to the energy of love.

To Donna Freed of Radio Gorgeous in London, for embracing my diamond philosophy with such positive enthusiasm and then agreeing to read the story when it was still in its infancy. Your encouragement and support is incredibly valuable to me.

And last but not least, to my own diamond family: Julian, Oliver and Joshua. Your patience, love and belief in me are my greatest strengths.